This edition © DOPAMINE 2024

Published by DOPAMINE
1139 N Summit Ave Pasadena, CA 91103
www.dopaminepress.org

Special thanks to Caitlin Forst

Cover Design: Faye Orlove
Layout: Hedi El Kholti

10 9 8 7 6 5 4 3 2 1

ISBN: 978-1-63590-212-9

Distributed by the MIT Press, Cambridge, Mass. and London, England
Printed and bound in the United States of America

EDITED BY
Michelle Tea

Contents

Michelle Tea

Introduction: A Vision for Sluts

SLUTS is the very first publication of DOPAMINE Press. When I was brainstorming how to start publishing books, I thought about all the really great writers I know, far and wide, from my own work writing books and touring them, and producing literary events and just from decades of being in literary community. I wanted to involve them all in this project, but of course know that, at least right now, we can't compete with what bigger, more established publishers can offer. I devised a collection of themed anthologies, to be published annually, as a way to involve these writers with DOPAMINE, and involve DOPAMINE with these writers. I dreamed that the anthologies could act as benefits for the press, which has very little moolah and is relying, currently, on the gen-erosity of queers who have more. I would ask that those who can please donate their measly fee back to the press. And the debut title would be *SLUTS*.

I made a huge list of a bazillion writers. You are probably on it. Every single name was an obvious potential contributor to *SLUTS* as well as the future anthologies *WITCH*, *CLOWNS*, and, should we all live so long, *CRIMINAL*. So many of the folks who turned up in this anthology arrived here a bit randomly; I sort of divined the Table of Contents, trusting that the book would contain all the writers and stories it was meant to. And, it does. I wanted this collection to be slightly enormous, and filled with different takes on the concept of *SLUT*. Putting this book together, as a cis woman and mom in a queer marriage that theoretically allows for some possible misbehavior but for all intents and purposes is totally monogamous, I was really interested in *slut* as a concept. If a slut stops being slutty, is she still a slut? Can one be culturally slutty? Can one be a slut within the bounds of monogamy? Is Slut an identity, like Queer, that can go through various iterations throughout a lifetime? Is being a Slut sort of like being a Writer, something you just *are*—born that way? I don't think I was born Queer; was I born a Slut? Did my sluttiness actually cause my queerness, or did my queerness cause my sluttiness? It certainly enabled it—I recall being young and sexual and understanding that it was sex with *men* that made one a slut; as a girl fooling around with girls I was, what? A fairy princess? That's what it felt like. Maybe, all things being equal for a Slut like myself, I migrated to queerdom, permanently, because it is such a free play to slut it up. A cis guy could think a girl was a slut for literally giving him the very thing he was hoping for—sex! What ingrates! Whereas likeminded queers got it. Sex was hot fun, like devouring a pizza. Eat up!

That's *my* story, I guess, but what's yours? That's what I was hoping to find in this book. The way *Slut* is weaponized at such a young age, the way it can be reclaimed in adulthood, the glamour and the heartbreak of sluttery, the pressure to be a slut, and maybe, at core, how sluttery is just about hunger—desire, hedonism. There are professional sluts in this book, among the bravest of the sluts, because though the literal word "slut" has become so mainstream that a person can use it to name a chain of breakfast restaurants, being committed enough to body and sexual autonomy to defy law and involve it in a strategy to survive capitalism—this is still, even today, boringly controversial, and dangerous. Everyone who shared their relationship with this word and, by extension, their relationships, with other people and their bodies, with their own bodies and senses of shame or entitlement, daring and embarrassment and power, I do think they are quite brave and wonderful storytellers to boot.

I hope you enjoy the book. I think you will. It is deliberately varied, and purposely not divided into categories (i.e. "childhood," "work," etc.). I wanted it to feel more like a ride, story after story popping up, providing multiple twists in the overarching narrative. I didn't want readers to get too comfortable thinking they know where this book is going; I wanted it to be like treasure box, a tome of surprise. I plan to assemble future anthologies similarly. The book itself pushes you to indulge in multiple genres and styles, creates a bit of a slut from everyone who leafs through its pages.

—Michelle Tea, Eagle Rock, Los Angeles, 2023

Amanda Montell

Slut Eras

Why is thy Lord so sluttish?
—Geoffrey Chaucer, *The Canterbury Tales*, ~1400

Do not trust her, she is a fugly slut.
—Regina George, *Mean Girls*, 2004

"i'm in my slut era," i whisper to myself as i curl up for a little nap.
—@bugsmaytrix, Twitter, 2022

As it happens, I am alone in northern Italy attempting to finish a book draft, and I've been calling myself a "cheese slut" since the moment I arrived. Every day at lunch servers ask if I'd like a bit of Parmigiano-Reggiano atop my tortelloni. "Tell me when to stop," they say, and I just let them jerk that wedge up and down the grater until my whole plate is doused in salty white stuff. The innuendos write themselves. It occurs to me that there's no accurate way to translate "cheese slut" into Italian, because in Bolognese culture, there is no such thing as censurable wantonness when it comes to dairy. The toothsome irony of the phrase would be lost.

It strikes me then how much this word "slut" has changed in general since it first entered my lexicon as an adolescent. Even just twenty years ago, "slut" contained little irony—it was a tool of public shame, a linguistic tomato hurled in the face of femininity. I heard it used privately on my best friend for the length of her jean skirts and publicly on the baby-voiced celebuttantes on MTV. I heard leading ladies in Y2K romcoms express their desperation to avoid the classification, like in the episode of *Sex and the City* where Carrie asks, "How many men is too many men? Are we simply romantically challenged, or are we sluts?" There seemed to be so few ways for a girl to pull off having a sexuality, I made an unconscious decision at twelve to opt out of one entirely.

For centuries, "slut," with its hissed opening consonant and the percussive slap of that final "t," served exclusively as a weapon shaped and sharpened for women. Now here I am in 2023, using it as a casual, hyperbolic garnish on my declaration of love for cheese. Linguistic change is a reflection of social change, and at the risk of too much optimism, I choose to interpret this semantic shift as a glint of hope for the future of women's sexual liberation—the brackish cream of freedom on the tip of my tongue.

About a decade ago, I began writing about feminist sociolinguistics, and one of the most enduring lessons I gathered from experts in the field was that word meanings and cultural beliefs work hand in hand. Where gendered slurs are concerned, a language's particular vocabulary of feminine insults says something about its speakers' attitudes toward women more broadly. For the 4,000-year-odd history of patriarchy, there's never been a way for a girl to come of age that didn't feel like some kind of trap. Our evolving rolodex of feminine insults, slut included, has always played a role in that entanglement.

Since it first appeared in English, "slut" has ridden a corkscrew roller coaster of semantic change. Etymologists' best guess is that its journey began with the comparatively benign Middle English term "slutte," which simply meant an "untidy" person—usually a woman, but there's evidence to suggest the term was also applied to men. In *The Canterbury Tales*, Chaucer describes one slovenly-dressed male lord as "sluttish."

It didn't take long, though, for "slut" to take on disparaging sexual connotations, reserved for women alone. By 1600, the word had devolved to mean an immoral, "sexually loose" woman ("To cast away honesty upon a foul slut were to put good meat into an unclean dish," penned Shakespeare in *As You Like It*). For generations, this cursed definition stuck, and it was only fortified by its heavy usage in pornography. In linguistics, this process whereby a word starts out indicating something fairly neutral or even positive and eventually deteriorates to mean something negative is called *pejoration*. Almost every word the English language has ever offered to reference femininity (from "tart" to "spinster" to "bitch," all of which once held relatively innocuous connotations) has followed this ill-fated route. The opposite process is called *amelioration*. And that, with delightful surprise, seems to describe where "slut" headed next.

By the late 1990s, some academics and activists were already making formal attempts to turn the word around. In their 1997 book *The Ethical Slut*, queer feminist writers Dossie Easton and Janet Hardy redefined a slut as "a person of any gender who has the courage to lead life according to the radical proposition that sex is nice and pleasure is good for you." It was a radical endorsement, but "slut" didn't ameliorate overnight. One can't change everyday speakers' conceptions of a word before they're ready. As the feminist linguist Deborah Cameron once said, "The struggle for meaning is a grass-roots campaign."

The next phase of slut's semantic transformation may have coincided with the rise of the term "slut-shaming." This coinage assigned a sorely missing label to the pattern of disparaging women for having violated some patriarchal standard for their sexuality. In an article for *American Speech*, lexicographer Ben Zimmer dug up one of the first recorded uses of "slut-shaming" from the comments section of a 2006 post on the feminist blog *I Blame the Patriarchy*: A reader had questioned if some earlier articles rebuking roller derby players were just engaging in a glorified form of "slut-shaming." The term gained wider traction through the late aughts during debates on sex-work legalization, and by the early 2010s, pockets of feminist culture were ready to embrace "slut" in a bigger way. In 2011, the SlutWalk movement was born. It arose after a cop gave a rape prevention talk at Toronto's York University, during which he proposed that young women could avoid sexual assault by dressing less provocatively. Outraged, students proudly scrawled "slut" across their chests and marched for the fact that women's sartorial choices were not the cause of on-campus sexual assault, and shame was not the solution.

At the time of New York City's first SlutWalk, I was attending college in Manhattan, and a few friends from my linguistics program invited me to march with them. At nineteen, my fledgling feminism still felt safer within the womb of a classroom than the hot throng of the streets. Skittish, I told them I had to stay home to finish a paper and couldn't go.

Until that point, slut's rebrand had mostly been serious business—feminist texts and protests. Then, something happened to lighten the mood: In the spring of 2022, a dimple-cheeked actor from a television series about a teen werewolf posted a tweet that read simply, "slut era." The phrase caught on like a Beatles song. Quickly amassing over 800,000 likes and 150,000 reshares, the tweet may not have provided a definition for "slut era," but the public quickly came up with one. A person's "slut era," according to KnowYourMeme.com, indicated "a period of time when one parties and embraces making questionable decisions." What fun.

Who knows if the TV-famous white boy came up with "slut era" himself, but if I had to put money on it, I'd guess likely not. Word provenances are always tough to trace, but when it comes to slang, linguists consistently find that young Black women invent more of it than anyone. Virginia Tech sociolinguist and lexicographer Kelly Wright told me, "Black women do language differently because they can, because they like it that way, because they seek to differentiate themselves from structures and systems that do not serve them, because Black individuality is a luxury, an heirloom to be protected and cherished." We have female speakers of African American English to thank for transforming all kinds of misogynistic slurs into beloved slang, like "bad bitch" (popularized by the '80s hip hop artist Trina), "hotation" (one's circle of casual sex partners, a playful portmanteau of "ho" and "rotation," which I first heard from comedian Issa Rae), and "WAP" (Cardi B's celebratory acronym for wet ass pussy). "Slut era" could be next on that list, but it diffused so quickly, we may never know.

As swift and meme-driven as internet communication is, it only took a few months for "slut era" to evolve to mean its precise opposite. "Language is a natural system," said Dr. Wright. "And thus it evolves as all other natural systems, in response to collective pressures experienced by the species or group." From the time of the teen were-wolf's tweet in April 2022 to September of that year, "slut" went from a celebration of social maximalism to a wry embrace of quotidian comforts. (When a phrase can mean either its literal or reverse definition like this, it's called a *contranym*. Another example is "hysterical," which can mean either funny or panicked and also has gendered undertones as it comes from the Greek word for "womb.")

A whole new genre of sardonic tweets emerged: "In my slut era (Eating 3 meals a day, only crying once a week, remembering to take my SSRIs)"; "'slut era' i say as i rot and decay in my bedroom and watch the years pass me by as i miss out on core experiences other people my age are having." That fall, *Rolling Stone* writer Miles Klee dubbed this "new" slut era "sort of a lonely time, a turning inward. We declare ourselves sluts in a flatly ironic way, knowing a hedonistic air is expected of us on social media, yet in the same breath admitting we can't (or won't) be putting in the work, which is too tiring and tedious."

Slut era, I might whisper, as I behold grated cheese falling onto my plate like snow and debate tossing my iPhone into the Adriatic Sea. "Sure, one-night stands are great," wrote Klee, "but have you ever remembered to eat and take your antidepressants?"

* * *

In 2017, I began writing a feminist linguistics book called *Wordslut*. I was so nervous to commit to that title. Even then, it was scandalizing. I was afraid to tell my parents. Once the book came out, reporters asked me in hushed tones how I convinced my publisher to go for it. While researching that project, I spoke to feminist writer Andi Zeisler, who told me that one effort we can make to mitigate the harm caused by gendered insults is simply to avoid using them abusively. That is, we can call upon them only in positive contexts ("wordslut" as opposed to "fugly slut"). When I interviewed Zeisler in 2017, that notion seemed like a pure fantasy; six years later, it's becoming more of a reality.

Alternatively, we can opt to give up slurs like "slut" altogether—after all, not every insult is destined for amelioration. Slut is one word that some feminists believe deserves to be abolished rather than reclaimed. One of the SlutWalk's own celebrity spokespeople, Amber Rose, confessed her resentment of the word. In 2017, the model told *Playboy* magazine, "My goal this year is to . . . get slut out of the dictionary. I'm going to find out where [*Webster's*] headquarters are, and tell my fans to come and protest with me." Storming *Webster's* HQ will no doubt be less impactful than choosing to eradicate or redefine "slut" in our own daily conversations; however, I agree that in a culture that did not spurn women's sexual sovereignty with such zeal, the entire concept of a "slut" would lose its resonance and eventually wither into obscurity. We've seen this kind of linguistic vanishing act before: The reason terms like "spinster" and "old maid" seem passé is because, as of the twenty-first century, so does the idea of criticizing a woman for being over the age of twenty-five and unmarried. Simply put, slurs go out of style at the same time the underlying belief in them does.

A recent Google Trends checkup revealed that web searches for "slut" have steadily dropped since the mid-2010s. It's a sign that the word might be fading from our vocabularies after all. However, we all have our own relationships to different slurs and personally, in sparing doses and flattering contexts, I've grown quite fond of "slut." Less than a decade after I began writing *Wordslut*, I tell people the book title with confidence, and sometimes an ironic wink, but no more shame. It doesn't feel like a coincidence that this linguistic shift dovetailed with my own personal journey toward sexual acceptance. As I was finishing my final draft of the book, at the height of the MeToo movement, I had relaxed enough into my own sexuality to assemble an exhilarating first "hotation" of my own.

The path to sexual freedom doesn't always seem to be pointed the right way. But it's been, dare I say, a thrill to watch slut's meaning ameliorate before my eyes online, like a time-lapse video of a ripening peach. It once took a word meaning as many years to evolve as it took to build a cathedral by hand. It could be centuries. Now, a 3D printer can make a house in a matter of weeks. Who knows what "slut" could mean in a decade or even a year. But our culture's larger relationship to pleasure will be what determines it. I consider the pasta in front of me. For English epochs, "slut" zapped the deliciousness out of sex for women the way words like "guilt" and "glutton" rob food. These labels are bars on a window, our bodies wrongly imprisoned. Whatever the next "slut era" brings, I hope there is pleasure and wordplay and liberation. And by god, I hope there are Alps of cheese.

Vera Blossom

A New Myth for the Slut

Sluts built this whole joint. The tapestry of history is awash with sluts; enterprising women who used beauty, wit, and sex to get what they wanted and not only that but build something bigger than themselves.

So many towns in the West Coast, my home country, were built up on the backs of whores. All the gold rush towns in the West weren't really towns at first. Just a bunch of sad dirt camps full of men sleeping, shitting, and seeking gold. This was where enterprising women saw an opportunity, offering their services and time to lonely, horny men in need of a good time. Brothels became so successful in the West that they could sustain entire towns around them. Women with money bought land and opened up stores, schools, and churches. It was women–sluts–who built the American West.

But who cares about American cities, right? That's all a bunch of settler-colonialist porn. Let's talk about something real: trans history.

Trans history is full of sluts taking care of each other. Sex freaks who found other sex freaks and took care of them like mothers. Trans women led the whole community of fags, dykes, baby transes, cis gays, into a brand-new future. And I know we like to #normalize-transpeople but a lot of us happen to be pretty slutty freaks, I'm saying this as a trans person who happens to be a slut freak. And we like to raise other baby slut freaks up to be big and strong; lascivious and licentious.

Just like the prostitutes and madams who used sex work to take care of themselves and their community, trans women often turn to sex work to take care of theirs. It's in the face of scarcity and violence where sluts can make some magic happen. Equipped with nothing but their bodies and street smarts, they build houses and families.

* * *

Recently, my mother came to visit me in Chicago, and I took the opportunity to ask her about her life. She's always been a bit enigmatic, perhaps because I never asked or perhaps it's because her sun is in Gemini. My sister, my mom, and I were all gathered together at a rooftop bar in my neighborhood, the one all my friends work at, and because they love me, they are sliding over heavy-handed cocktails that taste like spirits and smoke. It was the perfect environment to gossip about the past.

It's on this roof where I learned my mom was a slut, too. She was a party girl—is a party girl—seeking adventure and fun. She flirted with co-workers and customers at her job, she juggled boyfriends, she was a regular in the house party circuit of '90s Bay Area Asians.

This was incredibly thrilling. I loved that my own sluttery was a part of a grand legacy. Growing up, I knew my dad was a slut. He's a serial monogamist, sure and he's also an abusive narcissist, but he's also, as they say, got that dog in him. He's a total man slut that loves throwing big parties and flirting with every beautiful woman unlucky enough to cross his path. I always worried that I got my flirtiness from him, weary that I might be like my father (a nightmare, obviously). But now that I know my flirtiness could come from either parent—maybe even both—I feel a sense of relief. It's like something I was always going to inherit. I'm like a nepo-baby for being a hoe.

I've always thought that wanton horniness and a penchant for sexual freedom were natural feelings for humans to feel. I never understood why everything in this country was so staunchly anti-sex. When did the pursuit of sexual pleasure become something so loathed in this country when sluts have been so essential to its history?

As always, I like to blame the Puritans. But apparently, in some ways, Puritans were actually pro-sex. They encouraged women to have sex with their husbands—yes to procreate, but for pleasure as well. Sexual pleasure between husband and wife was an important tenet in some Puritan communities. Impotence and erectile dysfunction were considered solid grounds of divorce and communities would agree that a woman needed a man who could get it up.

However, any sexual act outside of husband and wife procreating was not seen as favorably. This is a pretty good means of control: keeping a subservient class of people who rely on men as leaders, forcing men into roles as breadwinners and homestead security. It does not allow for a lot of revolution, anti-monarchal action. It produces capital and it produces workers. The system at work.

Anything that requires heavy policing and laws to keep in action is obviously rather unnatural. Humans like to fuck. Humans like to fuck in all matter of configurations—tops, bottoms, sides, cucks, bulls, orgies, swingers, unicorns, subs, doms. We invented all of these out of pure human ingenuity. Surely humanity has proliferated as it has because of some ancient sluts who enjoyed the act of procreation. There were some cave whores who chased the pleasure of fucking and, perhaps, found pleasure in mothering, too, and now here we all are. The products of millennia of sex.

Policing free sex is the act of depriving us of life. It's like outlawing the purchase and sale of food, the criminalization of something as fundamental to human life as eating.

Obviously, as a devout hedonist I believe our time on earth should be focused on the pursuit of all earthly pleasures. But even as a pragmatist: sex is kind of essential for life, you guys. We need more humans to keep this earth turning. And sex is healing, it regulates our nervous system, it keeps us happy and functioning. It also connects you to someone else in such a primal way—something beyond language. To have sex is to directly interface with someone else's biological system, your spit entering someone else's ecosystem of spit. A spank sending electrical signals from your ass to your brain and making you feel at peace. To discourage this is to discourage life.

* * *

That night at the rooftop bar, I learned that my biological grand-mother, my mother's mother, was a bar girl in the Philippines, planted near one of the many US military bases that sprung up after Spaniards decided that they lost the war and sold the country to America.

There's a whole industry for bar girls in the Philippines. These are beautiful women who know how to dance, serve drinks, laugh, enter-tain American men whose pockets are lined with imperial money. This dynamic is one of the many insidious ways colonization mani-fests itself—here we have military men gawking at local girls like they're another one of the sights to see in this country they're occu-pying, and the girls help maintain the romantic fantasy of a settler taking up space in a totally non-violent way. It's hard to blame the bar girls for participating. There's an obvious opportunity here, the same opportunity prostitutes in the American West found during the Gold Rush. Plus, anti-imperialistically abstaining from fucking Americans for money is not going to pay the bills.

I don't know if my grandma was a sex worker, strictly speaking. It was more likely that she was a waitress or a dancer, maybe used her sexuality to make a few extra tips on the side. Regardless of her day job, she fooled around with a man—maybe he was a soldier, maybe he was just a foreigner from the West having fun in this neighbor-hood carved out of the Philippines for foreigners to have fun in.

This man is what my mother refers to as her "sperm donor" since that's all the information she has on him. He was not from the Philippines. He was maybe Puerto Rican, maybe German. My biological grandmother did not terminate the pregnancy, but she was not ready to raise a baby.

Instead, she gave the baby up to her good friend who happened to be the woman running a bunch of bars staffed by beautiful women— yes her boss. My actual grandma. This de facto madam took my mother in and raised her. She was extremely Catholic and extremely strict, despite running a business that required hiring eager women to entertain eager men. She was not a cultural slut; she was an entrepreneur and she saw an opening.

Still, I wonder where I might have ended up if my bio-grandma didn't sleep with one of the soldiers stationed by her bar. If my adoptive grandma didn't see an opening for the sex industry and decide to cater to the needs of a bunch of foreign men. If my mom wasn't a party girl searching for fun once she moved to America she might not have found my dad, a true Lothario. It's likely that I wouldn't be here if a series of women hadn't indulged in sluttery.

So, I posit a rebrand for the slut, a vibe shift if you will. Don't get me wrong, it's beautiful that sluts are dirty and salacious, but what if we added to the mythology?

The slut is a shaman, communing with the spirit of sexuality that lingers within you. They pull something primal out of you, they regulate your body, and bring you back in tune with our bestial nature.

Sluts are healers, massaging the emotional and physical aches and pains that come from being a human. They help unravel the knot that work, death, disease, trauma, and capitalism tie you into. They are bringers of light and soothing.

The slut is a planeswalker communing with oblivion. She calls upon that ether that we come from when we're born and where we go to when we die. She invokes an orgasm, a constriction of your muscles, the palpitation of the heart, the paralysis of your nerves. She calls forth la petit mort—a mini death. The slut sometimes risks her life, knowing that there is always a chance she might fall into the void of oblivion at the hands of a cruel Johnny or in a freak sex accident. She knows that the man might lock her up for her actions, putting her in a cage until she dies. She knows it's all worth it, if it's in the pursuit of pleasure.

Sluts are shepherds of life, bringing together people, creating new human beings, raising kids and each other. She keeps her community alive and thriving. She sees the shadows and the light and guides her family through life between the two.

A slut is a know-it-all. She knows where to find all the fun. She knows no life is worth living without some dirty fucking fun.

Fun

Ah, but a man's reach should exceed his grasp,
Or what's a heaven for?
— Robert Browning, "Andrea del Sarto"

When I was another boy, I was the boy-next-door. He was Jase, short for Jason: generic, but with a nickname just *off* enough to seem real. My lover—I call him Famous, which he is to me—became Jase's best friend, Chris, a name that needs no explanation. Jase and Chris weren't quite boyfriends, not like we were in real life, in which we worked very hard to be boyfriends. In real life, we had to stay below the radar of the Immigration and Naturalization Service. We had to figure out what domestic meant, as in home and as in argument. We were known to many for being adorable and codependent. IRL, we were gay. Because the way we were identified became an identity. Maybe that's how it works, for me anyway: I don't seek out identity, but consider my position, and articulate it like a mime feels their box.

Online, I could shake it off altogether.

Jase was just a body organized around his lickable ass, thick and juicy. If you could smell over the internet, you'd get high off the fumes. He did not have mammoth pores on his nose, like real me, or baroque ingrown hairs. He did not lose his erections. He was either unavailable or rock hard.

The term catfish wasn't yet used, but in a way that's what I was doing. I'm just not always sure what the difference is between that and my delusions. For one, I claimed I was nineteen and Chris had just turned eighteen. We were maybe six years older, and mid-twenties is a long haul from teen. We did not live in San Francisco—too fruity. I said *somewhere near Santa Cruz*. Lying close to the truth helped me feel convincing.

I was catfishing the catfishers—these two low-rent pornographers from San Diego County. I imagined them living in a condo. They knew how to build a website. It was called SaggerBoyz. It promised skaters, surfers, swimmers and plenty of sagging, all in the typeface of a beach cafe. The homepage was Tw!nk of the Day, a big new image with the archive below, and the rest of the site was divided into scrollable grids of clickable thumbnails in the categories of skater, surfer, swimmer, sagger. The images ranged from sneaky shots of brunette dolphins in Speedos taken by some craven attendee at a high school swim meet to full frontals of sun-bleached blonds looking with shock at their newly arrived erections.

The experience was one of anticipation. The photos took forever to load via dial-up onto our iMac, so it was a bummer if, for instance, you thought you were getting a detailed hairy crack but it was just shadow. The images appeared in horizontals, some sections thin glimmers, then suddenly a chunk, a nice bit of clavicle. We ate snacks, smoked cigarettes and listened to The Moldy Peaches during the interminable wait.

I'm not sure exactly what we wanted when we submitted our photos. To be objects rather than subjects. To be worthy of the grid. To be legitimate. As a couple, we were illegitimate. Famous only had a British passport and had overstayed his allotted time in the States in order to be with me. He could not leave for fear they wouldn't let him back in.

As an individual, I felt illegitimate. In high school, my mixed-race friends and I referred to one another as half. But half-what, which half did that mean? I was half-everything that gay men forbade on their Craigslist personal ads: fat, femme, Asian.

Online, using far fewer words than I did in live conversation, I could be an easier person to like. I could be an object. I could stop being over-analytical. I could emerge, as someone else, from shame. I cropped out half my big forehead—"an eight-head" as the dig goes in *Do the Right Thing*—and half my brain. Offering myself up through a limited selection of angles, I could expect to be told what I was: A good looking boy, so fuckable. You look like fun.

Jase and Chris did not need to *pass*, they just were so boyish they blended in. They were skaters, and rapscallions. Jase and Chris should be imagined skating away, and not just for the ass, but the departure, sailing towards their own horizon, not paying attention, turning their backs. The currency of Jase and Chris was in their elusiveness. Their allure was how they presented a challenge. But of course their corruptibility. And complicity. After all, they supplied these two men with a selection of graphic images.

These uploaded in horizontal bars, a too-slow striptease until finally there it all was, laid out for the two webmasters to behold—shaft and sack and, underneath, enough fuzz to make a man purr. My thick buns. Chris's cakes. My furry legs. Twenty toes. The canine faces. Two puppies. Noses like snouts. Hoodies unzipped, falling open. Two trails to adventure. Mouths agape. What pervert wouldn't want to wipe his ugly, impertinent cock all over Jase and Chris until they reeked, then send them out onto the streets. The world shall know they are objects.

I had by then understood that to be desirable you had to be a type. I learned by osmosis. The desirable types—jock, frat boy, surfer, all of them undiseased—were ideals. And to be convincing as that type, that ideal, is a matter of relativity. So to be this ideal skater, reluctant and delicious, I placed myself in a context where the suspension of disbelief was inherent, through these select images sent to faithful perverts. A fantasy was built by what was cropped out of the image. It helped that we were not audible; I wouldn't have to force a masculine grunt, swallow down my gay voice. The men only watched, never heard, Jase and Chris, in less and less clothing.

Our emails were taciturn and confident. *We're buddies. Always together! Thought you might like these pix we took.* They witnessed us shoot our wads onto the deck of my board, anointing the grip tape. They didn't observe us swish into Katz Bagels and dither over sundried tomato or chive cream cheese. Jase and Chris ate whatever. Jase and Chris did not know every word to all of *69 Love Songs.* They had never heard of Pierre et Gilles or Jean Genet. In order to be an object, I couldn't also be a fag—not a cultured fag. There was too much backstory in that, of overcoming and political liberation.

It wasn't exactly catfishing, because it was our actual faces and bodies, and if it was deceitful, it was a gift. We were naked before them. They could believe what they wanted from those pictures. I hadn't really considered they could do what they wanted with them.

* * *

The first known publication of the word *fun,* as a noun, was in 1699, in the first edition of *A new dictionary of the terms ancient and modern of the canting crew,* credited to the author B.E. Gentleman. The word *fun* was defined as "a Cheat or slippery Trick," as used by disreputable types who speak in cant, or coded jargon used within a socially marginal group. The full title of the glossary was: *A new dictionary of the canting crew in its several tribes of gypsies, beggers, thieves, cheats &c.: useful for all sorts of people (especially foreigners) to secure their money and preserve their lives; besides very diverting and entertaining being wholly new.*

Prior to this, the word made its way into print as a verb—also meaning to cheat, cajole, trick or deceive—in the sheet music for the ballad "Poor Tom the Taylor": "For she had fun'd him of his Coin; oh then he could have kill'd her."

The *Oxford English Dictionary* traces the evolution of *fun* within a couple of decades, though still classified as a "low cant word," to mean "light-hearted pleasure, enjoyment, or amusement; boisterous joviality or merrymaking; entertainment." By the time of my youth, this was the most widely used sense of the word, perhaps carrying over a residual slumming-it connotation, as in *Girls Just Want to Have…*

As *fun* came to be used as a synonym for sex, it retained a seedy, debauched quality. *Are you looking for a little fun?* says the television streetwalker into the blackness of the idling car. Eventually some gays on apps would separate themselves from hardcore cruising: *not looking for fun*—an amusing way of managing expectations.

* * *

We were unpaid sex workers. We were gaining something, I guess, by giving it away: a feeling of desirability, and the exchange of a particular type of desire, as if speaking in our own slang.

I had to think like the webmasters, which was actually pretty close to thinking as myself. I should look like a boy who might bully the webmasters when they were younger yet turned out to be gentle and amenable. Jase, a little tough. Chris, a little untouchable. Yet the men had access, even power. They could shoot a load onto the screen.

I think Famous was just indulging an exhibitionist streak, while for me it may have been a little more complicated, hence all the subterfuge around our identity. Unsure who I was, I could become a sex toy, a means to gratification. Exhibitionism was a way to disappear.

I figured my own self-vanishing was theirs, too, Jase would not remind these guys of struggle, oppression, self-hate and AIDS. I did not think I could make contact with them as a self-possessed young gay man with ideas and opinions. That wouldn't be sexy, I thought, not their sexy, which was not about a queer utopia, but the frisson within repression. Their sexy must stay in high school, continuing to seek the contact they never made.

* * *

In 1972, the *International Journal of Psychoanalysis* published an article entitled "Homeovestism: Perverse Form of Behaviour Involving Wearing Clothes of the Same Sex" by G. Zavitzianos. If I've matched his identity correctly with a *Washington Post* obituary, this Zavitzianos was born in Corfu, Greece, studied in Paris then taught at places including Georgetown University while maintaining a private medical practice and writing poetry.

His "homeovestism" article is composed of just two case studies: Both twenty years old, one female and one male, both apparently a little too aroused by wearing clothes that adhere to gender conventions. The approach and vocabulary of the article are obviously pathologizing. The shrink sees them as, I don't know, criss-cross-dressers. "In both patients," he surmises, "homeovestism stabilized a precarious body image, relieved castration and separation anxiety and maintained regressive object relationships."

The Boy was "probably an unwanted child," G. Zavitzianos says. His mother couldn't deal, and he was raised by his sister and in fear of his older brother. At the age of three, he began to wear his mother's and sister's dresses. His sister encouraged this, and by the age of six or seven it was a regular thing. He preferred the company of girls, in which "he had the tendency, because of the persistence of primary identification, to become like them, to think the way they did, to imitate their gestures, manners, etc. He could no longer feel that he was a boy. When he was in the company of men, it was different. They inhibited him because he was afraid of them, but when he had a homosexual relationship, he felt at ease, because his feelings of inferiority and of dissatisfaction with his self-image disappeared."

He had an intense relationship with his dad, "who was attached to him narcissistically, spoiled him continually, and promised him a marvelous future if he would love and listen to him." The boy, dependent and ambivalent, often hated him. As he hit puberty and hit the showers, he saw two athletic types wearing jock-straps and "got the impression that the jock-straps covered very large penises." His own, he felt, was not. He tried to masturbate wearing one in front of the mirror. This made it easier to get hard—his covered dick he could imagine being bigger—but he had trouble reaching orgasm. "Since puberty, he had always worn underdrawers similar to those that his father and older brother wore, which was an indication of his admiration for them and his desire to be like them. Here, then, we have a case of male homeovestism since the patient is using clothing of the same sex for his perverse behaviour. When he looks at himself in the mirror wearing this apparel, he reacts with an erection." The mirror, in Dr. Z's analysis, facilitates a simulated homosexual incestuous relationship in which, wearing his athletic-supporter, the boy becomes his own omnipotent father.

When having sex with a girl, the boy kept looking at her feet. But they were too small, apparently, for him to "overcome his castration anxiety," so he gazed at his own ("and not at his penis.") He wanted another dick to grasp and grind against. When he engaged in homosex, he could look at another penis. And: "When he sees handsome men, he stares at them as if he wanted to 'take in' their beauty and power. His glance finally falls to the genital area as if he wanted to 'absorb' the penis. At times he feels as if he wanted to steal it. He is dissatisfied with his own face and body and feels that if only he could get a good penis everything would change in him like magic. Sometimes he buys clothes, usually shirts, like those of the men he admires, so that he can feel a little like them."

He may have had a strong exhibitionist tendency—a component of homeovestism, the doctor tells us—but this was mostly repressed: "He compromises by a hippie appearance."

In *The Philosophy of Andy Warhol: From A to B and Back Again*, published three years later, Warhol writes: "So today if you see a person who looks like your teenage fantasy walking down the street, it's probably not your fantasy but someone who had the same fantasy as you and decided instead of getting it or being it, to look like it, and so he went and bought that look you both like. So forget it. Just think of all the James Deans and what it means."

What *does* it mean? I know gay men in this model became known as *clones*, a term that Wayne Koestenbaum has pointed out "subtly derides a gay male's nonreproductive sexuality: it defines homosexuality as replication of the same."

* * *

The undies that I purloined from my dad, when I was maybe fifteen, were see-through white bikinis that he'd been forced to purchase on a trip to Paris because he'd found himself short on clean underwear and they were "fast-drying." Everyone in my family agreed they were funny. The bunchy elasticated waistband was annoying. But they were as sexy as I could get.

When I was maybe thirteen, I had tried to shoplift a set of tiny briefs—with a torso-to-thigh photo on the box —from JCPenny's. The security guard had no time for my excuse, which was that I nabbed them for my father who was in great need. When my dad showed up, looking not needy, the head of security knew I was a liar, but did he really have to go through with all the paperwork? It seemed prejudiced considering the loot had a retail value of seven dollars or something.

My dad and I were forced to go to an anti-shoplifting workshop, like traffic school, because the law was: if you could afford to pay the fee, and had the time to attend the session, the incident would be wiped from your record when you turned eighteen. And I could legally say, we were told, that I have never been arrested. The kids whose parents could not afford it, I guess, still have to legally say they have been arrested to this day. Even if they actually had stolen for a father in need.

"Permanent record." We heard this warning all the time when I was a kid. I never imagined anything good could possibly go on my permanent record.

I wish upon all adolescent homeovestites your success in shoplifting underpants more skimpy than any you'd be willing to purchase openly.

So you won't have to resort to pilfering your dad's French fast-driers. Which I was wearing in spite of the fact, not because, they belonged to my father. They were so skimpy, I figured, he was unlikely to notice their disappearance. They were the kind of item destined to slip down the back of a chest of drawers or washing machine.

The fabric was silky. My nub bent over like a defensive slug. I wore them under my shorts on a walk behind our property, through the former orchard, past the Boo Radley house, into the construction zone. There were already gently winding streets, looking like a new track for go-kart racing. The incipient houses lined up like naked adolescent androids: boxy, two-story frames. The name of the development was meant to sound French, like a type of wine. The homes were already selling, and progress seemed to be going apace, although weirdly there never seemed to be many construction workers around. The sounds the few guys emitted fell into a mellow rhythm, not obstreperous like the pneumatic drill from some movie about a dynamic metropolis.

The reverberation from a single hammer bounced off the hills. As if it belonged to the last of the gold rush prospectors, still loony for gold. But really, I imagined at the end of the hammer there'd be a burnished, hairy arm and at the end of that arm a tawny laborer just into his twenties with vocational muscle and a willingness to molest me just to shake the routine.

I'd wait until the men broke for baloney sandwiches, which they chomped over legs akimbo, then slink by soliciting a wolf whistle but earning nary a glance. On other occasions I wore nothing beneath my shorts but a condom hanging loosely off my dick. I struggled to keep it affixed while walking. I pictured the drooping cap of Dopey, the seventh dwarf, squirming down there. I thought: if they are not elves or gnomes, just tiny miners off to work, why are they adorned in those baggy hats that seem to allude to arcane powers, like some Deadhead wizard beanie? Anyway, I felt positive that with my sheathed dick I emanated desirability and the builders could tell that underneath my clothes I was dissolute and free. Why no catcalls, then, no following?

I sat upstairs in my choice of the unfinished houses. The builders were on another site uphill so I could climb this one's exposed stairway unobserved and claim my concrete corner. To amble through the shell of this typical two-story was like feeling one's way through a floor plan in 3-D. In just a few months, the walls would be plastered, insulated and wallpapered, and eventually there'd be a piano upon which would sit frames, and in the frames would be photos of the people who called the place home. The first family to live in this boring house in the bend of the road. Each member of the family would be represented atop the baby grand, some appearing more often than others. (Only one of the dad.)

The photographers will have been hired by church or school. Each will have been selected as the best of the options provided, though the person in the photograph will have liked none of them very much at all. The mother and daughters would say *I hate that picture of myself.*

Then the daughter would get the one-time treat of a portrait taken in a proper studio in the shopping mall, with additional fussing reflected in the price. This photographer takes the teenage girl by the chin and points her face at three-quarters towards the future, like a mermaid figurehead on a great American ship.

As a result of this posing and titivating, with not a hair askew, plus the subsequent retouching, in which the edges are blurred like the start of a dream sequence, the sitter would be sure to look frosty and beautiful. Another effect was to depict the sitter in double, facing forward and hovering behind herself in silhouette. Despite how it sounds, this will make the girl look not crazy, but important.

Even my family, disinclined to bells and whistles, eventually capitulated, but the double-portrait commission was literally two of us: my sister's face in the foreground and mine sideways behind. I never saw anyone else do it this way, and I suspected it was a little cheap of my parents, and also seemed to miss the point, which surely was narcissism.

The quality of production in the most elite cases was indicated by a gold signature in the corner: Alan J. Milner, at a tilt with flourish, both reliable and Hollywoody. I was under the impression the actual Alan J. Milner shot each of these photographs personally until some sagacious acquaintance explained that it didn't matter who took the picture, Alan J. Milner was the name of the chain.

In the unfinished house, the decoration would be brand new and deliberated over by wives who would go through catalogs saying *that one.* The interior would involve a lot of white. You were obviously a more refined person if you were able to maintain a domicile vulnerable to the ravages of a spill. There would be no stains. The kitchen would be spotless and shiny, and the enormous, gently humming refrigerator would be stocked full of victuals for famished teenagers to heartily consume after school, before they did or did not play the piano upon which were displayed their photographs in frames.

I took pleasure in knowing that the family moving here was unaware I occupied the spot where they planned to put a wing-backed chair. My toes explored the boundaries of rooms whose measurements the husband and wife knew by heart. But I knew the actual space more intimately than them. I made contact first, and it was with the concrete skeleton under the thick carpets that would lie servile beneath their feet. I was touching the bones. Imagine their faces if they knew I sat there smoking cigarettes in the stairwell, dangling my scrappy legs over the edge, where an external wall would be. I could look out through the whole of it, when they'd suffer the limitations of viewing only through window frames.

I decided to leave behind the condom for the construction workers to find as an invitation or clue. I pried the thing from my crotch and tossed it to the floor, where it splat despondently. The texture was powdery. I pushed myself up, swanning around in a proprietorial manner then juddering forward on the balls of my feet with a sense of jazzy superiority. My fly remained open. For the present it was I who lived in this house. I knew it prenatally. I was more at one with it than they would ever be, because I knew it not as something fore-closed, but a potentiality.

I was insatiable for the sound of the hammer to stop, for the worker to lay down tools and wander bow-legged to this site on the bend, first enraged by my presence, engorged and veiny. I had never really shot a load. The cum just leaked out, usually when I was lying prone and picturing the one from Wham! who wasn't George Michael. He'd be wearing his white tennis shorts. I had a sticker of Wham! on my bedroom door, the outside edge of which had lately found itself at the mercy of my groin, rocked back and forth on a hinge that creaked its disapproval. I was only vaguely aware of the possibility of really gushing, whether through atavism or word of mouth. It was like there was an orchestra forever tuning in my testes.

I pictured the sheet music on the piano. I needed something pre-scriptive like that. I imagined being forced by the hammerer. Did that mean I was thinking about being raped? Is that what it would take to relieve this immense pressure? I did not know what it is to surrender. In the meantime, if I could be an unwilling participant, maybe I wouldn't feel ashamed.

When would I be ready to spew forth, viscid and sticky? Splatter all over this rudimentary floor. Something held me back. If only I could contribute my semen to the agglutinant that would keep the plush carpets in place. Or better still, me alongside the tanned hammerer . . . tomorrow or the day after—for he certainly does not seem to be coming over today. Only we would know the extra ingredient in the adhesive. A part of us would be a part of what glued the house together.

* * *

Years later, I found my glue. Famous and I made glue all the time. Why did we want other men's eyes on us? Because we were gluey, we did not just stick together, other things stuck to us, too. The literary scholar Steven Connor has written of how childhood is like the sticky side of tape, whereas adulthood is akin to the gloss on the reverse. When we're kids, we've got our last two meals on our face and bits of sandcastle in our hair and who-knows-what beneath our fingernails. Adults don't like this. It's a faux pas just to have a bit of oat milk foam on your lip. We were not ready to gloss over, to turn away from the world.

So we sent the photos. In the ones of Chris, he could be thirteen years old, looking at his photogenic penis as if he's been given a trophy. As if it was his essence, somehow, his identity. Mine, delicious, but photographed sinewy, like beef jerky.

I figured if they were going to put the photos up on their site, there'd be some discussion, maybe compensation, certainly an ID check. What would we do? There was no Jase—just a Jeremy, older, with an Asian last name. Chris was actually an English scofflaw with no work visa who couldn't give his real name.

Turns out we didn't have to worry. They just threw the photos up. Jase, broody, his thick head and soft belly. Chris, looking inappropriately young. The other boys were off guard, horsing around or showboating. We looked maybe a little too sensual and artistic. Still, we *passed*, blended into the grid. I wondered how many people were slowly loading the photos, if they waited for the complete image, left it open while they masturbated. Anyway, we'd gone public, if not exactly with consent. After too much coffee, I began to fret about my permanent record.

When I had to be at work at the video store (quite Jase) or the community college French class (not Jase at all), I burned to get home and take more Polaroids, send them to the two guys. It was just me who wrote the emails and just one of them, Paul, who responded. He'd refer to the other guy, Danny, as if he was in charge. I'd created a separate hotmail account with an address that used the phrase woodpusher. Paul mentioned in an email we should visit them in San Diego County, they'd fly us down, we could sit in the hot tub with them.

IRL, we were becoming more like Jase and Chris. I took to wearing a striped polo over a long-sleeve t-shirt, puka shells around my neck, a Fuct Skateboards cap. All very Jase, meaning an attempt at Josh Hartnett. Which came first, this self-identification or the photographic representation? I couldn't tell anymore. It felt fake but real, and it felt good, and hot, but also kind of half-assed, like how Dr. Z's young man compromised with "a hippie appearance." We still had to look indie enough to stay credible with friends. We couldn't go the way of Abercrombie & Fitch. Famous had not long ago experimented with *Rocky Horror*-ish weirdo femme looks, painting his nails and eyes and lips and hair, wearing mesh and making video self-portraits smoking sad cigarettes. But somehow as Chris he was perfect. The ten pounds the camera puts on remade him into everybody's all-American just-eighteen dream.

I had no idea at the time about Dr. Z's diagnosis, thankfully. It would have fucked me up. Or rather taken away the feeling that I had the right to be fucked up in my own way. I had started considering my gender in variations like a snake eating its own tail: Was I, for instance, a femme boy's mind trapped in a woman's soul trapped in a butch boy's body? This went nowhere, but that was totally cool, because the permissive culture of San Francisco allowed me to send some ripples through my gender, and to laugh at my reflection.

So why was it that what was turning me on was the imagined condo, the hot tub invitation? Suburbs had become my fetish. How could I be a truly hip San Franciscan if my fantasy life wasn't Radical Faeries or fisting, but SoCal surf camps and stolen fumbles between the two-car garage and kidney-shaped pool?

A lot of us spend the first part of our life with our heads down. I'm not talking about fellatio, but discretion. As we surmised we were unable to be fully dimensional beings, we acquired another layer, some kind of fakery. When I was Jase, even as I leaned in, I chafed against that layer. With time, I came to respect it, live alongside it, a part of me.

Around the time I conjured Jase, I had mostly abandoned contemporary fiction. I found new novels too often rang false. I liked old novels because I didn't have to decipher their authenticity—they were too far removed from my own experience.

Contemporary porn, on the other hand, I admired very much. We watched Dink Flamingo's *Active Duty* series, in which military boys, or those pretending to be, tug on their cocks boastfully, and gradually succumb to each other's curiosity. Were the dog tags authentic, or provided by Dink? Did it matter? There was an insatiable anticipation to the parts of these videos where the pair (or trio) sits on the couch or bed together, becoming increasingly horned up from their own and the other's hesitation.

My other favorite studio was Defiant Productions. It delivered straight skaters. They looked stinky. The armpit bushes and greasy hair were throwbacks to a raunchier homosexuality, yet made safe by the fact that the dirty boys were supposedly not gay. If gay men had become epilated and wholesome, and gay bars ice-cold and wipe-clean, all of it telegraphing *disease-free*, the skaters made it possible to indulge the grungy, bruised and scraped, the ripe, foul and filthy. As if straight guys didn't already have enough privilege, they were now the ones entitled to be unclean, too. At some point, Defiant adopted the slogan, "the best in horny, all amateur, skater boy action, proving that you don't have to be gay to have hot man on man sex!"

* * *

One morning, I brought up the SaggerBoyz site as usual, and there was Chris, his familiar blue hoodie and checked shirt falling open, his pale penis hogging the foreground. His dick was chewing up the scenery. He was Tw!nk of the Day. I went hot in the soles of my feet and my cheeks, which is my first reaction when someone has undermined or offended me. I was envious. Jase may have been on a clickable grid—skater section—but Chris was the homepage.

Yo Paul, I emailed later. *Saw Tw!nk of the Day, so cool. —Jase*

Hey Jase! Yeah!, he responded. *Don't forget to log on tomorrow. It's going to be YOU.*

Aw, man—but Chris is better. So hot! —Jase.

Yeah, Danny thinks he's great. Gets him off! But I like you. Very handsome! —Paul

I checked SaggerBoyz the next day, and again, for maybe a week or two. Jase was never Tw!nk of the Day. Why the empty promise—was I being strung along, unaware I was only a pimp for the truly marketable Chris?

Soon enough, Famous insisted we go camping. We needed to get away from screens. And out there we breathed in redwoods and heard brooks babble. We drove home smelling of campfire. We listened to Cat Power. We noticed boys on the freeway, drivers and passengers, that looked like real saggers, with a girlfriend or a group of other dudes or their families. An arm steering the wheel, or leaning against the window, headed towards front lawns, towards condos and hot tubs, their heteronormative lives, our homosexual fantasy.

I stopped checking SaggerBoyz, and the hotmail account. We left behind the names Jase and Chris. But we had *taken in* their beauty and power, *absorbed* them, like a happy version of homeovestism. Not long after that we began having group sex with other fags, who had also taken in and absorbed the essence of handsome males they have seen. Like Dr. Z's case study, they bought similar shirts to the men they admired. We took those shirts off. We learned a different form of surrender. It felt real, and *enough*, and we had fun.

Cyrus Dunham

Sorry

In my green bedroom there are three of us. The other two are blonde and I am not. My parents are asleep at the front of the apartment. The lamp is on and we're whispering. We end up in this place: show us. Giggling, begging. "Come on, show us." He's wearing athletic shorts and high white socks. He pulls the shorts down and pulls it out. We're twelve and he's shorter than both of us. But he grows in front of us and it's adult. It's giant compared to him. We want to touch it but we're afraid because it's alive and has its own will. We touch it like it's someone's pet lizard or snake. Reaching into the glass tank, quickly tapping it and then pulling our hands back, squealing. We calm down, reach back in, touch it for a bit longer.

I had the sense it was separate from him. His name was Jasper. The living thing was an extension of Jasper, but it also wasn't Jasper. It was his, and it wasn't me or mine. The skin was like sticky paper, wrapped around something hard. A new kind of skin I hadn't touched before. He didn't seem to enjoy it at all. "Ouch," he said. "Too tight."

His parents were young, cool—a soap opera actor and a photographer. They wore black leather jackets, lived in a loft in the East Village, drove him to school on a motorcycle. He had long hair he kept behind his ears and wore a chain around his neck like a grown man. I imagined myself in his outfits, with his hair, in his chain.

The other girl sat behind him, her legs jutting out at an angle matching his. She reached forward like she was reaching around and grabbing herself. He held her hand inside his and moved it up and down. Faster, harder. His face had no expression, but he periodically licked his lips. I reached forward and held the tip. "Your hand is clammy," he said to me.

"Sorry," I said, "I'm sorry." I stopped and just watched, unsure what or how to be.

He says he's going to finish, like the end of everything is near. Now he parts his lips, closes his eyes, and exhales a small sigh. She says, "Ew, I don't want to see it." She doesn't want to see the end. She doesn't want the world to end. I do, but I don't speak up. I want to be the one providing the ending. He says he has to or it will hurt. We tell him to go to the bathroom and do it in there. We say do it in your hand and show us. He goes in there for a minute. The bathroom has turquoise tiles, my older sister's makeup covering the counter. He comes back in with his hand cupped. The end looks like glue. A white, shiny puddle. She jams the tip of her pointer finger into the end and then mimes throwing up. I do the same. The end is hot, sticky. "Ew, ew, ew, ew, ew."

Now he's soft and a kid again. He washes his hands off in the bathroom and comes back with his shorts pulled back up, hunching over. We are laughing, rolling around on the bed. I have green sheets, a green comforter, to match my green walls. He asks us not to tell anyone. We keep laughing, rolling around. "Seriously," he says, "Don't tell anyone." We fall asleep with the other girl in the middle and in the morning we pretend it never happened. I hold the image of his sigh in my head for a long time, I zero in on it and replay it, a mantra I imagine is me, is mine.

His dad's show was *One Life to Live*. His dad played Kevin, a violent, sociopathic rapist so handsome that no woman could resist him. A few months after the green room the dad took a group of us to set. We watched from behind the camera while Kevin cut his hand with a shard of glass to try and convince a woman to stay. He winced as he sliced his hand. After the scene was over he showed us a little plastic sack of red liquid. What looked like blood wasn't blood. Eventually the dad won a daytime Emmy for playing Kevin. They kept the Emmy on a shelf in their loft. Jasper got an older girlfriend and started having sex before the rest of us, before he grew any hair on his face or body. He started working out, getting bigger and stronger, like his dad.

I don't have a green room anymore. I haven't seen Jasper in a long time. I heard he's a soccer coach, married to a Scandinavian nurse. They have a baby. Recently I was in a small room off a red-lit hallway. The hallway was wet, and so was every little room off the hallway. In each room naked men congregated in the red light. The walls between the rooms didn't go all the way up. The space was full of sticky sounds. I stood with my back against a black wall, my friend bent over in front of me with his ass against my groin, his mouth around the cock of another man I was kissing. My friend moved back and forth like I was inside him. The third man didn't know us, didn't know our names, didn't know what wasn't there, what I didn't have. The third man was skinny but strong, with a hairy chest, a gold chain around his neck. We didn't speak the same language, so all we'd said was "Hello." I held my friend's hips and the harder I slammed against them, the more he swallowed the third man. We stopped kissing and I watched the third man's face. He became a little boy. He licked his upper lip, closed his eyes, and breathed a long, quiet exhale. He pulled my friend up and held him, finished with his own hand. I watched their embrace. He came on my friend's stomach. I watched him sigh, but didn't get to see the end itself. There was no end for me.

The green room is next to the red room. In both rooms there was something I didn't have, something that wasn't mine. In both rooms I watched the end from afar. I wasn't a part of the ending. I saw myself as separate. As long as there is separateness, I will be more what I'm not than what I am. I will be creating difference, I will be differentiating, and I will suffer. What I want to say is I'm sorry. I'm sorry for being separate from the ending. I'm sorry I said sorry. I am not saying I am sorry I am saying I *am* sorry, that is what I am, all I am. I am sorry for my fixation on what I'm not and what it's like to be close to someone who isn't where they are and is attached to what they aren't. I'm sorry I haven't been able to offer an end.

Taleen Kali

Slut Diaries

January 2020

I'm all for sluts, but I don't do rebounds anymore.

The exquisite grief of taking comfort in another's body used to appeal to me. Now it just makes me cringe. It's been two months since I last had sex and right now, it doesn't interest me at all.

It would be too soon to call it anything but a rebound. I don't need a physical witness to my pain, and my stillborn emotions need no mirror to receive recognition. Until I'm ready to love again, I want to languish in this grief like a sort of masturbatory act; a slut unto myself and no other.

February 2020

Instead of going out, I play music every night in my tiny bedroom.

During the day I take long baths and too much Xanax and book a tour for my band.

The past few weekends I invited friends over and we watched movies on the projector in my living room while we had snacks and wine. *Cleopatra. The Decline of Western Civilization. Sliding Doors.*

March 2020

It's ninety degrees in LA in Pisces season and I'm finally starting to take myself outside.

Today is the third hot day of the month so I pry myself away from my morning pages and slip into my turquoise swimsuit to hit the poolside while my roommate is out at work. With no job, no partner, no sex, and no schedule to speak of, it feels especially good to get into my body with the help of this fucking heat.

Getting over a breakup is easier when the sun's out. It makes some people crazy when this kind of thing happens (both the warm winter weather and the happy mockery of good weather in the midst of grief), but it's healing me. I'm slowly emerging from my primordial funk. Where quitting coffee failed to make me less stonewalled and anxious, the hot tub under the sun has become my deliverance.

I glide down into the water, a glimmering of jet streams. My body is unnaturally slim for this time of year so my swimsuit keeps swaying underneath the surface, floating an inch away from my skin. The shock of being tricked into a false love, of missing someone who was never even real, led me to fasting in addition to quitting coffee. Anything to mitigate the old wounds of emotional freeze that have been stirred. Now there's no attendant winter layer, not even on my bones, to keep me warm. Thus the sun, my savior, and also apparently, the random guy who's decided to join me in the tub.

It feels like a criminal act to interrupt my navel-gazing, especially since no one else is out at the poolside and he is quite large—especially in proportion to the small hot tub—taking care to mention that he doesn't live in the building. He's down to fuck. It would be such an easy lay, but I've got stranger danger and I haven't had sex with a cis male in a long time. He can't be the first fuck back. I start to feel uncomfortable so I make with the nervous small talk. Somehow I tell him my name, that I live in the building, what neighborhood I used to live in, until I realize I can simply get out of the fucking water and go back up to the apartment.

I've told him too much. Fuck. Oh well.

A few weeks after this encounter the entire world shut down, as did my one window of opportunity to have my post-breakup, non-rebound sex for a long, long time.

April 2020

It feels so strange for the world to suddenly empty just as I've begun to reopen. The tour I booked for my band is being cancelled. All of this is happening with no one to really talk to and important emotional changes are going unwitnessed. They feel like they're getting trapped inside and desperately need an outlet.

Thankfully I still have access to my rehearsal studio, which is a fifteen minute walk from where I live in Echo Park. I can cut through the park on my walk with LeeLoo the pup and enjoy the lake and the comically violent geese. Even though the swan boats are out of commission, there are girls in thongs laying out on the grass six feet apart and the sight of them makes me feel alive again.

I've been listening to the sounds of lesbian roommate sex and lesbian roommate fighting so much this month that I think I finally gotta move out.

May 2020

New apartment. I've examined every single article of clothing I own and then I washed and sun-dried it all on my beautiful new patio which has secret roof access so I can hang out in the sun whenever I feel like it, without any creepy intruders. I forgot my latex bra out in the sun and it has shriveled into a small melted mass. Is this what happens to a pussy when it remains unfucked?

June 2020

People are starting to go on virtual and outdoor dates, but the thought of trusting anyone with the dialectics of Covid disclosure doesn't feel palpable to me. I feel stuck in a grief that couldn't get fucked out of me, right as I was on the precipice of moving forward. I'm at a loss for how to safely connect.

Curious about my slutty desires and the state of my stutitude, I read about CDC's guidelines for safer sex, which includes curtain barriers (glory holes), masks (BDSM), and the like. Instead of intriguing my kink side, it makes me never want to touch anyone ever again.

I start reading other things voraciously, a veritable book slut. I read Wendy C. Ortiz, I read Dennis Johnson, I read Alice Bag, I read Maggie Nelson, I read Claudia Rankine, I read the Debbie Harry memoir, hell, I even read Thich Nhat Hanh. *Slut era*, I whisper to myself, as I buy another book to stay in and read. Maybe I'm becoming a spiritual slut, a tantric temptress, a holy whore.

October 2020

In October I shave my entire pussy and dress up as Cher for Halloween. "If I Could Turn Back Time" era Cher demands a bush-free crotch area for that badass bodysuit, ca. 2011 American Apparel edition, so here we are.

February 2021

Winter has delivered an interesting surprise. I've been freelancing for my first photo retouching client. Work is my new mojo. Making money fucking rules. A substitute for love.

May 2021

Newly vaccinated and filled with wanderlust, my family and I decided to fly to Armenia and Lebanon to visit with relatives we haven't seen in three years.

Being in close quarters with my parents in Southwest Asia/Middle East, I wore longer dresses, put on pantyhose even though it was blazing hot out. I even started to cover my arms.

The covert shame followed me home as I continued to cover myself in the heat, obscuring newly found evidence of my efforts at substituting food for sex.

June 2021

I've been gaining some weight and a change of state feels novel, so I want to commemorate it. I've started posing for some virtual shoots with my friend Kristin and yet I feel tight all over. Maybe it's the repression I felt in my travels manifesting. An unyielding feeling of constriction around my neck for lack of anything resembling sexual human contact, for lack of release. It feels safe to have parties again and so I hugged my friends and I kissed my bandmates and left lipstick stains on their sweet faces and I danced and I danced and I danced until I turned nearly blind and yet the tightening refused to release me.

Kristin tells me about a six-hour posing class she took online, so I take it too. I contort my body into new shapes as I learn what the camera wants, much like being with a new lover's body and discovering its unknown pleasures. Ass out is slimming. Tits to the side means a more interesting silhouette. Making angles with your arms and hips creates the illusion of negative space and thus lends itself to a more dynamic subject. These are all the ways you can make your body communicate to the camera, anticipating the exposure of its literal and metaphorical phallus. These are all the ways you can be captured.

My bandmate Royce invited me to Joshua Tree to celebrate his girlfriend Seajean's birthday. A bunch of us went. A friend took my picture in Pioneertown wearing a cowboy hat. Arms up, ass out, tits tilted. Yeehaw.

On the last night I walked up to a cowgirl at the bar and asked if I could wear her hat, my silly little pickup line for wanting to dance with her. She said no.

July 2021

I kiss the bar manager at a music venue on my birthday. A year later, he screws my band out of drink tickets at our first show back in LA since the pandemic. He is shorter than I remember. (This is surely a type of fucking.)

August 2021

In the apex of summer, inching just below one hundred degrees, I go to the plant store near my house with Royce, and Saejean, and our friend Emma. It's so hot that I'm surprised how many plants are thriving. We're there for less than five minutes before I faint from the heat and fall facedown onto the asphalt. The only thing saving my skull from impact is Roycifer rushing to the rescue. The irony of a riot grrrl-espousing feminist having a Victorian fainting spell is not lost on me, nor is it new to me: I've had vasovagal syncope since I was very little. Trips to the dentist and extreme heat can cause me to completely pass out and surrender to the black void. Once I come to, I drag myself to the car with bloodied knees while my mom maniacally thanks Royce over FaceTime. I feel equally shameful and grateful to have felt something so visceral in the company of fellow humans.

September 2021

I've been writing about my emotional pain all year, but I haven't been able to find a way to fully deal with the physical pain it's manifesting into. And the recent fall I took last month is taking its toll.

The fresh, shiny new pain has begun writhing its way into my body commingling with the dull, old pain and awakening something feral as it tears through me like a terrible lover. I love the pain and the pain loves me. I'm its little slut.

The pain is fucking devastating. The only thing that gets me out of its portals, or through them rather, is going to my bandmate Miles's house. It's too lonely to make music at home anymore.

The songs need to be witnessed by another human, and we need to make demos of the new music that has been swirling around in my head.

I go over to Miles and Vivian's a few times a week and play through the pain for four hours at a time, no more, no less, and never alone as I show Miles new melodies and chord progressions and potential song names. He patiently nudges me into places the songs want to live and breathe, he tells me when a chord isn't working, he supports me as I journey through Western and Eastern scales for the right chord to serve the song. Miles is my brother, my creative confidant, my rock and my pillar for this process. What happens here is a sacred creative act. Pain can't touch it. Nothing can.

Some of the lyrics are here in my head, and others are written in my notebook at home. I always finish them off on my own later.

October 2022

Summer turned into fall and fall into winter as the songs began to take on their final forms. I've been living and breathing these songs. I'm still working on my freelance stuff, but I don't see my friends and family as much. They notice when I withdraw and it's not always easy. Still, the pain to music pipeline is extremely transcendently beautifully taxing and this slut needs rest.

January 2022

The album is starting to take shape and we're deep in pre-production rehearsals smack in the middle of the holidays. Literally no one in the band minds because we're all starved for musical connection—the non-verbal communication it proffers, the exacting way it matches up your brainwaves when you play together for long enough.

Feeling accomplished, I cut myself some slack and start going out more and—surprise!—get my first case of Covid two weeks before we hit the studio. Out of sheer quarantine boredom I go on Hinge and find a bisexual-looking guy with a feather earring and a pet pig. Between talking about his freeganmism and my abstinence, he walks over to the bathroom and starts casually taking an on-camera leak. I'd only barely started trying again, but I've already had it with this bullshit. Unmatch. Unfuck.

March 2022

The pain has followed me all the way through these songs and into the recording studio. I am creating an artifact of it now. If I couldn't fuck my way out,* at least I've sublimated it into something beautiful and terrible. A divine trade.

I haven't had sex for 2.5 years and I still consider myself one of the most sex-positive people I know. Yet at this point giving this energy to anything other than music feels futile, cause shit's starting to feel downright tantric. In December I told Miles and Royce something like, "There's marrow deep in the hips of my bones that feels like it's entered my bloodstream just for this," just to help me create this new thing. Now we're alive in it.

We are decimating amplifiers with guitar feedback and walls of sound. We're floating on some kind of wave that's hell-bent to finish what it's started, that needs to be heard to unfurl its grasp. We are tuning and retuning and returning.

---

* *The author finally has sex a year later, in March of 2023, the same night the record is released.*

Lyn Corelle

Sildenafil: A Love Story

fist fist fist all morning long I fisted that hole till I myself almost melted into it rotting starving to the floor make from me a fleshy tube of you orifice into orifice limited but by an inner expanse of yet-to-be-charted sub-dermal pleasure pulsing woven bodily structure collecting screenshots of thirsty holes with no communication skills posting incessant why is nobody fucking me the exact way I need without me having to tell them or help to build a container within which my shit could get rocked railing railing pining for it to happen if you really want to as if calling oneself bottom grants exemption from the imperative to speak one's desire in as precise terms as possible thirsty thirsty everything you want is here for you if you can but ask

pfizer's patent on viagra lapses 2020 culmination of years-long crisis over replacing little blue cash cow generically dubbed sildenafil but happy endings come for us all as super-virus shakes untold billions into pharma giant's coffers what were those executives up to in 2019 we could fashion a more compelling conspiracy than lab-leaks anyway my girl and I prefer the more feminine sildenafil spinning ad copy via pillow talk sildenafil the lady's choice sildenafil mommy's helper of course there were feelings attendant with popping the pill but amazing to learn that railing hot sluts moaning mommy is the best solution known to womxnkind for my personal strain of dysphoria

I have come to reaching slippery bottle out to hungry hole bumping lip with finger nitrates spill across his face pause move to stop worrying chemical burn no no no don't stop fucking this ass don't stop who am

I to argue so a brief wipe with the top sheet will do watching that blank look bloom out on his face my favorite sight slack expression past all register of volition become flesh become hole stretching ass skin to not skin pushing out from inside bend over suck face while pounding lipping cheek ears chin gum lips and now now yes yes now that familiar rush coming on for me too residue upon skin oops bursting forth anxiety and ecstasy in equal measure back then we used to joke about the two genders poppers and sildenafil and never the twain shall mix but here I am holding on for life keeping pulse under control regulate breathe still pronging deep deep deeper cock into him heart pounding sweat pooling the small of his back my forearms forcing weight through sternum into mattress into mattress yes

sounds like a skill issue do you feel solidarity towards people less happy than you notice who is telling on themselves cracking jokes about golden showers and viagra thought you had a sure-fire dunk on old cis men but only betraying your own lack of imagination as regards fractioning the refractory period and fucking for a good four to five hours sildenafil my favorite party drug yes baby yes ready to take mommy's cum in that hole once more at this point no more substance to my spasm but both perfectly happy to pretend the long slick plane of belly against back my bed a canvas littered with small bottles a lube for every season and two wrung bodies

of latex aluminum polyester best age any at which to feel your pleasure itch underneath passenger seat arms sore twist fist through crack past unknown fiber to reach what's lost left there bumping on head against collapsing felt roof making out to takeout light lower hatch to stretch squirm ridged plastic pressed lines in expansive ass stippling a blanket in back shooting over lips edge licked can be coated I'd coated liquids won't separate once spilled together across skin not a blanket but tarp we'll need now spit piss almost anagrams but for that elusive t slash s savoring that loose slippage of signs as well as of my hand across your torso up to cheek ear hook grab press pull grind face to surface sip between grooves don't worry my hand will stay here firm clasped close to roots until you lap it all my old trick demanding don't break eye contact till I do but you don't do well with eye contact so we'll save that one for someone else and I need to be able to trust you to talk to me I'm stating once again that the top shortage is a myth the only shortage is of communication skills but as a top I sometimes benefit by the misconception never getting over how much there still is to learn about bodies relating in space and time thinking as we frot on the lineage of lovers' lovers accumulating and passing on this knowledge leading to us blowing each other's minds some skills can only be learned in the doing summer is here I need you bent forward in child's pose singing gently back come let us fist holes all round nay let us all fist ourselves into each other let us fist ourselves universally into the very milk and sperm of kindness let us

---

As this piece in part describes an experience of accidentally inhaling poppers while also being high on sildenafil, a.k.a. Viagra, it feels important to note that these two substances are dangerously contraindicated and should never be taken at the same time.

DL Alvarez

Union

Monday, May 16th, 1994. 8:02 p.m.

I'm off to my "union" meeting. It starts at eight and is a block and a half from where I live. We're a collective of sex workers, mostly male. Our group has three women so far. We try to be punctual because occasionally people have to run to work afterwards. Monday nights are traditionally slow but sometimes you get lucky. These meetings are held at the Faerie House on 14th Street and a little more than half of our members have Radical Faerie names and allegiances. The friend who first told me about these meetings is named Nettle and our hippie-esque group moniker is Sacred Horses. I keep meaning to ask if that references a mythology or has meaning beyond the obvious homophone of Horses and Whores.

I'm not a Faerie but know quite a few: from this group, solstice orgies, and readings at the bookstore. My taxable job is at a queer bookstore in the Castro. We host events and the faeries often show for things with spiritual leanings. Before I became a Professional Dominant I wore lots of monochromatic shirt-waist dresses. My aesthetic was butch 1940s garden lady. The faeries enjoy genderfuck but they have more of a Ren-Faire and tie-dye vibe. Still, it's enough common ground to get conversations going.

At the meetings, we pass a talking stick decorated with colorful ribbons. Each of us share the ups and downs of our week. This job can be isolating, so having this pulpit is restorative. Monday nights are our office water cooler. If you do any kind of sex work, your friends who aren't in the biz won't be able to relate to the sort of things you want to unload come the end of the day. Gripes that are confusing or mundane to civilians fall on understanding ears here. Outsiders fish for titillation. They beg you to make them blush, or maybe they want to prove themselves jaded enough to not be shocked. "What's the weirdest thing you ever did?" It's the most common question. I struggled with it at first, then felt mildly annoyed. Something in the way it's asked feels like they assume you cringe the whole time you're at work, but the opposite is true. I like my clients. Exploiting their fetishes for laughs doesn't sit well.

These days I deflect the question, unless it's a close friend. In those cases I've formed stock answers that check the boxes they're hoping for. In the course of telling the story, I make sure to humanize my clients and remind the listener that none of us behave in our day to day the way we do during sex. Imagine wearing your sex-face to the local cafe! That said, when I was still trying to find the scandal that people were fishing for ("No, I mean *really* weird") I discovered many were fascinated with Gunther. He identifies not only as a canine (or K9, as it's written in the pup-play scene) but specifically as a German Shepard alpha. He's obedient to my commands but dominant towards other K9s. This hierarchy dumbfounds those hearing about it for the first time, especially when I tell them about Tabasco, a beta that Gunther brings with him to sessions. Tabasco is a life-size Cocker Spaniel plush toy. Sometimes, when Gunther is excited he mounts Tabasco. For that, he's disciplined.

If I brought up Gunther at the Sacred Horses circle, it'd have to be because something unusual happened. Like the time he was over and two girls got into a fight on the street directly in front of of my storefront-dungeon. The shrill yelling of onlookers and the intermittent sounds of someone being knocked into the wrought iron that guards my windows took Gunther and I out of our play headspace. The detail my colleagues were focused on was my concerns that this episode—not out of character in this neighborhood—might cause Gunther to think twice about rebooking in the future. Gunther is a regular, who thankfully does not scare easily. Regulars are the gold of any business; you know how to please them going in and they get you through those times of the year when tourist traffic drops, as it will from late-November until about mid-January.

Jennifer, my Dominatrix mentor, says the weird parts for her are the things that have become quotidian. One afternoon, at the BDSM house where she works, she noticed the dishwasher being unloaded of its carriage of dildos and rubber cock rings to make room for coffee mugs, measuring cups, and a muffin pan. The Head Mistress of the house baked chocolate zucchini cupcakes for everyone and the scent hovered in the air. In that vein, I've come to anticipate the routine of making adult men lick my boots, or bending them over my lap and calling them "son" or "boy" even though they're older. There's Michael, whose fantasy is to visit to the doctor's office where things go wrong—with him I take on the role of an unscrupulous physician who blackmails his patients in order to run sexual experiments on them. Even those sessions are now all part of the job.

The curveball was discovering that to personify the macho archetype of a Master/BDSM-Top I had to learn a whole beauty regimen. I can throw a fabulous "fem" look together in under an hour, but it's a full-scale production to sustain a stoically macho facade. A person digging for weird stories would be disappointed to know that the weird part is I've perfected the art of shaving my balls. They'd never seen a razor before I "manned it up." Now I trim everything. I exfoliate and hydrate my face twice a day. Previously it was enough to wash it in the shower with the same soap I use on my body. Once upon a time, riding my bike on errands checked the box for exercise. Now I lift weights past the point where my body's natural pain receptors beg me to stop. What's more, I'm at the barber twice a month to maintain a profile that suggests militaristic.

Another thing that stands out is the overlap. Sometimes I get a page from a john while I'm installing an art show at New Langton Gallery, where I'm on the board, or at my bookstore job setting up folding chairs and introducing guest speakers. My hip buzzes and I hurry into the office asking anyone in there if they can give me a few minutes privacy. I shut the door behind them. This particular view of myself—a moment in which I have a foot in two worlds at once—underlines how flimsy each environment is. In creative circles, people call me Dee or DL and the conversations are mostly a series of opinions: on art, dinner, friends in common, politics, weather, songs, movies, books, the person at the other side of the room. Sexual innuendos are used for laughs. When I'm in my hustler mode, I'm Luther. Words are few and mostly statements of fact or instructions that support the power imbalance fantasy.

"You're late." "On your knees, pig." "Show me that hole."

When I'm at the gallery or bookstore, surrounded by forms of culture and aesthetics, and suddenly have to rattle off my kinks and physical stats, I'm conscious of the humorous discord of this state of limbo. Certain words that are erotic in the context of hiring a Pro Dom feel silly spoken in earshot of customers browsing books on spirituality or psychology, the two sections closest to the office. We do have erotic books here—the works of Larry Townsend, Phil Andros, Pat Califia, some of Dorothy Allison's short stories—I could go on and on—but it's one thing to purchase sexy literature to read before bed, another to hear a clerk use such language out loud on the company phone.

The same is true to a greater degree at the gallery. If we had a neon work on the wall at New Langton that read LOW HANGERS, people would take it in with a giggle and consider the poetic and political implications of those words during our time. On the phone however, those same descriptors get the client worked into the desired state of committing to booking my services. "I'm especially good with impact play, I have a thick, seven-and-a-half-inch tool, and a nice pair of low hangers. Now tell me how naughty you've been."

* * *

I'm just a couple of homes away from the Faerie House now. There's a photo on the ground and I stoop to pick it up. I have a collection of found images. For the majority, it's obvious why they're tossed: poor lighting, out of focus, the subject is not at their best. Though as I see it, all the things that are wrong with the photo are what I'm drawn to.

This pic, however, is perfection. It's a black and white shot of a young couple taken in the late-fifties or early-sixties. Both are incredibly good-looking and dressed neatly. The sun illuminates their calm, smooth faces. They seem to be in a rowboat, behind them is a river. The shore is bursting with spring blossoms. She's white with lips painted dark, probably the rose-red shade of that era.

Her black hair is done so that it puffs out at the side—along the lines of a poodle cut only more casual, something a person could run their fingers through without destroying the effect. Her eyes shine with confidence. Her feet aren't in the frame but you'd imagine flats or a biscuit heel ready to go on a hike. I could even envision her kicking the shoes off to climb a tree. The man is some racial mix: full smiling lips parted to show straight teeth. His clear eyes are cast on the object of his affection. His hair is trimmed short and has a tight wave, black like hers.

I tuck the photo into my shirt's patch pocket, then walk up the steps to the Faerie House and ring the chimes.

* * *

At tonight's meeting there's a new member. His name is Ares. He anticipates our assumption and clarifies that Ares is not a faerie name but his birth name. "My mother is Greek," he tells us. "My father is Italian. That's the combination giving me these good looks." He laughs, but the joke is not that he doesn't look good, rather that he's poking fun at his own conceit. "And yes, I am an Aries: fiery, passionate, determined, confident, independent, and impatient." The circle hisses their approval (hissing being faerie applause).

Ares continues, "So, I came here with a question. I got this page, right? I call back. The guy wants to know, will I do a trade? At first I think, he's asking am I trade? You know, because I have a picture ad." He says this to point out that if you saw him on the street, you could mistake him for a straight. The word *trade* (as a noun) refers to straight guys willing to to things for cash. If the guy is especially sketchy—perhaps turning tricks to support a habit or so detached you get the sense he might roll you—they're called *rough trade*. Ares could pass: those dark circles under his eyes, the square jaw, the short and unfussy haircut. Even the voice is absent of gay accent. The illusion ends, however, as soon as he's in motion.

He goes on. "But then the guy says he's got an ad in the paper as well. So now, I'm really confused. Like, is this guy claiming to be trade?—*Do you do trade meaning: will you do me?* Anyway, no.

Neither situation. He's got this ad in the bodywork section and wants to know if I can 'trade' my service for his."

"Bentley!" says Hamir. Only the person with the stick is supposed to talk, but this break causes the room to chuckle. Then we all laugh harder as the obvious becomes clear.

Nicolas asks, "Did you go?"

"No," says Ares. "A friend of mine said I could ask here to see if this guy's legit, figured one of you might have had the same offer. I didn't imagine all of you had."

* * *

Like Ares, my introduction to the concept of trading was via Bentley. Since then, I've received a few more offers. It makes me laugh when guys who do standard sex work use the euphemism. In those cases, they're saying, "Do you want to get each other off . . . for free?" The so-called trade happens concurrently. This is hustler framing, the penchant to monetize sex even when no currency is exchanged. It aligns with a mythos that sex for cash is hotter and more taboo. Sometimes I wonder what these guys think about the sex they have in off hours. Do they picture it as an act of charity? Ares might subscribe to this reasoning. He points out, in a tone to suggest he's kidding, "Going to Bentley would be an uneven trade because people pay more to get fucked than they do for a massage."

The value of anything is relative. I love sex but it's not my only pleasure. Some of the things I'd choose over sex include swimming in a summer lake, a laid-back dinner party with close friends, seeing a good movie in the theater, getting that twice-monthly haircut from the barber on Castro Street who always gives the full treatment and only charges only for a trim (I tip big), and definitely receiving a massage. When Bentley called asking if I'd trade a fuck for a "deep-tissue massage from a licensed professional," I agreed without second guessing. He sounded sincere and his ad has no erotic overtones. It names the massage school he attended and his prices are based on lengths of time (one hour, hour and a half, and two). He definitely wasn't one of these naked guys who spin their fingers around on your back a few minutes before giving a quick handjob.

It wasn't knowable how good a masseur he might be, but it was obvious he'd make an effort. Plus, he's good looking. His headshot evokes a 1950s album cover: sincere eyes, a collared shirt and sweater vest, the background blurred. I went to Oakland, where Bentley lives in an apartment near Lake Merritt. It was a trek. To make it an even trade, I hoped he wouldn't grouse about visiting my playroom on the day he came to collect his service. One in-call for another in-call, that's only fair.

In describing what he was into, he said he wanted "to be pounded by a dominant man who was a little kinky."

"No scat, no snuff, no children or animal-born-animals," I said. I intended to fish out more details about what he was into, though from his word choices (*a little kinky*) it sounded standard: probably some nip play, some verbal, maybe a few ass smacks with a leather glove. Bentley told me he loves leathermen though he has yet to make it to the Folsom Street Fair. I pictured a guy who owns a harness but never wears it in the light of day.

At his place he led me directly to a warm candle-lit room. There were silk shawls draped on the walls and the air was smeared with wispy trails of incense smoke. He left while I disrobed. Once naked, I laid face down on the massage table. When he returned, Bentley kneaded my muscles with the perfect balance of a smidge of oil and a lot of pressure, never attacking the knots but working them loose slowly and completely. The room was piped with the typical new age chimes I hate but have learned to tune out. I dissolved in his grip. By the time he was done, I knew I'd sleep like a rock.

That's when he said, "Whenever you're ready, I'll be waiting for my part in the front room."

All I could think was, "Is he kidding? TONIGHT? I have to reassemble myself into human form within the next few minutes and perform a kink scene, the very work that made me need a massage in the first place!?" A deal is a deal, however. I should have asked upfront how this worked instead of assuming we'd conduct two separate sessions. He did me right. Now, it was my turn to pull it together and show him a good time. I prayed it would be something simple, like a spanking followed by a quickie. I took a moment to enjoy the sense of a body freed of tensions and did some deep breathing until I was present enough to take on my half of the bargain. I opened the door and went down the hall towards the dim glow of the front room. It was large, empty, and had a polished wooden floor. The space was lit by a single wall sconce. Bentley was naked. The only object in sight was a large blue rubber ball the size that some people use as a chair.

"How are you feeling?" he asked.

"That was amazing. You're very good at what you do. I have to say, I was happily surprised. A lot of the massage guys in the *BAR* (*Bay Area Reporter*, the LGBT newspaper where our ads are listed) aren't um . . . well, they sort of make it up as they go along." My eyes returned to the ball. "You said you like to be fucked?" Did he plan to straddle that thing? Why was there no other furniture? Were we going to have vertical sex? That would be fine. I wasn't keen on getting on my knees on hardwood.

Then he said, "Yes. I like to be fucked while I'm riding the ball." That was when I noticed two phallic handles. I think the brand name is Hippity Hop; The grips are the ears at the top of a bunny face. The logistics were still unclear. He must have been used to this confusion because he continued. "You ride the ball as well, sitting behind me."

"Ah! I'm behind you. So, my cock is up your ass?"

"Right," he smiled, "and then we bounce."

The mechanics of it were not as impossible as I imagined. I held Bentley at the waist to keep him pressed against me while he more or less drove the Hippity Hop in a tight circle. Some of the others said they had a difficult time staying inside Bentley, but because they felt so relaxed from the massage, each time they did slip out it became a shared point of uncontrolled laughter, like when you're crashed into on bumper cars.

* * *

There's a lot of giggling at tonight's meeting. People share stories about Bentley as well as other trades. Turns out we all had the same reaction of dread upon hearing Bentley's line: "I'll be in the next room when you're ready." By the fourth time someone mentions it, my mind drifts to wondering which part of the evening turns Bentley on most. Is it really the bouncy fuck or does he get off on the reveal? The whole time he is turning his clueless victims into jelly, he gleefully harbors a secret.

This is another aspect of Sacred Horses that makes it such a boon. Having a group like this undoes those surprises that make our work challenging: little speed bumps like Bentley's blue ball, guys with bad breath, and non-tippers, as well as the bigger road blocks like johns who will attempt to underpay or go over the agreed amount time. Top of the list are the men to avoid completely—those who pose a threat to you or your livelihood. They go on the Bad Trick List that gets updated regularly. There are jerks who will get off on getting away with shit, like doing something you hadn't agreed on, trying not to pay at all because they couldn't cum or some other flimsy excuse. Messy, violent, guys who think it's not rape if they're paying for it, especially if they try to force you into unsafe sex.

Recently we started printing these out. I take the list to Kinkos and put it on the bookstore's tab. We circulate them at places such as the Tuesday late-morning gathering in front of the *BAR* when the guys are placing their weekly ads just before the noon deadline, or on the streets in the Polk. This in turn adds names to the list, because as soon as we tell the guys what we're doing, everyone has their own story about some asshole.

* * *

After the meeting some of us hang out for a soak in the backyard hot tub. Ares sinks in next to me. "So with your clients, how do you set the rates? Is it a per-fetish request? Like, what if a guy wants to do role play AND be tied up AND pissed on? Does each item figure in?"

"No. I have an hourly rate that's higher than standard. I anticipate that there's going to be lots of prep and scene setting, the use of equipment, and extra clean up. Sometimes it's more work, usually not too much. Guys who call are pretty focused on what they want."

"Yeah," he nods. He thanks me and rests his arm behind my back. I don't think he means to flirt but I get aroused regardless, maybe more so because the contact is seemingly without intention. Luckily no one sees my excitement under the shroud of bubbles.

* * *

Back home I pull out the photo I found earlier. My collection started organically. The photos attract me with their stories—both the readable narrative in the picture and the obtuse one of how that image lost its way. Someone held onto this particular photo for at least thirty years. Surely the couple themselves kept it in a book, shoebox, or perched on a shelf. What happened to the safe place where it lived? Did one or both of the subjects pass? Did the photo simply fall out of a dresser drawer during a move? Normally I keep these treasures in a binder, but this one gets taped on the wall near my vintage 1972 calendar from an auto shop that no longer exists.

I'm not a hopeless romantic but sometimes wonder if that's exactly what a romantic, hopeless or otherwise, might think. Before turning tricks, I was in a relationship for nearly five years. That relationship slowed to a putter. We both still like each other but the spark fizzled, maybe for the best. After the breakup I pursued art with resolve, which required investment (art supplies, traveling to install shows, the time needed to make work) and so too, a much more substantial income. As they say, it takes money to make money. So here we are.

Pro Dom work lifted me from a poverty-level income to sampling middle class luxuries overnight. I wasn't hurting before, but did skip an occasional meal because I was too embarrassed to pay in nickels and dimes. Now I happily and immediately deposit all coins into tip jars along with whatever paper money gets the total to twenty percent. Not a penny weighs my pocket. I only have to do one scene a week to get by. If I do three, I'm rich. Not only does it pay the rent, it enables me to workout with a trainer, buys travel tickets, and elevates my gift-giving game come birthdays or Christmas: nothing ostentatious, but a huge step up from the homemade cards of yore that promised a home cooked meal or a shoulder rub. For her birthday this year I got my mom a kitchen table and chairs for the nook in her new apartment.

I guess I'm a practical romantic; I admire love and people in love to a fault, but am currently too busy for that distraction. Relationships are postponed until I have a livable income from art alone. It's hard to even imagine the guy who'd be fine with me as is.

He'd have to settle for very little time together and be unbothered that I regularly exhaust my sexual energies with aging businessmen and German tourists.

Most sex workers I know abide with a single life until this job is past tense. In movies, the hooker (stripper, pornstar, whatever) is rescued by the one john who truly sees her. In reality, we save up until we have a degree of financial security. Maybe we retire at that point *and then* find a partner . . . or maybe we don't, depending on our inclinations. Some workers are involved with other sex workers. That's less complicated. One couple in fact emerged within the Sacred Horses. My thoughts go round the circumference of the Horses' meetings. It's a good collection of people, sweet and attractive, but until tonight no one really caught my eye as a potential-crush. Even this new guy, Ares, though physically hot—compact body and those long dark lashes—gives me some pause. I need a better sense of his personality. He seems stuck on himself. For a relationship, even a casual one, I'm more into a sharing-is-caring dynamic.

Not that it matters. I doubt I'm his type. He couldn't take his eyes off of Alexi and Spicer: the skinny early-twenties boys who look like members of the British band, Blur. The only musician I was ever compared to was ten years ago when I had long greasy hair and dressed in tatters. A punk couple (a guy and a girl) tried to pick me up by telling me I looked like Iggy Pop. Anyway, the reason I'm not trying to see anyone isn't that I'm too busy for someone else's liking; I'm too busy for my own good. The art shows, the bookstore and New Langton Arts, my clients, the committee meetings and actions with ACT-UP (I'm not as involved with them as I used to be, but still) . . . It's already too much.

* * *

At the next Sacred Horses, Ares has returned. It's rare that anyone comes to one of these meetings and decides it isn't for them. Before this group formed, I had two short windows of social exchange with colleagues. The first was those micro-conversations that happen in line at the *B.A.R.* on Tuesdays. They're limited to anyone directly in front or behind you and hindered by the fact that none of us are totally awake yet. The second opportunity was rarer: it was those trades. Now that I have these weekly meetings, I decline requests for a trade, which exposes why I said yes when I did. The post-coital chat was the gravy on that business lunch.

This week when Ares gets the talking stick he lets us all know, "I decided not to bounce-fuck Bentley." Ares confesses he loves the economy aspect too much to engage in give-aways. "Once a john paid me to piss on him. Since then, whenever I piss on my own it feels like I'm flushing money down the toilet." He laughs harder at his joke than anyone else. Then he gets serious. He's losing his shelter. "My friend who has been letting me stay at her place, she's moving to LA. I'm not on the lease. I can pay rent, no problem. It's hard though to find a place when you don't have a job on paper."

The unspoken is that people aren't eager to live with us. They have a hard time conceptualizing intimacy as a job. They picture us getting whore-juice on everything or confuse us with other criminals. After all, if we're willing to engage in one illegal act, what other laws might we break? Our existence is a red flag.

"You don't have a bed?" When it's my turn to talk I have a one-way conversation with Ares. It's me thinking out loud, so the group hears me Lego together an idea. "I have space but no extra bed. Well, that's not a big deal. I have a sofa that's comfy. You could stay with me until you find something normal—my place isn't normal. It's just one big room with the windows all in the front. I share the bathroom with the print shop next door."

I can tell by the faces that I'm rambling. What is it I want to say? Am I inviting Ares to stay with me? Part of the problem is that I do in-calls. I tell him that, "It's just one or two a week and they book at least a day in advance. Most of 'em. I'd need you to clear out during those sessions. They're usually around noon or five p.m. I can mark them on a calendar so that you have warning."

I take a breath. It's the stick that's the problem. I feel compelled to cover everything while I'm holding it. "The rent is pretty cheap, if you want to pitch in but . . . you know what? Don't worry about rent, because you'll need to get a gym membership for showers. I have a membership at Gold's Gym, which is on the same block. In other words, it's not ideal, but what I'm trying to say is you can consider me a safety net if nothing else avails itself." The group hisses for my generosity, even if it is conditional. Ares nods a thank-you.

After the meeting he approaches me. "It would just be till I find my own place. I only do out-calls so no worries there, and I workout at Muscle Sisters—you know, for the showering." The gym he refers to is actually called Muscle Systems, but because it's in the Castro it's 100 percent gay men. Their nickname grew from their tradition of going out as a group on Halloween, all in drag: an entire mob of muscle-queens busting the seams of thrift store dresses. It feels like the personification of the gym floor chatter: this parade of testosterone poured into backless gowns, clicking down the pavement in high heels.

* * *

Ares sits on the edge of my metal desk and takes in the room. "I love this space," he says. "We should have sex." He presents it as a two-fold proposition. "To get any sexual tension out of the way, but also it can be a test run. You know? In case one of our tricks wants a pork roast or some three-way situation."

I laugh. "So we're working out the bugs ahead of time? Are you afraid we couldn't improvise?"

"Yeah, I guess that's stupid. I was thinking of those guys who do the act for voyeurs."

"Alexi and Spicer. Is that why you were staring at them?" Alexi and Spicer look so similar they run an ad as a brother team. Their gimmick is that they have sex with each other while the client watches.

"Yeah. Their whole thing freaks me out. The idea is hot but I don't know."

"You know they're not actual brothers, right?"

"It's not that. It's because they have sex on the regular. That basically makes them a couple. A couple who only do it for other people's pleasure."

"Maybe they're exhibitionists."

"Sure," Ares shrugs. "For me the whole perk of being a prostitute is the variety. Did you know they have a routine? They go through the same moves every time. They told me!"

"That won't happen to us," I say. He shoots me a puzzled look. "I do the Pro Dom thing purposefully to minimize sex with clients. I mean, sometimes penetration is part of the gig but usually it's just running them through their paces. Most of the time I don't even have to undress. But they feel rewarded if I whip it out at some point to show them I'm hard."

Arie looks crestfallen. "So we're not having sex?"

We definitely are, but it's fun teasing him like this. "*To break the tension?* I mean we could, but I'd say it's more so that we can get to it while the tension exists. After a week of seeing you before you put on your face in the morning, anything sexual is going to fade."

Ares laughs, "You're an ass! I knew I liked you. Thanks for letting me crash in your whore house. Do you want some weed?"

* * *

Sex with Ares isn't difficult to decode. Maybe he has my number as well. The more I give him the spotlight in words and attention, the more he comes to life and proves himself worthy of the pedestal. It's a 50/50 call. Some egos respond better to being put in their place. They enjoy the respite from having to always shine. But once you get to know your narcissist, you can meet them on the level they need. Some are over-compensators. They're the dicey lot. From day to day they waver between needing praise—truly needing it—and wanting secretly to be called on their bullshit. Then there are people like Ares who simply recognize their worth; they see what others see in them and are tickled by it, wanting to make sure you see it too because, "Look how cool it is that I've got all this going on!" Which is not clinical narcissism so much as immodesty. It's only the tone and frequency of self-promotion that gets annoying.

What Ares really has is self-confidence. I hold it against him out of envy. I like to believe that I'm handsome, charming, and sure of myself—that's the front I put on when I'm Luther—but behind that facade I'm desperate for validation. My top skills are an extension of a near pathological need to hear from others that I am as amazing as I think I might be, if I weren't also riddled with insecurities.

I let Luther come out to play with Ares, even finishing with a classic porn-style pull out. I rip off the condom and shoot a load into the nest of black hairs on his chest, leaving him slathered in cum, his and mine both. He says, "That's what I love about sex workers; we know what we're doing!"

Since it's his first night, I bring out the *special occasion wash bucket*—a big metal bucket that I've used in the K9 scenes and home bathing. I put it in the center of the girl's bathroom (my neighbors are never in the building this late) and use a hose attachment to fill it with hot water. The room has a drain in the floor, so after his bath we dump it and then I give both bathrooms and their connecting hallway a mopping. He smokes a few more tokes and we settle into our respective beds, his on the sofa downstairs and mine in the loft.

A few minutes pass (ten at most) when his voice calls up. "Are these your parents?"

"What?"

"The couple in the boat?"

It takes me a half-minute before I realize he's talking about the found photo, the gorgeous newlyweds.

He says, "God they look so sweet on each other. And you totally look like your dad."

I breathe in, so relaxed from the pot, sex, and the clean up. My eyes are closed as I answer, "I do."

Gary Indiana

My Hole

B takes photos of an Irish jock type who does a little urban land-
scaping, J also uses him in his art work, he's usually pictured jerking
off his fat average-length cock, in a trance of lubricity, the artful thing
being his total lack of self-consciousness. When I run into J at a party
he says, "You should try him, he'll have sex with you for $100." So I
call the kid and say I might want to take photos but mainly want to
have sex with him. "What am I running now, an escort service?" He
asks what I want to do. "Uh, suck your dick, get fucked by you."
"You can suck me, that's cool, but I don't fuck, I get fucked." I'm not
the only one who finds something intriguingly contradictory in this.
When B (who likes to be fucker and never the fucked) talks about it,
he's vague on the subject of how far he goes with the kid, who's asked
him on occasion to screw him "bareback." "He said, 'Shoot your
come inside me,'" B says. "Which you have to wonder, what does he
mean by that."

R has been boning me for years. He's so beautiful that it hurts. We
fuck and fuck for hours, all over the apartment. My sheets are an atlas
of his ejaculations. He's a flake. If he shows up at all it's an hour late,
we've had arguments about it, or rather I've had the usual one-sided
argument with a passive-aggressive. "Haven't you ever heard of
Colored People's Time?" he offers with deliberate lameness. Inside
me, he's brilliant. But even his big dick isn't enough to control me,
when he wants me to know how much I want it from him he uses his
fingers, his fist, his toes. One afternoon he shows up with a camera,
says he's documenting himself with the guys he fucks. "But I don't

have any with, uh, footfucking," he says, almost apologetic. "I won't show your face." Next he's greasing up his left foot with ForPlay and working his toes into my rectum, snapping away. Soon we're thickly connected at an improbable angle and I tell him it's okay to shoot my face. "You wouldn't find it embarrassing—?" "Why should I find it embarrassing? You're doing it too."

But I wonder about R, who routinely sabotages himself in the real world, and whether having these pictures of me with half his foot up my ass represents some sort of imaginary leverage over "my image," i.e., this is as abjectly bottom as you can be. But since I like it, where's the abjection? He should know by this time that I can't be embarrassed or compromised by anything sexual, that the concept of "secret" means nothing to me. If anything, I'm in the business of selling off my secrets, of not having any. In the real world, I'm the one who's the top, maybe this is why I need to submit, to open my ass to his entire body—for psychic balance. He calls up one day and asks me if I'd help him get his work into one of the art magazines. So I set up an appointment with an editor who's hard to get to, and he stands her up, for which I have to apologize. He has some insane excuse and asks me if another appointment's out of the question. I say no, but if you miss this one don't ever ask me to do anything for you again. And sure enough, he calls me the day before to cancel. The next time I see him, he makes it clear that he wants his asshole scoured with my tongue, sits on my face for half an hour, tells me to lick his balls while he shoots come all over my stomach.

Fucking someone in the ass is supposed to be a metaphor for power relations, so it's strange that so many of the most sexually virile people, if virile's the word, are powerless or passive in their dealings with society. I used to drop into Hombre near the parole office in the afternoons to find ex-convicts, guys who'd just done time for armed robbery or assault, but usually just for narcotics possession, who often went all dreamy and wetly masterful when they slid their penises in, and later I'd see some of them on the street, working hard to stay losers, puffing on crack pipes, eyes rolled up in their heads. My parolee period ended when one of them insisted on sucking my dick:

I could see they were all on a slide away from their "masculine" top position, that I was the last fuck on the way down to grand theft auto and servicing some daddy in Dannaemora.

What about the real world (taking sex as an unreal world)? Who's the top? Does top apply? I'm not a big fan of metaphors, actually. (The real world is an articulated metaphor of sex, as Marcuse used to tell us, but as he also used to say, it's more real than what it's a symbol of.) I mean I'm not sure we need metaphors to live. If you need money you're always the bottom, which I learned through years of pennilessness, when I actually needed, for example, the $400 that *Artforum* paid (and still pays, like the aunt who still sends you $10 for your birthday and thinks you can have fun with it) for a "featurette," and the editor, a dyke with visions of world domination, would force me to sit beside her in the office long into the night as she mutilated whatever I'd written with her red pencils, you do it my way or I push your face in was always the subtext despite the atmosphere of exhausted good humor. If this editor knew you had a plane to catch, she'd schedule your edit in a way that forced you to agree to every cut as it came up or risk missing your flight. Getting fucked over, though, isn't the same thing as getting fucked, and rather than call this type of person a top (which she'd find flattering, no doubt), I'd rather call her a pain in the ass.

B is the West Indian man I see in Los Angeles, whose cock is probably the biggest and thickest I've known that was completely functional. Those "humungous" guys with the fat foot-long hoses usually can't manage a hard-on. I went home with a Cuban man in San Francisco once whose penis was so monstrous, I really had doubts about my own capacity. For sure I couldn't blow him. His bedroom was completely mirrored, I watched this enormous black rod pushing into me and expected to see the end of it emerge from my mouth. Once it was in he immediately went soft, and after a great deal of squishy effort pulled out, went to the closet, and came back with the largest dildo I'd ever seen. "Let's try this," he said, "it's about my size." Writing this, I'm overwhelmed with longing for B's massive prong and pick up the telephone. "I hope you're calling from here," he says. I confess that I'm not, that I can't come to LA for another month and a half, ask if he's going to be in New York at all. He tells me how nice it is that I'm thinking about him, and about it. "When you get out here," he says, "I've got a surprise for you. It's the same surprise, but now it's bigger and longer. I've been doing things, I'm sure you're going to like it." What on earth is he talking about? Piercings? A cock pump?

B used to be this skinny mocha-skinned kid who kept his sneakers on "for traction" when he fucked me, usually at the Chateau Marmont, with me bent over the back of the sofa, or balanced against a chair. He smiled a lot. We always had perfect communication physically, and at the same time some kind of aphasic verbal dysfunction together, I could never make myself understood about even simple stuff like dates and times or whatever, and when B talked about anything he got entangled in the English language to the point of complete opacity. In the last two or three years he's buffed up as if he worked out full time, now he's so muscular his whole body feels like one taut muscle, and he's become a genius with his donkey prick, he takes control in a way that lets you know that he knows exactly how much you want it to hurt (with him it can hurt) and where your pain threshold is: it's thrilling, I leave his place fucked enough to feel just-fucked for days. Strangely or not, it isn't fun with B any more, at least not in the same way. Even the first time with him he yanked off his condom in the heat of things and fucked me without it for a few minutes, then put another one on, muttering something to the effect that he hadn't meant to do it raw that long, as if the only risk was his, or we'd already agreed that fucking raw very briefly was an acceptable risk. Now he rolls it off in mid-fuck surreptitiously, so I don't even have the opportunity to object (though it's true I'm so gone with what we're doing that I wouldn't anyway). That isn't exactly what is wrong, though it's obviously a really bad idea, and gives a pretty wretched meaning to the concept of "top." What's wrong is that he's perfected fucking, even the way it doesn't feel mechanical is, how to put it, scientifically calculated. He used to sing the praises of my hole, tell me how happy he was to find somebody who could take all of him, in fact he would talk about this with great excitement; now he's sure of himself, sure he's giving me as much pleasure as I could possibly get from a dick, and there is nothing around this pleasure at all, no context, not even the ridiculously baffling conversations we used to have.

R asked me once why I like to get fucked, and I couldn't think of an answer. I think it's natural, but I don't know what nature is. Sometimes I like the idea of it more than the act itself, when somebody's a lousy fuck, for instance, and I just get off on the idea of having them in me because it means they're not in anyone else. Sometimes I'm totally turned off by Hispanic boys I pick up in the streets, who make a big thing about being straight, and ask if I've got any straight porn they can get hard with; and sometimes I really get off on one of these sweet morons fucking me from behind while his eyes are glued to a straight video, and my ass becomes this conceptual cunt, or a woman's ass. But I hate these guys, somewhere, they're invested in fooling themselves, their narcissism lacks charm. And I know they live in a world of idiotic relationships, having fathered unwanted babies and married unbelievably stupid, shrewish girls whose manifold sufferings hold no compassionate interest for me whatsoever. Ferdinand, very verbal, asks me do I want to be his bitch, he's pumping his prong in up to the balls so I say Yeah, I'm your bitch, next he's slapping my buttocks and muttering Take that cock, you love that big dick don't you bitch, etc., are you my bitch, yes you're my bitch, and then when I see him a few weeks later in a bar, he walks over and interrupts a conversation I'm having with another guy, and starts acting as if I really am his bitch, so I tell him to go fuck himself. "Don't you dare order me around," I tell him. "I'm old enough to be your father." If I'd still liked him, I would've said I was old enough to be his mother.

When I was growing up, everything was butches and femmes. And then for a while things got muddled, everybody was "versatile." And then they were clones. Now they're … nothing. I liked those versatile days, and I liked fucking people, and then much later when I travelled I found a whole world where the old-fashioned codes of masculinity still ruled, and knew I wanted to be on the dick. The Hispanic world, the Islamic world, though ruled by archaic codes, also offered the desperate urges of socially inhibited straight men, the same carnal frenzy produced by repression at home in the '50s and '60s. In places like Quito or Tangier you were gay, a puto, only if you were penetrated, and macho if you weren't. Which still fascinates me for what I can get out of it without having to be some tiresome "First World" fag's image of perfection. I want to be the hole he wants to fuck, but why, exactly. Because I want sexual things to stay at a certain place, not spill out into role-playing and learned sentiment, I want this guy's boyishness and the feelings he has immediately before, during, and after the sexual connection, but not most of what goes on outside that connection, I don't want his slop, his emotional retardation, his bullishness, I don't want his masculinity except in the form of his hard dick. I want his macho expectations of life to be disappointed and I want my ass to be his consolation prize.

I'm only interested in sex that has the possibility of opening a door into another world, the world of men I was never going to be.

The butch and femme thing in the '60s was: the femmes are homos, the butches are trade. This isn't the standard in gay bars anymore, but it still operates in slightly different form in the places I go. The difference is that femmes are no longer feminine because nobody is feminine the way people were in the '60s, and not so many butches are that masculine either. (All "masculinity" means any more is violence.) At least they don't have to maintain the fable that they're essentially straight, though some do, and they're boring. Being a dick is always the dick's problem, a fact never recognized by the dick himself. Unless you are totally full of shit, there is nothing problematical about being the hole, the receptacle, the fuckee, if you like it, because just like the masochist, the bottom is always the one in control. On the other hand: being gay was really an unusual thing when I was growing up, you met interesting people, and lived in the seedy margins of sex with all the excitement that brought with it. You learned how to talk and be brilliant and defend yourself by being smarter and more sophisticated than other people, especially smarter than the straight dumbbells whose jockstraps you managed to get into. The effulgence of gay culture has made this a club that virtually anybody can get into, and so it's lost its edginess and alas the stolid dumb allure of trade. (Who were, of course, always guys who eventually turned gay, not just gay but nancy-gay, and took it up the ass themselves.) Are people returning to the old model of things out of screaming boredom with their own acceptance? Or is it just me, up in the country with my cat, eyeing the cable television installer and the guy who mows the lawn with the stirrings of my childhood's vulpine, manipulative, ridiculously submissive lust?

There's a throwback to the '60s on the internet now, www.streetlife.com, which is basically a ponce service that shows nude portfolios of rent boys, complete with florid biographies and contact numbers. Most of streetlife's models are described as having girlfriends, but "don't mind" doing it with guys, bottoms only. Well, whatever, but come to think of it, fuck that.

Robert Glück

Ed's First Sexual Experience, June 1967

I grew up in Tacoma, Washington. I turned seventeen in May and I was so horny that everyone could see the need in me, I was made of glass, the need to be touched was an emergency, a frantic accident: 911FUCK. Cars slowed down, drivers could see it. My heart was thumping but I jumped in a car and we dropped acid and drove into the woods—the wilderness. Acid was an old friend coming on in the dark.

Jim was at least thirty and he did not say much. We walked into the forest—huge feathery hemlock trees, the slight skittering of their needles—and he brought me to a halt in front of four stumps, except the stumps rose above our heads and supported a treehouse. Vines twined up the stumps, looping before my eyes like the curlycues and exquisite filigrees that cover Sleeping Beauty's castle. Would I be going to sleep?—or was I sleeping and here's Prince Charming? The dark firs swayed and bowed down to us, we were going to have sex so we were the center.

I'm describing my first sexual experience. The woods surrounded us with multifaceted silence. The cabin made my nose itch. Jim lit a kerosene lamp. An atrocious clubfoot hung from the ceiling, its shiny eye was glaring at me. On a moldy mattress, Jim pulled my butt onto his mouth and that was weird. I mean, did he forget about my cock? And it was a week since I'd taken a shower. He spread my butt cheeks like parting the curtains before the diva's high C, so I guess he didn't mind and really that smell is part of nature, right? Then his tongue was squirming inside me, reshaping me from the inside. My anus was spinning clay on a potter's wheel and Jim was making vase shapes with his tongue. He said, *Shiva owns the place*, and I thought, that seems right: throwing pots with his thousand hands. Jim's words were muffled by my butt and because he was huffing. The thousand arms of Death lifted our treehouse to his fanged mouth and crunched like we were hard candy. That made me laugh and I said *Death* in greeting. Jim nodded so fast my ass felt like a snapping window shade in a cartoon.

He said, *Shirt is an ace*. That was strange because we were naked and my shirt was balled up in the corner, a plaid flannel I got at Goodwill for free because there was a red stain on the back. I said, *Thank you*, and that made Jim so happy. He said, *Shit on the race* and I had to agree—the whole rat race, you could have it. We were turned on, tuned out, whatever. He was bucking under me. He said, *Shickon my ace*. Shickon my ace? That was code for something. Chatting away like this was a part of sex I had not foreseen, it was distracting. I thought sex would be like going to a library: when you have something to convey—I love you very much, or, Will you be my boyfriend? —you whisper it. Jim tipped his head out of my butt and bellowed, SHIT ON MY FACE.

It took a second to realize what he wanted while a turd sprinted through my intestines and out like a dog responding to his master's voice. I jumped off the boogey man's roaring shit-covered face and grabbed my clothes and ran into the forest, too scared to stop and put my sneakers on.

Strays

Shane had been gone for three days. He would disappear for a day sometimes but never this long. He couldn't call, we didn't have a phone. Someone said maybe he'd gone to Chicago with this guy they'd partied with at . . . he couldn't remember where. Someone else said Shane had gone to the burbs with a business guy and his wife. "They like to share boys."

I was too concerned. Chill, I told myself. He'll come back or he won't. If he didn't, I could find someone to move in. I could ditch the place. No need to panic, no need to spin out, but I couldn't sleep.

Shane reappeared a week later. He didn't want to talk about it. He found me at the diner. I'd moved out of the apartment. I didn't know what had happened to his stuff. Rent was due. I didn't have it, and no one would commit to moving in and paying. I moved in with an older guy, a painter. Shane was shocked I'd done anything without him. I could see his surprise and disappointment, the fear. I was no disciple.

"How's that?" Shane said.

"Fine. He paints, sleeps, and does coke."

"He keeping you?"

"No, we don't fuck. He likes having someone there. I'm still working. Hey, order some fries and we can split them."

"I was going to see if you could float me some cash," he said.

"I'm broke, man."

Telltale knee bounce. Shane was agitated I'd moved out and left his stuff—a small suitcase of shitty clothes and toiletries.

"There was no time and you weren't here," I said.

"It was one suitcase though," he said, moving his thumb along the bent aluminum lip where the tabletop was cracking.

"Here," I reached in my pocket and handed him a little packet under the table. "It'll set you right."

He took it without touching my hand and got up, turning his back to me. I watched him. While he was in the bathroom, I emptied my change on the table and counted out my coffee and tip. I got up and left.

* * *

Gray lather from black tar soap and the smell of cheap cocoa butter. Dead insects and browned flower petals on the sill. The shades pulled almost all the way down. Envelopes and birthday candles on the table. Crayon stick paints mashed like bright stubbed cigars in the big room where canvases were set up.

The painter had models sometimes. Strung out kids. I went for walks to the diner or bookstore when they came over.

At the diner I bought a plate of fries and a bottomless coffee. I was flush with a fresh pack of cigarettes and people came over to bum them.

"Thanks man, thanks. Whatcha reading?"

I flashed the cover.

"Is it good?"

I nodded. The exchange reminded me of childhood in the house of the Bible, *McCall's*, *Ladies Home Journal*, and *Reader's Digest* where reading was viewed as rude.

I checked the big clock over the register. A john had given me a watch, but I'd sold it. I avoided him after because I didn't want him to ask about it.

"So, you sold the watch for money and then lost the money you'd make from the guy by not tricking with him?" Shane had said.

"There's always another guy," I'd said.

All I had to do was look outside and see two boys waiting to get picked up, waiting for a long time by the look of it, and know that wasn't true. At some point beauty, novelty, and youth were gone, and all that was left was sour will.

Almost midnight. I had gut rot from the coffee. The junky boys were probably gone. I reached into my pocket for money and found a two-of-diamonds playing card. No idea how it got there. I paid and idly played with the card on my walk home.

I opened the door, and two naked boys were standing in front of a green wall. The smell of fresh paint was strong.

"You wanna join?" the painter asked.

"Good night." I kept moving to my room and closed the door.

I turned off the light and got under the covers. I watched the shadows under the door. I couldn't make out the voices, but they whispered outside. I closed my eyes.

I heard the door open and the painter said my name. I opened my eyes in the half-light and could see one of the kids crouched beside me. He touched my hair and I rolled away from him. The other kid was on that side but standing. His cock was by my face and he shook it and made a weird high whistling laugh. The painter crawled on top of me.

"No, no, no."

"You sure? They wanted to meet you." He was still on me.

The boys had already backed off. They didn't care. They wanted more drugs. He had his face right by my ear.

"Get off me."

He got up and joined the two silhouettes in the door.

I waited as their voices left. I heard laughter and got up and placed a chair under the doorknob. I lay awake listening to the voices as I did with my mother's card club when I was little but this night I wasn't lulled. I was thinking about the knife in my bag.

* * *

"We put cocks in our mouths and asses. They're never going to be okay with that," Shane said too loudly. The other diners looked over.

Shane had brought a quiet kid named Arlo. He ordered a burger and Shane berated him for eating animals. The kid blinked back tears.

"Lay off," I said.

"You think the animals didn't cry when they were killed?" Shane said.

Arlo got up and went to the bathroom.

"Stop being an asshole."

"I am a professional asshole," he said.

I asked about Arlo.

"He's puppy-dogging after me. Can't do anything for himself."

"Aww, he's your new foster kid."

"Fuck yourself. I'm going for a walk, man."

When Arlo returned, he asked where Shane was.

"I pissed him off and he left. I'm not sure if he's coming back," I said. "Can I have a bite of your burger?"

"Sure." He pushed the plate my way.

I bit in and chewed and smiled with meat showing.

"He fights with everyone because he doesn't want anyone to get too close?" Arlo said, looking at me through thick bangs.

"Yup." I took another bite and held the burger up to him. "Bite?" He shook his head and gestured for me to finish it.

"You in love with him?" I said between bites.

"No, he's . . . it's hard to . . ."

"Got it."

"I was supposed to stay with him tonight but now, I don't know."

"You can crash at my place but it's not the best."

"What?"

"I mean you can crash tonight but you have to fend for yourself. I live with an old freak who loves guys like you."

"Okay."

"You can sleep on the couch in my room. It's small. There's a bigger one in the big room but he'll bother you. How tall are you?"

"Six feet."

"Yeah, it's small."

Arlo looked ridiculous on the little couch, which he called a love seat. He kept saying he was fine, but I could see him shifting positions, trying to not make the couch creak. I remembered my nights like that, trying to not take up space, to disappear.

"Just sleep in my bed."

Arlo joined me and slept. I woke with his arm over me. Be careful. These small moments were how people got in trouble.

* * *

Arlo started tricking. I tried to talk him out of it, told him to get a straight job. He was too sensitive, too young.

"Creeps will eat you up in ways you won't realize until it's too late, man."

I always called him man because his eyes brightened at the word.

Arlo told me about a man who took him to fancy restaurants and watched him eat. The man enjoyed the discomfort of the other patrons. He was old and rich and therefore untouchable.

"My grandson has an appetite," Arlo said, imitating him.

"Free meals," I said.

"Oh, he pays me to eat and there's no sex."

Another guy paid Arlo to beat him with a belt. He had feeder and masochist regulars. At first, I was suspicious, but I realized it was true, or true enough. The kid was smart either way. I ordered us burgers.

* * *

"This garbage you eat will make you fat. It's very bad," the man said. He was gesturing at a bag of chips and a soda.

"These crisps and fizz?" Shane said in a ridiculous accent somewhere in the vicinity of British by way of a Chattanooga theater troupe.

"You can laugh but you are what you eat."

"Do you eat old goat?"

The man sputtered. I was worried we were losing him and his money.

"I try to watch what I eat. It isn't easy though." I smiled a little and held his eyes when he looked at me.

I knew he wanted Shane more than me. That was where his attention had been, but I could see him reappraising the situation. Shane was in an impossible mood. He would be mad at me if the man went off with me instead of him, but he was doing everything in his power to lose the guy. This wasn't a game we could afford. Who cared about some shriveled old cock that had to be coerced to half-mast in some dreary room? I did. At that moment. It was late and I wasn't in the mood to go find another guy. Either I would have him or Shane would. This was the end of the night. The long Thanksgiving weekend loomed during which every suburban closet-case would either be in town visiting family and in desperate need or every ring-fingered dad stuck in an endless loop of Black Friday holiday buying would need attention. Good money, bad times. A lot of repressed amateur hour fuckery.

"It's getting late," I said.

I touched the man's hand and smiled again. I could feel Shane's eyes. I was leading the man away now and would probably pay for it later. Shane didn't seem to care. He had turned his attention elsewhere and I realized he had done this on purpose. I was getting his castoff. I could still bail out. I could turn and say forget it. But I thought of tomorrow, waking and feeling out of sorts, maybe even sick. I turned and said, "Let's go."

* * *

Shane listened as a woman told a story about her young son with a heart condition. She talked about his medical expenses and her long nights with him at the hospital between her grueling waitressing shifts.

I had grown up among women like her with genuinely hard lives. They had learned how to turn a good tale out of their misery and win sympathy, which was as close to compassion and understanding as they were going to get. Sometimes sympathy led to a helping hand, something as small as a meal or a ride to an appointment. Sometimes to something as glorious as free babysitting or secondhand clothes.

This woman was shrewd. She surrounded herself with a mix of former middle-class types and artists, the demographics that were people likely to be bohemian enough to be fun yet still have memories of comfortable upbringings that could be exploited for guilt.

I slipped away to snort a line and when I returned from the bathroom, she was regaling someone else with a story of her sassy comebacks to problem-customers at work and Shane was gone.

"Where's Shane?"

"Who?"

"My friend."

She looked at me. She acted as if she hadn't been pouring her heart out to a stranger only moments before but years ago: how could she be held responsible to remember something that far in the past? She turned back to her audience.

I walked outside and saw Shane in the street with some man. I called out his name and he turned and squinted. He told me about a party, told me to call him, told me it had been a fun night. The man stood behind him waiting patiently, swaying to an invisible song.

* * *

I had joked about the Pony Express for no good reason. Whatever the conversation was, a space had presented itself to show off some wit.

"You're the smart one, aren't you," the man said and ran his rough hand across my cheek like I was a cat. His pet. Fine.

The man said, "You know the Pony Express only operated for two years. All these years later people still talk about it, but it only existed for a brief time. Do you know why?"

The telegraph, I thought.

"No," I said.

"The telegraph," he said.

"Oh." *You're the smart one, aren't you?*

I was unbuttoning his shirt. He made little noises.

"I'm glad . . ." He looked at me. "I'm glad I came with you."

"Me too."

I opened his shirt and saw the big scar. I'd seen that kind before. Heart surgery.

"Heart surgery," he said.

"Oh wow, that must have been something."

"It was," he said and began the story. He rambled about his doctor. "It's a big scar but I'm glad just to be alive."

"Can I touch it?" I already was.

"S-sure."

I pushed his shirt back and touched the ridge of flesh that parted his chest. I ran my hands over his shoulders. He'd shrunken some from his drunken chatter. He was quiet and hesitant.

I unbuttoned his pants and slid them off. The paunch, the good underwear worn for tonight. The mismatched black and midnight blue dress socks.

I stood and undressed and let him look at me. He reached out and his hand shook.

"Do you want the light on or off?"

"Off? Is that okay?"

"Sure."

We were in darkness and I went by feel. A mixed blessing. I didn't have to see him, but I also couldn't take any facial cues. I had to pay attention to his body and mine. I had to be present. *I am here.* That would pull me into the future of it being over.

Tom Cole

Excerpt from the play
The Tyranny of Structurelessness

My sponsor told my ex-boyfriend I was shooting up meth after we broke up.

I challenged my sponsor on this—he said:

> *I don't think I wanted to tell Doug that, he said.*
> *Go to a meeting. You are tied up in personality.*

You don't THINK you WANTED to tell him, I say? And he says:

> *Well, I am sorry you are upset. I think, however, you have other things to worry about than this . . . Doug needs to be out of your head, believe me he's not renting you any room in his.*

He is all gaga over his new boyfriend, his career.

And I think, *You don't know how jealous I am. You must love me to death.*

Then I shot up and got gangbanged by dozens of men all on video, the largest gangbang in history: call Ripley he won't believe it.

When I think of how easily it could have been avoided, happened in a less cruel way.

I think I must believe in a God—a vindictive one.

And I realized this is what it takes to get me interested . . .

Maybe it was daddy. Maybe it was mommy. Maybe it was the American dream.

Oh, and it doesn't count with men who want to have sex with me. I've never had more, they like to be around self-destructive energy. Darwinian. Like childbearing hips only in reverse but hotter even. They want to fuck me into extinction.

We weak ones, we are better fucks. We really know how to swallow and moan like pigs. We have therapists and secret drug use and holes that just won't quit—deep, deep tides.

What made me a negate, what made me realize I wanted to be the lowest of the low? What made me lean into that?

Abject is the place where meaning collapses.

FLASH FORWARD FIFTEEN YEARS and I'm talking to my friend Susan— she tells me about a conversation she had with that ex-boyfriend where he says, referring to me,

"Oh, do you mean the contortionist with the drug problem?"

And she says, "I defended you, I told him that's not true, he's not a drug addict," and I yell back at Susan, "but it is true, that's not defending me, because it's true."

I hate whoever did this and I thought—I can hate too.

And now I'm interested. And I'm so taken with this phrase, "The contortionist with a drug problem," that I want to use it as my complete bio.

Even my psychiatrist said that, in theory, extreme objectification is not necessarily pathological but the fact that I was doing it with street drugs and strangers I described to him as "mean" demonstrated a lack of good judgement.

I seem to be a very special person—I'm in the middle of a strange adventure.

Light Change

This guy with the steel cage in his basement—he wanted to knock me out, a total KO scene like where the submissive takes twenty Ativan but he found out I was sober and couldn't, so, he wanted me to be his slave. At first I thought—hot—until he said:

> "My roommate has this silly idea of paying a maid to clean our apartment."

Suddenly the idea didn't seem so hot.

He said he also likes the idea of abusing a cop—to degrade a *nice* cop with integrity—this I can get excited about.

I go to a special cop store to buy a badge, aviator glasses—plastic night stick from a leather store on Christopher Street—it has to be plastic because if you are going to stick it in you have to be able to clean it. I ride my bike to his place, in Harlem. When I enter, I'll give him a citation, we will fight, fuck, then I'll bike home.

So I'm ready, when he answers the door, I'm ready with a scene, dialogue—but instead, we are not alone, his roommate is at the kitchen table making pie crust. I hide the night-stick—suddenly—a gay sitcom. These guys have money.

He tells me to take off my shoes so as not to dirty the apartment.

And the roommate, before looking at me, turns to the guy, (whose name I still don't know) and says:

"Tell *it* to go get the brown sugar."

Against my better judgment, I go to get the brown sugar.
Or I should say, "*It* goes."

I look in three different bodegas before I find any.
I feel like Carrie, all dressed up in a prom dress, tiara, cop gear I had spent hundreds of dollars on (going to a prom would have cost less) and the brown sugar—pig's blood.

Hence my therapist's point that I masochistically seduce the aggressor in the world around me, until, no matter how hard the world tries to make things turn out otherwise, I end up being Carrie. And by the way, looking like a cop in this neighborhood feels strange—I desperately want to explain to the shopkeepers that I'm not a cop . . . but . . .

When I get back dinner is served and there is an expectation that I will sit at a different table and wait on them while they eat.
I ignore this and sit with them—
my one act of rebellion.

I wish I HAD sat at the little slave table . . .

The salad has alfalfa sprouts on it and they start talking about Musical Theater.

And I think—WHAT IS THE SAFE WORD.

And I still don't know his first name and at this point it I'd rather not learn it.

What had been hot about this: the steel cage he kept in the basement, and he told me he knew someone in Washington who wanted to be killed.
He didn't use the word kill—just that the guy wanted to be taken out altogether, to end it for good, and this guy discussing musical theater, he wanted to help him do it.

They start talking about WICKED, and the meanings of the songs therein. Any other musical would have been . . . better.

Gypsy?

Godspell?

And I'm thinking, is this a kind of new-fangled perverse sadism? A scene they've devised to bring the torture to a new high. (singing) *Popular, I want to be popular.* THERE ARE NO SAFE WORDS HERE.

I stayed.

And dinner is over, and the roommate starts clapping like this: (demonstrates)

> And singing a clean-up song,
> (clapping and singing)
> *Clean-up clean-up clean-up—and now we clean it up! Clean up clean up clean up!*

And I realize this song is meant as a prompt for me to clear the table for them.

And I think what Fassbinder film is this.

Chinese Roulette?

And, like the brown sugar, for some invisible reason, I clear the table. As if moved by my own
remote control.

Am I a monster? Or is this what it means to be a person?

I'm not sure why I submit—maybe to see how far I can take it—how Carrie can I get, how far I can push that line, and none of this is in my erotic lexicon but I'm interested. This is what it takes.

Eventually—his bedroom. He has rifled through my bag when I wasn't looking and retrieved my nightstick. I let him beat me with it, but he doesn't really.

He puts me in a strangle hold and as he chokes me out, he whispers into my ear,

"Say good night faggot."

And I say, "Good night faggot."

A vain repetition—that's what it is, a vain repetition.

. . . that sounds like something an addict would say.

. . . this is what it takes . . .

There was no particular feeling around this. No fairy-tale degradation, or dark night of the soul.

Just brown sugar, pie crust.

You are a victim. There's no endurance in your face. Victims are necessary so that the strong may exercise their will.

And I don't believe alcoholism is a disease any more than depression is.

Light Change

I met Tattomuscledad online. In order to meet, he required a letter of introduction—a request for a beating, a formal letter—like something out of Jane Austen or an epistolary novel. And the idea of having to write this letter—this interests me. I submit this letter (I saved it) as Exhibit A as to "Why I No Longer Want To Be A Slave."

(typing)

Letter to Tattoomuscledad.

Hello Sir,

I'm in the mood to be tortured. It's an odd feeling, but I'm focusing my thoughts, driving me to seek you out to hurt me and then care for me.

Got a good beating on Tuesday night and it has put me in the mood to get more pain.

a small note after a large orgy

I am looking for you—someone who likes to inflict pain, to torture.

I've been with this dominant guy who lives in Hell's Kitchen.

Our time together unfolds like this—he sends me a text—*put on combat boots, spandex underwear.* I get the restraints, gear, ready. Rings my buzzer, let him in, wait in position, blindfolded—ass up in the air, face in bed. He plays with it, flogging, whipping, but he's left few marks, doesn't do it hard enough, but the setup is hot, I'm blindfolded, don't know what he looks like. He completely objectifies my body and when we are together, I do not make a single physical action that is self-motivated nor utter a word not in response to a prompt. He talks about my holes—he's never encountered any like them. This makes me feel special, unique. He lies back, still blindfolded, I give him head, he comes in my mouth, I fall asleep in his arms, his cock in my mouth because I never sleep I am afraid of sleep and dreams—this is the only time I let myself, when I do finally sleep, he sneaks out, like a ghost.

I find it intoxicating, knowing there is lots of visual information occurring, most of which is unavailable to me.

When I was little I remember being tied to a tree while we played, "Tickle Dick," and under the gaze of a huge yarn God's eye, my brother kneeling on my shoulders, spitting. I remember dodgeball, locked in a closet with holes, a broomstick thrust through—a medieval torture device. I remember.

I thought it was romantic.

Tuesday night—someone I met online—when he saw the bruises on my ass he goes wild, gave me a good satisfying beating. What he didn't know was how much I can take, and by the end he was hitting me as hard as he could, and I was like:

I can't feel it, whatever are you even doing anything back there.

You know, egging him on . . .

And he was beating me and beating me and finally I broke down crying, at which point he comforted me. Here is a picture of my ass the next day. These bruises look better in person, much more colorful, they have depth, and then he sent me on to the next person.

Next time I see the Dom guy he'll react to the bruises.

I even had bruises on my actual sphincter I've never seen that before.

But it didn't hurt very much—

Any mark can set off the next sadist—a roving punching bag—stumbling from place to place—beat by whomever needs it and I train for this—the sheer cardiovascular effort of travel, pain—I wish I were travelling in a replaceable skeleton.

I am transcending, taking in the pain of the world, transforming it, releasing it.

This brings me to my fantasy—to be tortured, bruised, pissed on, the things in your profile—I want you to take me out of consciousness.

And what happens while I am out, and where and how I come to are completely up to you.

I send this letter I've just read to Tattoomuscledad and it works! He agrees to meet me for lunch—I'm at work—I step out. He orders me to wear a butt plug and I do, but it keeps falling out and as I am headed out the door at work it pops out and creates a tent in my shorts. The receptionist asks, *"Are you ok?"*

In this moment, I think this lunch might be a bad idea, but I'm interested—I force myself—follow.

A fancy upscale diner, Meatpacking District, and he had this thing planned out like Desdemona's handkerchief—he'd drop a bottle of vitamin water I'd pick it up, keep it, open the door, pull out his chair—let him sit first.

And you are thinking, and I was thinking, why the vitamin water.

So he drops it, I pick it up, open the door—but the vitamin water is a shade of yellowy orange I've never seen before and as I am bending over the butt plug falls out again and I'm almost scared it will slip out of my underwear, fall to the ground. But God is on my side because it doesn't, it hangs in the elastic.

When he tells me the vitamin water bottle is filled with piss, *"Take a sip,"* I show no visible reaction, put it in my backpack, tell him I'll save it.
    And at this point we are sitting down so I don't have to worry about the butt plug slipping anymore.
    And he is a finicky eater—lots of dietary restrictions.

And this is when he drops the bomb—
    He's a member of a Leather Family
    of five men into heavy fetishes. There is a master
    a sub-master
    a pig, a sub-pig, and a
    boss and I could be the boy! They need an "Oral Pig Boy."

What do you do when a man says that to you? Laugh, clearly. And even then I had a steadfast notion I'd always be lost in it—the world—conquered.

And I'm thinking now I'm interested. I don't know about you, but I had never heard of a Leather Family.

And I think of Mormons—sister wives, Idaho—how wonderful it would be—I could turn over my 250 square feet on Ludlow for my own wing in a McMansion.

Maybe the polygamists are on to something.

And I want to disappear into this completely suburban-sounding leather family—bad shag carpet and a washer dryer—somewhere in deep New Jersey.

Leather couch, flat-screen tv.

And when I'm bad I'm kept in the space beneath the porch.

I think of my normal relationship.

After a while you stop falling in love and just become irritated.

Sound Cue—Isn't it Romantic

And he tells me that meeting me, at this point without permission from above, goes against the rules of the leather family—that the master, who lives in Michigan, controls the family—the members all of whom are submissive to Michigan—can't really do *anything* without consulting Michigan—beatings orchestrated via Skype as punishment for breaking these rules. This meeting *must* be kept under wraps. If I want to meet him again, I must meet him and the sub-master for an interview to join their family and pretend we had never met heretofore. Tattomuscledad used to be the master, but now he is the sub-pig and his former slave is the sub-master and the guy in Michigan—he is now the master. Tattomuscledad tells me he had testicular cancer, also is sore because Michigan had the sub-master taser his balls fifteen times, all broadcast on Skype—it really hurt and he feels Michigan is trying to ruin his relationship with the sub-master who used to be his slave (and is, in fact, his longtime lover of twenty years) but he is going with it because Tattoomuscledad and the sub-master live together and really can't afford to separate.

~~End Music~~

Typical New York real estate story.

But I tell him, I have to tell him, that the tasering of his former cancer site, I tell him I think this is mean.

And when I think of Michigan choosing the cancer site as the place of torture—I begin to wonder if Michigan may *actually* BE a sadist.

And now I'm interested.

I take my bottle of piss back to my office and throw it in a drawer and look forward to my interview, perversely.

I've haphazardly stumbled across something I can't turn away from, but it feels like staring into the sun.

I imagine myself splitting in two—leaving one of me behind with the Leather Family while the real me, the me who goes back to work carrying a bottle of yellow vitamin water, his heart draws back at the power of the other's will and its commitment to destruction.

And all the while the other me is behind a locked door getting spanked, or beneath my bed, all tangled up in a bag of cuffs, tape, clothespins, shackles. This other me is always behind something.

I find the vitamin water a few months later in my desk drawer, make the mistake of opening it …

Finally, the Leather Family Interview.
    That Sunday I go to breakfast with Sir Austin (sub-master), Tattoomuscledad, and although Michigan isn't present, Sir Austin

keeps getting up to call him on his cell, and whenever this happens, Tattomuscledad sits quietly, ashamed? Embarrassed?

And in this instance—my bones—my marrow—my intestines—they feel very private to me, but maybe they won't be, if I join the Leather Family. I am instructed to open doors for them, sit last, let them order for me, eat last.

And I am reminded of the Charlotteans—a cotillion-type social dance program for teaching manners I attended when young—the girls wearing gloves, the boys greeting them on the way in, I knowing I was gay and my mom bringing me here in the hopes that contact with the other sex, no matter how formal, how twee, how in fact, gay—that this contact would lead to further contact, and I loved it, but for the wrong reasons, and in the end, we would all dance to Lynyrd Skynyrd, Fleetwood Mac, Freebird and boogie on down boogie on down, (or could she have sent me here because of the reports the teachers sent home to my parents about my "nasty habits," which involved playing with my balls and smelling my fingers, picking my nose, tweaking my nipples in math—my bad habits of scratching the inside of my ear and then smelling my fingers—could this be why they sent me?) This is where my mind went, not to the future glory of being a member of a Leather Family but rather to my childhood, me always home, eating Cheetos, NyQuil poured over ice cream, gum rolled in sugar then chewed again, living for the *TV Guide* (obsessively circling what to watch) *Fantasy Island—The Love Boat* (oh, look a double episode special). The TV won't die even though it is essentially murder and there is a TV in every room and it is always on.

And in some deep current of my psyche I knew I wasn't done with drugs yet. This isn't available to me consciously at this lunch, but I knew I knew I knew I was worthy of a grander destruction and viciousness of vices, that my destruction should and would be more luxurious than a leather gag and a mouthpiece connected to a toi-let—some sort of human urinal.

I wait for everyone to sit down, and then sit down myself, take out my handkerchief, lay it upon my lap, then fold hands, and suddenly feel self-conscious about my clothing choice—tan shorts and a gingham shirt, shaved head but I think I may have missed a spot, and I look up to the huge mirror at Balthazar, and imagine it falling, breaking, a shard piercing the jugular of the girl having brunch at the bar with her date—they've been up all night doing cocaine, they are having oysters, martinis, can barely talk—sunglasses, slurred speech.

In what way is a Leather Family any different from the typical American family, really, when you take the longer view?

They portend to teach me what it means to be in a healthy and com-mitted S&M relationship. But I don't know, it all feels like mentally ill people clinging to each other through pain. Or like being a 1950s housewife. And I begin to wonder if there is such a thing as a healthy S&M relationship.

Why can't I find someone to just beat the shit out of me, fuck me, and leave?

Sir Austin and Tattomuscledad have interesting things to say about punishment and torture—how to gut punch with a bruise, how to gut punch without a bruise.

This is all so depressing.

And I wonder, and I hope, that other tables can hear this conversation.

After another hushed and stuttering cell phone call on an old flip phone to Michigan, I come to understand that if I am to meet with Tattoomuscledad to play on our own, he will make the rules, but these things will be reported to Michigan and Sir Austin.

Eventually, Sir Austin goes to Michigan to spend a week polishing Michigan's leather and ends up sero-converting (Michigan had lied about his HIV status) and after that Michigan drops off the face of the earth completely—turns out he had a traumatic brain injury causing violent outbursts and disappearing acts, but that all came later and felt tragic, sad —all of this torture and anger an extension or weird symptom of a brain injury, fetishized.

When I finally do get a one on one with Tattomuscledad, it turns out all he wants is for me to fuck him mercilessly with a dildo for hours—he never comes because of the testicular cancer—it goes on and on and on until his asshole looks like late abstract expressionism, a wounded Georgia O'Keeffe flower? Finally he puts on a glove and sticks one finger up my ass for one second. That's it.

Oddly my KO fantasies faded. Write it out and it goes away.

And in retrospect all I can think of is the sero-conversion and not to mention Sir Austin asking me if I knew where to get some Special K that *there is nothing like being fisted on K*, and I said, "I'm sober but give me fifty bucks and a cab voucher and I'll get you whatever you want." WHAT'S WRONG WITH THESE PEOPLE WHO CAN'T FIND DRUGS FOR THEMSELVES.

So much for wanting to be a slave.

Kamala Puligandla

The Slut Factory

Before I started working at The Slut Factory, I had been a respectful regular—the kind who knew to tip extra on anything with the intention to be ostentatious, regardless of the outcome. It wasn't any less hot to me if a dancer went hard and didn't land their pole dismount, and it wasn't a big deal if a bartender gave me a glass full of lime garnishes, rum, and crème de menthe because they didn't really have the ingredients for a mojito.

The essential thing about a slutty queer bar was gratefulness. It was a built-in part of the establishment. You always appreciated every effort, were always overly gracious about the inelegant parts—and there were always inelegant parts—not because it was "our place" or because we were "lucky to still have these bars" but because committing to sluthood means giving yourself permission to sometimes be the inelegance in a room.

For example, The Slut Factory was the place where I could meet some hottie and try to impress them by embellishing facts about myself in front of a bartender who knew I was none of those things, then come back several days later to detail the hottie's many unforgivable deeds until closing, and THEN come in with that hottie the very next day, deeds forgiven. And the same bartender might simply suggest that I try today's special, "Amnesia Much, Bitch", before we all moved on with our nights. I think we were all grateful for that, it was its own unique kind of elegance.

I was trying to explain all of this to the men in suits, who were stiffly arranged around the bar, trying to look at home in their new investment. When Gwen and Mateo, the only queer Latinx bar-owners in town, found themselves unable to shoulder a recent rent increase, it seemed that someone's straight cousin and his fellow venture capital buddies popped in with an interest in backing "a project for the community." I couldn't stand them. I knew they had some horrible scheme up their sleeves. I wanted them to know that their presence was bringing down the value of the place, that we were all at The Slut Factory precisely so we didn't have to be wherever they were.

"So, who are you?" they asked me, when I was done with my soliloquy.

"Nobody," Gwen said at the same time that I said, "I'm a VIP."

"Not quite nobody," Mateo came to my defense.

"Thank you," I replied.

"You feel strongly about The Slut Factory?" asked one of the suited men.

"I do!" I exclaimed with great enthusiasm.

"Well great, we need people with that kind of spirit. There's a role that you seem like a natural for." The man raised his beer to cheers with me, but my drink had yet to be poured and I just stared at him until he lowered it.

I looked over at Mateo, whose brows were furrowed, and at Cid, who was there just as often as I was, but who had remained eerily silent.

"Look, Pepper," Gwen said to me gravely, "there's gonna a be a few changes around here."

The scheme was both more and less evil than I imagined: these venture capitalist bros were buying up local gay bars all over the country, infusing them with cash, and creating a sanitized version of the gay bar experience that catered to straight people, who were more than willing to pay high prices for an exclusive step into a previously unsafe and inaccessible world. "The LGBTQ themed bar is the hottest new concept in town," I heard the bros exclaiming to each other on their way out.

"Okay, so The Slut Factory is becoming like a sleazy gay Applebee's?" I asked.

Mateo nodded. "Classy though, like The Slutty Cheesecake Factory."

Gwen sighed. "We couldn't not take the deal, okay? They're allowing us to keep the name, keep our performance schedule, our staff, and everyone will get paid more. Plus we'll still get to do strip and karaoke nights, with the regular crowd at regular prices."

"Oh, so you're a responsible sell-out, I see," I said.

Gwen glared at me. "Pepper, you can fuck off."

The rancor in Gwen's voice reminded me of the time, at least fifteen years ago, when we'd had a molly-fueled hook-up at a terrible pride party because her actual crush had ditched her, and I was waiting for my ride home to finish getting railed by some basketball player with a broken arm, which was why, I had to assume, it was taking so long. Gwen hadn't ever been particularly lucky in love, and she was always in a bad mood—it was hard to say which begat which.

"I'm sorry," I said. "You know I love this place. I'm just feeling sensitive about having to do my slutting in front of a straight audience."

"I know, it's macabre," Mateo said, tapping the bar between us. He paused to brush his fingers through the thick beard on his chin. "But it could be a good thing, Pepper, you know? Maybe it'll give you the chance to really hone your approach, work on some new flirtation material that's entertaining and somewhat vulnerable? No pressure, but there's always room to improve the craft."

"Wow," I laughed. "Okay fine, I'll accept that challenge."

Cid seemed rather unmoved, I figured because they were still young. "At least this place isn't immediately turning into soulless condos? We still get to come here, even if it is overrun with creeps."

"Thank you, Cid!" Gwen exclaimed.

"Plus, like these douche bags said," Mateo added, "since you all are already here, you might as well get paid to be in the circus."

"That is, Pepper, if you're not exceedingly and overwhelmingly busy 'writing your book'," Gwen added with vicious air quotes.

"Such a shame that the Angry Dyke role has already been claimed," I said, looking at Gwen. "That could've shaken things up for me."

"Take your bad jokes to open mic night," I heard Gwen grumble, but Mateo and I were way too busy laughing at my bad joke.

* * *

If I'd had any better way to make money, I probably would have just continued to frequent The Slut Factory as a patron, who enjoyed a healthy discount, and stayed out of the Slutty Cheesecake Factory business. However, as it was, my main paid gig was writing interviews of dogwalkers for an app, and I had run out of gentle ways to ask what kind of desperation had led them to dog walking. So when I received an email from Sandy@thegayborhoodbargroup.com, asking me to come in for an interview, I agreed. I've always said that my ideal job was getting paid to be myself, and this wasn't not that.

When I walked in, Sandy was seated at a table on the small stage at the back of the bar and didn't take any time getting down to business. "How familiar are you with our theme, LGBTQ?" she asked. I took in her faded tie-dyed t-shirt and her long hair in a low ponytail. I couldn't decide if she was one of us, if she was already in costume, or if she was simply a person who had spent the past several decades focused on practicality.

In response to her question, I considered my gay resume. "I think I'm pretty well-versed in the theme," I replied. I wasn't sure what exactly would be impressive in this scenario. I thought about the gay peak of my college years: hooking up with three girls in a hot tub at a queer co-op, after baking vegan pizzas together.

Sandy looked me over hard, from my lilac Docs to what seemed like the tips of my soft mohawk. "Okay, we'll do a run-through and see how natural you are."

"I can do whatever you think is best," I said, suddenly wondering if I did have any familiarity with the theme. I still had a strong memory of my first visit to a Benihana for Jessica Sclamberg's eighth birthday party. It had been described to me as a Japanese restaurant, so I was shocked by the showy, eagerness of the Asian men behind the grill, batting eggs around in the air and lighting everything on fire. Nothing there remotely resembled anything I had experienced as Japanese or Japanese American in my family, so what did the queer version of this entail?

"Personally, with your stature, I'd pick you for Lesbian Door Guy, though I have a note here from the owners that they'd like me to try you at Slut Regular, so why don't we give that a shot?"

I nodded and sat down at the bar. Davia, a real regular bartender, sauntered over and did her real regular thing of silently staring at me while she unloaded the dishwasher. She knew it was an impressive turn-on to me that she could do it without looking.

"I love your new hair," I said.

"Thank you," she replied, "it wasn't cheap."

"It really highlights your cheekbones, I'd say it was a worthy investment."

"Well if it isn't Pepper, checking out my cheekbones like I'm wearing this bustier for nothing. You know this rack was more expensive than my hair!" Davia side-eyed me, she was such a Leo.

"I was working up to the bustier, it's like 3 p.m. I wasn't sure if you were ready yet for me to say your tits look luscious."

"Luscious?" she asked and started putting ice in a glass for my negroni. "Say more."

"Ravishingly luscious," I said. "Like a pair—"

Suddenly Sandy stood up and clapped her hands together loudly. "Well okay, that's enough, I think you're exactly the right person for the role. Pepper, is it?" she asked me.

"Yeah, Pepper. So what exactly is the role?" I asked, confused.

Sandy was matter of fact. "Your job is to make the ladies feel good. Include them, give them The Slut Factory treatment. Whatever it was you were doing there, do that with them." She wrote down an unintelligible figure in pencil on a piece of paper and placed it in front of me. "That's our offer. You're on 5 nights a week, 7 p.m. till closing, you'll be emailed a service guide that we take seriously, and we start trainings next week."

"Sorry, what does that say?" I asked for the purpose of clarity.

Sandy looked at me like I had just asked for a ride to the airport. "Fine. We can go 10K higher, but that's it."

As someone used to begging for $100 checks from my publishers, I had the good sense to not ask any more questions. I shook her hand, "Sandy, thank you, I won't let you down."

* * *

I planned to hate The New Slut Factory. During training week, I got the entire staff to refer to the training team as Senseless Breeders, and reduced one young man to tears by asking if this was his professional foray into grooming or if he'd had a lot of experience in training the oppressed to accommodate the sexual curiosity of those in power.

But the truth was that we all naturals at our jobs. It was easy to be the most extreme version of ourselves at our favorite bar. At our best, the fags made you suddenly aware of your body and thrillingly question your own decisions; the dykes left you with hot tips to improve your life and a sense of your own power and beauty; the bisexual bartenders were just flirtatious and elusive enough to keep you coming back for more; and the performers made you wish the show were, in fact, intended for you.

By the night of the grand re-opening, I almost didn't recognize The Slut Factory. The drink menu had been revamped, the booths had been reupholstered, the bathrooms boasted expensive herbal-smelling soap—thankfully the graffitied stalls with decades of sexual gossip remained—and there was soft, warm lighting, so unlike the harsh red glow of beer signs, that it made my whole existence feel rich.

"It's such a nice brothel," breathed Cid, now one of my fellow flirters, who winked at me through an eye hole in their latex hood.

"These booths are smoother than my face," I exclaimed, rubbing my cheek over the buttery leather. "Who wouldn't be horny on this?"

I heard two claps and Sandy's voice calling "Attention!" and that's how the night began. It was unheard of for the place to be packed at seven, but there was a sizable early crowd flowing through the doors. I wondered how our investors had lured in these straights in their business casual, still talking about the day's meeting drama. I watched a pair of "girlfriends" walk in and cover their mouths, scandalized by the strap-on porn playing on the TVs perched overhead.

"How are you girls doing?" I asked. "What brought you in this evening?"

They looked around carefully, trying to avoid eye contact with me, but still wanting to look at me, to gather some kind of information. I had been prepared by the tearful trainer to answer any questions, including ones that I would never answer without that extra $10K, but theirs were far more innocent than I imagined.

"How do we know where to sit? Does it mean something?" asked the one with a short haircut and a sharp blazer.

"And what do we do, exactly? How does the slutting work?" asked the other, as she adjusted her blouse for an ideal cleavage peek.

"We like the name," added the first. "It's very sassy, very sex positive."

I had always thought of The Slut Factory as an unsentimental read on what happened to anyone who hung out here long enough, but I wasn't upset about the aspirational quality these women were attributing to it. Maybe there was some glamour to being transformed into a slut.

"You can sit anywhere, but personally, when I'm coming here with a friend, I grab a booth," I said, guiding them over to the one next to the jukebox. "So you can privately discuss what kind of slut you feel like being, or you know, pull in someone you're intrigued by." I adjusted my mesh vest and tried to sound authoritative. "How it works, is you drink, you dance, you say yes or no to the experiences people offer you, or you approach the people you like. The drag show is at 8:30, and if you want a pool lesson, let me know, or just find a dyke with a stick." I touched both of their elbows and made eye contact, until they seemed reassured, then I borrowed Cid's wink and strode away to nurse my comped negroni at the bar.

"First impressions?" asked Mateo, who was working the bar in a classic leather cap and chest harness. It was such a different look than his usual grandmotherly hipster ensembles that I didn't recognize him at first.

"They don't seem so bad," I said. "I almost feel sorry for them. Can you imagine never having been casually fingered under the table while eating a chicken finger?"

"Wow," Mateo shook his head. "To be denied of such poetry."

"That's your contribution to the world, Mateo, the legacy you and Gwen built."

"No, Pepper, that's too generous, that's all your legacy."

By ten, when the drag show was over, I was busy encouraging Reckless Rachels, flattering Anxious Ashleys, and returning invasive questions to Curious Cassies. I was pleased to see several business casuals, including my booth girlfriends, dancing and rubbing up against Cid, Lucia, Randy and each other in non-hetero formations, all to the pounding rhythm of La Bouche's "Be My Lover."

There was a part of me that was filled with hope and joy for these young caterpillars, who, in the moment, were less straight, so much as new, who were about to be changed by the firm touch and prolonged gaze of someone they both wanted and wanted to be, for the very first time. There was another part of me that inwardly barfed as soon as a bachelorette party rolled in. They hung onto every person in the room, like all of us existed for their consumption—because, here, we did. The group of them chanted for shots in front of the bar, and as Davia swatted hands away from her hair, I watched the bachelorette—announced as such by her penis-studded crown—try to shove her lime wedge into Mateo's mouth and go for a body shot. Cid and I got her sandwiched between us and sucking tequila off of Cid's latex-covered chest in about five seconds flat, and as we high-fived over her head, I briefly hated myself for feeling accomplished over this.

I was back at the bar, having some water, remembering that this was just my job and every bad encounter with an awful straight was the exact fodder I relished retelling, loudly, in places full of straight people.

"Nice save," I heard Gwen uncharacteristically compliment me, and turned to find her closing a check at the register.

"If we can't queer a bride in under a minute, how would we qualify to work here?" I asked.

Gwen laughed, and I was touched that in the midst of her worst nightmare, I could still entertain her. "Pepper, you didn't hear it from me," she said. "But this patron at the end of the bar has been eyeing you for a minute, and I get the feeling she doesn't care to hear anything remotely truthful."

I looked over, and the "patron," a pretty South Asian woman with dark wavy hair, was gently watching me over the rim of her wine glass. It was so classy and composed, not an open stare, but a careful observation. Her legs were crossed, and there was a subtle annoyance in the tap of her platform sandal against the bar rung.

I wandered a bit closer. "I wasn't aware that The Slut Factory served wine," I said.

"The Slut Factory does serve wine," she answered. "But nothing I would drink." She opened her fancy leather bag and showed me a peek of the bottle inside. It had a cute purple mushroom stopper, which I felt like she was showing me too.

"I love a good skin contact Gamay," I said.

"I kinda thought you might," she said. "Does that make me psychic?"

"Or does it make you a wine snob?" I asked.

"I thought the LGBTQ experience wasn't about binaries," she said with a smirk.

I laughed. "Wow, I'm being called in. I apologize for limiting your identities. But from one wine snob to another, please tell me how you're getting away with drinking this nice wine in a dive best known for well drinks?"

She reached over the bar, pulled up a glass that she placed in front of me, and started pouring. "It just so happens that I'm married to the primary investor in the new and improved Slut Factory," she said, and waited until the glass was mostly full before looking up for my reaction.

As a professional, I betrayed nothing, and anyway, people had confessed much more disloyal things, which hadn't diminished my interest in our vibe. "And what's that like?" I asked.

"The marriage?" she asked.

"Yeah, marriage to the primary investor in, not just the new and improved Slut Factory, but I hear many other successful LGBTQ experience ventures?" I sipped my wine. "This is delightful, by the way, thank you."

She laughed with exasperation and propped her head up with her fist. "This, me here, now—this is the experience. I know it's fucked up, it's such an embarrassing mid-life crisis project for him to put us through. You don't have to be so nice to me about it. I probably deserve to be sitting here alone, thinking about what I'm complicit in."

I took a deep breath and took her subtle bait. "You're far too gorgeous to be sitting here alone, if you don't want to be," I said. "And if it's punishment you're looking for, we can both be grateful your idiot husband saved this bar from closing, because there's a spanking room/green room behind the stage that I could show to you."

I saw the way her eyes agreed before her hand slipped around my wrist. "Maybe we should just take a look."

We had hardly stepped backstage, amongst the disarray of costumes, wigs, and make-up caboodles, when she pulled on my vest so we were pressed against each other, and started kissing my neck. I was undeniably turned on, but I absolutely intended to punish her. "You think I want soft kisses from the wife of the gay bar colonizer?" I asked. I grabbed a fistful of hair at the back of her head, pulling her face away from me and leading her toward the couch. I pressed her face into the cushions, so she was kneeling. "You're a disgrace," I told her. "A blight on humanity."

"I am, I really am," she said in a quavering voice. "I deserve to be punished; a spanking is the least you could do."

Her pleading eyes told me everything. I instructed her to pull down her pants, and admired her beatific ass, so exposed. Then went rummaging around in cabinets, until I found Mateo's lucky paddle, which I knew he kept around in case of emergencies—this was one I bet he hadn't even planned for.

"What's your name?" I asked.

"My real name?"

"Or whatever you want me to call you," I said.

It came out like an admission of defeat. "Rekha."

"Rekha, I'm Pepper," I said. "I'm gonna spank you now, so say 'red' if you want me to stop, okay?" I whispered in her ear. "I'm not gonna stop if you say 'stop' because I want you to protest and I want you to hurt."

"Okay," she said weakly.

But I could see she was trying not to smile, and it fueled my angry spanking performance. I thought of all of the men in suits smugly standing around our bar, and it gave me great pleasure knowing that I was going to get to hit one of their wives, at her request. I was filled, once again, with that signature Slut Factory gratefulness, it hadn't been extinguished!

I began lightly, slowly building up strength, watching her body absorb the strikes, her skin reddening, until she was groaning loudly into the couch and confessing all of her great shame into the green velvet. "That's right, come clean, you flagrant, complicit slut! You enjoy this sick game of getting off on the very business you pretend to be ashamed of."

I was basking in the formal diction of my insults. I was getting riled up. I was deep in the zone. She was begging to me to stop and I refused. Her hair was stuck to her face, and she was panting something that I couldn't quite make out.

"I can't hear you, you feeble coward. Louder!" I commanded, and then turned around, because I heard the turning of the door handle behind me.

"Fuck me! Fuck me now!" Rekha screamed, at the same time that Gwen opened the door and a group of men in suits entered the room.

With great amusement in her voice, Gwen continued her tour, like this was perfectly normal. "So as you can see, this is our green room, where our performers warm-up and get ready."

Rekha hadn't moved from her prone position on the floor, so I continued to stand over her, cradling the business end of the paddle in my left hand, and smiling politely.

"Rekha?" asked one of the men.

"Uh yeah, WHAT?" she retorted in a clear, challenging voice.

"Oh, uh, maybe we can talk about this later?" he asked.

"Get the fuck out of here, Josh!" she screeched. "And Pepper why the fuck did you stop?" she hurled at me next. "I did NOT say the safe word!"

* * *

I figured I was most certainly getting fired. I left The Slut Factory that night with Rekha all over my hands and the rest of her bottle of wine in my backpack, feeling satisfied in a new and different way than I'd ever left the bar before. I fully expected an email in the morning from Sandy@thegayborhoodbargroup.com, informing me that I had violated our service guide—though I knew I hadn't, nothing in it said that you couldn't, at their vehement demand, fuck the investor's wives. But no such email came. So I went about my morning, and even sat down to write for a few hours, before showing up for my shift at The Slut Factory.

There was the usual buzz about the place, nothing remarkable, and nobody except Gwen indicated that anything unusual had happened the previous night. Even she just poured me a negroni and said with a little more pep than usual, "I like to see that 'fuck you' spirit in action." I could tell she was proud of her double-entendre, so I gave her some credit for it and relaxed. Cid picked out some porn to play on the TVs, while I put on some jukebox songs to get the night going, and we opened to the same kind of happy hour rush of the previous day.

"Hey, psst," Mateo tapped me on the shoulder, while I was leading a pair of young newbies to a pool table.

I motioned, frustratedly to the guests, and he called out to them, "I'm gonna borrow Pepper for a minute, but I'm sure Lucia, can give you a lesson with her stick."

He walked me over to the bar, where a group of three women stood nervously, adjusting the coasters under their martini glasses. "These women, ahem, ladies, were asking for you," Mateo said. "I'm sure you'd love to meet them."

The one closest to me touched my shoulder and leaned in close. "We heard what you did for Rekha. And how much she liked it. Are there other kinds of experiences here that you can offer?"

Another piped in. "We would like it to be a bit more discreet, however. We're not entirely sure what our husbands would think about us being guests at their bar—you know, husbands."

"Oh, absolutely," I reassured them. "And are your husbands investors too?"

"Yes, they're all extremely passionate about supporting the LGBTQ community, but it's not lost on us what it means for a bar like this. Having outsiders inside."

"We're really sorry," said the first one again. "Very sorry."

"Right," I said, looking over that night's staff, deciding who else might like to engage in some cathartic guilty wife play. "Let me see what I can do for you. You know, as VIPs here."

They all collectively purred into their martinis and shivered.

Much to my surprise, Rekha came in by herself just before closing. "I have a bottle of wine I want you to try."

"I'm intrigued," I said. "But it's late, I have to start cleaning up soon."

"Actually, I was thinking we could drink it at my hotel room? When you're done?" she asked, then winced. "Unless I misread everything about last night, and you do really think I'm a feeble coward and don't want my, um, soft kisses?"

I laughed. "I'm a sucker for having my lines repeated back to me."

"They're unusual and pretty funny," she replied. "They've been stuck in my head all day. Well, a lot has been stuck in my head."

"Wow," I said. "So one night at The Slut Factory and you're a full-on gay slut?"

Rekha rolled her eyes. "Let's not get ahead of ourselves."

"You're the psychic wine snob," I said. "So I'll let you tell me whether or not I'm genuinely interested in your offer."

* * *

It wasn't more than two weeks later that I walked into The Slut Factory, to a wild round of applause from the entire staff.

"Oh no," I sighed. "I'm fired, right? The investor's wives? The green room? I'm really sorry guys, I didn't mean to. Is the bar—"

Gwen had the biggest grin I'd seen on her face in the entire twenty years she'd been forced into community with me. "Pepper, will you please shut the fuck up?"

I put up my hands in surrender and shut my mouth.

It was Davia who beckoned me over to the bar and placed a negroni in front of me. She had placed it on one of the original The Slut Factory coasters with the cursive neon sign font, and two open mouths on either side.

"What happened to The Slutty Cheesecake Factory?" I asked.

"The investors mysteriously needed to sell the bar back to us ASAP," Mateo reported proudly. He was back in his normal clothes, a hideous illustrated cat t-shirt and some preppy seersucker shorts—I almost missed his cliché leather daddy getup. "In their desperation, they seemed more than happy to sell it for less than half of what they bought it for."

"Not to mention what they paid for in renovations," Gwen added. "And I know not everyone likes all of it—Cid—but our new lighting and plumbing are not going anywhere."

"Okay wait, so am I fired? Or am I not?" I asked.

"I mean, technically, your position has been eliminated," Mateo said.

I shook my head. "I knew it, it was all too good to be true."

To my great relief, Mateo continued. "But we think you'd make a great bartender if that's what you'd like to do."

"Regardless, you're officially a VIP now," Gwen added. "I'm sorry that I wasn't able to see that before."

"Thank you," I said. "That's really big of you. And I'd like to try my hand at the bar. I love this place, I'd fuck many more wives for you to keep it."

"We know," they said together.

"You really embody the soul of The Slut Factory," Gwen declared, which was, to this day, one of the greatest compliments of my life.

Jen Silverman

Appetite

She'd only had someone die on the massage table once, but once is enough to change the course of anyone's life.

It happened simply, quietly; she wasn't even sure when it happened. He lay down; she covered him with the thin blanket; she asked him if he was comfortable and he said yes. He seemed calm. He was an older man, his hair shock-white, his girth spilling over the table. She liked people in the realness of their bodies—their fat, their wrinkles, their strange spots and skin tags. She felt her imperfect body speaking to theirs as she listened to the contours of their muscles, the place where tendon knotted and blood slowed and everything had to be coaxed into looseness. She was a good listener, and so she did not understand how she could have missed the moment in which he passed from life into death.

He was pliable under her hands, yes, but he had been from the start. He was silent, but he had been that as well. And he was lying face-down so it wasn't until she asked him to turn over—and she asked several times, shaking him gently to wake him up—that she would have had any chance of seeing his chest fail to rise and fall. He did not turn over. He was, by then, no longer there.

When she quit the massage job, she did not say it was because of him. Her employers did not ask her about him; they did not even mention what had happened, though of course it was on everybody's minds. She said she was going back to school—this was a lie—and they wished her luck, while guessing that she was lying. She was nearly forty, they thought, what school would possibly take her?

* * *

After that, a great hunger seized her. She was a person who had always been restrained in her desires. She had never wanted more than she needed, and she had whittled her needs down past those of most other people. The hunger arrived like a revelation.

The day after she quit, she awoke in the middle of the night, ravenous. Moonlight poured through the bedroom windows. She got up. She walked into the kitchen. She wondered if she had come for a glass of water, but instead she opened the refrigerator door and she began to eat. When she was finally satisfied, she found that she had consumed: a peanut-butter sandwich with Bonne Maman apricot marmalade; two bananas, one overripe and the other still green; a small container of Greek yogurt; a larger container of regular yogurt; a box of rosemary-and-salt crackers with a wheel of brie; a medium-size bag of baby carrots; a container of olive-flavored hummus; the remainder of a box of Corn Flakes, and a chocolate-chip cookie from several days ago that she had forgotten and that had become regrettably stale.

She returned to bed and slept a deep and dreamless sleep. Her stomach did not hurt, nor did she feel particularly full. In the morning, she was starving again.

The other hungers came subsequently. They did not replace each other but were cumulative and additional: a hunger for music, for books, for sugar, for alcohol, for soft things, for sex. She imagined herself as a giant bag, expandable and unstructured; she put things inside.

* * *

She dreamed about him, the dead man. She didn't remember his first name, just his last: Sorrell. She had called him "Mr. Sorrell" when he first walked in; he had said Hello; she had asked him to undress and lie face-down, and then she had left the room. When she had returned, she had begun the massage and they had not spoken beyond that point. She tried to remember the sound of his voice when he said that one word, "Hello." She thought it had been low and a little rusty, the voice of a shy man, but she wasn't certain about this. It had not been a very remarkable voice. But perhaps no voice made itself remarkable with a single word.

When she dreamed about him, he was silent then as well. In one of the dreams, they were walking companionably along the shoulder of a long road. The sun was behind them, casting their shadows straight ahead, as if they were following their shadows to some undesignated meeting place. In another one of the dreams, they were in a large indoor city pool. He was beside her, doing the backstroke, and she was floating, with her legs stiff and her arms out. When she started to sink, she cried out in alarm and woke herself. Once she dreamed that they were in her little kitchen, cooking together. She was stirring the red sauce and he was pouring hot spaghetti into a colander in the sink, steam rising off it in billows. Working away beside him, she felt the sort of intimate contentment she had not felt for years in her waking life.

She didn't look him up online, nor did she look for an obituary. It was too easy to know things about people these days, and they were always the wrong things. Most of the time, you knew somebody best when you didn't let other people describe them to you; that way you could pick up the details that clarified and not the ones that obscured. When Mr. Sorrell's husband showed up at her door, she was unprepared, because in all of her many dreams, there had never once been a husband.

* * *

The second Mr. Sorrell was a pale matchstick of a man, with eyes like chips of ice. He sat in the most uncomfortable chair in the living room, though he had been offered the couch. He had gold-rimmed spectacles that were both restrained and stylish. He introduced himself and then he thanked her for letting him stop in.

"Joanna," he said. "Thank you for letting me stop in." Though he put them on first-name basis, the second Mr. Sorrell did not follow up by offering his own.

"You're very welcome," she said. As silence expanded between them: "Can I get you anything? Tea, or?"

"No thank you," said the second Mr. Sorrell. Then: "Maybe some water if you had it."

"I have water."

"Or some coffee? Only if you had it."

"I have coffee," she said. "I'll just—I'll just be a minute."

She went into the kitchen; she boiled water; she poured it over granules of instant coffee. She wished that she had better coffee, but yesterday she had had a great appetite for coffee and so she had ground the entire bag of good beans and drunk it, cup after cup after cup, until she was dizzy with caffeine but still unsatisfied. This had been a new sensation: overpowering thirst that wasn't really thirst.

When she came back to the living room, the second Mr. Sorrell was standing by the window, staring down onto the street. She realized she hadn't washed the windows or watered the plants in some time, so the glass was streaky, and the plants were dying. She handed him his coffee, wondering if she should apologize for the state of things, though this was always the state of things. Looking at her life through his eyes, it looked shabby and a little sad.

He thanked her for the coffee. He took a sip and then put it down on the windowsill. "You were with my husband," he said. "When he died."

"Yes," she said.

He nodded. "It comforts me," he said. "To know that someone was with him."

"I don't think he was in any distress," she offered. "He seemed very peaceful."

"He was passive," the second Mr. Sorrell corrected her. "It was a problem of his."

"Oh," she said.

"I spoke with him about it often. His passivity."

"Oh?"

"He found it very hard to take a stand. I would say to him: Jonathan, I would say. Take a stand!" The second Mr. Sorrell sighed and adjusted his glasses. He seemed as if he wanted to sound admonishing, but a tendril of wistfulness had crept in. "Especially where his mother was concerned," he added, as if he felt the need to justify himself.

"Oh," she said. She wasn't sure what else to say. "Well. It can be hard."

"I don't know," said the second Mr. Sorrell. "I've never found it particularly hard to just say what you think, to just say it directly and without obfuscation." He took his glasses off, breathed onto each lens, and scrubbed the edge of his sleeve around the lenses before putting them back on. "Can I ask you something?"

"Okay."

"Could you tell that he was loved?"

"I'm sorry?"

"When you met him," said the second Mr. Sorrell. "I know it was a brief meeting. But if somebody is loved enough—you can tell at a glance even, that they're loved."

She was quiet. He was quiet. His eyes fixed on her, and she saw that his narrow chest was rising and falling under his blazer as if he had been running. Someone shouted on the street—the screech of bicycle brakes, more shouting. They listened to the shouting, and then it stopped, and then she said: "Yes, I could tell."

The second Mr. Sorrell let his breath out all at once. "You're sure?"

"Yes," she said. She was lying. "Yes, I'm absolutely sure."

"Thank you," said the second Mr. Sorrell. She could not tell whether it was his eyes or his lenses that were blurry. "Thank you," he said again, and saw himself out.

* * *

On the matter of love: it was around this time that she began to want it. Not sex—although sure, sex—but someone to pour hot spaghetti into a colander while you stirred the red sauce. She said this to her sister, Elga, who was in town from Ontario. They were having dinner at a place that had billed itself generously as a "wine bar with tapas."

"Love?" Elga repeated.

"Or companionship."

"Well then you should go on more dates. Or any dates. Do you even date?"

"I stopped dating," she admitted.

"God, I knew it! How long has it been?"

"Nine, ten years." And to forestall Elga's howl of despair—"It just got too depressing! And I was busy, anyway. And it just sort of—it's not like I *decided* to stop, I just . . . stopped."

"I loved dating," Elga said. "And I loved marrying, I just don't love *being* married."

"Are you and Henry still talking about a divorce?"

Elga shrugged. "Oh, we're always talking about divorce. It's one of the few methods of foreplay that we both still enjoy." Elga drained her vinegary glass of house white and gestured for another. "Anyway, dating is a must. You don't find people unless you go looking for them, or unless you're very, *very* rich and they go looking for you. Do you know Dakin? Dakin Moss? Have we talked about Dakin?" They had not talked about Dakin. "He's newly single, you should meet him."

"I don't know . . . Where does he live?"

"Around here. Somewhere. Maybe Philadelphia. On the East Coast, definitely."

She briefly had a vision of the East Coast rolling from Maine to Florida, and at each end of that long snaking coast, the only single man and the only single woman still left in the world. In her vision, the situation had been deemed so dire that an introduction between these two endangered creatures was of vital importance, no matter the distance. She did not like this vision.

"Maybe," she said noncommittally. Her sister was a great forgetter, and so she assumed that this was something about which Elga would soon forget. "We'll see."

But Elga did not forget.

* * *

Dakin lived in Paris, which is not proximal to Philadelphia or the East Coast of America. He came through New York once a year to see his mother who was elderly, though in savagely good health. After his wife had asked for a divorce, Dakin had considered leaving France—she was French, he had moved there for her—but he still had a weakness for French women, and it became impossible to imagine romantic satisfaction with any woman who was not also French.

He explained all of this briefly and succinctly, over appetizers, before their entrees arrived.

"Sometimes I ask myself what I like so much about French women," he said. "Other than, you know, everything. And I think what it really comes down to is that they know what they want and then they take it. Whereas American women—no offense but—there's just this constant dance, this game, like, *so* many apologies but under every apology is this little rock-like core of hatred and resentment."

She considered this. "You mean sexually?"

"I mean everything," Dakin said. "Like: *Oh no, I shouldn't, I won't have dessert*—but then there's this absolute rage because they never order dessert. And the rage builds. If they just had dessert, they wouldn't need to own guns, you know?"

"What about the men?"

Dakin shrugged. "I don't have a lot of interest in men," he said. "Socially, emotionally. Culturally. They're undercooked. Why have raw hamburger meat when you can have a steak?"

"Women are the steak?"

"In this analogy," Dakin said, "women are the steak." And then he smiled—"But *French* women," he said, "are steak and *frites*. Just that extra bit of *bon appetit* tucked on the side."

By the end of their date, it had become clear to her that Dakin did not have much to give her, other than the feeling that she needed to find a French woman.

* * *

It was not easy to find a French woman in upstate New York. Either they lived in the city, or they lived in France. She went on several dates with women whose names sounded French—Celeste, followed by Sandrine—only to find that they were American after all. Celeste's real name was Chelsea, and Sandrine had received the name of her French grandmother. A third woman said in her bio that she was from Paris, but it turned out to be Paris, Texas.

Slowly, little by little, defeat crept in.

She thought to herself: *maybe I ask for too much.*

She created a new profile. She named herself *Johanne*. She said she was from Lyons.

* * *

She met Claire by accident. She was in the parking lot of the Shop-Rite; she was backing out of her space; she was not looking; the back of her car crashed into the front of Claire's slowly but undeniably. They stood in the parking lot and examined their cars. Hers was dented, but Claire's was fine, and for this reason Claire was friendlier than she might have been. Claire was not French, but she was French-Canadian, and this became evident as soon as the topic of exchanging insurance information was raised.

"The car's a rental," Claire said. "And also, it looks okay. I don't care if the front drops off after I've handed it back in—I'll be back in Montreal."

"Montreal?"

"Yeah, I live there."

Did a French-Canadian woman have the same virtues of a French woman? She wasn't sure. It seemed possible, but then at the same time it also seemed like the sort of mistake an American would make, conferring the virtues and vices of one group of people on another.

"Do you want to get a drink?" she asked.

Claire glanced at their two cars—the one dented, the other unblemished. Claire glanced at the Margarita Monday in the strip mall behind them. Claire shrugged. "Yeah, a drink, why not."

In the Margarita Monday, she introduced herself as Johanne from Lyons, but she got a little shy and pronounced it *Lions*, and she didn't do an accent of any kind. Claire seemed to take all of this in stride.

"I'm Claire from Montreal," she said. "Well, actually Claire from Québec, but now I live in Montreal."

"I've heard it's a good city."

"It *is* a good city! Wait, which one?"

"Both," she said lamely, "I hear they're both good cities."

"Now you're lying," Claire said. "Nobody talks about Canadian cities that much, let alone both of them." Claire gave a wink, flagging the joke.

It became quickly evident that Claire was a practiced drinking companion. She was as adept a drinker as she was a conversationalist, and over bottomless margaritas, Claire provided the names of her present and former cats, the name of her neighbor who sometimes fed the cats, and a funny story about the first time Claire's boss ever visited America and found it to be as awful as he had expected. And then Claire mentioned her near-death experience a few years before.

"That was the last car accident I was in," Claire said. "That one was my fault—this one was totally you, no offense. I was thirty-three, so it was my Jesus Year and I was driving to my best friend's place, I was already late so I was really flooring it, and this *deer* runs out in the road. Full antlers, so cool, but: in the road! Also, I'm a little bit high at the time—you know, just a little weed, not *so* bad—but my reflexes are not great, and I slam on the brakes, which you're not supposed to do, and I sort of panic so I'm screaming and I think whipping the steering wheel back and forth, I don't know—but I end up flipped over on the embankment. Car upside down. They had to cut the door off the car to pull me out; I was in a coma for a couple days. I don't remember a lot of it."

Claire took a sip of her third margarita, the salt chunky around the rim. She licked a large salt crystal off the back of her hand with a delicate tongue. "I have this memory—but I don't know if it's real or something I saw it on TV? But I'm walking down this long hallway and there's light at the end. I'm walking and walking toward the light at the end. And the next thing I remember is waking up in the hospital. With this feeling, like . . . I almost got somewhere. I almost found something. Like something had been lost, that I hadn't even known was lost, and I *almost* . . . but it was gone.

"After I got out of the hospital, I had this year of being a complete ho. Like not in a bad way. I was just . . . DTF as the kids say. I tried all kinds of things, even stuff I never thought I'd be into, and I met some awesome people. It was a great year." Claire finished her margarita and set it down on the table. "It was actually just a really great year."

Joanne from Lions considered the story. She considered having presented herself as Joanne from Lions, which had given her a patina of unknowability to hide behind. Presented with Claire's unselfconscious honesty, she felt guilty and anxious. And so, before she could think it through, she said: "I was in a room with someone recently, who was going through a . . . a big change. The biggest transformation he'd ever had, probably. I didn't understand until it was too late. And ever since then. I can feel in me—this hunger for . . . I don't know. Something."

Claire studied her with interest. "Something like what?"

She shook her head.

"If you don't know what you want, how will you know when you find it?"

She shook her head again. "After your year ended—your great year . . ." She hesitated. "Did it end because you found . . . whatever was lost?"

"Oh no," Claire said. "No, I just . . ." She considered and then shrugged. "I guess I just started looking in new places."

"Oh."

Claire smiled. "I don't know much about finding anything, but I'll tell you one thing: I've really enjoyed looking."

* * *

She went home. Home was a quiet place, though she had not noticed for many years just how quiet it was. She watered her plants and cleaned her windows. She called the shop and made an appointment to get the car looked at. She called her insurance company and sat on hold and gave up. Early evening fell. Shadow pooled at the corners of the room. She was not married and she did not have a dog or a fish or a roommate or even a job. It is so easy for things to slip out of your fingers, she thought. You don't even realize they're lost. At what point in the past four decades had her life slipped out of her fingers? At what point in their hour together had the first Mr. Sorrell's life slipped out of his?

* * *

That night, she dreamed about Mr. Sorrell. They were in a canoe on a great body of water. They sat companionably, lulled by the still summer air, the sound of insects far away throwing up a smokescreen vibration of song. Neither of them had oars, and as she sat, it occurred to her that they were getting no closer to the shore. She turned to ask him what he thought they should do about it, but he was gone. She was by herself in the boat. Gentle ripples spread on the placid surface of the water. It was hard to tell if she was moving at all. She thought: *I can panic, or I can enjoy being in this boat.* In the distance, birds.

Cheryl Klein

Woman in Background

The first time I heard the word, it was in reference to the two Shaunas. Shauna M. was known as The Slut, and Shauna K. was known as The Slut With The Last Name. I don't remember what her last name actually was. Maybe something difficult for our waspy sixth-grade mouths to pronounce.

I didn't know Shauna K., who was new to our elementary school that year. Shauna M. had been there since first grade, and I associated her with her talent show numbers. As a six-year-old, she'd belted out "Cabaret" in a black leotard and gold sequined wristbands. Her voice was big but nasal, projecting to the back of the house. The "house" was our school cafeteria. Even with the tables folded up for special occasions, it still smelled vaguely of canned green beans.

That year, the year of "Cabaret," I was reciting a poem about ants competing in "the jungle Olympics," curated by my mom from a collection of poetry for children. The ants did very badly in the Olympics because they were ants. Like Shauna M., I wore a black leotard, but mine was complemented by foam balls attached to a headband with pipe cleaners to represent antennae.

What I'd *really* wanted to do for the talent show was reenact the entire made-for-TV movie *Nadia*, starring myself as gymnast Nadia Comaneci. Directing other second graders to play silver medalist Teodora Ungureanu and stern coach Bela Karolyi proved difficult, and the show had fallen apart.

If I was cute and a little funny as a poetry-reciting ant, Shauna M. represented the world of *real* talent. My parents explained to me that a first grader singing about a roommate who "rented by the hour" was funny because it was a "grownup" song. But I didn't see a small child singing about embracing hedonism in the shadow of impending fascism in Weimar Berlin. I saw a star.

Shauna M. had an agent. One day she missed school to do a voiceover for a Polly Pockets commercial; that was how I learned what a voiceover was. There was, in our beachside LA suburb, at least one kid in most grades who skirted the edges of Hollywood, going on auditions and occasionally appearing on screen—playing with Workout Barbie or chomping a Kentucky Fried Chicken drumstick. Shauna M.'s older sister, Misty, appeared on a sitcom. Her line was, "Hi, I'm Candice." They were better than the rest of us, who did not have careers yet, who played with toys in the dull privacy of our own bedrooms.

* * *

The year I was in sixth grade, Shauna M. was in fifth. We weren't friends, and not just because we were in different grades. In fact, the sixth and fifth grades were close that year. A group of sixth-grade girls had grown tired of the boys in our own class and turned to younger men. My best friend Bonnie was going out with a fifth grader. What "going out" involved wasn't clear to me, and probably wasn't clear to them. Maybe some phone calls. Definitely a lot of playground drama.

I wasn't going out with anyone. Sixth grade was the year that Bonnie semi-ditched me to become besties with Hillary, who was in Advanced Gymnastics and wore a lot of Guess clothes. Once, Bonnie mused, "You know how everyone has something they don't like about themselves? Like how you don't like your nose and you're too tall? And I don't know what my thing is, but I'm sure I have something. Hillary doesn't have anything wrong with her! She's perfect!"

I wanted to remind Bonnie that she—Bonnie—had those little white bumps on her upper arms. But instead I just acknowledged Hillary's perfection.

I seemed to be sinking into a different social stratum. I'd never been popular, but back in fourth grade, I'd been confident, which was almost as good. Suddenly I was too tall, my nose was too big, my hair was frizzy, and I wasn't into the right things, despite my best efforts. I bought Debbie Gibson's *Electric Youth* album and played the cassette on the stereo in my dad's study over and over as I sat in his brown velour armchair, puzzling out how to *be*.

"Electrocute?" my dad said. "That sounds violent."

I explained that it was *electric youth*. In the dull privacy of my own home, I could be the voice of Cool Young People.

But at school, Hillary and the girls in her radius had gone in for Debbie back when *Out of the Blue* came out. I couldn't quite keep up.

I think Hillary went out with a fifth grader that year too. All the popular girls did. And so the popular fifth-grade girls became threats.

For the talent show, Shauna M. and Shauna K. did a duet of Tiffany's "Could've Been." Shauna M., with her half-grown-out blonde perm and dusting of freckles, passed the hand mic to Shauna K., who had brown hair and a round moon face. They wore blazers, jean skirts, and tights, and did choreography in unison. Step-touch, step-touch.

I wore a train engineer's hat with my leotard and tights and did what I billed as "gymnastics dance" to Kylie Minogue's cover of *Locomotion*. I wanted to do The Snake, a move that required isolating one's ribcage and curving to one side, then the other, with a little snap in between. But my body just didn't move like that. So instead I step-touched while making a roller coaster motion with my hands, a sort of *allusion* to The Snake.

I thought popularity was a recipe I could perhaps reverse engineer, one dance move at a time.

I don't know who started referring to the Shaunas as The Slut and The Slut With the Last Name. I didn't know what the word meant, though I wasn't about to admit that. It was clearly an insult, and yet it was equally clear to me that the Shaunas were popular, and that popularity was in fact a prerequisite for being a slut.

Popularity didn't mean a person was especially well liked, although some popular girls were. In movies, popular girls were pretty and rich, but everyone in my town was middle- to upper-middle class. Our dads were engineers for the local defense contractors. Our moms were teachers and librarians and homemakers.

Maybe popularity was elusive because it couldn't be lab-generated. It was a diamond to my cubic zirconia.

* * *

One day in the cafeteria line, Craig L. shoved in front of me. His body was doughy and heavy and pale, and I recoiled. No one liked Craig L. As recently as fourth grade, he'd cried in class almost every day. He still cried too much.

This was 1989. There was no Brené Brown telling anyone that vulnerability was brave. There were no anti-bullying campaigns. Once at a school dance in the cafeteria, I'd seen Hillary nudge a popular boy and tell him to dance with Tiffany, a bulky girl with big lips and greasy blonde hair, who was even more adrift than I was. I marveled at Hillary's brilliance. Imagine your title being so secure you could dabble in the lives of peasants. It was like she'd invented niceness. Mostly, it was every kid for themselves; if people shat on you, it was probably your fault.

Craig L. was an easy target, not like Craig F., who was tall and knowledgeable about heavy metal. No one would come to Craig L.'s defense if I was mean to him.

"You're such a slut," I growled at him.

Immediately, someone behind me piped up, "A guy can't be a slut."

I had vaguely thought it meant something along the lines of "slob." Certainly the Shaunas were not slobs (and they probably weren't sluts either). The point was the insult, not its definition. Except I'd gotten it wrong. Again.

* * *

In high school, I was an extra in our school production of *The Outsiders*. I attended rehearsals religiously, even though there wasn't much to do other than root around in the green room for possible 1960s costumes. The stuffy upstairs rooms hadn't been properly cleaned out in twenty five years, and the cupboards were full of unintentionally vintage costumes. I found a long dress made of brittle cotton and sewn with little blue flowers. It would be perfect for my role as Woman In Background.

I studied everything from the wings. Not just when Kym, a redheaded senior with big, dimpled thighs and a loud drama-girl voice, performed her monologue as Cherry Valance, but when she spoke to me and the other underclassmen, gathered cross-legged in a semicircle on the dusty wooden floor backstage.

Time stretched out between scenes. Especially if you had no lines. Someone found a boom box and played the Beatles. I crushed on Denito, the dark-haired sophomore playing Sodapop Curtis, but I told no one.

These shadowed evenings had a truth-or-dare quality to them, though it was more truth than dare. Kym asked, "Okay, when did all of you lose your virginity? And if you haven't lost it, that's totally cool. I wish I'd waited."

I didn't buy that she wished she'd waited. It felt like a humblebrag, although that word didn't exist yet. But I believed she didn't think we were inherently losers for being virgins. I didn't mind being a virgin. I was only 14. But I wished I was a little farther along down the path. I wished I'd kissed someone, at least.

Two sophomores named Michelle said they'd lost their virginity last year. Neither was very popular, not even drama-popular. Michelle J. was skinny and hyperactive, a cross country star, but cross country wasn't anyone's favorite sport. Michelle N. had big ears and a foghorn voice. But they spoke coolly, and I saw them as a pack, pulling away from me.

I had better hair now than I had in sixth grade, and I'd grown into my nose. I had tits; I didn't really like them, but I knew guys liked such things. I laughed easily. Why had no boy, ever, not even one, asked me out?

Kym had another question. "What's your favorite body part on a person of the opposite sex?"

It was presumed we were all heterosexual. I worried that I wasn't. But the heat that consumed my whole torso that time I saw Denito playing basketball on the elementary school playground one weekend, his arms pale and muscular—that had been real. So what was my deal?

I looked at Billy, a tall, slender senior who was such a drama kid that he had starred in *another* high school's production of *A Chorus Line*. He seemed undeniably gay. Would he deny it? No one at our school was out.

"I love that area just below someone's belly button, on a girl, on a guy, it's just so sexy," Billy announced.

I held my breath. He had gold-blonde hair combed in a wave, as if to support a tiny surfer. Girl or guy. No one recoiled in disgust or shock. They just nodded in agreement: That part of a person was sexy.

* * *

I had wondered if I was bisexual, of course. That would explain my love for Denito as well as my . . . what? I wasn't *hot* for any girl I could think of. I cared about my female friendships a little too much, but so did my friends. I thought about girls' bodies too much, but I thought about my own body too much, and the two seemed intertwined: aspiration and passion. I channeled any passion I might have had into aspiration.

Bisexuals were sluts of a sort, right? I was too sheltered to have encountered any myths about bisexuals being incapable of monogamy. It was more like they'd checked "all of the above," and I could only imagine queerness through the lens of lack. Not having a boyfriend. Not being normal. Not being able to relate to my straight friends. Not being able to have a life at all, really. If I landed on any definitive evidence that I was gay, I would probably need to kill myself, I supposed. I didn't have a plan or anything like that. It was just an option. The opposite of "all of the above." A big black patch of none of the above.

And so I resisted finding definitive evidence. I didn't date boys because what if I didn't like it? I didn't date girls because what if I did? My chastity was a layer of bubble wrap between me and the world, but maybe it also saved my life.

I did not come from a family of experimenters, although my dad was a scientist by training. When it came time to choose a color for the wooden beam in the dining room, my parents held paint samples in varying shades of brown to the ceiling for months.

We believed in sticking with things. When we signed up for Parks & Rec classes, we stuck it out for all six weeks, even if the swim teacher was mean. My mom had grown up with an alcoholic dad who moved her family from house to house in search of a fresh start. He was a slut for houses, or at least a serial monogamist, and so my parents gave us the gift of one house for our whole childhoods.

I heard about girls kissing girls at the high school parties I wasn't invited to. Drunk girls who "wanted attention." I knew if I kissed a girl, there would be no turning back. Turning back was exactly what these girls did. On Friday nights sweet with wine coolers, they got sloppy with girls, and on Monday they were honors students and soccer stars with boyfriends.

I had the usual fears about coming out, but I also believed I needed to be very, very certain. Dating was not a buffet. I could not pile my plate with possibilities and take a little bite of everything until I was full, or until I decided what warranted a return for seconds. Easier to sit the whole thing out and wonder what I was missing.

* * *

During college, I fell for gay man after gay man. I would have devoured a buffet of gay men if I could have, even though the whole point was that I couldn't. I fell hardest for Juan, a fellow English major who belted showtunes while swinging his shower caddy, walking the hallway to the bathrooms. I transferred into classes he took. I helped him run a successful campaign for Sexiest Man Alive in our school newspaper, a title usually reserved for celebrities.

I was a slut for gay guys. Juan was my true love, but I was also very interested in my roommate Tommy, whose boyfriend slept over every night; my graphic designer coworker at the dot-com that hired me to rewrite *Variety* articles and post them as news; and actor Wilson Cruz, who was playing Angel in the touring production of *Rent*.

In them, I watched my own desire ignite and build. For the first time, I admitted my crushes to people. Not to my crushes themselves, but it was a start. *But he's gayyyy*, I would always lament. Straight girls getting "safe" crushes on gay guys was a thing—I knew that even then—but I didn't quite fit the mold. First, the guys I was into weren't exactly straight-acting. They were feminine or androgynous or *flaming*. It wasn't what made them safe that I liked; it was what made them dangerous, a part of a world that had always been off limits to me for multiple reasons. They took up space. They were unapologetic. They knew the words to "Cabaret."

When I finally started dating girls after college, I still wasn't a very good slut. If I couldn't imagine myself being with someone long-term, what was the point? (There was a point. There were many points. If I'd followed the mantra of *Rent*—"No day but today"—I would have fucked more people.)

After my first long-term relationship ended, I tried to date a few people at once, mostly because I'd signed up for Match.com and it seemed rude not to reply to anyone who responded to my profile, assuming they weren't assholes.

I met C.C. while I was also seeing Demi, a sweet, quiet girl who wore black hoodies and lived with her grandma in East LA. I was also exchanging messages with Jen, who was witty and bold and always jetting off to somewhere like China with her business school classmates.

I liked all of them, but the minute I met C.C. in person, the rankings became clear. C.C. was my people. She'd grown up in Southern California, and a few minutes into our first date, over vodka cranberries and the din of a Northeast LA gay bar, we learned that we had relatives buried in the same Orange County cemetery.

We weren't sure our first date was a date. On our second, I almost choked on the cruda topping my pupusa at Grand Central Market, and she kissed me in my car anyway parked at a steep tilt on a Downtown hill. ("You kissed *me*," she said later.) We fucked on the third date. I'd only had one martini, but it was big, and I was lightheaded, floating happily above myself.

On the fourth, she seemed antsy, and confessed her preoccupation with a woman she'd met on Nerve.com. The woman was her type: dark haired, light skinned, androgynous, South American. She even spoke Spanish. I was a blue-eyed part-Jewish femme who couldn't say much beyond "Donde está el baño?"

I braced myself for the "let's be friends" speech. I'd heard it before.

"I hope we can stay friends," I said preemptively.

"No, that's not what I'm saying," she said. "I want to keep seeing you, I just want to . . . keep it casual."

"Oh, okay. Yeah. Obviously, I'm pretty into you."

We fucked again. I promised myself I'd keep dating the other people I was sort of dating.

C.C. mentioned her ex, Jen, who was now in business school.

I messaged Jen to ask if she'd perchance dated a woman named C.C. for a couple of years?

"Ah," Jen replied. "I respectfully bow out."

So that just left Demi. We went to see an Amy Sedaris play in Long Beach, and the whole time I squirmed, perplexed by how genuinely cute and cool I found Demi, and how much I wanted to be with C.C. instead. So I gave Demi the friend speech, and she took it quick and well, and said she kind of just wanted to do this whole Match.com thing to meet new people. "Totally," I said.

That weekend, C.C. said, "Hey . . . stop seeing whoever else you're seeing."

Her tone was playfully bossy. She knew how much I liked her. She was telling me now that it was mutual. I glowed. Why sample the buffet if you knew what your favorite dish was?

Later she joked about how she'd initiated the "keep it casual" policy, while dating only me, and I—good girl that I was—had tried in my tiny way to slut around.

We've been together for seventeen years now, married for thirteen. Sometimes I have dreams that I'm with my ex—still dating her or fucking her, or getting back together with her, or trying to break up with her. But in all of them, I'm trying to find my way to C.C. Even my subconscious is no good at being a slut.

Carley Moore

My Big Slutty Essay

Prelude

How big is it? How does it taste? How does it fold in on itself and open up? How wet? How dry? What does their skin feel like? Hair? Where is their hair and how do they cut it, shape it, shave it? How is it wild? Where does it grow? Not grow? How do their lips feel? How do they taste? How do your faces fit together? Your bodies? How do they look at you? How do they look away? Big spoon, little spoon, both spoons? How do they smell? What happens when you touch them there, there, and there? What sounds do they make? How do they touch you? Move you around? Make space for you? What do they say? How do they say no? How do they say yes? What do they like? What excites them? When do they cry? How do they listen? What sets them free?

1

What if we're all sluts? Can we really say we're not given the ways in which sexuality has been repressed, punished, and controlled? Yes, some of us are asexual and/or less sexually focused than others. Libidos vary. But what if we were all allowed to be our fully sexual selves without shame, punishment, fear of pregnancy and disease, and/or surveillance?

Shut up, you little slut, is a sentence I sometimes like partners to say to me.

There is something infinitely paradoxical about taking on, wearing, writing about, embodying the word *Slut*. The fullest ownership of it, requires an acceptance of an always just out of reach vanishing point on the cultural horizon. You can love fucking, pleasure, love, sex, bodies, orgasms, desire, flirting, make-outs, kink, BDSM, romance, masturbation, sex toys, monogamy, polyamory, fantasy, porn, sex work as work—I really don't know where to stop here—you can love it for yourself and anyone who wants those things. You can write about it and make it the center of your work and life. You can be your most sex positive, slutty self, and yet—and I see this for both my daughter and myself, Fifteen and fifty-one respectively—there is always going to be some slut shamer throwing the proverbial Slurpee at you from the car window of the shame mobile. A well-meaning friend who calls you an exhibitionist, a post on Instagram about how Janelle Monae is trying too hard to be sexy, or having to explain your bisexuality to a date for the thousandth time.

You can give no fucks whatsoever about what anyone thinks of you and your slutty self, but there is always someone out there who's got a not-hot take on it, some variation on the same theme: *You're a whore. You like it too much.*

So while I mostly aim to write this essay as a celebration of my sluttitude, I can't deny that there is always the lurking voice, a deep ideology around bodies and sexuality, which is that they need to be controlled.

2

It started early for me.

I don't know why I found cartoons so sexy. It wasn't all cartoons, but by the age of four or five, I had the hots for Mighty Mouse and Underdog. Their heroines—Pearl Pureheart and Sweet Polly Purebread—were equally alluring, but what really got me was when the villains. Oil Can Harry and Riff-Raff tied their sexy (but pure!) mouse and dog lady captives to the railroad tracks or in the back of a car. The ties were intricate and pretty, not unlike Shibari.

I was hot for a few rare episodes when Woody Woodpecker cross-dressed, for Pop-Eye flinging Olive Oil over his shoulder in almost every episode. Later, I had crushes on Herbie the Love Bug and Optimus Prime. Maybe this explains my love of sex toys, which I think of as cute little robot helpers, not unlike my animated crushes in color and scale.

One morning my mom found me touching myself while watching Mighty Mouse. As I remember it, she said, "I know what you're doing," and left the room. I stopped or maybe I didn't. I can't remember. It was an early shaming, and I think after that, I buried and hid many of my sexual desires. They went underground or I understood that they were supposed to be private, which is perhaps what my mother meant to impart all along.

When I started therapy as an adult and began to work through much of my childhood trauma, this moment really pissed me off. Like, for twenty years. I was just being my little unconsciously sexual self. Now I see my parents for the flawed people we all are. I've done a lot of work in therapy, and I'm too tired to carry around these hurts.

I can recognize my mother reacting out of her own sexual struggles, narratives, and trauma, and I get it. We are all also products of our time. She was unconscious when I was born—drugged for two days in a naval hospital and so confused when she came to that she didn't believe I was her baby. When I gave birth, I was hyper-conscious. Pain blocked from the epidural, but terrifyingly, joyously awake!

It's possible, too, that I misremember this sexy moment with Mighty Mouse. My mom and I have recently decided to stop rehashing the past, so I won't ask her about it. My memory of it matters to my sexual formation, I know that much, but I'd rather have calm with my mother now, more than the absolute truth of a morning when she was likely so tired and overwhelmed as a mom, she didn't know what to say. I do know that I was determined to never shame my daughter about masturbation, and I made good on that promise. Culture got in there anyway, but I kept the Slurpee from hitting her for a good long while.

Our parents' sexualities imprint on us. My mother, a curious mixture of funny scold and feminist freedom. My father, horny and not quiet about it. As I shoved my own childhood sexuality underground, I made it stronger, and I became sneakier in hiding it.

I'd like to take mothers out of this altogether, but I have a mother, I am a mother, and now there are MILFS. Thank goddess for this porn trope, as I have benefitted from its placement in sexual fantasyland for quite a few years now.

3

Sluttiness is also a chemical situation. As I worked on this essay, I asked my neuroscientist lover if orgasms actually create dopamine. As is the case with many of my "brain" questions, the answer is far more complicated than I could explain here, even if I had neuroscientist language at my command. But basically, sex *does* create more dopamine, or rather it allows for the release of dopamine into the synapsis, which feels good. Really, really good.

My neurological disorder, Dopa Responsive Dopamine, is named this because I don't make enough dopamine, and my treatment is to take synthetic dopamine.

If orgasms make dopamine and I don't have enough dopamine, my slutitude might be explained by this lack. For much of my life, even when medicated, perhaps I was on a chemical hunt for dopamine. One easy way to get it was through sex, preferably sex with orgasms.

Many of us disabled people, especially with neuro and/or mental illness stuff have complicated chemical lacks and excesses in our brains. Serotonin. Dopamine. So many more chemicals I can't name. Many "manic" people are described as hypersexualized. I have had manic episodes, and they were also some of my sluttiest times. Now that I am on a more stable mix of Sinemet (synthetic dopamine), Lexapro, and Wellbutrin, my urges to fuck are more controllable. I'm not entirely driven by sex, as I sometimes used to be.

I used to experience falling in love as an utterly manic experience. This could be really fun and exciting, and also very scary and overwhelming. Some lovers have said being with me is like being in a movie. Hyperreal, fast moving, dramatic, and cinematic. I used to think this was a compliment, but now, if someone says that to me, it feels more like a warning. I am not being read as real, but as character, object, fantasy, slut. MILF in the porn, but not in life.

I am real.

The MILF in the porn is older, experienced, knows what she wants and how to get it, and will take care of you. She also has a porn-friendly body.

The real-life MILF has a body that held babies inside of it, is older, experienced, knows what she wants and how to get it, and will sometimes talk about her teen's friend dramas, and that she has to leave so that she can pick up her kid or cook a dinner or be home to do mom things.

I am a MILF, but more accurately I am a MWLTF, a mom who likes to fuck. Doesn't roll off the tongue, does it?

But once I was a little girl, who found her clitoris while watching an animated muscled mouse speed down through the pale blue sky with fists ready to punch. She moved her clitoris back and forth, and she smelled her fingers. She liked the smell. Salty, and a little like pee, but completely unique. Her. Self.

Here I come to save the day! Mighty Mouse is on the way!

He punched Oil Can Harry and he untied the screaming Pearl Pureheart from the railroad tracks. He flew her in his arms back up into the sky. She stopped screaming and clung to his muscled neck. His cape flew out behind him, and her hair curled perfectly around her mouse ears. She was beautiful and rescued.

I moved my clitoris back and forth. All was well in mouse world. Had Pearl had an orgasm? She did finally stop screaming. Had I had an orgasm? I don't know. But I was content, self-soothed, and completely absorbed in story and body.

To this day, two of my favorite things.

4

I played doctor with several neighborhood boys. Mostly it was of the variety "I'll show you mine, if you show my yours." Usually I asked them to go first, and then ran away laughing when it was my turn. I was a brat or tease. In sexual scenes, I love being chased and punished to this day. There was one boy I brought to my bedroom closet. Once there, I asked him to slide his pants down, and I brushed his penis very gently with a hair brush. He seemed to like that. There was another boy who I met behind a garage in my neighborhood. We liked to take off our clothes and touch our butts together. In retrospect, he was probably too old to be doing this with me. In most of these situations I was the initiator. Or at least that's how I remember it.

My father kept his issues of *Playboy*, *Penthouse*, and sometimes *Hustler* on the coffee table in the living room. Sometimes my mom would yell about this, and he'd put them in his den, still splayed open, but just on a different table. They were always readily accessible, there for anyone who wanted to look. I did, though too much looking gave me a queasy, shameful (Slurpee?) feeling inside my stomach. It was the '80s, and *Playboy* had these soft-core couple spreads. The man's penis was always flaccid, but still, there he was lying next to a naked woman on a beach with her legs spread open. Sometimes his face was posed above her pussy. I could not imagine what he was about to do. I don't remember any men in *Penthouse*, just a lot of labia and clitoris. The cartoons in all the magazines confused and titillated me. *Hustler* scared me and made me worry about the women.

After the morning cartoon incident, I stopped masturbating. Or maybe I was too sick to masturbate. Ages six to eleven, before I had a diagnosis and medication, were very painful and sad years. Maybe my sexuality went underground because of that. I didn't start masturbating again until I was twenty, in my best gay friend's bedroom, where I found my clitoris again. It was a marvel. Until then, I'd felt utterly dependent on lovers to make me come. At that time, they were all young men, with varying degrees of skill. How had I lost myself for so long?

Learning how to make myself come did not slow me down. It made me want more sex, more orgasms, and more adventures. I was on my way to Madrid to study abroad for a semester. I wanted to become fluent and have adventures. I had an older boyfriend back in the states, but once I arrived, I decided that I wanted a Spanish boyfriend. It would help my Spanish and it was kind of a badge of honor—to snag a Spaniard. One drunken night I let two Spanish men flip a coin for me. We'd met at a club drinking whiskeys and Cokes, which was the Spanish drink of choice in 1993. The whiskey came almost to the top of a tall glass with a small bottle of Coke on the side. You drank the whiskey and added the Coke as the whiskey went down. It made everyone very drunk. Angel and Adolfo. They told me they were best friends, and we talked and danced well into the night. Eventually, I got in one of their cars with both of them. They said, *You have to choose.* I said I couldn't. I probably wanted a threesome, but did not have the language for such things, and perhaps rightly sensed this wouldn't go over. Angel won the coin toss, though when we dropped Adolfo off at his building, I made out with him in the lobby while the doorman looked on or looked away. I sensed then the coin hadn't been the best decision maker.

Angel was erratic, doing his military service, extremely hot, and not very good at sex. Once he tried to use a bar of soap as lube. Still, my Spanish improved with him, if only because I had to explain so much to him about sex and my body. He complained sometimes that I didn't act enough like a girl, that my shoes were too mannish, my hair too short, and I didn't wear sexy lingerie. I felt bad about this, but I refused to change. I didn't have the money for those things anyway.

I sensed there were vague rumors among the other American students that I was a slut or would make out with anyone. My coin toss story, which I'd thought would impress my best gay friend, had the opposite effect. He was worried about me and a little jealous. I did get drunk often and make myself available to most anyone who seemed interested. Often my friends dragged me home. My true love that semester was a blonde woman from Poland by way of Syracuse. Astrid. We were often very drunk together, and I hoped by proximity we would have sex or at least make out. It never happened, and I sensed, in the way that sluts can, that she also thought I was too loose, too free with my body, an American whore in the land of Spanish virgins.

One night in a very small Spanish town, our professors brought us on a trip. We had many of these trips throughout the semester, and we loved these visits, older customs, and the conversations we could have with non-city dwellers. We had a meal together, drank a lot of wine, and listened to La Tuna, which are all-male university student singing groups throughout Spain. They dress in traditional clothing and serenade. When I Google La Tuna now, I don't even understand how we could be expected to not want to fuck these dudes. They are so hot. Still. They serenade!

I remember a series of brick streets and passageways. I was following Astrid. I was following a Tuno. Either one would do. The musician caught me first, pressed me up against a brick wall, kissed me hard and well, and left me there. I wanted more, but in Spain most young people lived with their parents until they married, such was the economy. There was often nowhere to go. Sometimes too, there was an unspoken code in Spain I couldn't figure out. My eagerness, my straightforward desire to make out or fuck sometimes backfired on me. Or perhaps this young man wasn't ready or wanting to have sex with a wild drunk American woman. Sometimes I took it personally, sometimes I didn't care, but how smart was that dude—giving me a fantasy to write about almost thirty years later.

Astrid had been watching maybe, or watching out for me. Was she angry? Was she ready finally to kiss me? She said something to me. It's very blurry, but it was something about me being too easy, a slut, not discriminating enough, and that meant she would never be with me.

On another trip, this time to Valencia, I gave an Irish man a hand job in the back of our travel bus. We were there for Las Fallas, when the city burns satirical wooden sculptures, sometimes five or six stories high, to celebrate the arrival of spring. We spent the day wandering the alleyways of Valencia, looking at the sculptures, and drinking wine. Eventually, late at night we converged in the town's biggest plaza to watch the tallest of the sculptures burn. The drunken crowd surged and for one terrible moment, my feet lifted off the ground and I thought I'd be crushed. A friend pulled me to safety. Later, when I saw the Irishman, he wouldn't look at me. I was hurt, but I shrugged it off. Now I see that I might have scared people with my forwardness, my sexual abandon, my sluttiness. Or perhaps he was a guilty Catholic. Who knows? It's not like I had the language to communicate much of what I was doing. It was 1993. Communication about sex and desire was non-existent. Our sex ed classes consisted of two messages: if you have sex you will get HIV and die, or if you have sex you will get pregnant and ruin your life.

I have never put all these stories together in one essay, and if this were online, I likely wouldn't do it. Print allows me to hide a bit, and sluts still need cover. The world still hates sluts, and a free woman is the most dangerous woman of all. I have Googled and researched this famous sentence which I thought belonged to Audre Lorde or Emma Goldman. I am dismayed to find out it may just be Instagram and/or meme content.

I am Don Quixote but in girl form, wandering the Spanish countryside, fighting my windmills, I mean, lovers. I wanted to live in Spain, to stay forever and become fluent, but I knew somehow that my sexuality would not work there. I felt the patriarchy shoving me into my place in a more oppressive way than I'd experienced in America. As my best gay friend and I searched for gay bars that required secret passwords and knowledge we couldn't access, I gave up on that country. It may be that in Spain, my queerness was more visible to the people I slept with and tried to sleep with than it was to me. It may be that these are the normal behaviors of a young woman studying abroad.

It might be easy to leave this section feeling like I was a sad, misunderstood slut in Spain. Occasionally, yes. But I was also wildly free in a way I had never allowed myself to be, and I loved it. It didn't always work out in my favor, and the shame mobile and the wet Slurpee were hyper vigilant, but for the first time in my life I wasn't trying to be monogamous. I chased who I wanted to chase. I did the wild things that came into my head. When I let Angel and Adofo flip a coin for me, I was asserting something I never had before. Power. I was the protagonist of my own life. *I* came up with the coin idea. It was hot *to me*. It was my fantasy, and I made it come true. I was writing my own story for the first time in my life. It may have been a messy, precarious one, but it was mine.

I'd found my clitoris. If someone didn't make me come, I could do it myself. Mostly, I wasn't trying to make anyone else happy. I was on an adventure in another country. I could walk anywhere I wanted, because I had medication. I felt sexy in Spain. I was becoming fluent and living in a city! I'd always wanted to live in a city. Men chased me, but more importantly I chased them, and as a disabled person that was a big fucking deal. For years, disability had rendered me undesirable. I was inhabiting my slut self for the first time, and sex was a way to claim my body fully and use it for my own ends. My body felt powerful instead of broken.

I didn't seduce Astrid, but it was the first time in my life where I let myself desire a woman. I didn't write it off as a silly friendship thing or a phase. I let myself love and want her, without reservation.

In another country, at twenty, I was my true bisexual slut self.

It was also in Spain, having a conversation with my "Spanish mom" —a feminist psychoanalyst, Gemma—that I first explained what I wanted in a partner. She didn't approve of my older boyfriend and had noticed me lingering by the answering machine.

I thought and thought, looking for the right Spanish words and gender agreement for the noun and adjective, which didn't exist for what I wanted to express.

"Cabellero feminista!" I'd finally found the words.

Gemma laughed until she cried, saying the phrase over and over again.

I was delighted to have made her laugh in Spanish. The literal translation is *feminist gentlemen*, but what I was trying to say was that I wanted a not specifically gendered feminist cowboy. I still want that. Gender doesn't matter to me, but the cowboy part does.

How privileged I was to be able to have that semester in Madrid. It was my greatest escape from my straight, monogamous, good-girl self.

5

I buried my true bisexual slut self again when I came back to the US. I tried nonmonogamy under duress and hated it, a five-year-long relationship with a bisexual man. Did basic New Yorker things like getting mugged and robbed. Spent a couple more weird years dating before there was internet dating, which meant I mostly had crushes on random people in my neighborhood that I never spoke to, but lightly stalked. I fell in love with a woman who had a partner and was monogamous. Our flirtation consisted of lesson planning together, driving in her pick-up truck around the upstate college town where we taught in the summers, and laying on her dorm room bed stoned for hours, hoping she would ravage me. Around that time I met my now ex-husband and fell in love with him as well. When my upstate woman crush asked me if I was sure I was straight, I said I was because I liked "dick too much." I believed this, I really did. What I couldn't understand then was that I liked *penetration* with a dick, fingers, or a toy. The flesh dick was just one of many options.

I was in love with my ex-husband and I wanted to get married and have kids. I was steeped in straight people's ideology, even though for most of my life I'd been in queer spaces and had gay and lesbian best friends. My crushes on women, trans people, nb people confused me. Heteromantic, a more widely used term now, might have helped me understand myself better, but it also doesn't quite fit who I am or account for all the romantic feelings I've had for people who are not cis men. From what I can tell, this kind of confusion, self-hiding, and delusion is common for bi/pan people my age. I had also swallowed a lot of biphobia by that time, and I truly believed that I wasn't officially bisexual until I had eaten pussy. Absurd! But lesbians told me that, and gay men, and straight people too. There was even a *Sex and the City* episode about it. Maybe that's just what we all believed in the way-back times.

Perhaps there is another version of my life where the upstate woman had ravaged me, and then she left her then wife, and I came out, and who knows? But I wouldn't have my kid in that version, or I'd have a different kid, and that idea hurts my heart. I loved her. I loved him. I love a lot of people. It's just who I am, but I didn't know that then. I was convinced that I had to choose one someone, and in choosing that someone I had to lose someone else. Some might say I took the easier, heterosexual route, but burying your identity because your experiences have led you to believe the world doesn't get you isn't easy at all.

For a long time, I loved being married. My ex-husband and I came from difficult families and we needed one another, in all of our codependent glory. We had a lot of fun together—hanging out with our friends in New York, teaching and trying to get books out into the world, being a couple. When we started to try to get pregnant and couldn't, we began to unravel. Infertility treatments can destroy the strongest of marriages. We miscarried once and eventually had our child, but it was grueling and reduced sex to a laboratory of sperm and eggs. The pregnancy was difficult, and I emerged fearful, freaked out, and disconnected from my body. Later, I realized I likely had postpartum depression, but I couldn't see it then. I didn't have the time or money for therapy in that first year of my kid's life. She had trouble latching, she had jaundice, and for that first year I was afraid she would die, like her twin had. Until she was four, we were always broke. We traded off taking care of her, and hardly ever saw each other. We both encouraged the other one to see our friends, but we weren't friends anymore. Our sex life was pretty dead too. Mostly, I felt trapped, by monogamy, straightness, and being a mom.

When my daughter was two, I went back into therapy to figure out why I was walking around Brooklyn crying all of the time. I was supposed to be happy. Why did I always feel so lonely? I'd made my life, hadn't I? Why couldn't I live it?

The therapist I started to see to try to save my marriage told me I could be a slut for just one person, my husband. Given that I had already fallen in love with *him*, and was treating our sessions like hot dates, I was skeptical.

What I wanted was to open up our marriage, but my ex-husband was very monogamous then, and didn't want that. When I asked for an open relationship, it was too late. Our trust in each other had unraveled.

Interlude

Phew. Sometimes in the middle of writing an essay, I need a break. I hadn't meant for my slut essay to turn into my autobiography. When my students try to cram their whole lives into one personal essay, I never let them.

But I'm a cheater.

Or a hypocrite.

Or I want it all the ways.

Or I break my own rules.

Slut stories are complicated and messy. The first entry for slut on Entymology.com is, "c. 1400, *slutte*, "a dirty, slovenly, careless, or untidy woman," first attested in the *Coventry mystery plays*." Don't you want to read those Coventry mystery plays? I do. Perhaps the slut essay as a form is a dirty, careless, untidy thing which wanders the countryside or inns of the page to deliver maximum untidiness and hotness.

6

On pine needles and dirt behind a white clapboard church after a meandering walk. In the grass under a blanket, mosquitos buzzing. I snuck out of the house. In twin beds, dorm room beds, double, queen, and king-size beds. On the floor. In the kitchen. On my beautiful deep blue sectional, often. In that car, in that car, in that car, in that car. In so many cars. In pick-up trucks. On benches in Madrid and New York. In Florence in our yellow apartment on the grounds of villa where we didn't belong. After, we opened the window and I pretended to be Lucy Honeychurch in *A Room with a View*. In hotels by the hour and for a night. In the shower. At dive bars where a shot of whiskey and a can of Pabst cost five bucks. In the bathroom stalls of fancy restaurants. After swimming. Near the ocean while she napped in her Pack 'n Play. By a dumpster. On the stairs outside of a bar. On stoops while smoking a joint. In a cabin. After dancing. In the morning. In the night. In the graffitied room on a bar in the East Village. After long conversations. After short ones.

Touch. Curiosity.

Are these your places or are they mine?

I'm running out of space!

There's too much!

 It's too big!

That's what she said.

I got free. It was painful, awful, and necessary.

For a while I kept banging my head up against monogamy and straightness because, though I can be very smart, at these two concepts I am incredibly slow.

For the DJ who saw me one night as not a mother and not a wife, who didn't care who I was but wanted me with animal abandon. I was stuck. You didn't flinch and you did a job no else would do. You pulled me through the looking glass.

For S, who was there the whole time, guiding me. My bisexual Cancer twin who made a path in the dark woods for me. Or maybe you left me breadcrumbs to follow. You were right next to me with a big gluten-free sandwich and dogs to protect us. You said, *Anything is possible. Don't give up.*

For J, the wolf, who taught me to ask for what I wanted, growled at me when I was bad, spanked me hard, and said let's try to be poly. You were the first person to say that to me, and you let me be jealous and you told me over and over again, *There's no one like you. You're special. I love you.*

To A, the first woman I kissed, and the best dreamer I know. Thank you for letting me have summers with you and for sharing your poly family with me.

To S, the first woman I fell in love with. Let's keep saying, *You are the love of my life.*

To K, the first woman who let me eat her pussy. My first girl-friend. Thank you for all the delicious egg breakfasts and for breaking my heart so spectacularly.

For A, you complete me, Baby Slut. You are a dirty little whore and you know it.

To C, my first truly poly partner who wants to do this with me for a long time and also believes in love. I finally found you! What fun we're having. You're right, I am a slutty little minx.

I'd like to do this last bit in the style of Bridget Everette, queer icon, diva, and hot genius. To everyone I've fucked or loved even if just for a night, thank you for your service. You did a really good job. If you made out with me by a dumpster and then listened to me scream when once again, I inexplicably found myself making out with someone by a dumpster, thank you for not freaking out. If I picked you up at a bar during a snowstorm and a recession, and then ran away from you when you admitted you had no heating, thank you for your service! To everyone who has made out with me in bath-rooms and cars, you are so GGG, and wasn't the tightness part of the excitement? To all the people I've made out with at parties and on a dare I made silently to myself, wasn't that fun? Or at least we have a story that unites us forever! Thank you to the four people who have given me the joys of threesomes. You will never be forgotten, you beautiful dreamers! Lastly, to all of the people I was monogamous with for various lengths of time, I tried to be good, but I'm not.

I'm bad. I'm a sneaky little slut, bitch, whore who loves to get caught. Go ahead, say it. You know you want to.

Zoe Whittall

The Sex Castle Lunch Buffet

Emily sits on a wooden bench outside the Common Cafe, scanning the obituary section. She blows her coffee cool, begins a slow scan of names and dates. Her therapy homework is to read every death notice and then record her anxiety using a numbered scale until her physical symptoms decrease. She's been doing it for six weeks, as a cognitive behavioral exercise intended to help with her panic attacks. She initially thought she was afraid of the grocery store, the subway, crowds of hands and faces, but at the hot heart of it was a fairly mundane fear of death.

"But doesn't our mortality terrify everyone?" she'd asked her therapist.

"Not to the extent that they are no longer functional," the therapist responded.

Emily paused just as long before repeating back, "Not functional?" Emily liked to use active listening techniques on therapists, just to throw them.

She dresses well for therapy, pleated skirts and tall brown boots. She feels ashamed of the not-functioning label. It was true that before this latest exercise, she'd been late filing freelance contracts, she'd started ordering her groceries online, and she'd stopped calling her friends. All signs.

Now Emily's anxiety is in remission. She feels silly recording *zero anxiety* in the appropriate box week after week. Her therapist is pleased. That's real progress! At first, she'd read the obituaries as fast as she could, to get the task over with. Now, the exercise feels like an opportunity to enjoy tiny, concise memoirs. She especially likes the old photographs. She lingers on the sentences. Today she comes across a name she recognizes: *Hiram Johnstone, 1952–2018.*

She sips her coffee, blows a kiss towards a puppy tied to a nearby bike stand, as though she has to fake being casual with herself, before turning back to his photo. Even after death, his photographed smile wanted something from the person who looked at it. The dog shifts his weight, whimpers and sits. He looks like a small bear. Hiram fucking Johnstone. She wonders if she can hug the dog. She doodles a circle in hearts and stars around his obituary, but is reluctant to read it.

Twenty years earlier, when Emily was a dancer at The Sex Castle, she spent many hours astride the pyramidical lap of Hiram Johnstone. If he'd walked by her on the street, probably even back then, he wouldn't have recognized her. To most customers, dancers only existed in three-minute intervals and then disappeared into suspended time until the next visit. Pierre, the *Sex Castle* DJ with the rat face and aggressive neck pimples, would cut every song off at three minutes because he was an impatient kind of guy. It worked for the dancers, economically, at five bucks a song.

Emily hasn't thought about that summer in years. She wishes she were still fit enough to do side splits on a pole, but is very happy to never have to make small talk with men as they thrust palms full of sweaty bills towards her breasts. Even more relieved to never have to watch them gorge on the all-you-can-eat shrimp lunch buffet before curling a finger in her direction for a private dance. Even now she shudders at the memory of their gaping, saucy mouths, their front teeth like high-beams under the black club lights.

She stares at his photo, takes another sip of her coffee, now lukewarm, and places her palm against her chest. She tries to name five things around her that she can see, three that she can feel, two she can smell or taste. A mindfulness exercise that is supposed to prevent a panic attack, one she can feel skirting the periphery of her body like a lion, waiting for her to be limp enough to pounce.

At the start of the summer of 1995, Emily's first serious girlfriend kicked her out of their shared apartment. The girlfriend, whose name

Emily can't even recall in this moment, had broken her heart and insisted on moving the woman she was having an affair with into the living room before Emily had even packed her stuff. "This isn't non-monogamy," Emily had wailed, "this is sadism." She overheard the ex calling her "emotionally unevolved" to the new lover. Before she left the apartment, Emily snipped all the phone wires with her nail clippers, taped a bright red sock to the inside lip of the washing machine, and gave Emily's name and address to the local republican candidate, urging them to always put up election signs on their lawn.

She handed in her final Women's Studies paper, Lesbian Fractures within the Riot Grrrl Movement, which was basically a long diary entry with lyrical annotations, and then moved onto her friend Cori's couch. She skipped her graduation ceremony because she thought it a meaningless custom. (Now she regrets it, wishes she had a photo in cap and gown for her album.)

After that, Emily found it difficult to go to her waitressing job. She called in late, then sick, then forgot to call in. The day she finally went in, she found a new girl wearing her nametag and apron. When Emily resorted to returning bottles from the alleyway for spare change, Cori suggested that Emily join her at the Sex Castle to work a few shifts. "You could make your rent in two, maybe three shifts, tops," she said, taking a bite of an onion like an apple and sipping pickle juice from a jar. Cori sat on her long kitchen counter, wearing the one-piece pleather dress she'd fallen asleep in. Cori had perfect skin, which she swore was a result of drinking pickle juice, and said strippers make a lot of money using a different accent.

"My fake Scottish accent makes me the most bucks for some reason," she said.

Until that first night, Emily had a lot of stripper friends but would laugh if anyone suggested she take a swing on the pole. She was cute but not beautiful, short with small tits. Emily assumed that strippers had a kind of god-gifted femininity that Emily didn't think she could fake. But then she thought about how if you hang out with whores, it starts to seem normal. You realize that the actresses who play sex workers on TV and in the movies are beautiful, but real hoes look like almost every kind of woman. When you hang out with drug addicts, doing a line on top of your *TV Guide* after work is normal. Or when you hang out with softball dykes suddenly waking up on Sunday to play in the park wearing ugly team t-shirts is no longer so bizarre. If you hang out with strippers and you're she stuck rolling quarters before pay day to afford milk, while Cori was pulling hundreds out of her bra and sleeping in until 2:00 p.m. Emily didn't have any religious or feminist hang-ups about it, so why not? That was her rationale.

"You only have a 20-year-old ass for a year. Why not make it lucrative?" Cori asked somewhat rhetorically, handing her a pair of heels one size too big. Emily took off her sweaty combat boots and thick socks, buckled herself in and tried to stand. Cori brought out a full-length mirror, leaned it against the far living room wall and pressed play on the cassette player. TLC's *Crazy Sexy Cool*. Emily shook her ass in the mirror and laughed. Cori showed her how to move her knees in a way that made her ass wiggle, then squatted down and crawled across the floor dramatically, finally flopping on her back and arching.

"I call that the wounded animal crawl," she said, "Do it whenever your feet hurt. The guys love it."

* * *

The Sex Castle was not a high-end place where rich guys hosted bachelor parties. There was only a slim door at street level next to a trashy donut shop. There was a small sign bearing its name above the awning and that was it. You had to be told about it or notice the sign in the second-floor window. Cori had big hips and spiked purple hair and Emily had a tattoo on her back, and so the classier clubs ruled them both out. This was the '90s when tattoos were still considered a sign of outsider status. Construction workers came on their lunch hour, alcoholics lingered away their afternoons in the front row until they fell asleep and got kicked out.

Emily walked up the steep staircase and followed Cori, noticing how her youthful slouch shifted when she ducked through the door. Emily tried to mimic her, pulling her own shoulders back as she reached the final stair, and then stuck her tits out and adopted a side-to-side sway. The Sex Castle smelled like any other bar, beer and smoke and sweat and drugstore perfume. Emily followed Cori up to the bar to introduce herself to the manager. She tried to stand in a feminine way, which threw off her balance and forced her to grip the wooden lip of counter.

"This is . . . Lily," Cori said, "She's over eighteen. This is Pierre."

Pierre had a throat slash scar across his neck. He took her ID card and scanned it, then her.

"You look much younger than you are," he said in a thick French accent, "If you can't hack it tonight you'll have to pay me thirty bucks to leave before last call. Three song sets. Give your CDs to Pierre, the DJ. Don't shoot up." He motioned towards a greasy looking metal-head smoking by a pair of speakers. Emily nodded, as though she wasn't completely out of her element.

"They're both named Pierre?" Emily asked Cori in a stage whisper.

"We call the DJ Little Pierre because," she said, making a motion with her pinky to indicate *small penis*.

Fucked up things Emily learned about strip clubs that night: Despite being the era of identity politics, the bar would only allow one Black girl to work on each shift. A woman with a brunette bob named Tina was called "the Asian girl" because she was Italian. Tampon strings glow in the black light. You can get a yeast infection from the pole. Men had eyes like tiny televisions when they watched you. It only takes one shift to make your thighs feel strong. It starts out terrifying and humiliating and then becomes normal. That process takes approximately six stage show rotations.

Men loved The Sex Castle because they could be kings. Once you crossed the threshold of the lightbulb bordered door at the top of the stairs, it was like stepping into 1977. Their sexist and racist jokes got laughs, their boring work stories were listened to, and they felt like the most attractive men in the world, with girls vying for their attention. No one was going to remind them who they really were.

The club was practically empty—it was a Tuesday night. During Emily's third rotation on stage, when she'd finally perfected one twirl around the pole without falling, her first lap dance customer walked into the bar. He looked comfortable, knew everyone and wore the kind of business casual clothing typical of suburban commuters, meant to be unremarkable. He patted the waitress on the ass when he ordered a drink. He was immediately transfixed by Emily as she hobbled around the small stage to The Waitresses' classic, "I Know What Boys Want."

Looking back on it now, Emily realized that she was a terrible combination of middle class, lazy, and filled with third-wave feminist mumbo-jumbo about stripping being the new road to empowerment. And while she had emerged from an average suburb, she had thousands of dollars in student loan debt, a propensity for being fired from any job, and parents who had the attitude of middle-class people without the money to lend her in a crisis. At the time she would've said she was tough, edgy. But she wasn't the sharpest pencil in the box in terms of basic life skills. This was a time when the term executive functioning wasn't commonplace. The rent at her previous apartment was only $130 a month. Even in those days, that wasn't much. That's the kind of person she was. She could never just get it together.

A decade later she'd be diagnosed with ADHD, and it all would make sense, but back then she just felt kind of stupid and inadequate.

"The root of it is your anxiety. So much of your time is consumed by worrying, it exhausts you. You have trouble managing your time," her therapist had said, recently.

"Maybe," Emily had responded, though inside she was worried she was just generally defective, achievement-wise. Even now, with a thriving freelance editorial business, she is haunted by the feeling that she'd ever be lazy again. It's why she insists on coming to the same café bench every morning before returning home to work, to purposefully mimic a commute to an office so she that when she returns home, she sits at her desk, and is productive.

The puppy has been outside so long she begins to wonder if its owners are neglectful. She glances inside, assumes they are stuck in the long latte line. She pictures the dog in her apartment. She could get him a cute bed to put near the window. She takes a sip of her coffee and begins to read Hiram's obituary. Her pulse accelerates, her fingers tingle.

She mouths quietly:

I see a red bicycle, yellow daisies, mint gum on the pavement, rusted bike lock, lonely dog.

I feel the softness of this skirt, the smooth coffee cup, the grit of this newspaper.

I smell spring mud, car exhaust.

I taste old gum and coffee.

Emily takes three deep breaths and keeps reading.

After her sixth set on stage, Hiram approached Emily with a coupon for one free dance that they were giving out at the donut shop downstairs. Emily raised her eyebrows after reading the coupon.

"Uh, seriously?" Dances were five bucks a song. In those days, that wasn't much either.

The bouncer, who also had an impressive throat slash scar—did the owner meet him in a support group for failed mob hit victims?—came over to Emily.

"You have to accept those coupons, new girl. Sorry."

Emily strode over to Hiram, took his hand and walked him to the VIP section of the room, a dimmer area with arm chairs bordering pushed against the mirrored walls. She began to dance in front of him, worrying how she might casually and gracefully end up on his lap. She leaned in half-heartedly, looking down past his face, while climbing up to place one knee on each chair of the arm.

"You have sad eyes," he said, as Emily moved above him, sweaty fingers puckered to the mirrors behind his head. She tried to mimic what she'd seen the other girls do. She was awkward. He seemed to like that she didn't know what she was doing.

"My whole family was killed in a chairlift accident," she dead panned.

His eyes widened, annoyed at being jolted out of a fantasy.

"Really, baby?"

Emily anchored both knees on either side of his lap, locking him in, "You're even more of a moron than I originally thought."

"You're a real bitch," he said, but he wasn't mad. He looked amused. "Did your daddy teach you to talk that way?"

"No, but my daddy did teach me to tip when you've had a good time," she said, as the song ended, using a line Cori had given her.

Hiram reluctantly parted with another five bucks. She tucked it into her G-string.

"You look way too young to be working here," he said.

"Maybe I am," she smiled. He handed her a business card. Hiram Johnstone. Talent Agent.

"Call me whenever you're working and I'll make a special trip to see you," he said.

Emily nodded, put the card into her impossibly tiny purse, and whispered to Cori who was in an acrobatic position astride a trucker.

"My first regular!"

Soon Emily found her look. She stuffed newspaper into the toes of her shoes, ugly navy blue pumps from the thrift store, along with a too-tight white polo shirt and a short, plaid skirt that was part of Cori's old high school uniform at Mount Royal Academy. Emily still didn't know what she was doing. She'd had a lot of sex, but until she met her first girlfriend, she'd never come with another person in the room. Sex was for someone else, even before there was money exchanged, she knew this. Even when the boys were nice and had read Andrea Dworkin, it didn't matter. When Emily had sex with a girl, who pursued her harder than any boy ever had, she walked home with her panties in her knapsack feeling like *oh well, I guess I don't like that either.* She told people she was bi, but really, she was nothing. Until she met her first girlfriend, who she fell in love with so intensely it altered her whole universe. She'd understood love, but desire had always seemed unnatural, until it didn't.

At the club, Cori and Emily would dance to The Ramones and Iggy Pop until the DJ rebelled and only played Def Leppard and Guns N' Roses. This was before it was cool in an ironic way to like heavy metal again. This was pure bad taste. They were above it, even though they were bad strippers. The real strippers—Cori had nicknamed them Silicon Valley—hated Emily and Cori and called them the *college bitches.* Silicon Valley dated the mafia men who came in at last call and had physical fights over who stole another girl's tampons in the dressing room. Silicon Valley knew that Cori and Emily were in it for the story first, and then the money, while they were in it for real.

Being around naked women wasn't very sexy. Except for one girl Lila, who would dance very slowly, slower than the song, and you'd think that would look awkward, but it didn't. It was exactly the way you should dance, except most girls were either nervous or bored or coked up, so they danced as fast as they could, trying to outrun their stage time. Not Lila. She took her time. Emily was always naked by song two, or else she wouldn't stop thinking about what she still had on, and how she was going to take it off, and what if she caught her G-string in the hook of her heel and fell? (This only happened once. Hiram brought her tissues for her scrapped knee.) Anyway, by the time Lila got to her third song you literally couldn't wait to see her pussy. It was like being denied food for days. She just knew how to hold on and smirk at you like, *What? Maybe you don't deserve it yet.* Lila always made the most money, but hardly ever took her panties off.

The only other dancer who could make as much money was Izzy, who was thirty-three. At the time Emily thought a thirty-three-year-old was basically a senior citizen and the most pathetic thing in the world, to be a thirty-three-year old stripper. Izzy had a mescaline face. But she raked it in.

Now Emily *is* thirty-three and she still feels seventeen, and she feels bad that she was such a jerk to Izzy, who was just trying to get by. It is easier to be kind in your thirties, she thinks. She writes that down in her anxiety journal. The dog pulls the leash as far as it will go and sits on Emily's foot, rubbing its head against her ankle. Emily loses herself in the feel of the dog's fur, petting his soft head.

Later they found out Lila was seventeen. She said she could work there because her uncle was in the mafia. But Emily never found out if that was actually true, because it was what every dancer learned to say when clients crossed a line. A whispered *My Uncle Tino's in the Hells Angels* was the quickest way to make a posturing man look like a tiny little boy, returning his hands from your breasts back to his lap.

Emily's moneymaker was the fact that at twenty, she looked fourteen. Sometimes people even mistook her for twelve. Guys like Hiram Johnstone, with certain predilections for age play, flocked to her. After their first encounter, Emily went down to the phone booth in the donut shop, Hiram Johnstone's business card in hand, and looked him up. He was listed. It was his actual name.

The next day, Emily went to his house. What kind of a pervert moron gives a stripper his real address? Emily sat on her skateboard on the sidewalk across from his house wearing baggy pants and a tuque. She smoked, read a paperback detective novel, and rolled backwards and forwards on the skateboard. Eventually, he drove up in a rusting Toyata Turcell hatchback.

When he got out of the car he looked right at her but didn't recognize her. Strippers are like teachers, when you see them outside the usual context, you don't really see them. She watched him unpack groceries from the trunk, and help his wife take a kid out of a car seat. An older girl, about fifteen or sixteen, got out of the car quickly and went inside, slamming the front door. His wife was beautiful. She was the kind of beautiful woman who would push ahead of Emily at the coffee shop with her big designer purse. His wife looked at Emily, who coughed on her smoke, got up, and rolled away.

As he got to know Emily, Hiram Johnstone became braver with his banter. How was school today, Lily? Did you do your spelling home-work? Emily would joke that her eighteenth birthday was swell! She wasn't into it, although there she was, in a school girl's uniform, giving him a little thrill.

One day he came during lunch hour and pulled her away from the bar where she was pretending to enjoy a watered-down ginger ale and reading a class assignment, *Regarding the Pain of Others* by Susan Sontag. "I don't like to see you reading," he said, grabbing her by the thin strap of her purse.

She began the usual banter, the regular moves. Because it was early, they were almost alone in the VIP room. Instead of sweetly asking about her day at school, participating in the ruse of an imagined high school life, he pinched her thigh and said she was getting fat, then he held her by the waist against his lap, not letting her dance.

Emily tried to go with it, rolled her eyes. "What's your deal today, Hiram? You're not usually such a grump." She lifted both arms, pre-tending to still be dancing with the top of her body, as her bottom half was in the vice of his arms, gripped against his bulging lap. She glanced quickly towards where security should have been standing.

He kept his hands on her waist long enough, staring at her so insistently, so murderously, even her teeth hurt from the chill. "Don't get uppity, missy. Do. What. I. Say." Then his faced looked like he was grimacing in pain. Was he having a heart attack? She wondered if she could remember the CPR instruction she'd received in junior lifeguarding. She'd never seen a man come before, only heard it in the dark, so it was a surprise to see the evidence on her skirt. When she realized it, she moved so quickly that her heel knocked his drink off the side table, crashing loudly enough that security popped his head in. She grabbed a cocktail napkin to wipe her lap and shuddered. An inventory of diseases scrolled through her brain. She flicked the straw from her drink toward him, hoping to hit his face, but it fell flaccidly against his arm and he didn't even notice. His eyes were closed, like he was napping, and he mumbled *sorry pretty baby*. She went back to the bar, shaken up. He walked by her on his way out, handed her a fifty, and said "Here's your allowance."

The next time he came in to the club and saw her, he picked out a new girl, someone younger. Emily was relieved and also annoyed.

The new girl put borage flowers in the dressing room, purple buds soaking in tap water and crowded into a plastic Pepsi cup. She snacked on them. "They're anti-depressants. They used to give them to soldiers to help them be brave!" She had a tattoo of Emma Goldman on her ass, but Cori and Emily pretended she wasn't one of their own. They made fun of her with Silicon Valley because she didn't shave her bush.

One day at the bar, the new girl said, "Hiram's a fucking perv, right?"

"It's all relative," Emily had shrugged. She thought about saying something more but stopped short. When she'd told Cori about him coming, she'd laughed and said, "Gross, dude! I hope he tipped big." Emily felt embarrassed that it had seemed like such a big deal to her.

Eventually Emily just stopped going to the club, the same way she'd stopped going to her other jobs. She started working at an office, got a master's degree, and moved to another city. Cori is a lawyer now. Lila is a documentary filmmaker.

Emily finishes the obituary, learns that Hiram died of heart failure, had three grandkids. She thought about the hours she spent naked with him, legs in a V, toes pointed and touching the mirror beside his ears. Every time she did this, she had a vision of snapping his neck with her ankles, and the thought would make her worry that she was a bad person. Later, she would learn this is a common symptom of OCD, an irrational fear of hurting others when you don't actually want to hurt anyone.

She writes zero in the box next to the day's date in her anxiety journal, remembering Cori's advice on their first shift, "If you fake it, you'll eventually feel it, your body won't understand the difference."

Emily places palm to heart and inhales.

Brown dog. Scooter. Hipster girls holding hands.

Drip of air conditioner on my shoulder. Itchy toe.

The smell of rain approaching.

Lydia Conklin

Truffle Pig

When Ronnie's new friend Helena kisses her, they're on the bike path after church. Last night's snow sugars the grass, a skin of glitter that melts when Ronnie breathes on it. The walk is normal except for one minute. In that minute Helena cups Ronnie's shoulders and their mouths join. The maple leaves—bent and soggy under the freakish September snow—blur to nothing.

Helena pulls away, her Coke-bottle glasses so fogged that Ronnie can't read her expression. "How was that?"

Before the kiss, Ronnie was just saying she didn't think kissing was a big deal, didn't get why their friend Samantha always IMs boys.

Helena shakes her fuzzy hair. "I thought you were like me. I didn't want to ask. But I thought so."

A knot of tissue loosens in Ronnie's chest. Did they really kiss? Helena is on the Gifted Track and can make up a story on any topic. She looks like no one else in eighth grade with her thrift store smocks, her nails painted in a rainbow. Her pig nose makes Ronnie think of the poem she chose for memorization this year in English, about a little lamb. People always think of the tiger poem on the facing page, with the brighter, scarier picture. But Ronnie thinks of the lamb. *Little pig, who made thee? Dost thou know who made thee?* Ronnie has ratty braids that dangle in wispy tails above her breast buds.

She reaches out to touch Helena the way she'd reach for a mirage. Helena shrugs away. Ronnie grins too big, not even fretting over her tooth stains for once in her life. For the rest of the week, Ronnie walks as if on cotton.

After school the next day, Ronnie visits the town library to work on her research project, avoiding the school library, where kids whisper about anal penetration. They use words Ronnie can't understand that keep her reading the same sentence forever: *The Puritans had a strong moral fiber. The Puritans had a strong moral fiber. The Puritans had a strong moral fiber.* If you pulled apart a Puritan, you'd find natural-colored cereal, like the kind her dad eats for digestion.

If Ronnie goes to the school library now, if she hears the kids debate sex, her brain will swell with the fact that she kissed Helena. Even though in health class the teacher announced that couples can be two women or two men, and Ronnie's classmates nodded seriously at the news, this is information to keep private.

Ronnie steps into the carpeted foyer of the town library. The essay topic is "Someone I Admire from Lexington." The teacher suggested picking someone from modern life. "A sports coach," he offered. "Or an industrious peer."

"Is that like the industrial revolution?" a kid asked.

The teacher rolled his eyes. "Exactly."

But Ronnie doesn't want to examine her contemporary life. So she scrolls through the microfiche until she finds a story from an 1801 *Lexington Sentinel,* in a column called "Ye Olde Lore" that revisits news items from the colonial period. Ronnie settles back against the wooden chair. This isn't some boring story about some mustached notable trading his horse cart or succumbing to diphtheria.

The story chronicles the life of a famous colonial girl who was utilized by bands of gravediggers to root for jewels. Her small hands ferreted through remains for the best rings and necklaces, so her nickname was Truffle Pig. The girl's tiny hands flashed through soil and bone right here in Lexington, maybe even in the graveyard of Sacred Heart. Her pig nose lit by moonlight, her neck smeared with dirt, an emerald glowing in her palm.

The story reminds Ronnie of Helena's stories. Helena has one about a fox that thrives on poisoned chicken meat and another about an oak that longs to unseat itself from the dirt so it can shuffle on its roots across a glade to penetrate a willow. This story is almost as good as Helena's stories. And it's real.

The next day, Ronnie is meeting Helena and Samantha in the grave-yard of Sacred Heart. As she turns down the bike path she thinks of the kiss, and her body goes rigid. She lifts a sneaker but can't bear to set it down. Samantha says horses behave this way in the evening, because they can't see in gray light.

The church parking lot is lit with potassium lamps, the bulbs buttered so thick with bugs that barely any light squirts through. The glow soaks into the meaty thoraxes, green wings and pencil-mark legs. Helena is new to the school and has never been alone with Samantha.

Ronnie dawdles at a grave. She traces the dead girl's name, soft from hundreds of New England winters. Florence is her favorite dead person, but she doesn't know if that's her first name or her last. Maybe both. Florence Florence, 1794–1803, four years younger than Ronnie.

"Ronnie," Samantha calls. There's Samantha's doughnut of bright hair, vibrating gold. She sits with Helena on a cheesy mausoleum, their thighs pressed together. Samantha scoots away. Her eyes are swollen under her blond bangs.

"You're late." Samantha wears a shirt with a bucking palomino. The horse has a speech bubble that reads I'M NOT PERSONING AROUND. The hemline of the shirt, draped over Samantha's leggings, is crumpled into a wrinkled pleat, hard as plaster, though Samantha claims not to suck her shirts anymore.

"We missed you," says Helena.

The mausoleum is carved like bunched cloth. Ronnie wonders if she should climb up and sit with them.

"What are you guys doing?" Ronnie asks.

"Hanging out," says Helena.

"I have to go." Samantha springs off the stone.

"Why?" Ronnie asks. But Samantha's already far away. She dodges graves, yellow shirt flapping in the fading light.

"Wait up," Ronnie calls, taking a few steps toward Samantha.

"You know," Helena says as Samantha shrinks into a yellow dot. "Samantha has a strange past." Helena draws Ronnie in with her story voice. "Do you think something happened to her?"

Ronnie shrugs.

"Maybe she used to have a lion where she lived before."

Ronnie pictures Samantha with a tawny, muscular cat. "But she's always lived here."

"Before that, though."

"There is no before."

"Picture this." Helena raises her arms dramatically. They're so skinny they look like they could snap in the winter air. "Maybe Samantha tamed that lion."

"How could she?" Samantha can't even tame herself. The whole time the lion waited to be tamed Samantha would be fidgeting on her seat, sweating about which boys like her. The only way Ronnie can calm her is by listening to her worries.

"You know how she likes horses so much?" Helena tips her pug nose into the fuzzy air.

"Duh." That's the main thing about Samantha.

"What if she called all the horses in Massachusetts, and the lion could eat as many as he wanted?"

"Wouldn't she be sad?"

"At first, yeah. But she'd have to respect him."

Ronnie leans back against the stone, watching Helena's skin dim as the sun dunks under the branches. She wants to crawl onto the mausoleum and set her head in Helena's lap as the story vibrates through her.

The drawing of Truffle Pig had Helena's same upturned nose. Ronnie pictures Helena's fingers smeared with dirt, jewels clutched in her fist. Helena has the same power in her voice that Truffle Pig had in her tiny, fast hands.

Next Sunday at church, Helena and Ronnie skip Curriculum and hide in the handicapped bathroom. Helena hikes herself onto the counter between bowls of potpourri.

"This stuff is so cool," Ronnie says, lifting a bowl. The smell of rose shoves itself into her nostrils. She tries not to look at the rest of the bathroom, prickling with equipment for disabilities. There are metal rails mounted to the wall, a plastic seat with Swiss cheese holes over the regular toilet. There's a hanging cord that connects to the administration, a red button that reads IN CASE OF ACCIDENT

EMERGENCY OR DEATH. Ronnie tries not to touch the buttons or cords, afraid that if she brushes one, the congregation will swarm in.

Leaning away from the emergency cord, she drops the bowl of potpourri. Broken glass mixes on the floor with old petals and thistle.

She gathers what she can, picking the glass carefully from the tiles. When she looks up, Helena is naked from the waist down. Her skirt, which is made of sweatpants material, is crumpled on the counter. Helena's body looks like Ronnie's, but if you changed each detail by one degree: the color, the shape, the coverage of hair.

"Hey," Helena says.

Ronnie knows what to do. She heard the kids in the library discussing it once. She would've thought she'd be terrified when the moment arose, but she's so calm that she's not in her body. She dusts the potpourri and glass into the bowl. She sets a hand on each of Helena's thighs, skin giving way under her. She presses her face between Helena's legs. Helena tastes like milk that's covered a bowl of tiny humans, absorbing their flavor for hours.

There's a sharp knock on the door. Ronnie's head springs up. Helena's eyes are still closed, head tipped back, mouth open.

"Helena," Ronnie says. "We have to stop."

"They'll leave."

Ronnie can't bring herself to continue. The person knocks again. Ronnie steps back.

Helena's face is drawn. She puts on her skirt. Outside the bathroom, the woman with Lou Gehrig's disease, the only disabled person at church, towers above, her hair a dark swirl over her ears.

"I don't know what's going on in there," the woman says. "But keep it off my toilet."

That night, in bed, Ronnie listens to the click of the radiator, remembering how the movements she made with her mouth fed Helena's happiness. She screws her face deep into the mattress pad, tries to settle the clopping in her chest that's like a tiny red horse.

She and Samantha met Helena last month, on the first day of eighth grade. Helena was the new girl, dressed in a turtleneck and a plaid skirt, looking like she belonged with Florence Florence and Truffle Pig and the other colonial girls more than in 1999 with

Ronnie. Helena had a star quality that glimmered under her glasses and through the nostrils of her turned-up pig nose. That nose that wiggled when she saw a friend, sniffing pheromones.

"Ronald, I presume," Helena said when they met.

For the first time, Ronnie was part of a group. The three of them were enough to take up a corner of a table at lunch, and they fit perfectly in a car with one chaperone. Ronnie never had so many friends before, loved the heat of it, the elbows, the festive, snarky jokes.

The whole school buzzes over Helena. "Are her glasses real?" "How's her hair so fluffy?" "She's so far above Tommy Lehman in Gifted that they had to make a whole new unit where she, like, learns things we won't learn for years." Girls ask each other if they've seen Helena's vintage smock, if they know Helena moved from Nashville, which is so cool. Though, in some ways, Helena is dorky like Ronnie and Samantha, she has a crazy charm that even popular girls admit. Ronnie might be prettier, but her only good shirt is one whose front shows guinea pig faces, their open mouths like cuts in the fur, and whose back shows guinea pig butts, anuses exposed like fleshy buttons.

Once a boy even asked Helena out. She said no, but she bounced down the hallways for the whole afternoon. And now Helena and Ronnie have shared a moment of deep intimacy.

After school on Monday, Ronnie invites Samantha over. She needs to discuss what happened. Plus, it's been weeks since Ronnie's been alone with Samantha. She misses her.

"When's Helena getting here?" Samantha asks when she arrives. The name makes Ronnie's nerves light in hot red tangles.

"She's not coming."

They pull chairs to the computer in the basement and Instant Message boys that Samantha likes and Ronnie fake-likes. The boys ask what the girls would do to them and Samantha types, *Touch your peen, touch your ball sack. Pinch your ball sack to see how loose it is.* Samantha slides the keyboard to Ronnie, but she shakes her head.

"Why aren't you helping?" Samantha asks. "Don't you even care about the guys?"

"Totally," Ronnie says, though she doesn't remember which boys from school the screen names represent.

The boys take their time responding after Samantha's description of sucking their privates as hard as a vacuum cleaner.

"They'll come back," Samantha says. "They can't resist."

They lean forward perilously in their chairs, watching the row of IM windows. Nothing lights up. Samantha's lips part, her blond bangs shagging over her eyes. In seventh grade, Ronnie and Samantha confessed to each other about getting teased at school. Ronnie for being a tomboy with stained teeth and Samantha for being obsessed with horses and for never closing her mouth. They used to make diagrams for each other's lives, scribbled maps of the future on rolls of parchment paper. Arrows pointed to boxes with goals like *Apartment with Carpeting* and *Five Pet Ferrets* and, in Samantha's diagram, *High End "Toys."* If Ronnie cried, Samantha would sit with her until she finished. She wouldn't tell her to calm down. She'd just peer out from under her bangs and nod somberly.

"Why do you like Helena?" Samantha asks.

Ronnie barely knows where to start. "Maybe because she'll be famous one day."

"Famous for what? Walking around in stupid clothes all the time? Thinking she's so great?"

Ronnie is taken aback. The graveyard was awkward, yeah, but otherwise everything's fine. "I guess."

"Thanks for finally inviting me over," Samantha says. "That's real charitable." She blows her bangs. For the second they're in the air, Ronnie sees her eyes are glassy.

In eighth grade, fewer people make fun of Ronnie and Samantha. The popular kids have their own business these days, like arranging parties in the woods. Bullying isn't cool anymore. When Ronnie walks down the hall this year it's almost like she doesn't exist. She needs another way to get close to Samantha. "I'm confused about something."

"Doy. You're always confused."

"No, I'm not." But Samantha's right. Ronnie never takes anything for granted. Like she wonders if Truffle Pig gave away jewels to hobos. Or caught a disease from a corpse and died young. The story can't have gone like the newspaper, laid out like a child's adventure book, ending with Truffle Pig happy forever with the band of gravediggers.

"You're, like, freaking out." Samantha uses her soft voice, the one for confiding. Ronnie should ask now.

"Do two girls ever do the stuff you talk about?"

"Can girls suck each other's balls, you mean?" Samantha's mouth lags open. Ronnie can see why that annoys people.

Ronnie puts her hands on the computer table and pushes off. Her chair rolls across the carpet. She's afraid to get too close to Samantha, doesn't want to look at those wisps of mustard-colored hair. One of Ronnie's parents is pacing upstairs. She can almost see the plaster swell in the shape of feet. "What's it called if one girl, like, licks another girl? You know. Down there."

Samantha presses her hands against the palomino. "You're gonna make me barf."

Ronnie's face heats. She would cover it with her hair, but it's in a French braid.

"You didn't do that with Helena, did you?" The way Samantha looks at Ronnie, she must know.

Ronnie can't stop thinking about what happened. "No way. We didn't do anything."

"Ronnie, you go to church. You're a member of Sacred Heart."

"Why do you care? You're Jewish."

"Your parents would care. Just think about that. It's gross, what you're doing."

Helena, half-naked on the bathroom counter. "What are you talking about?" Her vowels squeak.

"I have to go." Samantha picks up her sweatshirt and leaves, though her ride isn't coming for hours.

The snow melts and it gets warm. But the leaves are already crushed and ruined. Samantha doesn't call. Ronnie misses her voice, huskier than any kid she knows. Ronnie hangs out with Helena some, but they don't kiss. They walk the bike path, sit together on the same cold pew at church. Dissecting earthworms for a biology unit on Animal Science, Helena says, "Samantha's annoying. I'd rather hang out with you."

Ronnie can't help beaming, though she should feel sorry for Samantha. She leans in as Helena pulls a heart from the earthworm. The heart rises on a pin, glowing like a tiny ruby.

Ronnie and Helena have sleepovers. They go to Ronnie's because Helena lives in a Section 8 unit, and her room smells like cheese. Samantha is too busy helping her father roof a doghouse.

"Do you even have a dog?" Ronnie asks.

"We might get one."

In Ronnie's room, Helena sleeps on an air mattress and they talk through the molecules bouncing in the night air. Helena can make a piece of bread on the floor interesting. She can spice up a bad joke, a sad anecdote, their whole lives in Lexington. Their walks turn into journeys, their teachers become shriveled sages. Samantha's future dog becomes half-wolf. On one sleepover Helena turns a story about Samantha tripping on a pencil case into a whole novel where, by the end, Samantha has one leg and two eyes removed.

"Then what happened?" Ronnie asks.

"She hopped blindly into the future."

Ronnie misses Samantha, longs to kneel on the floor and draw up plans with her. But she doesn't heed Samantha's warning. She needs what happened in the handicapped bathroom to happen again.

Some nights Ronnie climbs onto the air mattress with Helena. They lie side-by-side, looking at the dark. When either of them rolls over, the mattress squeaks like a bag of overfull balloons.

One night, Ronnie asks Helena if it matters that her teeth are stained.

Helena makes a show of peering through the dim light. "I don't see any stains."

The whole bottoms of Ronnie's front teeth are yellow, even orange in one patch. She touches her mouth with her fingertips, pictures her teeth like Helena sees them, white and clean.

At school, Samantha runs up to Ronnie and slaps her shoulder. "You're it."

"What?" Ronnie asks.

"I'm joking." Samantha squeezes Ronnie's arm, friendly, but with pressure. "Oh, Ronnie. What can we do with you?"

Samantha's cheeks are bright, her t-shirt untucked. She looks like she must've looked years ago, before the social hierarchy.

Ronnie runs into Samantha walking home and invites her to a sleep-over. Samantha says she can't, that the dog roof leaks and she needs to patch it. Helena, who's walking home beside Ronnie, snorts.

"Just take a turd and sort of smear it around," Helena says. "It'll dry right up."

"No thanks," says Samantha.

One night, once Ronnie's crawled onto the air mattress where Helena was reading, Helena says, "You know the thing that happened in September?"

Helena has never brought up the incident. All the muscles in Ronnie's body harden. "Yes."

"Have you told anyone about that?" There's a steel edge to Helena's voice.

"No," Ronnie says. She doesn't want to scare Helena.

"Not even Samantha? Are you sure?" Helena sits upright, all her weight on her elbows. The skin of the mattress bends.

"No."

Helena sighs. "That's good. That's really good."

Helena hugs Ronnie. A shot of wet heat runs through her. She wants to tilt her face up, kiss until Helena's lenses steam. The kiss was the jewel Helena found, like Truffle Pig, in their friendship.

"I met someone, Ronnie."

Ronnie's heart squeezes. "Samantha?"

Helena laughs. "Are you kidding? No way. A high school girl. On IM. We're going to meet."

Ronnie rises on the air mattress, nothing left inside of her. Her head throbs. She won't think about it. She just won't think about it.

The next day she sketches Helena as Truffle Pig, tipping over the side of a grave. To get the details right, she imagines Helena leaning toward the computer screen, ready to plunge into another world.

The posters show up at school on a Monday, a URL centered on the page in Samantha's shaky cursive: TheTruthAboutHelenaClarke.net. Ronnie skips History and goes to the library. When a computer frees, she types the address. It fills in automatically, like it's been checked already.

Sitting on the plastic chair, as close as possible to the screen, Ronnie reads the long roll of blue and red chats between Helena and a user called IAmGay69Rainbow. The scripts start simple.

IAmGay69Rainbow: Are you Helena? I need to talk to you.
DecentPerson203: Why?
IAmGay69Rainbow: I have to tell you something.
DecentPerson203: You're gay?
IAmGay69Rainbow: Yes.
DecentPerson203: Doy.

IAmGay69Rainbow, who's obviously Samantha, claims to be a high school kid who's heard how amazing Helena is. Over the course of a few days, the IMs escalate. On the transcripts, extreme passages are highlighted in yellow. *I like the taste of girls*, Helena wrote. *They're the most delicious dinner.*

Some of the conversations on the website are so insane that Ronnie can't imagine them coming out of Helena's mind. Helena says she wants to press her face into the breasts of IAmGay, to lick her top to bottom. She says that she's been with girls all over the country, that no one at her old school ever made fun of her even a little bit. That if IAmGay would become her girlfriend, Helena would show her a passionate life.

But the worst part is the pictures. Ronnie recognizes Helena's open folds, her red gooseflesh, her curling, soft hairs. The glittered dark blue polish on bitten nails, spreading flaps of skin for IAmGay. Ronnie thought she was the only one who knew this part of Helena. Now anyone can visit the site with its toile wallpaper and blinking animations of pussycats.

Ronnie shakes her head so hard her eyeballs shift in her skull. One phrase burns so bright it shines out everything else. *You and me*, Helena wrote. *We're one girl.* Ronnie can't stop thinking about that. *One girl. We're one girl.* Even when she closes the browser, shuts down the computer and crosses the fake stone floors to lunch, Ronnie can't wash the phrase from her mind.

Ronnie storms through the halls, her cheeks burning. Wherever she goes that day, no matter how fast she walks, she hears Helena's name. And not Helena's name like people used to say it. Their voices rubber band from whispers to shouts.

Ronnie doesn't go to lunch. No one does. The kids mass in the hallways and open classrooms. Teachers pull down posters but seem to have no idea. On the way to the main hall, Ronnie finds Samantha. Her horse shirt is so chewed it's like there are tumors on her stomach.

"I know what you guys used to do," Samantha says. "Do you even know how your face smells after doing that? Here's a newsbreak. It's obvious."

The words tear through the skin on Ronnie's chest, dry school air racing into her. She wants to push Samantha down.

"She tried it with me too, okay?" Samantha says. "So you're not special."

"Shut up," Ronnie says, twisting her braid around a finger so hard that hairs snap off and float to floor.

"I made it easy. Now you can walk away."

"Shut up." Ronnie yells this time, louder than she's ever yelled in school. Samantha slinks into the janitor's storage and slams the door.

Ronnie can't stop staring at the metal of the door, like if her eyes could pass beyond the burnished surface she could understand. She's known Samantha for years. She loved Samantha. She doesn't understand how she picked a friend who'd do something so horrible.

In a defunct back hall where teachers never go, a crowd of kids watches Helena, who stands on a step stool tearing at a poster. Samantha affixed the posters as high as she could. She must have also glued them or used a whole roll of tape for each, because Helena scrapes at the edges without progress. People laugh and murmur below.

Helena has taken her glasses off. Her eyes are tiny and dark. "Can someone help?" she begs, swaying there, limp as a noodle. Then she spots Ronnie. "Ronnie. Please."

Helena is the smartest and most interesting friend Ronnie will ever have. Their conversations are a thousand times better than hearing about how Samantha wants to trim forelocks or squeeze balls. After what Samantha's done, Ronnie can never go back to their friendship, as old as it is. If she messes up with Helena, she'll have no one. She knows all this in her heart.

She can't breathe. Her skull is packed with cotton, like she'll fall hard on the tiles in front of everyone. She thinks of that phrase again. *We're like one girl.* She thinks of Helena and Samantha sitting together on the ugly mausoleum. She's going to be sick.

Helena's skin is gray, like oatmeal. The other kids murmur nonsense. Like when you play a member of a crowd in Drama and you say *Carrots and peas carrots and peas.* If she stands next to Helena, people will realize she's gay, too. Samantha knows what happened in the handicapped bathroom. If Ronnie doesn't keep her head down, she'll be next. The halls will become a gauntlet again, and this time she won't have anyone left to confide in.

With Helena watching her, all beady-eyed and needy, like a pet, Ronnie screams: "No." She screams it even louder than she screamed at Samantha. Everyone stares.

At home, she stands in her empty kitchen, clutching her book bag so tight a pencil snaps. She thinks of calling Helena, but she's afraid. She just needs to get through tonight, to breathe properly. Tomorrow she'll be her best self.

She logs onto the site. She posts comments saying Helena is a great friend, that the website is a lie. She posts all night, though her comments are swallowed by hundreds of *dyke, bitch, lesbo cunt, sicko, sister-fucker, dummy.*

Ronnie spends the next day at school with her head up, searching. But she can't find Helena.

"I heard she's in the hospital," one kid says.

"She joined a gay cult," another kid says. "Where they wear rainbow bathrobes and fuck."

Ronnie worries Helena hurt herself alone in her cheese-smelling room. She doesn't want to think about this, but maybe Helena even killed herself. Maybe soon there will be an announcement like there was for that kid Paulie who died last year, who had a weak heart that he was always picking at through his shirt, his skin gray because his blood moved like syrup. Ronnie pictures Helena in the soil of Sacred Heart, fertilized by colonial girls like Florence Florence and Truffle Pig. Girls who died with weeping sores on their faces, fevers shivering under their skin, black desires impacted in their chests.

Ronnie goes to the school office. The secretary says Helena's moving out of the district, to another system.

"I can't tell you more than that," she says. "Even that's confidential."

At home Ronnie calls Helena, though she imagines the landline already shut down, Helena and her mother already gone. Eventually, Helena answers.

"What do you want?" she says.

Ronnie gulps a huge breath, so floored is she by Helena's voice, high and thin. "I'm sorry about yesterday." Ronnie wants to say she hates herself, but she bites her lip.

"It doesn't matter." Helena sounds far away, like she's drawing the receiver from her mouth. "I'm moving anyway."

"Are you scared?"

"Why would I be? We move all the time."

"You do?" There's so much she doesn't know about Helena, and now there isn't time to learn. A breath sticks in Ronnie's throat, gummy and tight.

"I have to go. We're packing."

"Can I tell you one thing?" This is the last time they'll talk. That sends a bitter horror dripping down Ronnie's chest. They only have a few more seconds.

"Hurry."

Ronnie tells Helena about Truffle Pig. She shares every detail she knows: Truffle Pig was a teenager, she joined with a band of colonial men to find jewels sunken into the flesh of old wrists, soft chests. But she also makes up details. She says Truffle Pig was brilliant, that everyone loved her. Even though she was nontraditional she was considered cool by even the most popular puritans. In the graves, she'd slip one jewel into her underwear, baggy, canvas colonial underwear with plenty of storage. She saved up until she had enough gold to leave the gravediggers.

"She went to Florida," Ronnie says. "She lived there for a long time. She married someone she loved. And she was happy." Ronnie pictures Helena somewhere better. Somewhere where she could hold a woman by the waist and yell back at people who throw yogurt on her face and call her a pussy licker. A place with carpeted halls and green light bulbs. Beyond the gray skies of New England. Somewhere heated, where she's the boss.

"That story isn't true, you know," says Helena.

Ronnie flinches. She hadn't doubted it, but the illustration was so whimsical. She wishes she could unhear it. "I know."

"Why are you telling me?"

"She reminds me of you." Ronnie hears footfalls through the phone, adults talking.

Helena pauses, takes a breath. "Seriously?"

"She looks like you, in my mind. And you're both, I don't know. Brave, I guess. Is that a good story?"

Helena doesn't answer, but she doesn't hang up, either. Helena's mom calls somewhere in the apartment, telling Helena to get off the phone, to scrape her clothes off the carpet, to help pack. But for the moment she stays on the line.

Laurie Stone

Cat

I was sitting beside a stranger on a train when we passed the house where I had lived as a child. It was surrounded by tall trees whose names I didn't know. Limbs would fall, and I would crack them over my knee like bones. I held the stranger's hand under his coat. I could have left it at that.

He was drinking from a flask. He said, "What were you like as a child?" I said, "I stole other people's stories." He said, "All children do that." Did they, really? I was prepared to believe what he said. It was relaxing. I liked him. It was a sense of trust, whatever that means. He said, "One day when I was drunk, I fell down a flight of stairs and cracked my head. When I woke up, an angel was sitting on my bed. She had red hair and she said she loved me. After that, I stopped drinking, but only for a while." He smiled. Was it a sad smile? How can you figure out strangers? The pleasure of a stranger is the pleasure of nature. It's beyond our capacity to know it, because we are outsiders.

I had a friend her father owned a seaplane, and he would take her flying. I told people I had flown in this plane. I said that clouds and foam looked pretty much the same from the air as they did from the ground. I didn't want her father to be my father. He was a pretty unhappy man. He had one of those mouths that's a straight line. I wanted to have been somewhere, and I wanted what other people had.

I said, "What do you do when you aren't riding trains?" The man had gray eyes. He said, "I study *aging in cells*." When he said the words aging in cells, I fell in love. It felt like being swooped up in the mouth of something. I said, "How do cells age?" He said, "All organisms are subject to damage, but younger organisms have more stem cells, which repair damage. Aging is the failure to repair damage." This put a new light on everything. Do you know the sensation when you're in a strong emotion, and you have no idea why?

* * *

We passed a farmhouse. There were cakes of snow on the slanted roof. The sun was gleaming on the whiteness. It hurt my eyes, but it was impossible not to look at it. The snow was melting in streams. I could see into the rooms. In one was the head of an elk, mounted on a wall, its antlers branching out on either side, its mouth curved up at the ends like a smile, a coin of light glinting off a large glass eye. Maybe elks were happy most of the time.

I'd bought a ticket to the end of the line. I thought I would walk to the airport from there and fly somewhere new. I could see myself as a series of beeping lights, pulsing along. The stranger moved his face close to mine, and I smelled whiskey on his breath. He said, "What do you pretend to like?" I said, "Clothes." His hip pressed against mine. I could have left it at that. It was cold on the train. He said, "What do you do when you aren't riding trains?" I said, "I design sets for plays." He said, "You're an artist." I said, "I make frames for artists to work in."

Suddenly the man jumped up and pointed to the seat across from ours. A mouse had scurried up and was circling around with its thin, sad tail. It had a fat brown body. It moved to the window, and we followed its gaze to a baleful winter garden, studded with dead stalks. The stranger snatched up the mouse in a way not to hurt it. I could see its fur quivering in his large hands, and I tried to remember the last time I had eaten something. I wondered what those hands would feel like on me. He said, "I'll set it free when the train slows," and off he went to the end of the car and opened the door, leaving nothing behind.

I counted the seconds he was gone and thought of calling my mother, who was dead. In my thoughts I said to her, "Mom, have you ever felt suspense that comes out of nowhere? Suddenly, you're hanging by a thread. I love the sensation of not knowing how it will end." I remembered the man's face. There were deep, vertical grooves beneath his nose. One side of his face had been cast in shadow the whole time we'd talked. The dark side of the moon.

By the time the train pulled into the last station and the man had not returned, I felt a sense of heaviness it didn't seem possible to recover from. Love is love. I honestly liked that about love, and I didn't want to feel bad about liking it. Humans do this thing of retelling a story if the ending makes them sad. They retell it so they could have avoided the sadness if only they'd looked. All the signs were there, staring them in the face. We don't look. That's the fun.

I walked in no particular direction away from the train station until arriving at a row of tents grown up along the concrete embankment of a dry river. The tents were not really tents when you drew closer. They were blankets and sheets propped on tree limbs and other makeshift stakes. It had rained the night before, and the ground was strewn with the scaly remnants of clothes and packing crates.

I wondered about the people who had drifted there. The climate was mild, and I remembered a time I hadn't strictly speaking lived in a house. One summer I lived in a potato field with the friend whose father had a seaplane. We slept in a shed, becoming poisoned by pesticides. Our movements slowed, and the edges of colors faded until we returned to college in the fall. While we were being poisoned, I told her I had stolen her story, and she told me what basically the man on the train would later say—"The things we remember didn't happen to us." We brushed off the danger of the pesticides. We were young and didn't know how easily things ended. It made us carefree in a way you can't recover after a certain amount of time has slipped through your fingers. By then, you are just like an aging cell.

I could think of reasons the stranger hadn't returned, and the openness of the question moved up and down me as I breathed. He was a drunk. It made me think of all the things that were wrong with me. A certain kind of softness falls over you from failure.

As I stood there, wondering where to go next, a cat moved up from the encampment to the bridge where I was stopped. The cat was black, and sleek, and muscular, with white whiskers and gold eyes. The cat understood the radical rupture from the natural world that humans experienced because of language and the way they could makes things up in their minds. The cat rubbed its head against my leg, hard and insistent. And as I knelt to touch it, I lost interest in searching for the man. Not really, or why would I be telling you this?

Bradford Nordeen

From a story by Bradford Nordeen + Lior Shamriz

Going Green

He'd pictured their arrival like that scene in *Rosemary's Baby*, when Mia peers out the peephole and Ruth Gordon's heavily made-up face balloons in the distorted curve of the glass. But in actuality they looked nice: simply dressed church ladies. Both wore flats, slacks, cardigans. One knit was violet, the other royal blue. One carried a padded folio, the other a steno pad.

"Hello, Bradford! I'm Sarah! It's nice to finally meet you," the one in front said brightly, but also with business, from the hotel hallway. Her hair was blonde-gray and easily pushed back behind her ears. "This is Margot," she continued, opening her palm and waving towards her companion.

"It's nice to meet you," Margot chimed in.

They both wore cloth Covid-19 face coverings, which made him gesture towards his mouth. "Would you like me to put on a mask?" He opened a dresser drawer that also knew to contain drug paraphernalia and cursed himself for not having a mask at the ready. He pantomimed rummaging. Three years in and this was still a negotiation.

"Oh, you're fine! We won't be too long," Margot assured.

He quit that task. "Please, come in," he ushered. "It's so nice to finally meet you, as well. I appreciate you taking the time to come out today."

"I was about to phone you," Sarah chided with mild concern as she moved through the doorway. "The front door wasn't unlocked like you said, and there's no call box to reach you."

"Oh! I'm so sorry! There's a new guy—he's working the desk today, I think." This one was a tall, reasonably attractive blonde in his early twenties. He'd come to refer to him as "the bad seed," because of his resemblance to a former front desk worker, the way-hotter dopey surfer boy, Rudy. What Rudy lacked in skill he more than made up for in stoner charm—his stories would trail on aimlessly and get lost in the telling, never quite containing the resolution that they'd maybe once intended. And his manner of dress sealed the deal: he wore large Bob Marley sweatshirts or patterned paneled hoodies clearly selected from headshops. Once he'd paid Rudy a compliment on a pewter necklace with a dragon encircling a chunk of amethyst that hung around his neck, and the boy had thumbed the rock and shot back, "yeah, it's like . . . really powerful." But Rudy had to be let go when his meth use started to creep into work hours (typically the night shift). This new guy was a guileless substitute. He wasn't particularly outgoing (hence the nickname). "He doesn't really . . . like to work. They're supposed to put a pin in the door to hold it open for certain hours."

"Well, we made it, regardless" Sarah clapped her hands together and pulled them up to her chest, in half prayer.

As the women shuffled in, they moved their eyes about the room; there was a lot to take in.

He'd switched off the cheap little party light that Rita had given him, which normally danced colored circles about the room. And hid many of what he thought could be read as objectionable objects. Methodically, that morning had been spent selecting book titles from the desk like the 1960s trash paperback *Black Magick, Satanism &* *Voodoo*, Diamanda Galas' *The Shit of God* and the pulp fiction, *Night of the Sadist. The Gnostic Circle* and Kristeva's *Powers of Horror* had been deemed suitable. He was a grad student. And this had to be convincing, plausible. His mother had worked in Catholic healthcare so he knew that nuns could be pretty hip when duty called. And anyway, he figured that this visit was probably among today's more lighthearted.

"Please have a seat," he gestured to the couch and perched himself on the black pleather office chair. He dressed down, humble. He wore all black. Serious. Somber. *Poor.*

"I love your fabric," Margot softly padded at the arm of the couch with her hand. She must have been around sixty-five.

"Oh thanks—I got it from Santee Alley in LA—the garment district. Over the summer before I came back. That's where I live when I'm not here. It's my second year in the hotel program, so you figure out the hacks . . . what you need to make the space feel more like home." It was polyester black with orange polka dots. "Halloween circus," was Eric's read on it, but the text had arrived after he'd paid for it. He'd snapped some camera phone photos for help when picking out a pattern. "Halloween circus" made him instantly doubt the purchase he'd just made. Libra. But it worked.

Margot cocked her head cordially, receiving this information with smile lines deepening from the squint of her eyes. She removed a legal pad from her floral folio which she set on the coffee table.

A poster of Derek Jarman's *Sebastiane* was clipped over the hotel art in a frame behind the ladies, but he'd decided it was good to keep up in the purge earlier that day. His gay voice betrayed him instantly, so he figured he may as well play the part but keep an aura of clergy. Even if the poster was a little porno-chic. The 8-bit riso print of two brown men fucking in front of the Nine Inch Nails poster by Cocteau Twinks had to go, however. He kept nervously revisiting the

Jarman poster, his glances darting between the two charitable women poised on the couch to the curvature of Leonardo Treviglio's naked spine. He decided still that it was a good touch. Test their limits. It kept the room from feeling scrubbed. More real.

Sarah smoothed her hand over the yellow steno pad and began, "so we like to do these home visits simply to get to know you, listen to your situation and see how best we can help. You're a student . . . a grad student at the school?"

"At UCSC, that's right. It's my second year."

"Mmhmm," Sarah nodded, scribbling something down in her pad.

This meeting had freaked him out, frankly. Not just the bad financial straits in which he'd found, himself, and the need to ask for handouts. The incredulity of asking the Catholic church for help had actually made him say aloud, "why the fuck not?" But when Sarah spoke the words "home visit" over the phone, he balked. And when Monday morning arrived, he pretended to be sick and pushed the meeting off until later in the week. He let it sink in a little more and strategized. Overthought it, probably.

The glazed porcelain witch fingers by Courtney Cone displayed on a 3-D printed, pink hand mannequin purchased from Instagram had been carried carefully and shut up in the bedroom. The oven-bake Sculpey face he'd crafted on his kitchen table that bored, second week of lockdown in the image of Jacques Tourneau's namesake *Night of the Demon*, too. The assorted skulls, candles, pentagrams and that little wire devil he'd found on the street outside of his LA apartment were small enough to be stowed in the nearby paraphernalia drawer. He sat there, imagining the objects pulsing, goading him on, as he swiveled in the hot seat.

Underneath these hidden and the lingering secular tchotchkes was a mildly ugly non-place of a room, refurbished for the times—gone was the brown, patterned motor lodge carpeting, which had recently made way for blanched gray fake-wood laminate, watercolor wallpaper and black plasticine ottomans. Inkjet canvases of beaches, buoys and clipart landscapes were grommeted implacably into the walls. He'd covered them swiftly. The scuffed brown particleboard furniture somehow stayed on. But it was all dusted in a layer of objects that touted an outré lifestyle, he was suddenly made distinctly aware in preparation for their arrival. It could be less than helpful in this moment, but his judgement of the church ladies perched before him seemed to outweigh theirs for him. As usual, the Catholics had won. But on this he'd wisely hedged his bets.

"You mentioned on Monday that you'd had progress in securing other support? Which is great news! Who else have you been speaking with to line up additional funding?"

"Yes! Well, I think I first told you when we spoke, I was able to get $500 from Slug Support, that's like the campus slush fund. On top of that I was able to get a new writing commission; that'll bring in $1,000 before the end of the month. I'm still waiting on a couple emails out to folks on campus . . ."

"And what," Sarah calculated, as she scrawled his figures on her pad, "is the total amount of your deficit?"

His phone hummed twice, quietly in his jeans, sending his thoughts below, momentarily, into the parking lot, where Sir idled. He hadn't expected them to be early.

"$2,430. Which is due in the next couple weeks. Or else I'll have to vacate the hotel and . . . I won't be able to register for classes."

"What are you studying?" Margot chimed in with a smile that wrinkled her mask. Clearly, she was a chaperoning to lighten the mood. Good cop.

"Um . . . film."

"That's exciting! What kinds of films do you make?"

"I'm more of a historian," he tread, carefully. "Of LGBT movies and also queer urban histories . . . I'm . . . I'll be working next quarter on the concepts of utopia and the sublime." He lifted up a very boring-looking history book up off of the desk, smiling through the banality it likely contained. But just as chuffed to have the prop on hand.

"Oh," Sarah joined in. "It sounds like it'll be a lot of psychology as well!"

"Absolutely. I have to read a lot of Freud and psychoanalysis. It's not really what I do, but it's sort of the backbone of my field."

Sarah was amused but carefully turned her eyes back to the page. She was cool, in a way that wasn't hip, but sturdy and plain. Regal, almost. She conducted herself with curiosity and a comfortable ease that disarmed the morning's anxiety. Her pillowy facemask had the faintest stitched in pattern. Her eyes were warm and her posture, good. She was clearly in charge, but she wielded this role without sternness. She surprised him when she offered, "we worked very closely with a Catholic therapy center, through our previous assign-ment, in Brooklyn."

When his face displayed surprise, she looked back to her pad. Not unfriendly, simply mindful of the time. "So . . ." she tapped, "what we usually do is write a check directly to your landlord for around $300 to $400, but I think . . . since there's an odd remainder here, $430 . . . it sounds like that would help close the gap?"

"I know that I can come up with the last $500. I really do try not to ask my family for money—they're both retired now—but I'm paid at the end of the month. And then I'd be able to register for the spring quarter."

Her lips pushed out her mask with a smile as she scanned the hotel room again. "Well, this is wonderful. It sounds like we've got a *real* plan!"

"It is funny," Margot chimed in again, "that the school sent you our way. Here, you're literally just one block within our congregational lines. The school isn't at all. Usually, we're more at service to the hospital."

He sensed the moment to lay it on thick. And gladly pounced. "You know, when the school sent me that list of outside organizations, I was just as surprised to see a Catholic charity on top. But, actually . . . my mom worked in Catholic health care. She was from New Jersey. And even though she brought me up atheist, I was always surrounded by nuns. Growing up. But they were always doing business with my mom. So, when I saw Holy Cross, I thought . . ."why not?!"

Sarah was still smiling through her mask. "And do you have a faith presently?"

He shot a playful grin at Margot, then moved his address to Sarah, "Do I still get the money?"

The ladies laughed.

* * *

Sir fingered the carabineer that he kept his keys on. Twelve or so. They all spooled down from the ignition pad of the muddy white Ford Focus. Fall Out Boy was on but he wasn't paying attention. He was fidgeting. Waiting. Horny. The playbag sat in the passenger's seat. Ready. He pumped his foot quickly on the car's caked floormat. He looked at his phone. Then out the window, around the underground parking lot, then back down at his phone. Repeat. Until it roared to life:

Jesus… okay! Sorry. They just left 11:03 a.m.

And then in quick succession

I'm ready for u, Sir 11:03 a.m.

But he was already slamming the door when this second iMessage added itself to their already sprawling feed. With the reusable tote slung over his right shoulder, he broke into a near-sprint towards the entrance above the lot. But the exit door that was usually locked swung open in front of him and a student moved blankly out of it, towards her car. Sir caught the door behind her and bounded up towards the lobby two stairs at a time.

Rounding a corner, he clipped the shoulder of an older woman who was heading in the opposite direction, downward, accompanied by a second, slightly taller friend. There, time froze, for just a beat. A flutter, long enough to register an admonishing glare from behind the downy mask of the companion.

"Oops" he emitted, as they collected themselves, ignoring his articulation and continuing on.

In front of the door to room 104 he used his index finger to rap two quick knocks and waited. The door lined the interior courtyard of the hotel. Decades prior, it had been an indoor pool, and no swatch of bad wallpaper could cover the 1970s dream of what once was. The glass pyramid-shaped roof had been designed to part and open out onto the stars. That utopia had long since been sealed up and the pool floored over with tiling, so all that remained was a railed, two floor proscenium and a stairwell that snaked down into the breakfast bar. All coming-and-going was public here, as twenty-or-so windows fed out into the courtyard and the front desk faced it, too.

He opened the door on Sir's devilish grin and purred, "Hello, Sir."

"Hey boy," Sir strut in.

They'd met via the apps. This was their fourth play session. Usually, they hung late at night, as Sir was coming home from a night out with friends. "The boy" didn't like this. He always preferred to prepare for a scene. Rinse. Eat no less than six hours before, to ensure optimal use of both holes. Good sex was a science. But he made some exceptions, because otherwise he was without.

Sir moved his hand fast around the small of "the boy's" back and loomed in, brusquely. Rather than launch into an immediate kiss, he held himself there, inches between them, and searched "the boy's" face, inhaling anticipation, heat, musk. His smile broadened still. Agreeably.

He moved in for the kiss, hard, which twisted into a bite of "the boy's" upper lip.

"The boy" had been nourished the past couple decades on big city gay life. New York, Los Angeles, San Francisco, London. And the speed and variety that pulse could provide. Shifting to the rhythm of this small town took time. And a toll. He had to take what he could get. The irony in this instance was that seventeen years separated them, *not* in "the boy's" favor. But sex games contain a rhetoric so often untouched by humor. And they fell easy enough into this scene.

As was their custom, "the boy" dropped to his knees fast and Sir unbuttoned his olive cargo shorts. The dick was good. Seven inches, not too big, not small, and thick. "The boy" set to work then, swallowed the thing in full, adeptly. Taking it all the way down in a gulp. Sir smiled and let out a gratified chuckle.

"Good boy."

After several minutes of groaning, Sir used the utilitarian brown hiking sneaker that was still on his foot to nudge at the Trader Joe's play bag. "You ready?" he menaced down at "the boy."

Menaced is a word. Though in this scenario it proved perhaps a funny fit. Sir's youth mattered only somewhat. "The boy" was making peace with negotiation of this stacked economy. But Sir had also been shy to share his kink with "the boy. It took two sessions before Sir tested the waters.

6:05 p.m. This question is kinda weird, and you can totally say no but please don't be weirded out by me.

I'm intrigued 6:05 p.m.

6:05 p.m. Have you heard of the looner fetish?

I have not 6:05 p.m.

6:06 p.m. Damn haha

6:06 p.m. I don't like explaining it.

6:09 p.m. But essentially it's a fetish for balloons or inflatables. Using them for sexual purposes. I have a looner fetish and I have never been able to play with another person because I asked someone to try it once and they got weirded out and ghosted me. So I have been to nervous to talk about it with anyone. And the looner community is oddly exclusive and if you're not an internet content creator you're essentially not invited to any looner parties or meetups and it's hard to find em online.
　If you're interested in it let me know but no pressure.

I like to make my Sir happy 6:10 p.m.

6:10 p.m. Do you have any questions about it? I'm sure you're confused

Not confused 6:11 p.m.

I don't know what it is that you like done with them 6:11 p.m.

6:12 p.m. Let me see if I can find a good article explaining it, otherwise I might have to send some of my more spicy videos . . .

I looked online 6:12 p.m.

But tell me what you like. There's nothing to be embarrassed about 6:12 p.m.

6:26 p.m. Haha well . . . I'm not embarrassed as much as I don't know how to explain it. I can see why other people may not be into it, as we all experience sexual pleasure differently. I definitely have a lot of balloon fun on my own when I can get the house to myself, but I have never played with another person so the experience would be a bit different. When I'm on my own I get the most pleasure from blowing em up till they are tight, with a bit of a neck to them, and then tying them off and fucking them or sitting on them until they pop. I find people really attractive when they're blowing them up, sometimes till they pop, but I haven't been able to bring myself to that point yet, as it's kind of scary . Certain forms of popping can take some people time to get used to, so I wouldn't necessarily want to force you into it that far but if you're interested, could I maybe watch you blow one up while it's in between my thighs and you can tie it off and we could hump it for a little and then we can go back to what we usually do? Just so you can test the waters and if you don't like it, we don't have to do it again, but if you do, maybe we can incorporate it a little more into our fun time?

The next time they met was the first time they'd incorporated *the bag*.

"The boy" was game, however! He'd happily taken part in weirder shit. And while he was respectful of Sir's kink, he presently wondered if there was intentional irony in the fact that Sir's gear was stowed in a big-top themed grocery bag, illustrated with Trader Joe's signature tradesman (Joe?), floating away in a hot air balloon.

Sir removed the limp colorful forms like a kid at Christmas and blew them up, handing them to "the boy" one by one. But "the boy" hadn't really know what to do with them. He moaned and played the part. He surrounded himself with them on the California king hotel bed and clutched at them under his palms while they basically jumped right back into the same sexual scenario they'd played out two times prior. Just, now, there were pink, blue, green, and black balloons bouncing about the sheets.

He imagined himself in that web meme, "Cake Farts," where the bored brunette in a nondescript American kitchen flirts without affect into the camera as she lets her hair down: "What do I like the most? Cake farts. Mmmm." He made the balloons creek with contact and he performed moaning while he did so, stealing grabs at his twenty-one-year-old Sir's body, but his own arousal never really arrived. He started to feel inadequate. He was a bad liar.

He texted a request for more guidance before their next session.

Still on his knees "the boy" looked up and searched Sir's desire for next steps.

Sir lifted one foot towards him, gesturing for "the boy" to remove his shoes and he did. Then, the socks and the rest of his clothes. He thought back to all the tutorial vids that Sir had texted him that week, solo camera phone movies of balloon-sitting, blowing and popping, cumming on the stretchy latex. He looked up again.

Sir lifted the bag and turned, walking over to the polka dot covered couch. "Halloween circus." He placed the bag on the cushion then turned to face "the boy." He sat, naked, and padded on his lap for him to join. "The boy" obliged and slid one knee on either side of his, their faces coming together, close while Sir withdrew a white balloon from the bag.

"Blow this up."

Now, "the boy" was not a boy and had no children or much interest in their customs so he hadn't blown up a balloon in a good twenty years. The first attempt brought him beyond embarrassment. And the scene broke for a moment, as both laughed genuinely.

"It's harder than it looks."

"Fuck," but after a few tries he found traction. The white thing swelled up in front of him and Sir's breath got thick.

"Yeah, boy . . . " his eyes were wide. "The boy" wriggled his fingers around the balloon's nape and clumsily tied it.

"Get back on your knees," Sir commanded as he placed the white balloon beneath his thighs. "And keep going."

Another red balloon. He was getting the hang of it. He released it from his fingers and it dropped it onto the couch where it rode a current of static from the polyester sheet onto the floor.

Then another. And another.

Sir jerked himself, ferociously in front of him. His thighs starting to sweat where they clung to the balloon. He was panting hard, pupils wide.

"The boy" looked around the room as he dropped a blue balloon to the floor. The room that was still censored for his prior guests. Was that really only twenty minutes ago? Vintage gay porn videocassettes, the Joe Gage working man's trilogy, which usually sat underneath the living room flatscreen—more as décor, really—had been whisked away first and stacked up in the bedroom (*Kansas City Trucking Company*, *El Paso Wrecking Corp.*, and *LA Tool & Die*), where they were joined by James Bidgood books and one by Tabboo! He picked up another balloon. And so he continued, for some time, until, again, he began to get bored. This wasn't his kink. Maybe it was a little selfish, but he needed to escalate things a bit. For his own amusement.

Sir was clearly having a ball. He jerked and huffed. "The boy" traveled back in time to the last session, channeling "Cake Farts." The absurdly leaden "ooos" and "aaaahs" of the video. And how that became his interiority. It was up to him to make this fun for both of them. This time, he decided, he'd take on a more empowered surrogate. He decided he'd go full Sharon Stone. Nothing changed really in the way that he moved, but a bloom opened behind his eyes. The mood in his room shifted. He locked eyes with Sir, anew. He held still for a moment.

Then, very theatrically, he extended his index finger and moved it slowly downward, towards the white balloon on which Sir bucked. He traced a circle around curvature twice. Tugged at the little, knotted nipple a little, pinching between that stretched out finger and thumb. He kept Sir's gaze throughout this, and his eyes widened almost imperceptibly as he moved in with one forceful push and a loud pop echoed around the room.

His sensorium was struck by two adverse stimuli. There was the feeling of wet heat and warmth, as Sir's sperm gushed on his front like a crazed geyser, rushing in droplets literally all over the fucking place as he fell back onto the couch, convulsing in pleasure.

And then there was the knock. Three, actually, in quick succession.

Both things happened as if causally.

His head jerked to Sir, who was still convulsing, with a very distanced look in his eyes. One arm snapped up, tight in on his chest, as spasms quaked through his frame. "The boy" squeezed the top of Sir's muscular thigh with a weird smile, as much check in as it was tic of achievement.

That's when Sir emitted the simple warning, "oh no . . . oh no . . ." and then, like the balloons a few moments before, rolled off of the polka dotted couch and spilled onto the floor, taking the coffee table down with him. Its contents scattered all around the room.

"Fuck!" shouted "the boy." He knelt down to examine the body now splayed out on the grey laminate flooring. "Fuck," he repeated as the Sir's spasms grew more intense. He attempted to hold the body that shook beneath him. He used two fingers to lift Sir's eyes open, to find what he could see there. But after years of procedural viewing, he realized then that the professionals never really spoke aloud what they're looking for as they did this automatically, so he gave up there.

He heard that if you shout the name of someone into their face during similarly drug induced states, it can rouse them. And with that he realized, "I don't even know his name." He had only ever been informed to address him as Sir.

"Sir?" he tried, dubiously. It came out far more of a question than a command.

Then the knocking at the door started again.

"What the fuck," he shout-whispered into the room. Into this scene. And he slowly abandoned Sir to attend to the door.

Through the peephole he found Margot standing with her hands held at her lap, staring at the door intently, still. Waiting, polite but impatiently.

He swallowed hard. Sir's foot flailed behind him, kicking at a balloon that rolled all the way across the floor.

"Um . . . don't . . . die?" he turned and said stupidly to Sir. And then he scanned the room again, until his eyes landed on Margot's floral padded folio, which had gone down with the coffee table and skidded into a corner.

"Fuuuuuuuuuck," said "the boy" to the world as he reeled, thinking quick on his feet. Sir was hot. In shape, but not totally muscular. Still, he was 6'2" way bigger than "the boy" who was 5'7". He had the average anti-fashion of a male nerd who lived in small town in his early twenties. Maybe a hair more eccentric. When they first met up his brown curly hair had pink tips that trailed off into the golden fade of a bad bleach job months prior. He worked outdoors and had a degree in Adventure Tourism, which "the boy" didn't even know existed until they'd bedded. It was a perfect cover for Sir's sexual predilection, "the boy" had thought. But it turned out that this really meant that Sir spent his waking hours sending nearby office groups and corporate clients through zipline trails across the redwoods. Still, it kept him not muscley, but built.

He knelt down beside Sir. "Wake up! I need you to wake up," he begged, but there was no response just the jerks that were more spaced out now, and somehow deeper. Each second bringing greater and greater intervals. "What the fuck . . ." he padded his face, a few times, but very lightly.

Nothing.

Then a third trio of knocks.

"Um . . . um . . . um . . ." "The boy" sped into motion as if the movement was automatic, snaking one arm around Sir's chest from behind, and then reaching the other under the opposite pit. He was gonna lift him. He realized this to himself while he was doing it. He let out a strained, guttural noise as his muscles heaved from Sir's weight. That, he was sure, Margot had heard. Don't stop now. But neither could manage the lift.

Fortunately, carpet was no longer a thing in interior design and it proved possible, he found, to slide Sir along the floor slowly, pushing the mess that had been made of the coffee table out of his way as together they traced a long, arduous snail trail to the bathroom. It was only like ten feet, but this morning it felt a mile. Sir's unconscious body, still sweaty from the sex and from his contact with the latex, screeched as it was pulled along the laminate flooring. Each tug found a new pitch. Some just a rolling shudder.

Then the hotel phone rang, which made "the boy" burst into an uncontrollable laugh. His heart was in his throat. He stopped what he was doing. He went back to the peephole.

"The light changes when you look out!" he thought to himself. But he was too panicked to chase the thought. He found Margot still standing there but her head was bowed. She was texting.

"Sarah." He whispered aloud. Suddenly caught with a different sort of brevity. The blood drained from his face as he was hit with a sudden pang. Illogically, he felt like he was letting her down.

She was probably at the front desk now. And bad seed was calling to see if he was still "home." He felt an unrealistic pathos about this moment. Then the spell broke and he leapt over to the prostrate body he'd been skidding along the floor and made some terrible strained momentary heaves until he finally slumped it across the threshold, through the door to the inordinately massive bathroom.

Still whirring on instinct, he sprang the shower lever open and tore off all his clothes. (He was still dressed?) He doused his face and chest in water, tossed on a towel and jumped out the door, leaving Sir slumped over on the cold tile. Sorry Sir.

He fumbled with the chain, that prohibited the door from opening fully and slid his form so that it filled the slight vantage that the ajar door made for Margot.

"Margot!" he exclaimed hoping he sounded pleasantly stunned and not like some soap actor. His towel crooked across his waist. "Sorry, I just jumped out of the shower."

"There you are! I was beginning to worry we might have somehow missed . . ." she trailed off when she took in his face. Her voice suddenly sounded of genuine concern. "Is everything alright?"

* * *

After he managed to slip Sir into the shower and splash some water over him, he roused. "Oh . . . shit. Sorry," he made light. "I . . . have Tourette's and if I don't take my meds . . . and I get overly excited . . ." he trailed off. "The boy's" brows arched as he listened.

"Sorry."

Sir toweled himself dry and slipped back into his clothes. Left. The next time "the boy" texted him, his iMessage went green. He'd been blocked.

Miguel Gutierrez

Camboy Poems

BCM

He looks like he's had cheekbone implants, but it's just his face. His lips are always wet because he licks them a lot. He starts slowly on his bed, t-shirt on, smoking a spliff. His eyes get heavy from how stoned he is. There's a massive portrait of Amy Winehouse above his bed painted in thick strokes of purple, lilac, burgundy, blue, and black. It's hideous. He welcomes guys as they enter, casually, betraying no excitement, but you feel seen. You almost forget why he's there in the first place, but then you see the tip scales in the chat interface on the right and left quarters of the screen. When tips trigger the "lovense," his anal toy, you begin to understand his appeal. His breaths deepen, stop in intervals that match the rhythmic intensity of the vibrations, and come out in choked exhales like he's bearing down on something, giving birth to pleasure. His breaths echo the rise and fall of the pulses and indicate that desire is an inside job. You don't even see the toy for most of the session. After he hits the first tip goal, the shirt comes off. Eventually, his massive dick comes into view. Big, but not freakishly big. He cinches it with his fist like a tourniquet, distending the shaft into pinks and purples that stand out against his pale white skin. His jet black hair and eyebrows make the white whiter. He's a sex ghost. He's the only one I watch who's not in Colombia. He's in Spain. It makes his casual authority more upsetting. I submit to his conquering nature and he knows he's in charge, even when I'm in control with the tips. His favorite tip amounts are 101 tokens (32 seconds of wave-like pulses), 111 tokens (35 seconds of jagged, cliff-like pulses), and 222 tokens (75 seconds of increasing pulses). This last one shows him at his most virtuosic. Every cell in his body becomes carnal. For over a minute he's suspended in an undulating contraction that shapes his arms, chest, belly, and upper legs into a cartography of soft ridges. He's fit as fuck, but human. He's lap dancing the air above him. He closes his eyes. He's riding a funicular of sensation up orgasm mountain. The mountain is endlessly tall. Once the tips come in more regularly, he beats himself off ferociously for what seems like forever. I've never seen a guy who can resist cumming for so long while jerking off that intensely. It's not even edging, it's something else. Time loops and repeats into a promise of self-perpetuating ecstasy. Once he hits the final tip goal, he opens a private room for the top tippers where he extends the ride even further. His impossibly high cheekbones flush red and sweat parts his hair into athletic strands, like it's a soccer match, a fucking World Cup of delayed gratification. When he finally ejaculates, it's disappointing. For how epic the build up is, you'd think the computer screen would crack from the buckets, waterfalls, river rapids of cum. But nothing special happens. He cums, we cum, and Amy watches all of it, deader than ever.

JD

I don't feel drawn to twinks in daily life, but he calls to me through the screen. He cams from a small white room with metal beams that run across the ceiling. A blue, satin curtain, embroidered with silvery flowers, hangs over the window from the ceiling to the floor. I've never seen sunlight sneak around the edges. It could be a basement for all I know. So many of these rooms feel like they exist out of time, or like they're stuck in perpetual night. He must have a colored light under his desk, because the lower part of the wall shines pink as if the room were slightly submerged in a pool at a rave. Like BCM, he has a poster up, some of the same colors even. This one's a Buddha that looks like it glows in the dark. The room is so generic, the wimpy design gestures making it more so. It's probably a hotel. A lot of the cam work there happens in hotels that studios rent and sublease to models. Apparently it's worth it for them because the internet is stable and sometimes there are behind-the-scenes staff who give real time suggestions to get better tips. JD claims he's independent, presumably unmonitored, but I'm not convinced. How do you claim that you're not being surveilled when the whole job is about surveillance? Early on I found out he has a thing for older guys, or maybe it's that he sniffed out that I'm an older guy and shaped his responses accordingly. No, the start of it all was that I asked him to share a link of what he watches while he's working, and it was daddy/son porn. I swooned and decided it meant that we have a Connection. I responded with links of my own and with each click he smiled and said "Wooooow," all wide eyed and happy, like it was fireworks. One day I spent a good five minutes trying to understand why his profile photos are so pale when in "person" his tone is earthier. Not brown but a warm beige. You could imagine him laying out in the sun on a rock by the lake. You'd turn the corner from the trail to see him and think, "Who is that adorable, carefree looking boy sunning himself on a rock by the lake?" He has a curly fauxhawk, but he covers it with a cap, which gives him the allure of a skater boy, a classic erotic trope. Again, not something I've ever cared for but desire is a riddle. He positions his camera from below to accentuate his inner thighs and crotch, which are hairier than his upper body would suggest. His profile says he's in Bogotá, which comforts me, because I fear what might happen to him in a smaller town, though maybe it's different now. Maybe now in a smaller city like Altamira or Neiva you can be an overalls-wearing, femmy queer skater boy with a leather collar around your neck and no one bats an eye. His alleged excitement about bears and older guys emboldened me to do cam2cam with him once. I set myself up in what I imagined was the most favorable angle, aping his - leaning back in the chair, camera low, legs wide. "JD has started viewing your cam" flashed in the private chat and he let out another "Wooooow." I have no idea if he actually kept watching me or just clicked back to porn. But cam2cam only costs thirty tokens per minute and I told myself this was the kind of affirmation worth draining my cache for. The models only make about five cents per token, so during cam2cam they only make a buck fifty a minute, less than the cost of a phone sex line in the 80s.

CF

He's the most baby-faced of the lot, though he's not the youngest. Like several others, he has multiple screens in front of him, and the one where he reads private messages is different from the one he uses as the camera. He's also the second most pale, after BCM, but his skin is less blue white and more yellow white, like a faint jaundice. He has light brown hair, almost ginger. He sends private messages as soon as you join his room, and if you write him back, he responds vocally in heavily accented English. He rounds his vowels like a Russian who went to an English boarding school in Mongolia, stopping at the dentist's along the way. "Would you like to see my ass?" becomes "Wowed yow luhayck tew si mohay ayssss?" It's enough to kill the whole vibe, save for the fact that he does have a very beautiful ass and I do want to see it. My goal with him is to keep it non-verbal, though I made the mistake of asking him to call me daddy early on in our conversations, so now anything he does in response to my tips is punctuated with a "Dew yow luhayck daht, DEADdeey?" like he's plotting my murder through the screen. I hate it. So I tip him at the blowjob level in the hopes of keeping his mouth otherwise occupied. And while his big blue eyes are mesmerizing as he fellates the pink plastic dick, he still manages to get his death threats in - "Ayh lowf feehllingh yowrrh deekh ihn moy mowf, DEADdeey!" Each guy has their own signature set of skills. His includes inserting the dildo into his ass using his heel. There's a mind/body intelligence to it. He locks the dildo into place with his foot while he rides it. If the dildo plops out, his heel is there to redirect it back to his compliant hole. The mechanics are embodied. One time he suctioned the dildo onto the large, full-length mirror to the side of his bed and fucked himself that way, body and reflection in an accordion repeat of a long playing fucknote. He's so pretty but he doesn't have as many viewers as I'd expect. I think maybe it's the talking and the fact that he cums so fast. The small viewership means he always knows when I enter the room. I feel self-conscious about leaving once I'm there because I want to be a good audience member. But the numbers don't lie. He's a little boring.

SK

I feel a rush of excitement when he's online, because he's the least affected performer and most naturally sexual. He's the darkest skinned, a true moreno. His body is muscled and supple like the finqueros I used to lust over when I was a kid, if one of them had been a tattooed sex god. His shape and body hair placement evoke the Golden Mean. Everything's in perfect proportion. The Greeks would have loved him. He was the first one I noticed had a tip level where you can pay him to dance for you. I was resistant - I'm so judgmental about dancing, what if I didn't like the way he moved? I took a chance. He stood up and body rolled against the gaming chair as if I was sitting in it and I nearly came. Then he went to the doorway, leaned against it and folded his knee up like Tawny Kitaen in Whitesnake's Here I Go Again video. It shouldn't have worked, but it did. One time his mic inadvertently delayed his voice, turning his moans into a tapered echo. It was like a sex party at an experimental music venue. Yoko Ono for perverts. Of all the boys, he's the least distracted by messages and he's the least coy about cumming. No exclusive ticket offers or cat and mouse play with his followers. He doesn't even list particular tip goals. You could fool yourself into thinking he just does it for the fun of it, camming for camming's sake. All of a sudden, he's just cumming, jetting thick streaks into the air that plop onto his chest like wet ropes from the sky. Sometimes he seems surprised by his own ejaculatory power, though that's impossible because he's done this at least hundreds of times. Acting is being I guess. Sometimes he keeps going and, with all of the spontaneity of a miracle at Lourdes, he cums again. Same amount. How does his body do this? He either has the shortest resolution period ever or his orgasm manifests in serial form. He should be studied. If lustiness is a thing, he's been given too much of it. He could tour the world, literally disseminating. I start the planning for him: "You should come to the U.S. and work as a gogo boy!" I write in the private chat. He responds simply: "Oh yeah?" His approach to engagement is always genuine but minimal, which only proves my point further. He would do great here.

NH

So many assholes on the site, one after the other, like milestones on a highway. They blend into each other, but I notice differences between them - the starburst of wrinkles that surround the hole, or the pigmentation, or the different levels of yield each one has. NH is on another level when it comes to his anus. He has total control of its dilation and can will it to any size. And there's always something in his ass. He alternates between a large vibrator he can absorb into his rectum like a party trick and an array of dildos that line shelves across his back wall in varying sizes, like trophies in some alternate world where the only sport is bottoming. With his big dick and flexible sphincter, he complicates gender prescriptions regarding penetration and receptivity. I wonder what Andrea Dworkin would have made of this guy. I don't even know what I make of him. I draw him the most because he fascinates, titillates, and repulses me. I aspire to his level of anal elasticity. I also envy his ability to stay as hard as he does while so much activity occupies his backside. He's slim -- ninety percent of his blood flow must be in his enormous dick. I also draw him the most because when he sits back and lifts his bare feet to the camera, he's in a perfect one point perspective pose. His feet loom large and smooth, shiny from the abundance of lube that spatters to the ground while he furiously fucks himself as if his whole family were hostage and the only way to free them was dildo play. His handsome face recedes and becomes the point in the drawing, a sun on the horizon. Tattoos of cats, flowers, and vines adorn his arms, chest, and legs. He has the word "Sacrifice" written in script just south of his collarbone. His skin approaches ochre, a shade that registers as white-ish in South America and of-color in the north. He has symmetrical diagonal lines shaved into both eyebrows, like a Colombian Vanilla Ice. But back to his gravity sucking wormhole. I wouldn't be surprised to find Borges' infinite library in there or the string corridors of interstellar space, where Matthew McConaughey calls to baby Jessica Chastain across time and a bookshelf. I've always theorized about how being a performer you're mostly caught up in the subjective experience of interiority, how so much of what you experience on stage as the agent of the work is invisible to the audience. NH turns theory into practice in ways I could never conceive. His body is a site of new knowledge regarding internal/external perceptual relations. Surprisingly he doesn't ever fist himself. Or if he does, I haven't seen it. Which is a relief, because I couldn't handle the strangeness of thinking that the list of everything he can consume includes himself.

D_

One of the cam boys has a Twitter page where he wrote: "As Colombians, we actually only have four options: 1. Work at a call center. 2. Be a cam boy. 3. Live abroad as a waiter or nanny. 4. Work in the field that we studied and earn shit pay." The most entrepreneurial of the cam boys work for themselves, and in that world, D_ is Elon Musk. He's the most unabashedly capitalist, and the most convinced of his own ability to succeed. I'm pretty sure he's straight, even though he can keep up anally with the best of them. He jerks off so fast that his forearm blurs like a hummingbird's wings. He also makes the most dramatic facial expressions, which would be more off putting if he weren't so undeniably suited to the job in body and spirit. He's very white, the kind of white that gets leading roles in the telenovelas my mom loves. I used to watch him a lot at first, but I almost never do now. He's been doing it so long that every gesture looks too studied. Not that his energy has flagged at all. It's the curse of this particular job. Even if you're not into it you still have to be turned on enough to be hard. Maybe it's his drive that keeps him going. His Amazon wish list is astonishing: five synthesizers, four midi pads, two drones, five digital cameras, ten lenses, sexy underwear, sexy bathing suits, sexy singlets, sexy tights, sexy police costumes, a leather harness, professional grade headphones, Harry Potter box sets (three of them), illustrated Harry Potter books, multiple action figures from the Harry Potter series, two Harry Potter PlayStation games, a Harry Potter chess game, a box set of Game of Thrones, a box set of The Hobbit and Lord of the Rings, a box set of The Witcher, a box set of Goosebumps, a travel mattress, four Kitchenaid blenders, three gold watches, acrylic paint, a Santa Claus bathrobe, at least ten different cosplay costumes, swords, LED visors, a DJ deck, and three different cookbooks that focus on artisan bread. (He's a Sagittarius.)

Liara Roux

Cantaloupe Tits

My girlfriend Gabby was easy to resent because she had grown more popular than me over the years. She was sort of a loser our freshman year at Columbia, but I was *the* famous lesbian. My senior year of high school, I had gone viral after throwing bloody tampons at that bigoted loser senator Lindsey Graham. It was a total condemnation of his homophobia, his racism, sexism, etc.

Soon I was penning political screeds that were featured in the Huffington Post and Jezebel and made the rounds amongst the politically engaged youth of Twitter, Tumblr, and Facebook—social justice warriors, we were called, a name we welcomed. By the time I arrived at Columbia the student newspaper was eager to have me on board as a regular columnist. The ladies loved me. I had frizzy hair and wore shirts with edgy political slogans, was known for getting drunk at dorm room parties and sleeping with a new girl every weekend.

Gabby didn't go to these parties. She was in my Literature Humanities class, quiet, soft spoken, brutal and rigorous in her thought. I would overhear her talking with her friends at the library, arguing about Derrida. She seemed totally uninterested in me. She didn't even friend me on Facebook, like most of the other lesbians at school did. A personal offense.

She was dating Selene, a piano prodigy who had first played at Carnegie Hall at the age of fifteen. So when Selene was drunk and raucous at that weekend's party, I knew I had to take my revenge. I bedded Selene that night. It wasn't hard, and I relished the thrum of her talented fingers against my G-spot.

Selene and Gabby broke up soon after; I'll never admit it publicly but gave myself credit for that. Soon after, Gabby and I ended up at a gallery show in the Lower East Side. She was tipsy on free wine, flushed, chatting with the artist about the movement and the color in her pieces. Smooth as ever, I inserted myself into the conversation.

"Love the social commentary in your work," I gestured around the room, "Very bold."

The artist smiled blandly and thanked me. Gabby gave me a look that felt hard and thuddy like a thick wooden plank. Underneath her analytical gaze, I started to worry she knew about what happened with Selene. I dialed up the charm.

"I'm Emily," I purred, my hand out with surrender.

"Gabby," she took my hand in hers, holding it a little longer than might be necessary. Her hands were supple, strong, with delicate bones; a sensual grasp.

We talked and talked, tipsy as we walked to a ramen spot nearby. She ate like a maniac, slurping her noodles with abandon as she told me about a paper she was working on. She was so engrossed that her glossy brown hair dipped into the broth as she spoke, and I pulled it out for her. She smiled at me, eyes dilated from the dim lights and the booze. Our kisses were messy, her mouth all salt and umami from the ramen.

Rain had appeared so we huddled under my umbrella as I tried to hail a cab. I would take her to my family's empty apartment on Central Park East—that would surely wow her. Gabby is not from money, not like I am. Her parents are certainly comfortable, but they only had two homes. My family is *connected*. My aunt is a big-time movie producer in Hollywood. My cousin is engaged to a Kennedy. My first boyfriend, before I came out, was the grandson of a Supreme Court justice.

A flick of annoyance as little wet drops hit the back of my neck; she was crowding me out of the umbrella. Then there was a car; tumbling and wet we arrived in the humid backseat. We made out as he drove up the east side highway. It was late and the streets were nearly empty. Looking over at the Brooklyn skyline, this is exactly how I had always thought life would be.

We hurried into my building as I dug for my keys, scooting past the faintly disapproving doorman. Pretentious dick that he was, thinking working for all this old money made him worth anything more than his silence and loyalty, as though he was some sort of arbiter of taste. In the elevator I kissed her, grabbed her boob until she pushed me away.

"What if the doorman is watching the camera?"

"Oh, he's seen worse," I laughed, "Much worse."

She eyed me suspiciously, looking almost like my mother. I pulled her to me again, through the opening doors of the elevator, through the dim apartment to my bed. She was on top of me, straddling me, and slapped me on the face.

"Behave," she put her thumb on my bottom lip.

"Yes, Mommy," my bravado gone, leaving me suddenly bashful and squirming.

Broad smiles. We were on the same wavelength. She knelt down, tore off my pants and my underwear, and buried her face in my bush. I pressed myself into her and she drew back.

"No," she pushed me away, back into the bed, "I want to tease you first."

I had always thought of myself as a top, but that first night we fucked, Gabby outtopped me. At first, I struggled for control, hoping to bend her to my will, but she eventually pinned me down and fucked me so hard I was left mind empty. I liked it. She was small but mighty, and when she draped her arm around my shoulders, I understood exactly why girls liked masculine men. I felt exquisitely feminine. Finally the little spoon.

We fell asleep like that, her cradling me, protective and strong—me nestled into her like a baby. The sun woke me up before her. She was naked in my sheets, disheveled hair somehow elegant. I made us espresso in the kitchen. She must have woken while I was gone; she was looking out the window at the park. Morning light fell against her cheekbones, and I saw, perhaps because she was finally silent, that she was truly beautiful.

"Coffee?" I asked, handing her a cup.

She sipped it thoughtfully.

"Very Italian," she smiled up at me.

Oh Gabby! So easy to impress; almost too easy. She made scrambled eggs in the kitchen while I stared at her ass. The eggs were surprisingly good, fluffy and rich with cheese. There was a question I wanted to ask; how would she take it?

"Can I dress you in my mother's clothes? Or would that be too weird?"

She smirked.

My mother's clothes hang awkwardly on me, but they fit Gabby perfectly. She tried on one of my mother's old sundresses, a piece she hadn't worn since I was little. She grinned into the mirror. We strolled through the park, everything fresh and green after the rain. Daffodils everywhere.

"Where are your parents?"

"My mother is off with her lady friends in Spain and my father is with his mistress in Los Angeles."

I kicked at the smooth pebbles underfoot.

"I bet your mom is fucking all her friends," Gabby laughed.

"Don't say that."

I was suddenly cross, turning around, heading back.

"Sorry," Gabby apologized, helpless at the sudden change in weather.

"S'alright."

We walked silently back to the apartment.

Despite swearing I wouldn't get into a relationship freshman year, Gabby and I had something. Everyone saw it. Because of my celebrity status, we became *the* lesbian It couple. It was like my raucous behavior shone a spotlight on quiet, determined Gabby by my side. Suddenly, everyone wanted her.

She started going to those weekend dorm room parties with me and would bring along her acoustic guitar. She said it gave her something to do. I would roll my eyes, finding it trite, but everyone loved it. They loved her, that warm dark voice, and those strong fingers.

That summer Gabby met my mother, who was finally back in town after her misery tour of Europe, which she had embarked on after discovering my father's latest affair; she leapt at any excuse to ignore him for a few months. The three of us went to Café Sabarsky; my palms were sweating so much they left marks on my pants. Never before had my mother met a girl I was fucking; when I had come out to her in high school, she had lost it.

"Everyone has moments like that," she had lectured me, "*Everyone.* Once, when I was your age, my best friend kissed me in the stables, after we were done riding. That doesn't make me a *dyke.*"

But Gabby was charming, and my mother saw that when we sat side by side, she smoothed my rough edges, made me just a little more palatable. When Gabby was away in the bathroom, she put her hand on my knee and told me, for the first time in my life, she was proud of me. Typical of my mother to appreciate me only for someone else.

Whenever she was over, Gabby's gaze would linger on particular objects in my childhood home: the carefully preserved first editions ensconced in walnut bookshelves, the elegant oriental rugs, the generous views of Central Park. She was careful never to say anything or act too impressed. But she very clearly *was*.

She benefitted more than either of us could have guessed from my showing her off; someone recorded Gabby during one of her little drunken dorm room performances and sent it to their cousin, who was working at a record label. She was buzzing with excitement when she told me they wanted her to come in, play some of the songs she had been working on, record some demos.

My mouth frowned involuntarily. How could I explain to her that she would never be successful, that the only reason she glimmered at all was reflected light: the light I threw on her, illuminating her. Didn't she remember she was invisible before she met me?

But it was better for the guys at the record company to let her down.

"That's great," I said, "Just don't get your hopes up. I don't want you to get hurt."

It turned out she shone just fine without me. They loved her, in fact, they thought she could make it big time. They wanted her to drop out of college and focus on putting out an album, but she refused. She wanted to get her degree. She thought she could do both and so suddenly she was impossibly busy, writing her papers and her songs. I fought with her, angry that she no longer had time for me like she used to.

"I know this is hard, babe, but we'll get through it."

So, I threw myself into my schoolwork and began seeing other girls, privately, on the side. Gabby left me lonely and horny one too many nights; her mistake, as there were many ladies eager to pass an afternoon with me in bed. I got an internship working for the *New York Times*, my dream. My writing became more polished, less juvenile screed. I wanted to push the Gray Lady to the left, but elegantly.

Gabby would come over and we would sit on my bed in our pajamas, coffees on the nightstands, writing and writing and writing. We'd swap computers and read each other's work. I put a couple key lines in her songs, fidgeting with the wording until it was just right. In just a few months, her album was wrapped up, about to be released, and she was nauseous with anxiety. She kept pacing and leaning on the wall.

"It's so bad," she would say, "My god, it's so bad. The reviews will be so bad. What was I thinking?"

I would hug her and nuzzle her and give her some tea.

"I have a friend who works at Pitchfork, do you want me to put in a good word?"

She looked up at me, eyes open and vulnerable, like she was grasping directly at my soul.

"Would you?"

The album was quite well received, and I luxuriated in bed as she read the glowing Pitchfork review back to me.

"Thank you," she said, hugging me tight.

The next two years at school were a tight routine; we would work our asses off at school, she would write her next album, and I was freelancing on the side, racking up prestigious bylines. At the end of the year, she would release her album, then tour all summer. She was no superstar, but she had a deeply loyal fanbase. Some of her fans started following me on Twitter, would blog about us on Tumblr. #goals. They loved the two of us *together*.

We both got a little blue check mark by our names within a week of each other and went out to get omakase to celebrate. When the bill came, I grabbed at it out of habit, but Gabby stopped me.

"I want to pay it," she said, "You always get it. My turn."

Something cold in the back of my throat wriggled and squirmed.

Our senior year was when people started to really recognize Gabby on the street. Usually they would just look at her oddly, as if they thought she might be someone they knew. Some of them, though, knew exactly who she was and would rush to greet her.

Most of her fans were younger lesbians and she was usually kind and motherly towards them. Sometimes she would stop whatever she was doing, get coffee with them, listen to their pathetic sob stories about their parents rejecting them. She would nod and nod. Some of her fans were a little too obsessed; those ones hated me. They would tweet mean things at me on Twitter and I had to block them. Gabby would apologize, what could she do?

I leaned heavier into my writing, combative and angry. My new beat was tech; I wrote huffily about Facebook and Google destroying the world. I skewered the gender discrepancies in their offices. Emily Adams, verbal vigilante, that was me. I began to develop a healthy following myself, attracting just about anyone who felt threatened by the young, hotshot startup boys.

Gabby would sometimes get upset when she would see me hunched over my laptop, angrily typing out another viral Twitter thread.

"Let's go outside," she would tug at me, "Let's get lunch, let's go for a walk."

But I was glued, amassing followers at a rapid rate. Every now and then someone accused me of being addicted to the social media companies I loved to berate; this earned them an instant block. What better way to bring down these douchebags than proliferating my message through their platforms?

After I really nailed the formula for viral tweets, I convinced Gabby to let me workshop hers. Little jokes about being lesbian, New York, food, whatever. One of the tweets got hundreds of thousands of likes and I felt calm for the first time in months. I smiled as I watched her follower count tick higher and higher. At her record release party, she thanked me during her toast.

"To Emily, my guardian angel, without whom I would still be buried in a book deep in the library."

I felt superior as I sipped my champagne.

The record was a runaway success. People had said indie rock was over, but Gabby was single handedly bringing it back. Dozens of acts imitating her soft butchy aesthetic started popping up. She went on tour and kissed me goodbye, telling me to hold it down for her in New York. That was when I started being really bad.

Before, I had only been sleeping with girls as one-night stands, drunken encounters where I slipped out of their beds before morning. Now I was sliding into everyone's DMs. I would wake up to ten new messages, sometimes more. There were a couple girls in particular who made it into my regular rotation. My favorite was Samantha.

Sammy was fifteen. I met her on Tinder, where her bio said she was eighteen. She had big green eyes and big tits the size of small cantaloupes. She knew about my writing and about my girlfriend, Gabby, and said the first time we met up that she thought it was so cool that we were in an open relationship—no need to correct her. She was curled up on my sofa, sipping herbal tea. Her hair was frizzy and her skin was breaking out; she told me she was a freshman at NYU and even though she looked young, I didn't question it.

When I sat beside her, she threw herself at me, biting my lip so hard it bled. Jesus Christ, I cursed, and wiped it with my hand.

"Don't do that."

"Sorry," she looked down.

I cupped her face in my hands until she made eye contact with me again and then I kissed her, resting my hands up under her skirt, on her warm thighs, and pulled her toward me. She tumbled a little bit, our teeth awkwardly clacking together, before righting herself and kissing me again. Gentle nibbles on her lip, then I slid my tongue across the front of her teeth, and she made a soft and sweet noise as she let me. Receptive.

As I inched my hands up her thighs, I realized she wasn't wearing panties, and then that she had a yeast infection. Her pussy was wet, but with thick clumps that were white on my fingers when I pulled them out. Gross. But that wouldn't be a very body positive feminist thing for me to say, so instead I brought her to the bed, used a vibrator on her instead of kicking her out and shoved as many fingers inside her as I possibly could.

She must be faking it, the way she was writhing on the bed, her moans like a cheap imitation of some shitty Pornhub video. It had to hurt, my four fingers up to the knuckles in a pussy so clotted with yeast. Excruciating. I smiled. It was hot that she was so eager to please.

After her poorly faked orgasm, we laid in bed together and she tried to undress me.

"I'm alright," I playfully swatted her overeager hands away.

She looked disappointed, but she nodded.

"I think you might have a yeast infection."

Her face flushed.

"I'm so sorry!"

"It's okay," I placed a hand on her bare shoulder, my thumb resting in the cavity underneath her collar bone, "I have some suppositories you can use, if you want. It happens."

She nodded, said thanks, and I walked over to my bathroom and fetched one out of the medicine cabinet. I tossed it over to her, but she missed it and searched the rumpled sheets for the large pill.

"Let me put it inside you, actually," I smiled generously, holding my hand out.

She gave it to me and spread her legs for me, the look she gave me one of absolute comfort and trust. I popped it in, tucking the pill up behind her pubic bone.

"You probably shouldn't eat so much sugar," I played with her hair.

"Why?"

"It helps the yeast grow. Gabby has a bad sugar habit, that's why I have all those pills."

She nodded in disgusting admiration, her hero worship obscene, and was lingering, still naked, staring at my bookshelf, so I handed her her skirt. She flushed at the implication, that she was overstaying her welcome, quickly got dressed and left.

She didn't contact me for a whole week afterwards; had I been too mean? Was she too embarrassed? I sent her link to a movie she would probably enjoy and soon we had plans to meet the next day.

She was hungry for love and that made it easy to manipulate her. She wanted to be a writer too, she told me, and would email me snippets of her stories. I wrote to her that they were decent, that she showed promise, and privately I was angry because they were actually quite good, especially for her age. She was playful with words, leaping from one style to the next, leaning heavily on connotation and innuendo. Slippery. Hypersexual.

I told her a month later that I had passed the best of the stories on to my friend who was an important agent and she kissed me, pressed herself into me in a way that was somehow both shy and bold. I guided her to the bed, she seemed even more vulnerable than usual, pupils large and dark up at me, and I slid my tongue down her throat, then a finger, and I moaned as she took it all the way down her throat, tears in her eyes. She pressed against me and I ripped off her pants and her underwear and tasted her and then ran my tongue gently over the hood of her clit, down over her urethra, my hand squeezing her fuzzy inner thighs as she grasped at my head and my hair and then I began playing directly at her clit with my tongue, my finger inside her, convinced this time she would actually come, and she did, shuddering all over my hands, crying and crying out and holding me to her.

"That was so hot," I said, holding my fingers inside her still, moving her hair sticking to her face with tears and sweat to the side, gently regarding her. But she recovered too quickly—had this orgasm had been fake too? It was quickly out of my mind with the urgency with which she kissed me, then she flipped me, moved so her head was between my legs, her breath warming my cunt, and earnestly asked me to teach her how to please me.

I had told her that Gabby and I were open but that it was a Don't Ask, Don't Tell situation. "*Very French, you know what I mean,*" I said, and she seemed impressed at our sophistication. I said I was sure Gabby was out there fucking girls left and right on her tour and Sammy nodded and nodded.

Was Gabby fucking other girls? I doubted it. Gabby was very single-minded in her approach, not particularly sexual anyways, probably spending her nights alone in bed with her Kindle, reading. She latched on to a single person at a time, she had told me, and couldn't get off to anyone else but them. Ridiculous, I had thought, but I had grown to believe her. She was the most loyal person I had ever met, and besides, she was usually so distracted by her music and her research that she had barely any time for me at all, let alone some horny fan girl.

She would FaceTime me every morning and we would have breakfast together, her in some new hotel bed eating room service, me at the nook in my West Village kitchen. It was so comfortable, her warm voice and charming little anecdotes, still so earnest and excited every time a fan asked her for her signature, me bragging about my new job in the newsroom at the *New York Times*, how my boss loved me, everyone loved me, except for one resentful cunt who was mad that I had gotten hired right out of college.

"Of course I was hired immediately," I laid it on thick, "I'm privileged in every way except for my gender *and* I'm talented *and* I'm charming."

Gabby laughed a little, but she didn't take as much pleasure in my joke as usual.

"That attitude will get you in trouble one day," she shook her head.

"I'm not going to like, tweet that."

"Some people are more insightful than you think," here she had looked at me with concern, "You might not need to see it, they might just be able to sense it."

I agreed and reassured her, but I didn't *really* agree. Gabby had no idea just how good at lying I was, had no idea how I was manipulating even her. She thought my machinations surface-level, charming little schemes, but had no idea the complex web of lies and misinformation I had woven about myself.

Sammy kept asking about the agent and finally I had to let her down; the agent didn't like it. Of course, the agent had never even seen it, but she didn't need to know that. She sighed on my couch while I made her more tea.

"Should I give it up?" She asked me, exquisitely insecure.

"Well, you're only in undergrad. You haven't even done an MFA yet. Most writers don't get a book deal in their early twenties. It would be a miracle if you did."

"You did," she was eager to turn the conversation from anything that might reveal she was still in high school, "You published that book of essays when you were nineteen."

There was no inoffensive way to tell her that we were from different worlds, that I was both from an old, prestigious, wealthy family *and* a genius and she was neither, so I merely shrugged. The water was piping hot, and I plopped her teabag into the mug I had stolen from the office, brought it to her.

"That's only because I went viral. Publishers love someone with a following."

She pondered the bottom of the mug.

"Should I act more crazy on social media?"

I knew her and I knew she had no interesting thoughts, her brain dull despite her hot little body. There was no way she'd become any kind of sensation, just one of those tired teen girls with borderline personality accounts posting about how gay they are and all their traumas.

"Absolutely," a little wicked grin on my lips, "People love a show."

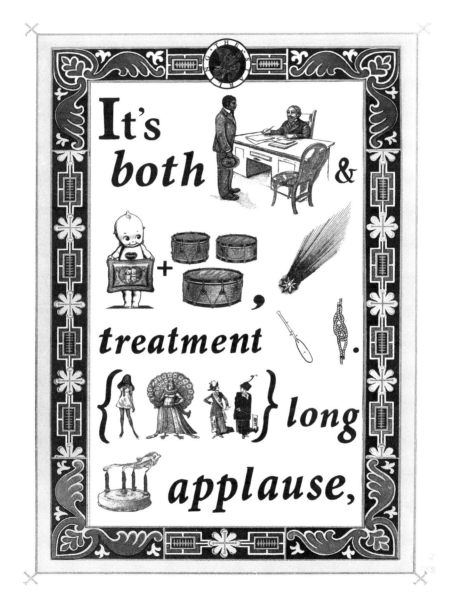

The British Invasion 1965, Age 14

New York, New York

Chaz pulls me to his narrow cot. Wrestles off my underpants. Lies me down on the scratchy blanket and lowers himself on top of me.

He grinds his body against mine. His hard-on hits my magic spot. That feels almost as good as the bathtub. I arch my back for more, but he's already moved on to pumping on my belly. That feels . . . rough. In a good way, and a bad way.

"You want this, don't you?" Chaz croaks out. Before I can answer, he wraps his arm around me, tight. With his other arm he peels off his Levi's and then his boxer shorts. His boxers are just like my father's. I know this because my mother makes me iron them, which makes me want to puke.

Chaz puts my hand on his penis. His *naked* penis. I've only touched him through his jeans before. He keeps his hand on top of mine and moves it up and down on that thick, lumpy log. He groans like I'm hurting him, so I stop. He grabs my hand and rubs it on his dick again.

"Do you feel that, baby?" he whispers. "How much I want you?"

"Yes," I say, which is true. I do know his penis is big because of what we're doing, same reason I'm wet between my legs. But in my chest, I feel dread. It's the same feeling I have when I watch *Alfred Hitchcock Presents* with my father. The same feeling I wake up with from the nightmare I keep having since Chaz and I started making out every day after work. I'm driving a car, but I don't know how to drive, since I'm just a kid. The car keeps going faster and faster. I know I'm going to crash and die. Just before I hit the brick wall in front of me, I wake up.

Chaz twists my wrists over my head with one hand, fumbles around between my legs with the other. I think he's trying to put his finger inside me, which he's done before. I don't like it, but I let him do it because he says it makes him feel like our bodies are one body. His hands and his penis don't do much for me. But his words do a lot.

"I want to be inside you," Chaz mumbles. "You want that too, don't you?"

He's put his fingers in me plenty of times before without asking. Why is he asking me now?

My heart starts pounding. Not in a good way.

"Ow!" I cry out. Chaz must be using a *lot* of fingers. "You're hurting me!"

Chaz covers my mouth with his hand. And then he's moving fast and hard, and my insides are burning like I'm ripping apart inside and I can't get away from him and I start crying, tears sliding down both sides of my face.

Suddenly Chaz stops. I'm waiting for him to comfort me, but instead he slaps his slimy penis onto my stomach and starts rubbing it even faster against me. It doesn't hurt. But it does not feel good. A thought keeps banging against the walls inside my head. *This has nothing to do with me.*

I open my eyes. Chaz's face is an inch above mine. His eyes are closed. His face is squeezed tight like a red fist. A blue vein throbs in his forehead, as if there's a frog under his skin. Sweat drips off his face onto mine. A big drop splotches into my eye and makes it burn.

"Stop," I whisper, because I can't seem to use my whole voice.

Chaz keeps pushing his penis against my stomach, faster and faster.

He's breathing hard and sweating hard and moving hard.

He makes a strangled noise.

He collapses onto me.

There's sticky white stuff all over my stomach. I know what it is. *Semen.* The gross stuff that comes out of Ivan's penis when I give him hand jobs. That's why I won't give Ivan blow jobs, which he keeps asking me to do but that is so disgusting when you think about it. I don't even like swallowing *milk*, which my mother makes me drink four times a day.

What just happened?

Am I pregnant right now?

When I was twelve, my mother sat me down and told me to stay away from semen. She said no matter where it lands, the invisible sperms in semen will keep traveling till they find my eggs. "If semen lands on the ground near you, it will find your foot," she said. "If it finds your foot, it will crawl up your leg till it finds your vagina."

Chaz reaches around me to grab his boxers off the floor. He uses them to wipe the gunk off his penis. Then he uses them to wipe the gunk off me.

He throws his boxers back onto the floor, lies down on his back, puts his arm around me, and pulls my head onto his chest. His chest isn't soft and puffy like Ivan's. It's hard and scratchy, like the blanket covering the bed.

"Do you see what you do to me, child?" Chaz says.

He makes it sound like whatever just happened was my idea, which it was not. I have a different question. Did I just have sexual intercourse for the first time?

Am I still a virgin?

Am I *pregnant*?

Are Chaz's sperm traveling around, looking for my eggs *right now*?

The room smells weird. Like the lion house at the Central Park Zoo.

I put my hand between my legs, then check my fingers. They're shiny-sticky, not red.

If that was really my first time, wouldn't I be bleeding?

I cannot possibly have just had intercourse with Chaz. Ivan's been begging me to do it since he gave me his ID bracelet almost a year ago. I told him I'm saving my virginity. For what, he always asks, and I never know what to say.

What if I'm not a virgin anymore and I didn't even give my cherry to Ivan, who's been waiting for it all this time? Asking for it, but not *taking it*, the way Chaz just did.

Chaz's eyes are closed. If he just took my virginity, shouldn't he be staying awake? Shouldn't he be excited? Saying "Thank you," at least?

I creep out of bed, pull on my underpants and my shorts and slide into my flip-flops. Chaz is snoring now.

Does he even know that was my first time?

Does he care?

My vagina hurts. I feel like crying. But I'm not doing that here.

I tiptoe out of Chaz's room and run down the stairs and out the heavy front doors into the muggy New York summer night. It's too hot to run but I keep running anyway, up Sixty-Seventh Street to Lex, right on Lex to Eighty-Second. This is almost exactly the way I walk home from school, but I never noticed that it's actually uphill. My legs are shaking.

Michael, the nighttime elevator man, frowns as he unfolds the rattly brass elevator gate. "You all right, Miss Maran?"

"Fine," I say, in the cold voice my mother uses when she talks to "the help." Michael turns away to drive the elevator, which gives me a chance to wipe the sweat off my face and neck with my Beacon Hill Neighborhood House t-shirt.

I wonder if Chaz and I will do what we did today from now on. I don't think you can go backwards once you've gone all the way. I mean, baseball players don't run from third base back to first.

I let myself into the apartment and yell Hi to my mother, who's in the kitchen. Where else would she be? She only gets to be in the living room after she's fed her family and nagged my brother and me into doing the dishes, which she then re-washes while nagging us to do them better. I go to my room and close the door. I wish I could lock it, but it of course I can't because then I'd have some actual privacy in my own home. So I shove my desk chair under the doorknob, a trick I learned from watching *Alfred Hitchcock Presents*. I pull my diary out of the back of my underwear drawer and I write down every single thing that just happened. I lock my diary and hide it in the drawer again. After dinner, I'll drag the phone into the hall closet and call my best friend, Cori. She always has a mature perspective. Her father died when she was nine. She's much more grown-up than me.

Writing everything down in my diary makes me realize I do know what happened. I just don't like knowing it.

I guess not everyone bleeds.

"If anyone finds out about us, they'll send me back to England, and you'll never see me again," Chaz whispers into my ear.

We're on a weekend camping trip with the kids, our first whole night together. As soon as the campers stopped talking and giggling, and the campfire burned down to orange embers, Chaz crawled into my sleeping bag and started kissing me. He smells like the campfire. He tastes like burned marshmallows. The combo of his British accent and the threat of getting caught turns *me* into a campfire marshmallow, flaming on the outside, sticky soft inside.

"You don't want that to happen, do you?" Chaz whispers, nibbling my neck.

He swallows my "No" with his mouth.

Chaz is twenty-two. He's visiting New York from Liverpool, England, running the Beacon Hill Settlement House summer camp for underprivileged kids. I'm his assistant counselor. A volunteer, because fourteen is too young to get paid. Chaz says he might move to New York permanently if he likes it here enough. Meaning, if he likes *me* enough. So, along with keeping the campers from killing each other all day, my job this summer is to make Chaz fall in love with me.

Oh, and to make sure no one catches us doing what we're doing. Not our bosses. Not my parents. Not my boyfriend, Ivan.

Fresh off the bus, wild and stinky from the camping trip, their little mouths lined black with burned marshmallow, the kids are milling around the Beacon Hill lobby, grabbing at each other's lunch boxes and light-up yoyos and ratty-haired Trolls, waiting for their moms or grandmas or pretend-cousins, who get here late every day, yelling at their kids to hurry up, *donde esta tu hermana*, get your drawings, *vamanos*, digging through the Lost & Found box till every bathing suit and flip-flop and kid goes home with *someone*, whether it's the right someone or not.

Finally, the lobby goes still and dim. Chaz catches me with his eyes, then starts up the stairs to his room. I know what to do. We do it every weekday. I give him a head start. Then I follow him up the stairs.

I tiptoe past the second floor, where the kids do arts and crafts, and eat their government cheese sandwiches on no-name white bread and drink their purple bug juice, and play jacks (the girls), and build houses with Lincoln Logs (the boys). I pull the third-floor stairwell door open and check both ways, creep down the hall and knock our special knock. Chaz opens his door and pulls me into his room and kicks the door closed with his big bare hairy foot. Same as every day, I feel excited as hell and guilty as hell, toppling into Chaz, because I have a boyfriend who loves me, and my boyfriend is not Chaz.

* * *

Lying to my parents is nothing new. I've been doing it all my life. They deserve it for trying to flatten me into a pancake version of myself. Not a hot, syrupy, buttery delicious stack of pancakes. One cold, dry, flat pancake: their imaginary perfect daughter, who makes my mother feel like a good mother, which she is not, and helps my father's career by putting on a perfect-daughter act at the dinners he makes my mother cook for his boring "colleagues" and their boring wives.

Lying to Ivan is different. He doesn't deserve it. He's the same age as me, cute and sweet, with a round face under his round Beatles hair-cut and round, amber-tinted John Lennon specs he perches on the edge of his round little nose. There are no sharp edges to Ivan. The one problem I have with Ivan is not his fault. In June, he got mugged in Central Park by three guys who knifed him in the leg, stole his gold necklace and his wallet, and ran away. Now Ivan can only walk with crutches, so he's stuck in his parents' public housing apartment on 119th and Broadway for who knows how long.

I hate to admit this, but I'm mad at Ivan because he got stabbed. I guess that makes me the world's meanest person, but I can't help it. I don't know why. I only know that the same thing happened a couple of years ago, with my mother. She got hot grease in her eyes while she was cooking and she yelled to me to walk her to the hospital, and my whole body filled with burning red rage, and I said, "No, I won't take you to the hospital. I'm your kid, not your mom."

My mother still talks about that. She looks at me and shakes her head and says, "Twelve years old, and you wouldn't help your mother when she was blind." When she says that I feel hatred for her, and I also think she's right. Since then, I keep having this nightmare: My mother is blind, and she's in a wheelchair, and it's my job to push her everywhere she goes, and I'll never be free of that job till I die or she dies.

There must be something wrong with me. I don't know what it is. But I do know that it's burning red.

The only excuse I have this time is that Ivan calls the guys who mugged him "*those Puerto Ricans*" in a voice that makes "Puerto Ricans" sound like it's a terrible thing to be. He used to call them *spics* till I made him stop, after I saw *West Side Story* and I realized what a bad word it is.

Ivan and his parents just got to America from Yugoslavia a few years ago, so there are things he doesn't understand. I try to be patient with his prejudice. I told him, "People of every color mug people of every color in New York every single day. There aren't enough Puerto Ricans in all five boroughs to do all that mugging." I reminded him that most of the campers at Beacon Hill Settlement House, including my favorite, Teresa Ortíz, are Puerto Rican. Not only are most of them perfectly nice. They're also poor. Poorer than Ivan's parents. I know that from first-hand experience.

I walked Teresa home one day when no one came to pick her up, and her mom invited me to stay for dinner, which was nothing but rice and beans on plastic plates, with nothing to drink but water in red plastic cups. I told Ivan about that dinner to make my point, that the guys who mugged him must have really needed the money. Ivan said, "I'm just telling it like it is, babe. You can plan on me hating Puerto Ricans for the rest of my goddamn life."

Ivan might be prejudiced, which I'm sure he got from his parents, but who am I to talk? If I were a better person, I'd be schlepping to Jackson Heights to visit Ivan after work, instead of going to Chaz's room and telling Ivan the same lie I tell my parents, that I get off work at 6:00, when I really get done at 5.

I hate cheating on Ivan because it makes me hate myself. I learned from rock 'n' roll songs that there are two kinds of girls in the world: the nice, honest ones who make men happy—like the one in the Beatles "And I Love Her." *She gives me everything/and tenderly/the kiss my lover brings/she brings to me.*

Then there are the lying, cheating girls who make men miserable, which Ivan would be if he knew about Chaz and me. Like the one in the Beatles' song "Girl." *The kind of girl you want so much it makes you sorry.*

I'd rather be a good person than a cheater and a liar and a whore. But obviously, I'm not.

Obviously, I'm the kind of girl who makes you sorry.

* * *

"I'm sure you know the Beatles are playing at Shea Stadium next weekend," my father says one night at the dinner table. "Well, guess who's going!"

"George, John, Gus, and Ringo?" I say. My mother says I got my sense of humor from my father, which must be true since I definitely didn't get it from her. But both of my parents hate it when I use it on them.

"*We* are!" my father says. "My boss is letting us use his box right behind home plate. Best seats in the house!"

Obviously, my father doesn't know the basics about music. Every girl *either* loves the Beatles or the Stones. No one loves both. I'm a Stones girl. The Beatles are too cute for me. The Stones are *rough*. The kind of guys I like. Not that my father would know any of that, since he doesn't know anything important about me.

"The box has five seats," my father adds. "So we can invite your boss."

"*What?*" I spit out a mouthful of chicken kiev. What am I supposed to do, tell my parents that I've spent the whole summer having intercourse with my twenty-two-year-old boss, so I don't want to go to the Beatles concert with him and my *parents*?

Not bloody likely, as Chaz would say. But what choice do I have? Once my father makes a decision, even if it's going to totally ruin my life, that's it. I have zero power. Childhood is a prison sentence. Which is one reason I cannot *wait* to turn eighteen and get out of here.

* * *

That's how, on August 15, 1965, I find myself at the first American Beatles' concert—with my nine-year-old brother, my mother, my father, and the twenty-two-year-old British guy I'm having secret sex with, surrounded by forty million screaming, crying, and fainting teenage girls.

Do you think I can actually hear the Beatles' singing in the middle of the baseball field over all that noise? No, I cannot.

Do you think I care? No, I do not.

I just want this hell night to end before it ends in complete disaster.

Finally, the Beatles run off the stage. We fight our way through the mob scene of beer vendors and crying girls and pile into the car. We drive to the Beacon Hill Neighborhood House and pull up to the curb.

"Thank you very much, Mr. Maran," Chaz says, climbing out of the passenger seat. He avoids my eyes, which he's been doing all night.

"I really enjoyed meeting you, Chaz," my father says. "We'll have you over for dinner soon."

Dinner? I'll die. I swear, I will.

"That would be lovely," Chaz says. "So nice meeting you, Mrs. Maran. And you, Drew. See you at work tomorrow, Meredith."

As my father drives away, he catches my eye in the rearview mirror. "Nice chap," he says, showing me how cool he is with his Beatles box seats and his British slang. He wants me to thank him.

For torturing me all night? No way.

* * *

A few days later when I come home from "work" (from Chaz's room), my mother greets me at the door. Her face is pale. Her lips are white and tight.

"Follow me," she says in a voice that's even colder than usual. For once, she doesn't tell me to take my flip-flops off before I walk on the clear plastic that covers every inch of her precious white carpet. Did you not know the carpet was white when you bought it? I asked my mother when she started unrolling the plastic covers. Were you planning on installing it on the ceiling so it would stay clean? She just glared at me and said what she always says: I can't wait till you're an adult. Finally we agree on *something*, I say back.

I follow my mother into my parents' bedroom. She closes the door behind me and sits down on the stiff corner chair that's only there for looks. I've never seen anyone sit on it before.

My father is propped up against the headboard of what looks like *their* bed but is actually *his* twin bed pushed against *her* twin bed, with one big bedspread covering them both to make it look like they sleep together, which they do not.

My father is *crying*.

I've never seen my father crying before.

Suddenly, I'm terrified.

They can't know, I tell myself. I haven't told anyone except Cori, and she'd never rat me out.

I drop my purse onto the plastic-covered carpet and slide down the wall so I'm sitting with my legs straight out and the wall holding me up.

"You've been having sexual intercourse with that man," my father says. "Your twenty-five-year-old *boss*. What kind of sick twenty-five-year-old takes advantage of a fourteen-year-old child?"

"He's only twenty-two," I say.

My ears are ringing.

It's happening. The worst possible thing.

My father reaches into his nightstand drawer and pulls out a fat little white leather book.

My diary. Its flap dangles unlocked in my father's hairy hands.

I look at my mother. She's given me the same diary in a different color for Christmas every year, starting when I was in first grade.

"How did he open that?" I ask her.

"With my key," she answers.

"But I always keep the key with me." I pull my rabbit's foot keychain out of my purse, with the tiny diary key dangling from it.

"Each diary comes with two keys," my mother says.

I'm looking at my mother, but she's just a blur. What I see clearly are the hundreds of pages I've filled in those diaries, day after day, year after year. The secrets I wrote on those pages, believing their blank whiteness was mine alone, my one private, secret, safe place.

"Do you even realize you could be pregnant," my father snaps at me. "Or you could have a terrible disease. Or both."

"Tomorrow I'm taking you to one of the best gynecologists in the city for a thorough examination," my mother says. "After which your father and I will discuss legal action."

"Legal action?" I mumble.

"There are laws against what that pervert did," my father says. "It's called statutory rape. Whether I have him sent to prison or not, know this: you will never see him again."

"You can't stop me," I say, automatically, the thing I always say when my father tells me what I can't do and who I can't see, which is pretty much everything and everyone I care about.

"To think I gave that criminal a *box seat to the Beatles*," my father says. "And he *took it*."

"Whose fault is that?" I cry out. "That was *your* stupid idea!"

"Your time at Beacon Hill is over," my father says. "Your employer will be lucky if I don't sue them."

I pull myself up on rubber legs, throw my purse over my shoulder, facing my jailers. I'm going to run to Beacon to see Chaz. I'm going to run away with him to England and never come back.

I start for the bedroom door. My father jumps up, grabs my arm, drags me across the hall, pushes me into my room, and slams the door shut behind me.

I yank my bedroom door open., ready to run. My father is standing right there, scowling at me. He shoves me into my room again. I hear a metal clicking sound.

I try my door again.

It's locked from the outside.

Andrea Sands

Hey Baby Take a Walk on the Wild Side

Janis Joplin once said, "There is no such thing as a male groupie." Janis—the first rock queen of the '60s, didn't get laid by some hot hippie fan every night? I didn't buy it. The only way I could justify her comment was to refer back to the year she said it—almost fifty-three years ago, back in 1970.

"My band members always fall in love with me!" huffed my friend Rita after she took a sip of her Jack & Coke at the Tiki-themed bar in Orange County. "That's why I don't hang out with guys alone any-more!" she snarled. We were drunk on a Sunday at 4 p.m. Rita fronts a popular band that recently has been getting attention, even a mention in *Spin* magazine. She has a cute round face, short black hair with a long blonde bang, is small framed, thin, and always has a full face of make-up with her signature red lips. We both took another sip.

I could not relate. My experience with men and music have been quite the opposite. No matter how many cocktails we share, I don't think she would ever fully understand. We're both singers in bands, both hope music venues can pay our guarantees, and both perform like motherfuckers, but there's one big difference—I'm transgendered, and she's the girl next door. In 2023, men don't fall in love with transwomen. No matter how great they look or how much talent they have, transwomen are god's burnt offerings.

I'll still listen to Rita's stories, and I feel protective of her; she's like a little sister. But I keep my stories to myself. I think she would melt into her bar stool if she heard half of what I've been through in this wild world of transexual love slaves and the pricks who use and abuse us.

* * *

Hey baby, take a walk on the wild side.

A lyric from my favorite Lou Reed song.

The original rock and roll trans chaser. He loved the ts dolls so much that he immortalized them in his most popular song. Lou was a badass.

* * *

I was assaulted at my company's Christmas party in 2019. My dear mother was gravely ill the night I got ready for that party. I stood in front of her living room's mirrored closet doors and pulled on the stretch fabric from the short black cocktail dress that I had altered a few hours before. My mom could see me from where she was sitting in her chair in front of her television. As I was walking out, I heard her say, "They're gonna fire you if you show up dressed like that."

Mom was always worried about me going out so flashy and femme. She even called me one time years before, when I first started femme-presenting. It was 1 a.m., after one of my shows and she sounded a little hysterical.

"Mom? What happened? You okay?"

She said, "Yes, I'm fine, I just had a terrible nightmare where these men beat you in the middle of the street and all that was left after they were done was your wig!"

I said, "Mami, I am safe and I don't wear wigs. I wear hair pieces, there's a difference!"

Bless her soul. My mother would die less than a month after that Christmas party.

That evening at my company's party I won "Star of the Night," announced before I had even gotten there. When I arrived I was handed a silver Kate Spade wallet and an Amazon gift card. My boss and her assistant went straight to me. Each grabbed one of my arms and *snap* went the photographer. All without warning. It was strange. I should have known peril was lurking.

The party was being held at this fancy vintage looking hotel downtown.

I walked up to the bar and asked for a beer and a whiskey on the rocks. "Twenty-two dollars," said the bartender. The price shocked me. I slammed the shot, dripping half of it. As I padded my chest and left breast with a napkin, I didn't see that my creepy homophobic coworker Ricky had scooted towards me with both elbows on the bar. "Got some beer on your tits?"

I looked up. "It's whiskey," I said in a deep, unimpressed voice.

"Too bad you wiped it, I would have licked it off," he snorted and let out a little giggle.

"You're hilarious," I said sarcastically.

"Let me buy you another one?" he asked.

I thought about how pricey everything was. Why not spend this asshole's money instead of my own?

"Sure, whiskey, double shot."

This time, I didn't down it like the first messy shot. I held it, reached over the bar and grabbed a sliced lemon, squeezed it and dropped it into the little glass. "Thanks!"

As I started to walk away, he called out to me. "Hey, wait a second!" I felt him grip my upper arm. "Ummm what if I had a room at this hotel, would you want to hang out after this thing finishes?" he whispered.

I turned my head and let out a big "Ha," big enough that it almost translated to *fuck off!* I kept walking. I didn't even turn to see his reaction. I went over to my assigned seat and ate my chicken legs and potato.

The night went on with more company group photos, selfies, and even a soul train style runway to Donna Summer and Bruno Mars. I had a hoot with Evelyn and Kacy, the two other ladies in my department. We danced together and pretended to twerk, really enjoying ourselves, no dates needed.

I excused myself to use the restroom in the lobby, only a few feet from the hall we were in. Right as I opened the hall door, I noticed Ricky standing there next to a window, drink in hand, red-eyed, and a little sweaty. We made quick eye contact and I hurried into the restroom.

After using the toilet and reapplying my lipstick, I hurried back out, but before I could open the hall door Ricky reached for me again and said into my ear, "Just give me head tonight, I'm hard already."

I pulled away, disgusted, and looked him up and down with my signature on-stage rage-face. "Aren't you married with kids?!?"

He quickly flipped his offer and insult. "I'm just fucking with you, don't get mad!"

I went back inside, I asked the girls at my table if they wanted to join me in a dance, some '80s Madonna song was playing. "It's my favorite song!" I shouted, trying to shake off the exchange in the lobby. I could see Ricky standing at the bar again, just staring. I could tell the wheels in his head were spinning.

My company gifted all of us cheap wine wrapped in red and white Christmas wrapping paper, green ribbons. Most of my coworkers were pretty tipsy. Many carpooled, and some took ride shares. I was part of the latter.

Standing outside holding my wine bottle, saying my goodbyes to the ladies in my department. I was alone, only one other lady stood some feet away from me, waiting for her ride. Ricky appeared, very drunk and holding three bottles of the free wine in one arm, a to-go box of food in the other. I opened my phone and saw I had three minutes for my pickup to arrive. *Lord help me.*

He stood there almost as if he didn't see me, but then looked up with those deep red eyes. He walked towards me like a zombie from *Night of the Living Dead.* "You think you're such a bad bitch, don't you?" He mumbled and spit. "Well guess what? I only fuck real women! I don't fuck fake fat tranny bitches like you!"

I was frozen. He continued. "You people belong in hell. You should be begging me for this dick." He dropped a bottle of wine reaching to grab his dick through his pants. The bottle, unbroken, rolled to the right.

Now with free hands he said, "I could have you if I wanted, you bitch!" He was in front of me. With rage-eyes, he grabbed one of my breasts, spit dripping from his mouth, and said "You bitch," full of anger and tequila.

Without thinking I swung my gifted company Christmas wine towards his face. I heard a smash and an explosion of paper and glass. We both were covered in wine. I rubbed my wet eyes. Ricky wasn't standing anymore. Now there were four bottles of wine on the ground, three unopened and one in pieces.

My car pulled up right in time. The driver put down his window and asked, "You okay? You Andrea?"

"Yes!" I said, as if I won something.

As I jumped into the car and I could see Ricky sit up, confused, as I drove away. On the ride home I wept and I smiled and wasn't sure of what was to come of all this. As we passed through a bright tunnel, I could hear music. A victory song played in my head. I could hear cheering, I waved my arm out of the window. I was proud of myself.

Sometimes trans people live on the intersection of sex and violence. We must learn to fight, or at least learn to swing something really hard.

At home, wiping off my makeup in my bathroom mirror, I realized I still had to go to work on Monday. Mom was right. A few months later, they did fire me. Last time I checked, Ricky remains employed there.

* * *

No more massaging of your prima donna balls like everyone else has to do for you. It's over.
     This was the last text my boyfriend sent me while we were breaking up.

He broke up with me because I accidentally snorted coke off a Cuban skater's dick in the green room restroom after one of my shows. He caught us walking out, and I said what any toxic girlfriend would say: "It was dark, I thought it was you! It was an accident."

He dumped me. That one I did deserve. I was twenty-eight, in my reckless teen phase, I suppose.

* * *

About a year later, I played a private party in a backyard, beer kegs stacked on both sides of the makeshift stage. The home owner was a fan but was passed out by the time we went on. Thankfully, he'd paid us in advance. The gig was fun, everyone cheered and moshed hard to our songs.

The restroom was located on the inside of the home, and you had to walk through the kitchen to get to it. Right when we finished our set I rushed inside, still out of breath and covered in sweat.

I saw a heavy-set man in a white muscle shirt and glasses standing at the stove in the kitchen. He was cutting up lines of coke on an iron skillet. People are always nice to us when we play shows, so I figured he would want to share. I said "Hey, let me get a line?"

The nasty drug chef looked up at me and said, "Give me money." I reached into my little purse, pulled out a dollar and waved it in his face. He grabbed my wrist, got real close to my face and said, "I want tranny dick!"

I pulled my wrist away, dropped the folded dollar. I was out of there like a bat out of hell.

* * *

I don't want to close this little memoir with violence, because I am grateful and super lucky to be able to travel the country performing and making art.

Some sweet spots do come to mind, like the time a femme fan helped me into a skin tight leopard print bodysuit in the janitor's closet of an abandoned diner somewhere up north. She zipped me up, said I looked beautiful and asked if she could kiss me. I was finally asked for consent, I thought, how exciting. I nodded and leaned forward. Our lips touched. She had the softest mouth that tasted like tamarindo. That memory has always made me smile.

I also remember David Darling, the only person who's ever offered to be my music manager. David used a cane, had a curled ringmaster mustache and black framed glasses. He was always waiting for me at my band's merch table after my sets to talk business. He warned me that he hadn't managed anyone since the early 2000s, when he was the original manager for one of my favorite goth bands of the '90s, Switchblade Symphony. That fact alone made me very excited. He assured me that he would learn all the current social media trends for singers and bands. We began to email each other, we talked about touring and recording and how he would be willing to fund some things my band might need. I was hesitant but open. Then the pandemic started, everything stopped and we all got locked into our houses. David, sober for twenty years, relapsed and died.

I was just starting to get to know David. He didn't want to fuck me or hurt me. He wanted to help me when he was the one at the end who needed it the most. The memory of him caring about me and my band has stayed with me.

* * *

The conversation with Rita at the Tiki bar continued, her voice muffled as I felt a calmness within me, the need to let go of certain resentments. I started to imagine myself standing inside of a burning building, looking for an exit sign, the roof above me starting to fall piece by piece, my clothes catching on fire, the heat blurring my vision. I hear Rita's voice: "Andrea! Hello? Are you even listening to me?"

I snapped out of it. "Sorry Rita, I got stuck there for a second, must be these hard drinks. Tell me again, please, what you were saying?"

Rita click-clacked her nails on the table. "I was just saying that if it wasn't for hot yoga, I would be completely lost."

I nodded, smiled, and kept drinking.

Carta Monir

Yellow Legal Pad (Undated)

I keep scratching at the side of my head, at the implant site. It's psychosomatic I'm sure because it's been healed forever, but it still feels itchy, like a bug bite that's scabbed over kind of. I hate this fucking shit. I'm writing this longhand on paper. My handwriting is garbage and it might be useless to treat physical writing as any kind of privacy, considering that my glasses could transcribe this text in less than a tenth of a second and upload it straight to some FBI database. But, ~~just for the fun~~ because I know I have to write about this, I'm sitting in my closet writing on this legal pad in my shitty handwriting. If you're reading this, you probably killed me the moment you looked at this paper. I hope I'm already dead. If you're reading this in anything other than my handwriting, goddamn you, I hope you die right at your desk. This isn't for you.

I guess first I need to start with the obvious stuff because I'm going to stick these pages into a hole in my drywall and pray that nobody finds them until after I'm gone. So in case you don't know what I'm talking about, there's a bug in my head, and a lot of people's heads. Some asshole working for Imperative Health invented them and they became basically mandatory for anyone on low-income health insurance plans. These dissolvable implants that you get replaced every five years—they're supposed to track your heartrate and mental health and brainwaves and shit. They were incentivized like crazy. So I got one. Lidocane shot, tiny drill, implant, some kind of glue, done. I was awake for it and it took like five minutes, took the day off work. Then like a year later it comes out that the early versions of the implants don't dissolve like they're supposed to, and what's more they will kill you instantly if you remove them. And kill you slowly if you don't. I get a big(-ish) settlement payout. And then maybe a couple years later? There's this big leak of anonymized data from claims, and it's like . . . a library of recordings of people's brain activity while horrible things are happening to them. And it didn't take hardly any time for someone to figure out that you can plug that data right back into your implant and get an incredibly fucked up high from brain-huffing people's death adrenaline. Imperative updated their terms of service to say that if they catch you doing it, they'll cut off your implant. They can't tell exactly what's happening or read the text I'm writing on paper, but if I were to write somewhere they could track me . . . I would become one of the death records of someone sitting at a computer and then, without warning, experiencing heart failure. If I'm going to die, I want to be deep in a wet hole, not face down on my keyboard.

[written in margin] I'm not going to try to make any of this writing pretty, because I don't think there's any way I can really communicate what it's like without being choppy. ~~You'll underst~~ It's just . . . this is my life now, my whole life, and I can't tell anyone. I can't talk to anyone about this in a meaningful way because they'll kill me, and I can't even keep a computer diary. This is all I've got. The only record of what my life is like now.

Fucking a cis man in the ass—I love twinks. I love finding younger guys, in that nineteen to twenty-two range, and hurting them in ways they didn't know they could be hurt. I met this one walking around the park—had my PA set to a proximity vibration for someone lQQking who matched my preferences, and all of a sudden there's that delicious little burning in the head of my cock as I'm walking close to this cropped-hair baby piece of ass. He's straight out of *Archie Digest*, swear to god, dressed like he's just left some kind of internship. He's stocky, not muscular, with a tummy and lanky arms. We make eye contact, I give him a little tilting "with me" head movement, he follows me to my car. I put up the privacy tint, recline the back seats, he's got his pants off, I open him up with my middle and ring fingers.

Kiss him, tongue down his throat, want him to choke on me. One hand in his hole, the other clenching that muscular little neck, the crotch of my thumb and palm right over his knife-like Adam's apple. I consider fucking him without lube so that it'll hurt him more, but my cock is still sore from the last couple days and I grab a little slide, not too much. Bend him over, face towards the door, tell him to hold his stupid faggot hole open for me. His cunt is brown, almost purple, shivering asterisk, taint fat and covered in light, curly hair. Push into him, god. Velvet, tight, a little sharp prick in the tip of my cock as I nudge some of his shit as I thrust deep. He whines deliciously, I smack his ass, start stroking. I feel the burning need in my brain, that waiting, that anticipation, that can't leave it alone feeling, that addict urge, and I roll my eyes back, navigate menus while I warm up his pussy. I'm looking at the buzzed nape of his neck, a mole under his barbershop fade, when the sensation floods through me. Car stopped on the train tracks. Focus on keeping an even tempo while I fuck into him. Car stopped on the train tracks, grab his waist feel those soft hips, calm but nervous. Car noises, doors not working. Don't freak out. He reaches under and starts to touch himself while I fuck him. I punch his ass, hard one two three four five times. Keep your hands where they are you fucking faggot. He grinds his forehead into the carpeting on the seat and moans, train horn. Oh my god, fuck. Okay, don't panic, I shift position and put my foot on the side of his face, pressing hard. One of my favorite tricks. Train getting closer, still far away, kick out the glass? Kick Kick Kick not working, I press harder and he tenses on my cock, his pain milking me. Kick kick kick kick oh my god I'm going to die. I'm going to die. I lunge over him and bite his shoulder as hard as I possibly can. I look desperately into the back seat, at my coat and realize it's the last thing I'll ever see. He screams. I'm about to die. Train bearing down. He screams I feel the impact I cum the world is a wall I die I cum I fill his useless ugly faggot ass with my hate my life my death my adrenaline, bite harder. Taste blood. He's crying and struggling under me, I juice the last of my orgasm into him grind grind grind, he goes limp, I go limp. I roll off of him, my dick is mostly clean, his hole is a screaming pit. He's crying, I feel like an angel falling asleep in heaven. His blood is on my lips, pooling in the corners of my mouth. I don't remember him leaving the car. Later he gives me a good review in the app, says I made him cum really hard which is news to me.

When I jerk off now I imagine someone else getting off to a recording of my death. I hope it's horrible. It would be kind of a waste for it not to be.

Pretty girl at a party, not lQQking, eye contact instead. Old fashioned. I get the idea as soon as I see her little scar, just a little keloided under her hair. She's my age or a little older, someone's mom maybe. She comes over, we talk, I invite her back to my place, we end up in bed together. Her name is A. She lies next to me, jerking off with a vibrator. Implant I ask? Yeah, she says. Do you ever..............? Yeah, she admits, but she's not proud of it. Let's do it together I suggest. I sync us up and set up my playlist. Lie next to me, still, I tell her. Let me show you my favorite one. We're both quietly jerking off looking at each other and just back to back to back experiencing "waking up and realizing the person next to you has died during the night." Wake up dawning realization horror denial checking horror adrenaline grief, switch to the next one just as "practical numbness" starts to set in, before planning, before the boring stuff. I make eye contact with her and we cry together, two of the most evil people in the world, cumming and cumming as we feel the loss of a spouse of decades, of a sister, of a child, of a friend, another friend, this one was a murder, this one was an overdose. Each of them has a different flavor and on top of that, our own feelings mingling—elation, shame, horror, ~~love~~, the deep intimacy of a shared criminal act. She begs me to stop and we stop. I hold her and then I'm fingering her and then she guides my cock into her and we fuck, no sound except for sniffles and gasping, the shuffling of sheets moving. I feel my cock rubbing so hard against her inner wall, friction like a thumb on the head of my cock, I cum. She cums shortly after. We hold each other, I slip out when I get soft. I ask if she wants anything, and we have tea.

I've tried a lot of different things during sex, dying during birth, industrial accident, dying while drunk, dying after being blinded. I like the ones where a sense is impaired, it's fucked. Processing data from what's happening to me as I fuck while I also try to integrate the numbness of a dead input, it's a sour feeling, it's a christ on the cross feeling. And the data really is anonymized as far as I can tell. There's not a way to tell when or where the sensations are from, you're exploiting faceless ghosts when you do this. It's a victimless crime that makes me cum so fucking hard and also makes me feel like I deserve to burn in hell forever, a special hell that's worse than the usual hell.

Every time something bad happens to me, I know that a computer program is going to turn it into an experience that someone else can jerk off to. I've started asking partners to hurt me, so much worse than I ever used to get hurt before. Those are the only times I don't feel the urge to consume insurance ghost pain, because I don't want to muddle my own brain signals. I'm creating something, I'm paying it forward. I don't know who is going to experience my agony in the future, but I want it to be as pure and horrible as possible.

I got really hurt a few nights ago. Trans girl and trans guy couple, buzzed me on the train. Looked them over across the car—the girl, L, tall, black jacket, ripped jeans. The boy, P, very wiry, elfin but worn, hair thinning, neon tank top. We chatted a bit, went back to their place. Something about them, so easy to talk to. I guess it's that thing about other trans people, knowing that there's some fundamental shared understanding. They had implants but neither of them was into the idea of using them like I do. Didn't get deep into it anywhere near potential microphones, but made a little aluminum tube from my mouth to their ears and confessed like I was in church about how badly I want to get hurt. They offered me sleeping pills, and the promise that they wouldn't stop no matter how much I begged. I almost cried on the spot, swallowed those pills so fast, stupid, they could have been anything. But I guess it wouldn't have mattered because I was looking to get hurt, the world blurred, I have a faint memory of resting my head down on the couch I was on, worrying that I would knock over the glass of water they'd given me. Then nothing, then knives, knives in my asshole. Brutal glass shard feelings that made me scream—I was getting fucked completely dry, with a gloved hand. One of those fucked up textured work gloves that feels like it's going to rip your insides out even with lube. I couldn't move, I felt so heavy, and realized that L was holding my head down, and that P was the one fucking me. My cheek pressed heavy into the fabric of the couch, and I drifted in and out of feeling present, studying a frayed thread in the fabric of the upholstery and living in the horrible inescapable burning. I barely noticed when L shoved her cock into the side of my cheek, artificially pulling my lip up into a half-smile. Her voice echoed down, "this is what you asked for," and even though I couldn't remember my own name in that moment, I felt some deep, insane satisfaction that I was being recorded, and that some other person might one day cum while drinking my helpless desperation, the boredom and horror and powerlessness that overtakes a body that cannot resist. Part of me hoped they would actually kill me, or at least come close, but that was probably too much to expect from a first encounter, even an intense one. P and L were nice people who were doing what I had asked them to, I think, not murderers. They fucked and used me, held a knife to my face, to my taint, kicked my ribs, joked with each other about how empty I looked. It was perfect. I wouldn't say I fell in love with them, but I also didn't . . . not?

It's starting to make me wonder, actually, if any of the experiences I've shared through this implant are from people like me, whose implant is killing them, who have decided to end their lives as extremely as possible, to honor this fucked up gift that's been imposed on us. I wonder if I would know one of those when I felt it.

You know, later I hooked up with P alone? He asked me to top him and I didn't mind obliging, and it felt right in a full-circle kind of way that while I put a fist in him and punched his stomach with my other hand, I was also letting the terrified final moments of a drowning victim wash over me. When he came, I was feeling water rush into my lungs, feeling the adrenaline surge as my body tried to muster a last kick towards the surface of the water, and right as the entire weight of the water crashed down on me, I heard P whimper that he loved me, and it felt like the devil had reached out of hell and pierced my heart with his long, manicured needle of a fingernail.

jimmy cooper

Boy

I have two dildos. The first is black & fairly small, maybe five inches, little sculpted balls. When I fuck myself with it I think of John Giorno's description of Andy Warhol's cock: "small, but very hard." Andy mostly liked to fuck around, or suck the poet's toes & get himself off later, alone. Andy was a pathetic thing. John makes that much clear. Naturally, fucking myself, I also think of you, your cock, small, but very hard, smaller even than this facsimile, & your own indifference to it. You had confessed that you don't usually really care about getting off, and how I changed that. Now, all you can think about is my pussy, how I shouldn't be empty, how you want to fall asleep inside me, for me to fall asleep and wake up full every day. Your obsession in this instance isn't even with your pleasure, but leaving something of you with me. I don't have the heart to tell you it's mostly pooled in my briefs by the time I get home, & what I'm left with after all is an empty feeling. I've never spent the night with you. I love you. I loved you instantly. You slow me down, build a wall around me recalling the cool stone of cloisters and dank libraries. Centuries of heads bent in study and praise. Kneeling, everything resembles stained glass, your dark eyes. Hand reaching through a black hole cut into some kind of alcove in time, space, presenting small gifts, a flower, a slap in the face. We were listening to Janet Jackson's *Control*, recorded not far from here, our small South Minneapolis bedrooms. Your hands move over my body slowly. Usually all energy, alert, physically, psychically, libidinally paranoid, I acquiesce, though it's hardly acquiescence. I knew I belonged to you the first time, ownership in the back of my mind despite every other cock that's passed through me since I met you. I feel as though I'm half your size, if that—you engulf me, everything in me attuned to more points of contact. As if there could be more. You touch me where it counts. I feel like a fireball, an overeager child. Your soft smile holding me down easily, with one hand I'm yours, I couldn't struggle if I wanted to. I don't. The way you own me is too easy: you just do. Your cock presses up under your belly, pricks my ass slick with what you made of me. You press into me so gently I don't even realize you were fucking me until you must have been for minutes already, but anyhow I had forgot where I ended & you're very still but your cock pulses and pulses and by now I recognize the difference between mere pleasure and the way it tells me you're about to cum though you don't say a word. My dick? Nothing, arrested development, bud of marigold, a new tomato green on the vine. I don't care. I was talking about fucking myself. You tell me I'm pathetic. The truth is these days I can't cum without imagining you shooting inside me. This feels too romantic to tell you, monogamy turned on its head, the closed space of this affair always an affair, the only affair. You hint anyways at fucking other boys. I don't care. They can't belong to you. I won't have it. The other dildo is pink—a bit bigger, softer. I don't fuck myself with it. I love you. I want you always.

SINK OR BURN

Excerpt

During the socialist bloom, privatized land became shrouded and untapped. Beneath the topsoil, the mantle, and the fertile, sacred grounds we lost to the regime—museums of nuclear assault rifles and rare tanks swelled. Silent, off shore, international pacts with neighboring, war-ravaged regimes multiplied, setting a global precedent for *New American* values. Underground, among newborn pipelines and concealed masses of land tucked along the Navajo nation, sat the seed of New America, back when it was still minimized as a simple-minded, lifeless threat—to *Make America Great Again*.

2110 wasn't only the year of the North American dissection, but it was also the year Fulanito and I were sluts. Simpler times.

Fulanito was heavily spoken for then, married for five years, as Generation Hex wore their god-fearing cowardice and mammalian needs for partnership on their sleeves. However, during those years, the newly wed, newly polyamorous couple painted the town red at underground sex clubs, and the monthly *Cheap Glitter 4 Cheap Blowjobs Fundraisers 4 Harm Reduction*. We called this our *bloom*—our blooming boners and elongated glances and Fulanito's bizarre attempt at polyamory which, in fact, did *not* include multiple lovers. It did not include connection or fucking around beyond the whirl-wind orgies we collectively fell into from time to time at nightclubs. Fulanito's game was a trauma bond roulette of performative prowess, but most controversially: staring at me.

He would stare when I walked, when I spoke, when I danced—peering from behind the stacks or DJ booth or otherwise focal point—like a nightshift stagehand looking for love and trouble.

Fulanito stared for years and I danced or laughed or sneered back. Throughout the most dismal nights of his and Narnia's marriage, Fulanito would stare beyond the abyss of compersion while Narnia fucked her other partner—Oracle—on the dance floor. Digging her fingers into Oracle, Narnia kissed her neck. Oracle moaned and Narnia laughed and heisted Oracle up towards our sky—a rotating disco ball that lit our most vulnerable parts. Fulanito snapped back into reality and raised a glass with the string of surrounding voyeurs.

We stared as I clapped and celebrated our collective freedom—a reclamation of our worst lovers, our most unforgiving organs, the undulating complexity of being queer and exhausted with our pride. We mostly feel unrest.

We stared on our walks home and our reprieves from being renown. We stared at dusk when we packed our gear onto the hatchback before every show. We stared during every drum fill and every climax of every word we wrote when things were softer and lonelier.

Playing live music was like fucking or masturbating on front of all of your friends but without the sexuality—if you chose to keep your clothes on. The penetrable rhythmic pulse of coordination kept it mystic and intimate, while the freedom of loving the words you are singing, the notes you are playing, kept it climactic and embodying.

Before the evolution of the colonized mind and body sensuality was about our carnal movement. On the best nights, a song could easily become a full body awakening, a prophecy, an orgasm. We scream our stories and destroy our tools for a sensory overload because our pleasure is not a threat, but a sacred gift. And during Cheap Glitter's electrifying pulse of synchronized breathing and yelling and noodling and blasting, Fulanito and I kept *staring*.

We stared when we packed up and set out and headed back to sleep. We stared in our dreams. We stared the morning after our crusades, on warm concrete porches in alien towns with bloody fingertips and doe-eyed wanderlust.

We stared on video calls during awkward band meetings where we got nothing done, nothing settled, and nothing advanced aside from the knowledge that maybe there was more to this *staring*.

Being single is not for the weak—for the traumatized—for the despairing. I can attest to this, as a weak, traumatized single woman in despair.

I didn't *feel* an end to New America, nor the tempered heartstrings between Fulanito's emotional unavailability and my nuanced free-dom. And so, we sat in them, tying them in gorgeous, complex, overhand knots, while we laughed about death and destruction. We wrapped them around our joints for cushion because we had so much left to learn about grieving our worst lovers. This helps us stay reactionary—fighting, singing, shredding, staring—but *not* fucking. Heavens, no.

We reached old Montreal at the peak of dawn and enjoyed a sprawling orange sunrise. If Dystopia did anything, it demystified state lines and blurred the bureaucratic dots between continents. We drove into town and felt at home in Montreal's reclaimed urban environments, half dilapidated, half thriving in their own bones and armor— string lights, city lights, local art, red lights, neon lights, families, vendors. Strategic survival with a collective town hall that peculiarly gave a shit.

We pulled up to our lodging on Rue St Laurent, above an abandoned bank with pillars like the regime, but worn and weathered. Rue St Laurent was a once overwhelming downtown, now subtle and pure. Half asleep and half awake, everyone except me and Fulanito ran up to their rooms like they had just won some battle or pissed off some gatekeeper.

"Hey! CT . . . wanna smoke this joint with me?" Fulanito spoke to me and I looked down at the fresh joint rolled in strawberry papers, matching the merriment of his hot pink curls. I smiled back. That meant yes.

"Do you ever just have no idea how to make a full sentence, so you like, do all kinds of stupid reactionary shit cause it's all you've ever been expected to do?" Fulanito exhaled and unfurled his can of worms. "Like, no one taught you better?"

"Hmm. Yes. But I'm full of sentences… to a fault." I smiled and ashed the strawberry joint onto the steps, shuffling the dust beneath my sandal, inching closer to Fulanito's bare feet. "I'm kind of obsessed with articulating everything for everyone because it's all *I* ever knew. That was my role, to hold my family together. To make them talk about shit. I think it makes me kind of annoying."

"Well maybe you can help me if it gets weird?"

"Oh yea?"

Fulanito looked into my eyes and paused, like maybe this, in fact, was the end of the world, but it was okay. It was the end of everything I had ever known and everything I had ever unlearned. It was light: motivation to do Demonixa's spell and drink the potions and do the ritual and honor the wisdom that I've been resisting because it's *beyond* wisdom, but a newfangled open wound. I let out a breath and smiled.
"*Mmm.*" Our lips were the closest they had ever been.

Fulanito smiled closer and I blushed, looking downwards at the curdling strawberry joint, then looking up.

"We should go to bed." Fulanito pulled back. "We're playing Canada tomorrow!"

"Yeah, totally, Canada! Another country." We snickered. I did not move my eyes away from his. I was exhausted with anything that

wasn't the awkward truth. Maybe we won't kiss, but I will continue to stare back, into his abyss. Like, maybe I found what I had always been looking for.

I woke up ecstatic. I opened my hellfire phone, messaged Reggy and Oracle and did three Hail Marys.

CT: YALL. FULANITO AND I HAD A MOMENT.

Reggy: Fucking jesus its 7AM

Oracle: Cool! …..Maybe you should tell him how you feel?…since were all bandmates?

CT: *eye roll emoji*

Oracle: btw Im up now— wanna roll me a J and meet me on the porch?

CT: Fuck YEA.

Reggy: Can you all please text on a separate thread? I just drove us down a dirt path on a mountain for 3 hours while we got chased by goats. yOUrE WELCoMeee. GOODMoRRNING.

CT: OMG REG WHY DO YOUR TEXTS MAKE SOUNDS??????

Oracle: (On a separate thread) Damn, left on read. 20 minuitesss?!

To kill 20 minutes I regressed in my nylon sleeping bag, silk pillow cases, and neon green vibrator shaped like some kind of space dick. My masturbation practice had started feeling like a cyclical state of purgatory—the same sleazy rock playlist, the same moment in fabricated time, where I'm making out with my ultimate crush who's unfortunately also my bandmate, on a circular velvet bed while all our friends sit around enjoying the evening as if it were any other. We're all turning full face, frocks, and plumage. Suddenly, Fulanito grabs my shoulders from behind and begins to kiss the back of my neck. Squeezing the despair out of me through a plunged neckline, Fulanito pushes his hands down my tits and towards my trail while his dick effortlessly thrusts against the soft plateau below my asshole. With two fingers, he massages my labia against my clit and to my pleasant surprise, begins to fuck me from behind, all to the wailing rock 'n' roll classics of 2069—*the year of the revolution*—and I am breathless.

Eventually, we nonchalantly break to contribute to the conversation as he innocently plays with my nipple. Whatever—it's *just fashion*.

Ahh. The good life. Partnership. The security of knowing who you will fuck at the party. Well, at least I have loneliness and trauma and something to write about and compare to the looming apocalypse that my generation was forced to desensitize—*goddammit*.

Fuck love, anyway, I often think after I have an orgasm by myself. Because nothing can *possibly* be as exciting as making myself cum by sitting on a barstool with my legs crossed while I gingerly enjoy whatever music is playing, whether I like it or not. This is easy after a double Kahlua Malibu. You know—a cafecito for lonely bitches.

Twenty minutes had not yet passed. I took a pause to reflect on the lighter side of apocalyptic despair and remembered last night.

Gabrielle Korn

Super Sick All Ages Rock Show

Susan Goldstein puts a salty, slightly stale tortilla chip in her mouth, and the moment she bites down on it, Katie says, "You're the loudest chewer in the entire world."

She's sitting cross-legged on the floor of Katie's bedroom flipping through the August issue of *Spin* magazine, the one with the Foo Fighters on the cover. There's a half-eaten bowl of chips beside her. Behind her, Katie is on her bed painting her nails navy blue.

"Do you want me to just suck on it?" Susan says, with her mouth full.

"No," Katie says, "I love your chewing. Never stop." Weirdly, Susan knows she means it.

The air conditioning is blasting so hard that they both have black hooded sweatshirts on. There's a glittering blue pool in Katie's parents' backyard but they've never used it, at least, Susan has never used it when she's hanging out here.

Susan doesn't have a pool. Her parents' house isn't as nice as Katie's, but they've never talked about it, they just hang out at Katie's house instead of hers.

Susan and Katie are both white, both Jewish, both seventeen. They like the same music and they shop at the same stores. Most of the time, though, Susan feels like she's a dimmer version of Katie; Katie is louder, she was cool first, it's her opinions that tend to dictate the shape of things. They both have brown hair, though Katie's is red in the sun, while Susan's color remains flat. Katie's eyes are wide and blue while Susan's small eyes are a muddy sort of green. Katie knows how to dress to look alternative, and Susan mostly just copies her.

There are four weeks left before senior year begins, which from this moment in Katie's bedroom feels like an impossibility. To Susan, life will always be exactly as it is right now; the year 2005 in the cookie cutter suburbs of Long Island, land of strip malls.

Katie says, "What are you reading down there?"

Susan looks down at the page. She hadn't really been reading, just looking at the pictures, but now she sees she has landed on an interview with the lead singer of a band they both like. In the black-and-white photo next to the column, it's clear that he's cute in that androgynous, gentle way all the indie guys are these days, and she brings the magazine closer to her face.

"It's the lead singer of What-What," she says.

"Hmm?" says Katie. "Who?"

"You know. The band name that's two question marks. It's pronounced What-What."

"How the fuck do you know that?" Katie is laughing.

"It says so. In the first sentence. *Jonny Lakes, the lead singer of the band pronounced What-What (written with two question marks), is only just getting started*. So fucking pretentious to name your band with symbols."

"I do love them though," Katie says. "I can't stop playing that one song."

"Do you have the rest of the album?" asks Susan.

"No," says Katie, "But we can get it."

"You want to go to Tower Records?"

"Yes, but not right now. Let's just go use the computer," Katie says. "We can kick Craig off of it."

Craig is Katie's twin brother, and it's easy to boss him around; at least, easy for Katie. Susan doesn't have siblings and wonders if it would be easy for her to be this mean to them if she did. At any rate, Katie is already on her feet and bounding down the hallway to the living room where the family computer glows in a corner with Craig hunched over it like some sort of gargoyle. Susan follows a few paces behind her and enters the room just in time to hear Katie say, "Jesus fucking Christ, Craig, what is that?"

Craig jumps, lunging for the mouse to close out of the open tabs but not before Susan sees it clearly: an image of a girl taking a photo of herself in the mirror, wearing just a black lace thong.

The image is immediately burned into Susan's brain; the conical boobs that look too large to be sustaining the angle at which they're pointed upwards, framed by tan lines, like the ghost of a very small bikini. An impossibly flat stomach, a belly button ring. The girl has long, straight brown hair that's partially obscuring her face but revealing enough to show lots of black eyeliner and clear lip gloss and bronzer. She's wearing a Tiffany necklace, the chunky one with the heart that all the girls wanted for their sweet sixteens last year—regular girls, not alt girls like Katie and Susan. A teenage bedroom is in the background, telling on itself with band posters and mess.

The page vanishes, whisked away into the ether.

"You're such a fucking perv," Katie says. "And on the family computer, no less!"

"What do you want?" he says.

"The computer, duh," Katie says. "Susan is here. You have to let us."

"Fine, ugh," he groans. "I hate you."

"Love you too," Katie says, blowing kisses as he gets up and slinks out of the room.

"Nice haircut, Suzie," he says to Susan, who promptly turns red.

"Shut up," she says, eyes down.

"No, I mean it," he says. "It's very Tegan & Sara."

Last week, Susan had taken a photo of a John Frieda shampoo ad to her mother's hair salon. She hadn't gotten a real haircut in ages and up until that day it was the same it had always been; to her waist, and parted down the middle.

"This is a horse's tail," the hairdresser had said, holding the split ends up. "You came to me just in time."

But the haircut Susan left with was not at all like the choppy bob in the magazine photo. It was more like a mullet, with short, uneven bangs and layers that ended just below her collar bone.

"It's a *fashion* mullet," Katie had declared when she saw her, which made her feel a little better. Katie would have said if it was hideous. Instead she told her, "You look like you're going to Misshapes," which was the nicest thing she could have said. Misshapes was a party in the city. Well, technically Misshapes was a DJ group, but there was a party with the same name that the DJs played (at least, that was Susan's understanding of it). They are too young to get in, so instead they'd spent many a Friday night looking through photos of the attendees, marveling at how ridiculous yet somehow cool everyone looked, and trying to emulate them.

Craig leaves the room and Katie throws herself into the desk chair.

"Who do you think that photo was of?" Susan says, when he's out of earshot.

"Could have been anyone," Katie shrugs. "Some slut."

Susan bristles at the word *slut*, but if Katie notices, she doesn't acknowledge it.

Katie pulls up the music pirating program and begins downloading the ?? album. Pop-up ads flood the screen and she spends the next few minutes X-ing out of them while the songs load.

"My parents would kill me if I did this on their computer," Susan says, and Katie rolls her eyes.

"You just don't know how to avoid getting caught," she says.

The computer makes a beeping noise to let them know they've successfully downloaded a free copy of the album, and Katie cranks the speaker to the highest volume while she hits play.

Over a twangy acoustic guitar, a man's voice begins to sing in the kind of whispery croon they can't get enough of.

"Fuck," Katie says. "He's the love of my goddamn life."

Susan smiles, closing her eyes. She loves this song; she loves how something sad can sound so catchy. It sounds like the inside of her heart has been transposed onto liner notes.

"Correct," she says. She lays down on the rug to better absorb the music. It smells like feet and carpet cleaner, but she doesn't mind. She spends a lot of time on this floor.

"Now that we've seen his face, you know who he kind of reminds me of," Katie says. She's hugging her knees on the desk chair and spinning it around.

Susan raises her eyebrows.

"Kyle Thomson," Katie says.

Susan groans. "No," she says. "Can't I just have this one thing?"

Katie begins to giggle. "Oh my god," she says, "That's why you love Jonny Lakes so much. He's a total Kyle."

"I don't even like Kyle anymore," Susan says. "It was too humiliating."

"For him, or for you?"

During their sophomore year, Susan had somewhat arbitrarily decided to be in love with Kyle, who'd been a senior at the time. Kyle was something of a social anomaly; his wheat-blond hair fell in a swoop across his face, and he always wore emo band t-shirts and jeans so tight they looked like a second skin. But he was a jock, too, a star on the lacrosse team, so he had a real body, with real muscles, not like the skinny emo boys that hung around Susan and Katie. He was friends with everyone; his appeal was kind of transcendent that way.

One day he met Susan's eyes as they passed each other in the hall and that was all it took for Susan to decide she was obsessed with him, with everything about him. The way his body looked in a t-shirt and the way other people looked at him. His effortless power, the way everything he did was cool. She wondered what it would be like to not have to try so hard, to simply be beloved because you exist.

She started doing things to try to get his attention, like listening to the music of the bands on his t-shirts and putting their lyrics in her away messages on AIM; hardcore and emo music that she hated, like the band Thursday or even Thrice. She stopped wearing dresses with combat boots and started wearing tight t-shirts with tighter pants, a black belt with silver pyramid studs, trying to look like the kind of girl he might like, lingering near his locker when she knew he'd be there. Finally, after months of this, he'd smiled and said hi, and that night she instant messaged him "hey."

The conversation didn't go beyond "what's up" and "nm u" but after that he did start saying hi to her in person every day, and because of that in her mind they were as good as together. Every night he messaged her about nothing, and her heart soared higher and higher.

"I can't tell if he likes me or not," she had said to Katie, who rolled her eyes.

"He wouldn't talk to you if he didn't like you," Katie had responded, but Susan didn't believe her. Why would someone like him be interested in someone like her?

But one night he messaged her, "wanna go do something."

"Like what," she wrote back.

"Idk maybe just drive around," he said.

He picked her up an hour later with all the windows rolled down and an Early November album blasting. She got into the car and smiled nervously. "Hey," he said.

He drove her to the lake, parked in the public parking lot and then they just sat there, listening to the music and looking at the moon.

"Have you heard the new Bright Eyes yet," she asked.

"Oh, I'm not really into that soft shit," he said.

"Right, you like screamo," she said. "That's cool. I like that stuff too."

"Cool," he said.

"Do you take all the girls here?" she asked, hoping to make him laugh.

"Just you," he said, not laughing. She didn't know how to take it. Was she special in some way? It was impossible to fathom.

Abruptly, he'd taken her hand and pressed it into the crotch of his skinny jeans, where she felt the lump of what she had to assume was his erection, though she couldn't be sure. It was smaller than she expected it to be. Really squished in there.

She froze, but kept her hand there, unsure what was expected of her.

After what seemed like an eternity he said, "Okay then," and took her home. When she got out of the car, she wasn't sure what to say or do so she said, "Thanks!" and then ran back inside. They did this several more times over the next month, each nearly silent drive ending with her hand on his dick and an awkward goodbye.

One night he messaged her: "are you ever going to want to h/u"

Instead of writing back, she hit the power button on her computer, paralyzed by a tidal wave of shame.

Susan didn't know much, but she did know that she didn't want to hook up with Kyle. The feeling was more like . . . she wanted to *be* him.

There was only one way out, and that was to go cold turkey.

The next time he said hi to her in the hallway, she averted her gaze, and after a few days of trying to say hi, he gave up. She stopped putting emo lyrics in her away messages and began listening to the folksier indie she preferred. She hadn't spoken to him since.

"Susan, I have to tell you something," Katie said one day, leaning against Susan's locker. "Kyle is telling everyone that you're a slut."

Susan felt all the blood rush out of her face.

"He called me a slut because . . . because I *wouldn't* have sex with him?"

"I think you can work this to your advantage," Katie said. "Your new reputation can be like, slutty music snob. That's kind of hot. Don't you think?"

The real benefit to this, Susan had realized, was that if people thought she was someone who fucked, they wouldn't know how desperately she did not want to be someone who fucked. Strategically, she did not try to defend herself.

Kyle went off to college and that was that, though Susan felt his memory in the whispers that every now and then made their way back to her.

Now, from the desk chair that's spinning round and round in dizzying circles, Katie says, "Whatever, Susan. You have a type. Kyle was just the original."

Susan's eyes are still closed. "Please just let me forget about Kyle and move on with my life," she says. "It's been two years."

"A lifetime," Katie agrees. "Sorry."

"I'm hungry," Susan says, sitting up, wanting to change the subject. "Do you want to go to the mall?"

"Yessss," Katie says, slithering off the chair, "I want pizza."

* * *

The taste of pizza is still on her breath as Susan wanders aimlessly down the "alt rock" aisle of Tower Records, trailing her fingers along the top edges of the CDs. A Fall Out Boy song is blasting through the store's speakers, a band Susan and Katie had liked for what felt like five minutes, until everyone else did, and now she finds their music so irritating it's almost offensive.

She visits the stacks where her favorites live, touches the names of The National and Broken Social Scene and Sleater Kinney and Clap Your Hands Say Yeah. She'll buy their new albums when she has more cash, at some point. It's all she spends money on, besides mall food, and, at Katie's insistence, sometimes clothes.

Her cell phone, clipped to her belt loop, buzzes. It's a text from

Katie, who is on the other side of the store. "Cute cashier today," it says. Susan glances at the front. She can't really see who is working, but that's beside the point. The point is that she only has 150 text messages per month and Katie has just wasted one of them. Katie's parents have her on an unlimited plan, and she seems to have no empathy for the limits of Susan's cell phone usage.

Then, a flier catches her eye.

The paper looks like a home-made collage that's been photo-copied and reads: SUPER SICK ALL AGES ROCK SHOW. And then, there in the middle, she sees two question marks.

"Katie!" she yells across the store.

Katie walks over. "What are you screaming about?"

"What-What is playing the Masonic temple this weekend. Look." She points at the flier.

The Masonic temple is twenty minutes away if she speeds on the L.I.E., in a neighboring town that she doesn't know the name of. Actually, she doesn't really know what a Masonic temple is, either, but this one has a large basement and they let local kids put on shows there, so she and Katie have been there a few times.

"I wish it didn't say *super sick*," Katie says. "That's so embarrasing."

"It's not amazing," Susan says. "But, still!"

"Why in the world would he play Long Island?" Katie says, tilting her head to the side.

"No idea," Susan says. "We should go." She takes the flier and shoves it in her purse, a black pleather messenger bag with pink zippers and pins. One pin has a coat hanger with an X over it. Another has a picture of the bird from the cover of the most recent Death Cab For Cutie album.

Later, when they've left the record store after buying nothing ("Why would we spend money when I can just download it?" Katie had said) they sit in Susan's old red Volvo station wagon in the parking lot, making plans for the weekend. Susan smooths the flier out in her lap.

Next to her, Katie looks over her shoulder, trying to read the details.

"So we're going," Katie says.

"Obviously," says Susan.

"Just promise me you're not going to wear that," Katie says, gesturing to the pink floral dress that Susan is wearing over her skinny jeans. The laces of her black combat boots are untied.

"What's wrong with this?"

"A dress over jeans is like, a *thing*," Katie says, rolling her eyes as though this is something everyone knows. "I promise you people will make fun of you. Like, older, cooler people."

Susan groans and throws her head back. Katie is wearing flared brown corduroys and a knit yellow cardigan with sneakers that look like bowling shoes. No bra, not that she needs one, and lots of necklaces; a look that might not have worked on everyone, but Katie prides herself on not being just anyone.

"Fine. What time do you want me to pick you up?" Susan puts her seatbelt on and starts to pull out of the parking lot. Katie pops in one of the burned CDs that are spilled on the floor of the passenger seat and turns the volume up.

"I don't know, seven? Do you mind if Jake comes?"

"I assumed he would," Susan says. Katie almost never wants to go anywhere without Jake these days, especially not now that he's in college and only home for the summer. This afternoon they are spending together without him is a rare treat.

Jake is artsy in the kind of way that means for most of his life, the popular kids liked to slam him into lockers and call him a fag. Which is funny, to Susan, because Jake is also one of the most heterosexual boys she'd ever met in her life. His long hair and tight black clothes don't mean he likes girls any less. And he likes Katie a lot; he'd liked her forever, and once she finally noticed him towards the end of freshman year it was like they were glued at the pelvis, making out and dry humping everywhere in a way that strikes Susan as disgusting and also kind of rude. But she puts up with him because Katie loves him, and at this point he's been around forever. She figures they'll probably get married, and she will be the third wheel for the rest of her life.

Susan says, "I have to run home to help my parents, but I'll drop you off first."

When Susan gets home, she sits in the driveway for a moment to rub what she can of her eyeliner off on her fingers, wiping her black-stained hands on her pants.

***

On Friday night, Susan picks Katie and Jake up first, from Katie's house. Katie takes the passenger seat and Jake flings himself into the back.

Susan has dressed in her best imitation of Katie; she's wearing tight black jeans, converse sneakers, and a knit green t-shirt from Urban Outfitters. At the last minute she decided to keep her black frame glasses on instead of her contacts. She thinks they make her look older.

"You look hot," Katie says approvingly.

"Thank god," Susan says, pulling out of the driveway.

"Can we go get my friend?" Jake says.

"Who?" Susan and Katie say at the same time. They know all of Jake's friends.

"It's a surprise," he says, and then Jake gives her directions from the backseat. "Two lefts and a right." He begins rubbing Katie's shoulders from behind her. "Mmm," Katie says. "Don't stop."

Susan fights the urge to gag.

Susan makes two lefts and a right. It's less than a minute before they approach a house that Susan has seen a thousand times. "This one," Jake says.

"I'll get him," Jake volunteers, and bounds out of the car and up the front steps.

"Is this . . ." Susan starts to say. She knows this house.

Katie calls out the window, "Jake, what the fuck?"

Susan turns to Katie. "Whatever is happening, I already don't like it."

She hears the sounds of Jake returning, and there's someone behind him.

It's Kyle Thomson.

He looks a little beefier than last time she saw him, but his hair is still in a blonde swoop and he's wearing a Thursday t-shirt that she recognizes.

Before she even has time to react, Kyle is in her backseat. Their eyes meet in the rearview mirror and Susan is fairly certain that she's about to die of embarrassment. The last time they'd spoken was in his car by the lake. She assumes he thinks she's the weirdest person on the planet. He wouldn't be wrong, she thinks. She wonders why she can't just be normal and like boys the way Katie does.

"Hi," she forces herself to say.

"Oh, hey Susan," he says.

Susan's face has never felt so red. She can't believe she's been ambushed like this.

"So you guys are in school together?" she says, when she can speak. Kyle and Jake were in different friend groups in high school. Different social classes, really. "Kyle, I thought you went to . . ."

"Columbia," Jake says, interrupting her. "We reconnected at a party and have been hanging out ever since."

"It was love at first sight," says Kyle, and they begin pushing each other and laughing.

"Cool," Susan says. "Okay, seatbelts." She's going to put on a smile and get through this.

"Wait," Kyle says, "Do you mind if we give one more person a ride?"

Susan looks sideways at Katie, who mouths, *I'm so sorry.*

"Sure," she says, weary. "Just tell me where to go."

"It's just one town over. It's on the way actually."

Katie turns the stereo on. A Bright Eyes song is next on the mix CD, and Susan raises the volume as loud as it'll go, her own private fuck you to Kyle for calling it "soft shit," though she doubts he remembers this exchange. She rolls down the windows as she gets on the highway. For a moment, she can forget the two boys in the back-seat, and it's just her and Katie.

Then Kyle is telling her to get off at the next exit and her reverie ends. She turns the volume down so she can hear him. He directs her through a quiet neighborhood and to a split-level house with a well-manicured lawn.

"You can just honk," he says, and she does, even though she knows it's impolite.

Within minutes the passenger door opens and a girl slides in.

"Hi!" The girl says. Susan feels Katie staring at her and chooses to keep looking straight ahead.

"I'm so glad you made it," Kyle says, and puts an arm around her.

Katie puts a hand on Susan's knee. Her face is pleading with an apology on behalf of Jake, but Susan ignores her. It's fine. She doesn't care that Jake brought Kyle and that Kyle brought a girl. She doesn't care about Kyle at all. She wants everyone to stop thinking she does.

Susan turns around and faces her new passenger. "I'm Susan," she says.

"I'm Eliza," the girl says. Looking her up and down, Susan thinks Eliza is deeply out of place. She's wearing black flared yoga pants folded over at the waist with a white spaghetti strap tank top and a chunky silver choker. Her brown hair has been straightened around her face, which is slightly orange, like a bad fake tan or the wrong shade of foundation. She's pretty anyway, though. Too pretty to be hanging out with this crowd. But that was always the thing about Kyle Thomson; the boundaries of cliques did not apply to him. So maybe it did make sense.

Susan squints. "You look really familiar," she says.

"I get that a lot," Eliza says, and next to her, Kyle is smirking, as though there's a joke that Susan doesn't get.

Katie finally turns around, her face full of judgment. "Hi," she says, "I'm Katie." They stare at each other. "Oh, wait," Katie says, brightening. "You do look familiar! What year are you?"

"I'm about to be a junior. You guys don't look familiar to me at all," Eliza says, and by the way she says it Susan can tell she needs to drop it.

"Okay," Susan says. "Sorry. Everyone ready?"

"I remember when we were juniors," Katie says, faux-wistfully, and Susan laughs.

"A hundred and one years ago," she replies.

"Oh please!" Jake shouts, from the back.

Susan gets back on the highway, wondering what Kyle is doing hanging out with someone so much younger than him. Two years younger is one thing, but three is another. As she merges, she meets Eliza's green eyes in the rearview mirror.

"Yes?" Eliza says. Susan is a little bit scared of Eliza and how direct she is.

"Sorry," Susan says, looking back at the road. "You just don't look like someone who would go to a What-What show."

Eliza tilts her head to the left. "A what now?"

Susan feigns surprise. "Uh, the band we're seeing tonight?"

Eliza starts to laugh. "That's how you pronounce it?"

"I don't know what you mean," Katie says, trying hard to keep a straight face. "Two question marks in a row is obviously pronounced What-What."

"I've been saying *question mark, question mark*," Eliza says, and at this Susan finally breaks, erupting into giggles. Eliza turns pink and looks out the window.

"I think your way is better," Susan says, softening at how embarrassed Eliza seems. "So," Susan says, to change the subject, "How long have you guys been going out for?"

Kyle says, "Since the summer began," at the same time that Eliza says, flatly, "We're not."

"Uh oh," Katie says.

"Kyle wishes," Eliza clarified. "I'm still thinking about it."

Susan wondered what there even was to consider. Kyle was looking hotter than ever now that he had one year of college done. They looked right together, squeezed into the backseat. More right than Susan would have ever looked with him.

Out of the corner of her eye Susan sees Jake fishing around in his jacket pocket but has to look where she's going and misses what he's produced until he hands it to Katie and she takes a swig.

"Ew," Katie says. "What is this, nail polish remover?"

"Sorry, but can you guys not drink in my car?" Susan says.

"What?" Kyle says, laughing. "Drinking and driving refers to the driver."

"I heard that if you get pulled over and there are under-age people drinking in your car, it's on you," Susan says. She's getting nervous.

"That's ridiculous," Jake says.

"Maybe you guys should just do what she says," Eliza pipes up. "She's giving you a ride, after all." Kyle pulls his arm back from where it's been around Eliza's shoulder.

"You don't have to be a bitch about it," he says.

Susan chooses to ignore this. "Thank you," she says to Eliza.

Jake sighs and puts the flask away. "We can wait until we get there," he says.

At the next stop sign, Katie puts a hand on Susan's arm. *Are you okay*, she mouths. Susan nods and forces herself to smile. She's very thrown off by Kyle's presence in her backseat. She doesn't know what to do with herself. And the addition of Eliza is an extra layer of awkwardness. Eliza is too attractive to be in her car, she keeps thinking, stealing glances in the rearview mirror. Like a movie star hanging out with normies. Glowing.

In the parking lot of the Masonic temple, people are strewn about. Since it's an all-ages show it's a young crowd, and everyone looks vaguely familiar; it's a small community of teens in Suffolk County with the same taste in music.

"Very scene-y tonight," Katie says, pleased.

At the door, a girl with a shaved head and cat-eye glasses sits at a small desk.

"Five dollars," she says, not looking at them.

Everyone digs around in their pockets to produce cash.

"Oh shit," Susan says. "I don't have anything on me."

"I got you, Sue," Katie says, turning to the door girl. "Two please, for me and my lady."

"Sorry," Susan says, and Katie waves her off.

Only once they are inside the big empty space does Susan finally relax. She feels at home here, with these weirdos who are leaning against the walls and glaring at each other. This is a world she understands.

Katie plops down, cross legged on the ground a few feet from the stage and pulls Susan's hand until Susan falls down next to her. Eliza, Jake, and Kyle stand awkwardly over them, eventually turning their backs and talking to each other.

"Why do I feel like we're the kids and they're the grownups?" Katie says.

"What the fuck is up with Jake bringing Kyle," Susan whispers.

"I'm so sorry," Katie says, putting her face in her hands. "I'm going to fucking kill him. He probably just doesn't remember, or doesn't know, what happened."

"I want to hide in a hole for the rest of my life."

"But Suzie, why?" Katie says, leaning closer now because music has started to play and the room is filling up, getting louder with talking and laughter. "He was the one who was an asshole."

"It's just so embarrassing that everyone knows I had a crush on him," she says.

"But that's how life goes," Katie says. "Humans like each other. It's normal and good."

"I can't explain it better than that," Susan says. "Can we talk about something else?"

"Definitely," Katie says. "Can we talk about Eliza?"

"Shh!" Susan says, and they both look up at Eliza, whose back is still towards them.

"She has a good butt," Susan says, eyeing Eliza's yoga pants.

"I know," Katie says. "And great boobs. I think I hate her."

Susan laughs. "It's like she's from another planet."

"Planet popular," Katie says.

"Planet JAP," says Susan.

"I don't think she's Jewish."

"JAP is an aesthetic," Susan says, and Katie snorts.

There's some commotion from the stage as the first band comes out. Katie jumps up and pulls Susan by the hand with her.

* * *

The opening band is three people. The drummer is a girl, which Susan thinks is cool. The other two look like every other boy in a band.

Susan turns to her left and sees that Eliza is the only person in the crowd not dancing. She looks almost shy.

"What's wrong?" she says.

"What?" Eliza shouts over the music. "I can't hear you."

Susan puts her hands over Susan's ears and shouts, "Why aren't you dancing?"

Eliza flinches. "Ow," she says. "My fucking ear drums!"

"Sorry," Susan says.

Eliza puts her own hands over Susan's ear and says, at a much more reasonable volume, "What kind of music is this?"

"Oh!" Susan says. She feels delighted. This is something she can help with. She feels, suddenly, cool, as though knowing something Eliza doesn't gives her a certain kind of power. "Prog rock."

Eliza tilts her head to the side. "They're from Prague?" Susan tries not to blush as Eliza's lips brush her ear lobe.

"No, prog like progressive."

Eliza glances around. "I don't understand how everyone is dancing to it. I don't hear a beat."

Susan laughs. She points to the girl in front of them, who is tapping her heel in time with the music. The rest of the movement in her body is coming from that momentum; it's making her head bob and her shoulders move.

"She's got it," Susan says. "Follow her heel."

They spend the rest of the set so close they're almost touching, heels hitting the floor in sync together.

When the opening band finishes, Eliza excuses herself to the bathroom, and Katie says to Susan, "That was nice of you."

Susan shrugs. "It's what you did for me, once." It's true: Katie is the one who taught Susan how to dance at shows without looking like an idiot.

"The student becomes the teacher," Katie says, and then Jake is wrapping his arms around her, and the conversation is over because she's turned and put her mouth on his.

Susan walks towards the bathroom. She doesn't really have to pee, but she doesn't want to be alone with Kyle, who was looking as awkward as she felt when Katie and Jake started going at it.

In the bathroom, a girl wearing black short shorts over ripped fishnet stockings is fixing her hair in the mirror. For a moment Susan is transfixed by the pale legs beneath the fishnets—the skin looks so soft, and her knees are bruised like peaches—but the girl catches Susan staring and so she looks away. A toilet flushes and Eliza emerges.

"Oh hey," she says, washing her hands.

Susan leans against the wall. "So what do you think of your first show?"

"Who says it's my first show?" Eliza says. She wipes her wet hands on her yoga pants, and then digs into her small Coach bag and pulls out a Lancôme Juicy Tube lip gloss. It's sparkly blue.

"Is it not your first show?" Susan says, ready to apologize.

"No, it is," Eliza says. "I'm just fucking with you."

Susan laughs, surprised that Eliza is funny. "Hey," she says, "Why is your lip gloss blue?"

"It's not," Eliza says, and when she puts it on, it shows up clear. "Want some?"

She gives it to Susan, who sniffs it. "I kind of hate lip gloss," she says, but puts it on anyway, handing it back to Eliza while licking her lips. "It tastes like candy."

"Exactly," Eliza says. "It looks cute on you. Try not to eat it all off."

"Should we go back out there? I think What-What is starting soon."

"I guess," Eliza says. "Or we could just keep hanging out in the bathroom."

Susan can't tell if she's kidding or not, but Eliza follows her out when she leaves.

The band is setting up and soon Jonny Lakes materializes, back-lit, like some sort of ethereal being who can only exist on a stage. Susan and Katie grab each other's hands and begin to scream.

"Hi, we're What-What," Jonny says into the microphone. His hair is falling into his eyes. "Thanks for coming out."

They open with Susan's favorite song. Instantly forgetting about Eliza and the others, Susan and Katie push their way to the front, until they're standing directly in front of Jonny. Susan puts her hands on the stage, looking up into his gorgeous face. She's singing along at the top of her lungs.

He looks down at her. "Hey, you know all the words!" He says into the mic, pointing at her. The next time the chorus comes, he takes the microphone off of its stand and holds it in front of Katie and Susan. He lets them sing the first line together before grabbing it back.

Katie hugs Susan. "This is the best night ever," she says.

For the rest of the set, Jonny smiles and winks at Susan, dancing at her with his guitar. She feels like she's dreaming.

When they finish, Jonny says, "Thank you, Long Island!" And then it's over and the lights are coming back on. Susan is drenched with sweat.

Kyle, Jake, and Eliza are all leaning against a wall in the back, looking bored.

"You guys are no fun," Katie says, when they rejoin the group.

"Dancing in the front is gay," Kyle says.

* * *

They're getting back into Susan's car to leave when Katie says, "You know what? I think Susan should go wait for Jonny."

Susan slides into the driver's seat. "Excuse me?"

"Yeah!" Jake shouts from the back, banging his hands on the headrest of Susan's seat. "Go get his number."

"No," she says. "First of all, he's old. Second all, no."

"I think you should," Kyle says.

"Wait," Eliza says. "Who? The lead singer?"

Katie nods vigorously. "He was totally into her."

Eliza starts laughing.

"Is it funny that he would be into me?" Susan says, her face beginning to burn.

"No!" Eliza says. "It's just, that guy is like, such a fag." The way she says the word fag is, somehow, not as mean as when everyone else says it; there's something affectionate in her voice that Susan can't place.

They all turn towards her. "What?" Eliza is still laughing. "Was it not obvious to you?"

"No," Katie said, shaking her head. "He's gay in the way Jake is gay, which is to say, in appearance only."

Jake nods. "I am the expert in this subject and I declare he is not gay."

"You wanna make a bet?" Eliza says.

Susan groans. "You're going to make me go talk to him."

"Someone needs to settle this," Katie says.

Kyle is quiet, looking out the window. Then he says, "You better go before he leaves."

"Fine," Susan sighs. "I'll go be a groupie and hit on the musician."

"Yesss!" Katie cheers. "Really? Oh my god Susan you're so brave. We'll wait here for you."

"You *have* to wait for me, I'm your ride," Susan says, rolling her eyes as she gets out of the car.

She can't be sure, but she thinks she hears Kyle mutter the word "slut" under his breath right before she shuts the door.

She looks back and sees all four of her passengers pressed into the windows, watching her. *This is so stupid*, she thinks.

When she gets back inside the temple, she finds the lead singer of the band packing up his gear. She leans against the wall, waiting for him to walk by, and when he does, he looks right at her and grins, putting his guitar case down.

"Hey!" Jonny says. "Thanks so much for coming."

She hadn't anticipated he would actually stop to talk to her, and she immediately turns pink, but tries hard to seem cool. "Oh, yeah," she says. "Uh, you're welcome. You guys were great."

He smiles. He's very pretty close up. "Thanks," he says.

"Can I ask what made you want to play out here? I feel like you guys are too big for a show like this."

"I'm from here," he says. "We like playing hometown shows. Keeps us humble."

Just then another man appears. He's shorter than Jonny, more petite in general, with a delicate face that strikes Susan as almost elvish and hair that looks like it's never been out of place. He loops an arm around the lead singer's waist.

"Baby, can we go?" He says, as Susan realizes that Eliza called it.

"Sorry babe," Jonny says, kissing the top of the man's head. "I'm coming."

The shorter man turns to Susan, looking her up and down. "I know how you love to meet the local baby gays," he says to Jonny.

"Oh," Susan says, "I'm not . . ."

The man cuts her off. "A local?"

Susan stutters. "Why do you think that I'm . . ." she can't finish the sentence.

"First of all, your hair," Jonny says. "But it's more of an energy thing. Do they still not teach gaydar in New York State public schools? You do go to public school, right?"

Susan is speechless.

"Don't bully her," the other man says. He's wearing a blue-and-white striped t-shirt and there's a red bandana hanging out of his pocket. "God, how old are you, honey?"

"I'm seventeen," she says.

"Well, you look twelve," he replies.

"So do you," Susan says, and he laughs.

"Thanks," he winks. "Botox."

Jonny puts both of his hands on Susan's shoulders and looks deeply into her eyes. "One day you'll get out of this town and your life will be amazing," he says. It sounds like a song lyric; so perfect, exactly what she needed to hear.

She doesn't know what to say. For some reason she feels as though she's about to burst into tears.

"Let me give you my number," he says. "When you move to Brooklyn to become a lesbian we should hang out." He writes his number on her arm in a black sharpie that he pulls from his pocket. "Seriously," he says, and she can tell he means it. "Call me. It's my sacred duty to help the queers escape Long Island."

Then the other man pulls him by the hand and they walk away, waving.

Susan is trembling so hard that she takes a minute before going to the car.

I'm not gay, she thinks. She wonders what would happen if her friends find out about this conversation, or, worse, if people she *isn't* friends with find out.

Lesbians are her gym team teachers with their mushroom hair-cuts and high-waisted khaki shorts. Lesbians are Rosie O'Donnell and Ellen DeGeneres. Lesbian was the word the popular kids sneered at her and Katie while they sat together at lunch. No, she wasn't that. She liked boys. She'd liked Kyle.

Unless. . .

She picks at her bracelet, a pink leather wristband with silver pyramid studs. She counts the studs. She tries to breathe.

After she's calmed down as much as possible, she walks across the parking lot and gets back into the front seat.

"Well?" Katie says.

Susan holds up her arm, showing the phone number. She doesn't need to tell them the rest.

"Wow," Eliza says, "I stand corrected." There's something in Eliza's voice that Susan can't place. It sounds a little bit like jealousy. Maybe she's not used to someone else getting male attention.

"I knew it!" Katie shouts, and throws her arms around Susan, who is still trying hard not to cry.

"Yay," Jake says. "Susan gets a boyfriend."

Kyle puts his arm around Eliza, who is looking out the window and not saying anything.

"Where to?" Susan says, desperate to change the subject.

"Diner?" Katie says, and everybody agrees in unison.

* * *

At the diner, everyone orders a grilled cheese, except Eliza.

"I don't eat carbs at night," she says, and sips her Diet Coke.

"So that's why you have such a hot bod," Katie says. Next to her, Susan laughs nervously. "What?" Katie says. "We were all thinking it."

"We were," Kyle says.

Eliza rolls her eyes. "Uh, thanks," she says. "Now that we've objectified me, can we move on?" Eliza seems like she's used to people talking about how hot she is.

"Yes," Jake says, and pulls his flask out. Looking around, he pours some of it into his soda, and then passes it under the table to Kyle.

Kyle passes it to Katie, who then passes it to Eliza.

"I'm good," Eliza says, giving it back to Jake.

"You straight edge?" Jake says.

"No, I just don't drink," Eliza says.

Susan doesn't know why she finds this so surprising. Eliza looks like she's the kind of girl who loves to drink and have fun. Instead, she's proving to be serious, thoughtful. It's unnerving.

Meanwhile, Jonny's words are still clamoring around in her head. *Lesbian lesbian lesbian lesbian lesbian lesbian.* She shovels food into her mouth to keep from having to speak.

Across the table, her friends are starting to seem drunk. Their voices are getting louder, and Katie is laughing uncontrollably at something Susan must have missed. Only Eliza is quiet, sipping her diet soda.

The weary waitress comes over, looking as though she'd rather die than be there. "Can I get you anything else?" she says.

* * *

Susan pulls up in front of Kyle's house and puts the car in park. "We're here," she says.

"Aw fuck," Jake says. "I don't want the night to end."

"I know you love going on dates with me," Kyle says.

"I'm in love with you," Jake says. "You're the love of my life."

Susan catches Eliza rolling her eyes in the rearview.

"Hold on," Susan says. The street is a dead-end. "Let me just turn the car so I can get out of here."

She puts the car in reverse. She rests her left hand on the passenger seat, twisting around to watch where she's going as she backs up. Before her gaze gets to the rearview window, though, her eyes get stuck on Eliza, who is staring at her from the middle seat.

There's a slow smile spreading across Eliza's face as she continues to look at Susan with her head tilted to the side.

Suddenly there's a loud scraping sound of metal on metal, and Susan slams on the breaks.

"What the fuck?" Kyle says and jumps out of the car.

"Shit," Susan whispers, gripping the wheel.

Kyle bolts from the car and starts yelling.

"Fuck," Susan says. She's frozen in place.

"Oh shit, Suzie," says Katie. "I think you need to go see what the damage is."

She shakily gets out of the car and sees that she's dented and scratched the entire side of a parked car.

"This is my dad's car," Kyle says. "He's going to kill me. Really nice job, Susan. Amazing work." It's almost pitch-black outside but for her taillights. She wouldn't have seen the parked car even if she'd been looking, which she hadn't been. All she'd seen was Eliza's slow smile.

"I'm so sorry," Susan says. "It was an accident."

"Was it?" Kyle says, walking closer to her, leering down at her aggressively. "Was it *a mistake*, Susan? Are you sure you didn't do it on purpose?"

She takes a step backwards. "Of course it was," she says. Her eyes fill up with tears. "I'll pay for everything." Susan has $900 in her bank account from her summer job. She will probably have to take all of it out to pay for the damage.

"You think?" He says, and now Susan does start to cry.

"You're such a fucking freak, Susan Goldstein," he shouts at her. And then his voice drops to a whisper, so that only she can hear him.

"First you practically stalk me for a year and then you basically *force* me to like you. And then once I do—and I did like you Susan, I really did—you start ignoring me? Who the fuck does that? You're a terrible person." He doesn't just sound angry now. He sounds hurt, too.

Susan is shocked. It hadn't occurred to her that she had the power to hurt Kyle.

"You're the one who told everyone I'm a slut," she says, in a rare moment of assertiveness.

He laughs.

She's trembling. She hears the door of the car open and shut.

"Kyle, that's enough." It's Eliza.

"Stay out of it, Liza," he says.

"I think you should go inside now," Eliza says, calm but firm. "Susan will call you tomorrow to deal with the car stuff, right Susan?"

Susan nods.

Kyle snickers. He suddenly seems crueler than Susan had realized.

"Kyle," Eliza says, firmly, "Go home."

"Aren't you going to come in with me?" he asks Eliza.

"Not after that display," she says. She puts an arm around Susan's shoulders. "Come on, Susan. You can drive me back home, right?"

Susan nods. "Yeah," she whispers.

"Fucking high school girls," Kyle says, and kicks a rock before turning and walking up the steps to his parents' house.

Susan and Eliza get back in the car, where Jake and Katie are sitting tensely in the back seat.

Jake says, "Well that was a fun end to the night."

Katie hits him. "Don't be an asshole," she says. "Susan, babe, are you okay?"

"I'm fine," Susan says. She's still shaking. She hates being yelled at.

Katie puts her hands on Susan's shoulders. "What do you need? Do you want me to fucking kill him?"

Susan shakes her head. "I'm fine," she repeats. "I just want to go to bed."

Katie nods. "We can just walk home from here, right Jake?"

"Totally," he says. "Hey, Susan, I'm sorry. That was fucked up of him. We all know it was an accident."

"Thanks, Jake," Susan says.

Katie and Jake get out of the car and disappear into the thick darkness, holding hands.

* * *

"How did you meet Kyle, anyway?" Susan says, merging back onto the highway with Eliza next to her.

"He crashed a friend's birthday party," Eliza says. "I thought he was the cutest thing for a while there. Now I'm starting to feel like maybe it was a little creepy that he showed up to a high school party."

Susan nods. "I used to think he was so cool. But like, why is he even hanging out with us? He's old now."

Eliza laughs. "He's nineteen."

"Like I said," Susan says, smiling. "Old."

They're quiet for the rest of the ride. The only sound in the car is its occasional turn signal. Susan feels awkward. She wonders if Eliza thinks it's weird that they're hanging out. They're so different.

Susan pulls up in front of Eliza's house and puts the car in park.

"Thanks for defending me," she says, turning to Eliza.

"Of course," Eliza says.

Eliza is holding her eye contact in a way that is making Susan's stomach begin to do flips.

"Um," Susan says. "So."

"So," Eliza says, and smiles again, in the same way she was smiling right before Susan crashed her car. "Do you want to like, come in? My parents are out."

Susan thinks she might have a heart attack. Instead she says, "Yeah. That might be cool."

She takes her seatbelt off and faces Eliza, who does the same. Susan can smell Eliza's vanilla perfume and all she can think is that cursed word from Jonny: *lesbian lesbian lesbian lesbian.* Was she a lesbian? Was Eliza? What the fuck was going on?

A lock of Eliza's straight brown hair falls across her face, and that's when Susan sees it.

"Wait," Susan says, pulling back, "I just realized where I know you from." She can't believe she didn't realize it before.

"Oh no," Eliza says, her shoulders slumping, all of a sudden looking very sad. "You've seen it."

"Katie's brother Craig has it," Susan says, shaking her head in disbelief as she remembers the naked photo on Craig's computer. Eliza was even wearing the same necklace she'd had on in the picture. "How . . . ?"

"I have to assume everyone's brother has seen it," Eliza shrugs. "There's nothing I can do about it now."

"But why does it even exist?" Susan says. She doesn't mean to be judgmental, but she knows that's how it sounds. Still, she can't help it.

"Because I took it," Eliza says, as though Susan is the dumbest person on earth.

"But did someone send it around?"

"I guess so." She folds her arms across her chest, which is turning splotchy as it rises and falls.

"But like . . . why take it in the first place?"

"Excuse me?" Eliza says.

"I'm sorry," Susan says, quickly, needing things to go back to how they were just a minute ago. "I didn't mean to offend you. I just . . ."

"You saw my tits and now you think you know me," Eliza says, her Long Island accent becoming more pronounced as she gets more upset; the vowels become longer, like there are W's attached to them, and her T's become harder and also more lispy, as though the consonant is formed in the front of the roof of her mouth. *Tits.*

Susan's eyes well up with tears again. "That's not what I meant. I was just worried, is all. I know how . . . I know how guys are."

"I can take care of myself," Eliza says. "Not that it's any of your fucking business."

This is the second time Susan has been yelled at tonight, and she's feeling very small.

"Anyway, Kyle told me all about you," Eliza says. "How slutty you are. I don't know. I thought it was cool. Not that he called you a slut, but that maybe you were like me. I guess I thought we could be sluts together."

"Do you want me to leave?" Susan says, and as the words leave her mouth she realizes she might have completely misinterpreted what Eliza is trying to say, but it's too late.

"Do you want to leave?" Eliza shoots back.

"Um," Susan says. "I don't know. I feel like you hate me now."

Eliza rolls her eyes. "Grow up," she says.

She can't see a way through this conflict with Eliza. So she does the only thing she knows how to do.

"I guess I should get going," Susan says.

"Yeah?"

"Yeah," Susan says. She doesn't really have to, but she's so uncomfortable she thinks she might throw up. "Okay, well, bye, I guess."

Eliza is shaking her head in disbelief. "Bye." She gets out of the car and slams the door. Then she leans into the window and says, "See you never."

"Okay," Susan says, feeling defeated. She puts the car in drive and takes off down the quiet street, tears running down her face. In her rearview mirror she sees Eliza standing exactly where she left her, watching her drive away.

"See you never," Susan whispers. (It's not never, though. Life is longer and the world is smaller than that.)

She drives home without music; just the sound of her turn signal clicking in the soupy suburban darkness, the Volvo's old engine humming, and the beat of her heart, which, despite the absolute failure of the whole night, is steady with the knowledge of who she is, or at least, who she might become, if she can ever manage to get out of her own way.

Chloe Caldwell

Summer of Strap-on

We were together for three period cycles each. It was the summer of strap-on, the summer of matchbooks from hotels, the summer of Malin + Goetz hotel toiletries. It was a summer of lingerie photos in the mirrors, of last minute plans, the summer of Amtrak. If I didn't know any better, I'd say I had the summer of a man.

When I learned my husband had been sleeping with prostitutes as I'd been going through fertility treatments for three years, one of my first thoughts was, *I'm too gay for this*. I left him and life changed shape dramatically, like a square shifting to an octagon. It was the summer of Marriott hotels on random Tuesdays or Thursdays to meet with the woman I was sleeping with. I identified as divorced, but was not yet legally divorced. The word "separated" didn't feel right as it implies hope. She was six years younger and told me the minute she heard me moan she wanted to continue to please me.

"Tell me what you want," she said.
"Talk to me," she said.
"Don't hold back," she said.

I swiped left on anyone who includes their vaccination status on Tinder. No thanks; Not here to be political, here to get laid. My friend always said about Tinder, the rules were "No Brads, No Chads, and no one from Connecticut" but the person I matched with was from Connecticut and I decided to break the rule, because the photograph of Avery in an orange suit on Tinder was making my spine tingle.

The first time Avery was about to fuck me, my soon to be ex-husband texted me from a rehab he is at called, if you can believe it, Seeking Integrity, about writing an impact letter. An impact letter, he said, would be about how his addictions to sex and alcohol had affected me and our family.

I hadn't seen his name text me in a month so for a second, I was confused about what his role in my life even was. Who was this person again? It all felt so far away.

"Can you send two pages of an impact letter? Diane@seekingintegrity.com."
    "Yes I can do that," I replied.
    "Getting fucked with a strap-on g2g" I followed with, because as I was responding to the text, I was watching Avery velcro down the strap-on and the moment felt so ridiculous.

Avery kissed slowly and deeply and touched my hip bone, and she had a tattoo of a watch underneath her real watch. The tattoo watch, to me, looked like it said 6:30, but she assured me it said 3:30. She's probably right. It was dark in the bar and plus I can't tell time that well.

Multiple times I asked Avery, "Are you real?" and "Where did you come from?" It felt like she had fallen from the sky into the hotel bed. I described the sex afterwards as "awesome" and she said she usually gets "great" or "nice" and that she'd never had anyone describe it as awesome, so then I wrote back with the words "unfettered" and "intuitive."

"Why are you like this?" she asked me every time before she devoured me.
    "Why are you like this?" I'd say back at the same time so we were in unison.

In the morning after our first time together she texted me:

Avery: How wet are you right now?

Me: I had to change again, not even kidding.

Avery: I really like that.

Me: I like it too, and you.

Avery: I like you.

Me: *puddle emoji*

Me: *sends voice note of orgasm*

Avery kept an audio message from you, my phone wrote back.

Avery: Good thing I have noise canceling headphones on. It is so hot when you cum for me, baby.

Later I got paranoid she'd leak it or play it for her friends.

"Any content you send me is just between you and me," she responded.

"It's like your private podcast," I text.

"If I had a daily digest of this, I wouldn't need podcasts," she writes.

I text my friend Maya: "I sent her another voice memo of me coming."

Maya: "oh my lord i need to get on your level."

"You need to get married and divorced first to get this high," I responded.

"This is why I can't be gay," I say to my friend Maya. "Because I get psycho."

"That's actually exactly what MAKES you gay," she responds.

Divorce makes me feel like I'm in high school again. Divorce makes me feel slutty. Wanna feel young? Get divorced! If the secret to staying married is to not get divorced, then the secret to the fountain of youth is to get divorced. Was it mean of me to text my ex that I was "being fucked rn g2g?" or was it transparent or irreverent? Unnecessary, definitely. I didn't mean to be vengeful, it's just that the moment was so ridiculous, like when two worlds collide, or the internal meets the external.

It was obvious Avery does these little sex dates somewhat frequently. In her Doc Marten tote bag she had been carrying a strap-on. People who don't have a lot of sex don't carry around a strap-on in a tote bag. They just don't. I appreciated her preparation. She even had lube with her.

My friend Sam texted me: "Being fucked with a strap-on is the best. It is so removed from men but also feels like a big fuck you to them— an extremely specific and powerful feeling! IMO."

A few days later I felt bad I had so irreverently writing "Getting fucked rn g2g" so I wrote, "Sorry, that was weird timing." Then I blocked him. It was also the summer of blocking.

"Have you ever had voice memo sex?" I texted Avery.

"Never," she said. I find it wild that people don't have voice memo sex; it is way less pressure than phone sex as you can erase the messages if you don't like how they sound.

She sends me a voice memo: "I want to see you in that seafoam green lingerie and have my hand deep inside you dripping wet. But you can't come. Then you'll have me in your mouth, but you can't come. I'm going to turn you on until you're begging."

Divorce feels like a second coming. I feel like I'm ten years younger. So what if I am a middle aged cliche—a woman finding her sexuality again? Like Kathryn Hahn in *Mrs. Fletcher*. Post-divorce it's been all white wine and random eating, eating just to be full, no effort put in, whatever is laying around like a bite of yogurt or crackers or a rogue frozen Twix bar. I can't remember the last time I cooked something or even assembled anything. I've been subsisting on sex adrenaline. Post-divorce the world looks brighter and birds chip outside my window. Life has never felt this rich or vivid. Post-divorce sex makes me so plugged into everything around me and my skin and hair look better than ever. All of that blood rushing to my face. I wake up and dance in the mirror to blasting music, something I never did while married. When I was married, my sex drive dissipated. I later learned from listening to sex expert Vanessa Marin that if you aren't desiring sex with your partner, it's not that you have a low sex drive, it's that you aren't desiring the type of sex you've been having.

Avery was meant to be a one or two time sex adventure, but one or two times turned into four months, and sex becomes something to do for pleasure again, instead of trying to get pregnant. For hours, I greedily orgasm, in Brooklyn, with a candle burning, to a playlist of fifty songs she made for our nights.

One August hot as hell morning I leave her apartment and walk to the Myrtle-Wyckoff L train. I am thirty-seven, seventeen years after I'd gone to the same subway stop for sex and air conditioning and a crush. How am I still doing the same shit? As I wait for the L train, a young kid, anywhere from nineteen to twenty-four walks by me holding a Strand tote bag, wearing glasses and converse; he is tall and skinny and looks like they all did when my friends worked at the Strand seventeen years ago. The cycle never ends. I get on the L train towards Manhattan and feel like there used to be more bagels and coffee on it.

When I begin having sex for fun again, I remember what my twenties were like. Sex as a hobby, sex as stress release, sex as empowerment, sex as relaxing, sex before sleep, sex as losing yourself. How can sex hold this dichotomy, become something so full of math and numbers and dread?

On my first date with Avery, I said that sperm was the only thing I needed men for. We were getting our bags and walking out of the bar.

"That's something I'll never need," she said.

"Go down on me," Avery said in bed.
    "I'm scared," I said.
    "You'll figure it out," she said.
    My journal a few weeks early had said, "Need to learn how to give head!!!!"
    June turns into July and then, in August, Avery fucks me even though I have my period. Before bed, I told her there is still some of my blood on her thighs, and she said she knows, shrugs and goes to sleep that way.

What is the word for going down on someone for the first time?

What is the word for when you begin calling each other baby?

What is the word for going to bed with your partner's blood on you?

"Sorry I bit your shoulder so hard," she said after she came.

"I didn't even notice."

The week of 9/11, I initiated a break up with her one morning while she was inside me and we both cried and then immediately got our periods and got back together within six hours.

Post-divorce lovers aren't meant to last, but they serve an incredible purpose of bringing you back to yourself. My friends all thought Avery was a rebound and a distraction, which, sure, but she was also the person to get me back in my body after six years. That's not nothing.

McKenzie Wark

Here She Comes

She is what enabled, but also what prevented, me from coming out. She is elusive. She hides. Sometimes it's hard to believe she has ever been around, or ever will again. She is the tip, the tip-off, to transsexuality, and not just for me. She comes to a few of us, it turns out.

For some of us, transsexuality is elusive, something lurking somewhere, hard to locate, hard to bring into a definite shape, hard to name. For some of us, it's going to come into focus in one part of life before it's legible in any of the others. Sometimes that place is sexuality. What are you supposed to do, when you finally perceive the edge, the shape, the tone, of the woman who could become you—and she is a slut?

I'd had the misfortune to read a very bad book about this. One that held that there are good and bad kinds of trans women. The good kind start out as gay men, maybe a little on the faggy side, but that's okay as they are going to transition into perfectly normal heterosexual women. The bad kind are not so much attracted to women, but attracted to themselves *as* a woman. I was the bad kind.

There's at least two meanings of slut, which might go together but don't always. Slut can be about fucking around, or slut can be about sexual intensity. There's quantity and quality sluttery. Some people who fuck a lot are not really all that present for it. Some people who fuck intensely don't necessarily seek that out all the time. Either way, its connected to femininity so it's supposed to be a bad thing, not least because a little threatening. This culture is not keen on women who fuck a lot or fuck hard.

I never fucked around all that much. Partly because of that tote bag of unnamed trans feelings I lugged around everywhere. Sex was rarely all that intense either, frankly. I focused a lot on the pleasure of sexual partners as I wasn't really there for my own. Except when she surfaced, like the outline of another skin under my skin.

It took a lot of coaxing to bring her out. She's a girl who appreciates seduction and situation. The ambience has to be just right, for she partly comes out of the air and partly out of this flesh. She surfaces from under the skin to meld into sex-saturated air.

What she wants, when she wants, she wants hard. She wants to be fucked. Not always to be fucked hard but fucked thoroughly. She wants to become her own fuckability. When she is with me, she's the intensive kind of slut. The kind that turns the totality of the situation into the act of fucking her.

Not everyone who fucks can handle that, as I learned through many disappointing experiences. The kind of slut who is the peak intensity of fuckability calls on those who fuck her to commit themselves to the task of serving this seemingly bottomless bottoming need. That's a lot to ask. Some recoil from it. For it calls for letting slip the sense of self-possession that most of those who fuck rather than get fucked do not want to give up.

The kind of slut with this kind of intensity can also be a lot even for the body in which she appears. She tears through the integrity of self-hood, pushing the flesh out through the opening she makes in it. She fucks the body by getting the body fucked. She's a lot.

I'm going to go with *she* for her regardless of the body in whom she appears, as somehow I think that if the slut has a gender, that in this culture, it's always she. That intolerable image, as Leo Bersani put it, "legs high in the air, unable to refuse the suicidal ecstasy of being a woman." Straight culture doesn't want us to fuck, just to breed. Any surplus sexual pleasure over and above what's needed for finding a compatible partner and stabilizing a domestic unit of consumption is somehow a bad thing in a femme kind of way.

She came for me. Came up out from inside, and from outside, forming another surface, a surface entirely turned over to turning on. She delighted and disturbed whatever was left of me. Delighted for as long as she was around, disturbed after she dissipated. While she was around, and I was her, a surface of excitability was all there was. A surface with a fold, so that it could be touched from without and fucked from within, and preferably both at once.

She liked to stay in an ecstatic state for as long as she could, or as long as she could coax intention and excitement from her partner or partners. She liked to make them cum first, so that then she could have their full attention to making her cum, making her shake and shatter, making her crease and crackle, pop off into shuddering, shimmery shards.

Sometimes an excess of sensation is only legible in an excess of language: To be a slut with language, to fuck with it too much, or too long. Even though when she appears she can only speak a wordless language of the body, or repeat stock phrases—*fuck me, fuck me, yes, yes*—where the body says what it wants without interruption.

The disturbing part came after. When she had come and gone. Who could I be after that? She came in part out of the noise of this body. The sex of the body is the music of the body. So-called gender dysphoria is noise, is the body unable to tune into itself. Here was a version of what this body could be, but only for a little while, only in situations of sexual intensity. One can't be a slut all the time. The world does not allow it. Nor does the body. It's exhausting.

She enabled me to perceive, through the noise, a possible tuning for this flesh. But barely. How could I play the rest of it? Who is she when she is not getting railed to oblivion? There weren't many clues.

And then: if I came out, lived my boring, everyday life in the world as a woman—would she still come? I put off finding out. For the longest time, I got by on those moments when she wrecked me.

Long story short: I came out. Became a woman in everyday life. A clocky, obvious, transsexual one, but a woman of sorts. There she is: riding the subway, shopping for cat food, walking the streets, leaning against a streetlamp, dragging on her weed vape. She lives the banality of everyday femininity. She cannot take up too much space. She smiles to smooth out social friction. She is an old woman, seen by most as past her fuckable time, and hence of no interest at all.

I might still have some hard, high slut moments, although frankly they don't hit with the same intensity. That went away. For a while, I traded intensive for extensive sluttery. It's surprising how many people want to fuck trans women, even if they don't particularly want to be seen with one of us in public. Or maybe not surprising, given the way transsexuality and femininity together coalesce into a kind of disposable hypersexuality in the straight mind.

When that got boring, I went in search of love, and found it—but that's another story. I still have my intensive slut moments, maybe not as intense as they use to be, because no longer edged with the tantalizing mystery of transsexuality. I stepped into that mystery, and now it's all rather commonplace. Its good, though. I can now perceive the little threads and glints of the erotic, everywhere. I can feel them I my body, in others, in the world, in language. The universe is low-key slutty all the time.

Daviel Shy

Loose Women

Dune sexualizes everything because, why not? Being the smallest of an already petite family, maybe she does it to escape that omnipresent word, "cute," hurled at her constantly. At least if you're sexy you're not cute. As far back as she can remember she always wanted to be a hooker. It could be that her sexual consciousness was developing in tandem with the release of *Pretty Woman*, but she thought to be desired enough that someone would PAY to have sex with you would be the ultimate validation. Fear and a vague sense of "morality" kept her from pursuing it. Plus years of rejection was enough to believe that even if she tried to sell her body no one would buy. She just wasn't seen as "that kind of girl." By the time she had age and a little more confidence, she didn't want to go near men and looked like a boy, mostly, but not enough to draw a whole different clientele, so she settled on being a slut. She desperately wanted everyone or at least women and queers to "see her that way."

Truth is she was always sexual. This freaks out adults to hear, but from three, four, five years old, her Barbie feet would find their way to her orifices and her imagination would furnish her with kinky scenarios to play and replay. Dangerous ground in a society that can't accept that the mere existence of a child's sexuality does not solicit its violation.

Dune's first fetish object was a pink and white marbleized t-shirt, totally threadbare that had probably belonged to her mom or an older sister, too big for her eight-year-old body to wear except as a nightgown. Eventually, too full of holes and thin even for that. That was when it got its real power: hidden in the back of a drawer for when she is alone and can pretend she has been left to look after a tailor's shop, given nothing to wear but this rag. Dune shifts around in the shirt to make sure her tiny nipple is framed by one of the holes—And always then some unexpected customer . . . The story always leads her to twist the shirt around in just the right way, getting the soft fabric to tickle her skin where it wasn't bunched and rub it where it was, pressing her body against an imaginary context unlocked by the garment in her hands. And then she puts it away. Back in the corner of her drawer to return to real life where she lives in a room with her sister in Reseda, not in a poor tailor's shop in olden-times.

On Shabbat the whole family naps after temple, which is really just structured quiet time for sex, masturbation, or fantasy. The day's services provide great fodder for a young imagination. The horny language of the psalms. *"Gird thy sword upon thy thigh . . . ride well . . . and thy right hand shall teach thee terrible things."* Today, Dune returns to the biblical scene where she left off like an earmarked book. Back at the well, she becomes Rebecca filling her urn in such a way that the excess water soaks her dusty linen robes, and the long glow of the desert light catches on her clavicle. The sight of her causes the hunk of a patriarch to fall off his camel. Dune as Rebecca feigns ignorance to the scene she has built, but inwardly flushes, knowing she has won an historic wet t-shirt contest.

Dune has a knack for endurance trials. She locks herself in the family RV parked in the driveway in one-hundred degree weather, vowing she will not come out until she has colored an entire *My Little Pony* coloring book, cover to cover. Hours later emerging sopping wet, quietly triumphant.

She favors the long game, strategizing over hard to crack personalities, making lists in the margins of her notebooks of who to crush on, being open to unexpected flings with strangers and friends, but hooked on the difficult rewards of effortful, often tragic romances.

For years, it works. Dune leads with her libido, getting herself into only a handful of situations she wishes she hadn't and a whole slew of beds she is glad she had.

But somehow along the way she perverts this pleasure, twists it up into a reflection of her worth. And when this goes sour for, she promises herself, the last time, she develops a rash under her boobs, her body's literalization of built-up resentment. It is never safe to have resentment toward her mother, so she chooses partners who can reproduce the neglect, gaslighting and unpredictable bouts of glorious adoration.

In the mirror, Dune examines her underboob. It doesn't itch or anything, but the discolored island spreads across the whole bottom crease of her left breast and forms a smaller oval under her right. Some days it's faint and some days it's prominent. When she recalls meeting up with her last lover at the farmer's market, it reddens.

"Hi! How was school?"

"Ugh. It was fine. The kids get so antsy in this weather and I get it, I just want to be outside, too. Are you . . . do you have something to cover up with in your car?"

"It's warm out."

"I mean, this neighborhood is kind of the danger zone in terms of running into parents."

"There's nothing illegal about having tits."

During the years of this relationship, her lover's body shame-blamed for being a school teacher would overflow into statements like these. Dune would protest, then immediately put it out of her mind, believing her life depended on this woman's attraction and approval. Now she was forgiving herself for these blackouts of judgment. Forgiving and tolerating the discomfort. Watching the moments replay in the months after their final split, as if seeing them for the first time. She labors at the questions they raise: how to keep her self-love, pride, embodied joy, but leave behind the shoddy boundaries? She knows the rash will clear when she figures this out.

The rash's placement hinders Dune from her favorite cut of shirt, cropped just to where her boobs end. She hadn't worn a bra in decades, and these crop tops offer a loose, nonchalant sluttiness. Living dangerously since the mere raise of an arm means a momentary flash of tit, plus the added benefit of the breeze on her naked skin while technically still wearing a shirt.

But the rash is making her uncharacteristically self-conscious. And resentment from the ongoing fight with her radical-on-paper ex-lover over her bodily autonomy turns a hotter pitch near the end, when the now ex-lover feels at liberty, having just quit her job, to give Dune tips on dressing slutty, the irony missing her completely.

The way Dune dresses is tactile above all else, opting for fabrics that feel good to the nipple, shorts that hug the hips and chains that thump at her heart when she dances. For her, choosing outfits is basically just a reverse striptease. Her sluttiness isn't an invitation for sex, it is an invitation for sexiness. She loves the way a certain cut of shorts causes her to move in just the way her body begs for. When you are built from two parents with thick thighs, wide hips and big asses, certain things need to be gyrated, moved, shaken, popped, jiggled and rotated, as much as possible. And when your ovaries are screaming, like Dune's are today, your body begs harder to move and stand and hang for maximal pleasure, which is coded as sexual.

Dune doesn't think any clothes are inappropriate for almost any situation. She doesn't think twice about wearing completely see-through thin tank tops to babysit her nieces. She doesn't want them to think that there is anything shameful in the body. Their mother Talia never polices Dune's clothes. But then, Talia is a slut herself.

Though they share no parents, (Dune's mom's second husband is Talia's dad) the embodied joy of sensuousness is perhaps linked to their time spent seeped in the Bible. But differently. Talia seduces with words and boldness. After marrying her first boyfriend, Talia's divorce unleashed her built up hunger, and she began to enjoy men and herself with them, copiously. For twelve days a year the sisters are the same age, and during this limbo time on the year Talia is about to depart their shared age for the wisdom of forty, they are dancing together in a park.

"Wow, you are so loose," one of the drummers says to the sisters, who are dripping with sweat, sipping water bottles against a tree in Griffith Park. The older man retreats respectfully to his post behind the congas. Multiple full drum kits line the haphazard circle. One man begins to play a large seashell, blowing the sound into a portable microphone. Dune and Talia happened upon this ragtag gathering of stoners, bikers, dogs, freaks, and music lovers a few hours ago. Down the hill, they had just finished celebrating Talia's oldest daughter's tenth birthday party and were crying together in the sun after all the kids and parents left. Dune because of her sister's grace, courage, and beauty. Talia because every day is still so hard.

Ten months ago she had the first seizure. A brain tumor, radiation, chemo, multiple unexplained seizures, hellish medicines and even worse side effects later, Talia was turning toward a mixture of alternative healing modalities. In the midst of tremendous fear and overwhelming physical sensations, she embraces this opportunity to pray with her body. Her moves are grand, elemental. A priestess whirling within a storm, bowing to and calming a tidal wave. This is medicine.

Dune's moves are smaller, precise repetitions and rotations, digging with motion where her bleeding pain points. The sisters are so comfortable in the center of this circle, being watched by the music, strangers, trees. Letting their bodies express their souls. They release from deep inside themselves any last dregs of caring how they look.

Dune can't care in the same way anymore. About anything. So much of her seduction strategy had been built over a well of desperation. What happens to a service top when all that has run dry? She has to come to beds now without anything to gain, just bodies in pleasure. "Just bodies in pleasure," she tells herself—to short circuit the habit of cultivating need.

So now, in post-date blissed-out text exchanges with a new someone, she stops herself from setting the scene for a "more" they can crave together. She sees how manufacturing longing can be hot, but actually devalues her alone time, her life without this new person. It would mean sacrificing her present for a hierarchy she no longer believes: one in which nothing surpasses time with the other. The very citadel that has just collapsed, based on offering her own severed limbs to her lovers, bloody and dripping for decades.

She had always been obsessed with the story of Isaac. So relatable when your own mom is hot and bothered for God. Abraham, too, wants to show God he will do anything. He brings his favorite boy up the mountain with all the tools of sacrifice, but one. But Isaac isn't an idiot. Each time his foot lands in his father's wake he knows he is one step closer to the end. He wants his dad to know he knows.

"Abba, where's the animal?"

Abraham nearly chokes.

"Oh, Hashem will provide it."

Dune as Isaac takes a deep breath, wipes the sweat from her face. She thinks her father is insane, but she has no practice in going against him. Her feet continue to follow. She does not struggle as the rope binds her to the stone. She feels held, instead by its tightness. Her fear boils over into arousal at the sight of the blade.

Dune paints a golden ram's horn on the back of her leather jacket for the animal that saved her ancestor from the God-obsessed father. While she can keep the rope and the knives, she knows she can no longer make every bed an altar. Anemic now, from shedding every last drop on the last one. This year, she prays, she will recover the vastness of a sluthood that does not depend on or even include the other.

Baruch Porras-Hernandez

Slut Cosmos

It was a slow night at the sex club. I had gone because I was a little down, a little disillusioned with life and love and San Francisco, and thought rubbing myself up on a naked stranger in a steamy den of deviancy and inequity in the heart of the city might cheer me up, at least a little. But just like the hopes and dreams of us poor people in San Francisco, the sex club that night was dead! Ever the foolish optimist, I enjoyed the sauna and decided to walk around in the empty club to at least get some exercise in, thinking, *Maybe the Gay Gods will be generous to me.* Then I saw him, in the far dark corner of the empty club: a big, sexy, muscle daddy, with salt and pepper hair, tall as fuck, towel hiding what looked like a huge present. I walked up to him, smiled, and asked politely if I could go down on him.

He said, "Of course, young man." I got on my knees as he pulled his towel away, revealing probably the biggest dick I had ever seen, with some salt and pepper pubes to frame it all. I got to work right away. We were really enjoying each other when I felt a light *nudge* on my temple. I turned to my right to see a thick, slim, pink erect penis right in my face, belonging to a tall, slim, bald white man in his thirties, with a nice stubble-bearded face. *Must be my lucky day*, I thought, and proceeded to suck on both dicks at the same time. I've had a lot of practice. The Daddy and Bald Guy both kissed and pinched each other's nipples as I worked, both moaned and gently pulled my hair and cheered me on as I made sure to service them as equally as I could.

The thought entered my head: *I love sucking two dicks at the same time, but I've never gotten to suck three dicks at the same time before.* I felt another gentle nudge, this time right on the left cheek of my face. I turned to my left to see a big, hairy, muscly, Latino Bear towering over me, with a mighty, angry-looking uncut beercan demanding attention. Being the polite gentlemen that they were, the Daddy and the Bald Guy seemed apprehensive to let the Latino Bear in and looked at me to make sure I was okay with adding a third dick to the party. I made a gesture with my hands and face that expressed *Sure why not!?* and waved the Latino Bear over, bracing for the girth. I was in heaven. I worked so hard to savor each dick, multitasking with my fingers up their holes, jerking off dicks that were not in my mouth, that the three men, really enjoying themselves, started to bond. There were high fives. I was high on the smell of man crotch. I felt very close to finishing myself, when, reader, would you believe it, a fourth cock nudged me politely, this time on the back of my head. I turned around, to see a tall, Indian man with soft skin, handsome features, wavy black hair, clean shaven face, almost no body hair and a very beautiful, big-headed cock. Shaved pubes, and heavy, *heavy* looking balls. He bent over, kissed my forehead and asked, "Room for one more?" The three men I was already servicing seemed pretty convinced I was going to reject him, but I thought, *three dicks are heaven, four might be too much, but I am up for the challenge!*

The Indian man was very sensitive and moaned a lot. The Daddy also got loud and verbal, saying, "Way to go, champ! You're doing such a good job, sucking four dicks! Impressive!" I was pretty impressed, myself. Pulling on balls, rubbing taints, taking few breaks to take deep breaths. I was on a roll, I was on fire, I could hear the spirits of San Francisco cheering me on, a big voice inside me saying—*BRING ON THE DICKS!* Ask the Gay Gods, and you shall receive. A couple came into the club. Finding it empty, they came right up to the party and just got in line, didn't even have to ask. It was two Asian guys, an older, muscly, jock bear, and a slim punk-rock-looking one, covered in tattoos.

There I was, in the middle of six naked men feeding me their dicks as they kissed and sucked on each other's nipples, saying beautiful things, like "He is a SUCK MACHINE!" Poetic things, like "AMAZING

MOUTH!" I felt on my knees on top of the world when I felt a hand shove me to the side a little. I don't like being shoved in sex clubs, so I tensed my body up and wouldn't move. I turned around, ready to say, "Wait your turn!" when a hot, Black guy leaned over my shoulder and started furiously sucking the dick I was working on, then the dick next to that, and then the dick next to that. He hadn't even politely asked if he could join us, he had just crashed the party—not that there are any cemented rules to a sex club, and if there are they are unspoken rules, they're to be creatively adapted and rewritten, but still. I had worked for these dicks.

The man probably sensed my feeling of *excuse me?* He responded, "HAHA! That's right, I'm stealing your dicks! I'm stealing your dicks! HA! HA!" Making us all laugh, every single guy in the circle and me, our laughter ringing throughout the empty club. I scooted over, and patted the ground next to me, motioned for him to take the spot next to mine. *Why not, this is America, dicks are for everybody.* The Hot Black Guy kneeled next to me and said "Hi there!" Very high energy.

"Welcome to the dick party!" I said.

"Thank you!" he said. "Now, let's get to work on these dicks!"

And so we got to work on the dicks.

We made quite a pair. The men seemed overjoyed with the extra mouth. We made the white Bald Guy cum, with a combination of him sucking on the tip of the head and me lightly sucking on his balls. After Bald Guy came in his mouth, my partner-in-head shared a wet, jizzy kiss with me. Everybody cheered.

We got to work on the Asian couple and made them both cum at the same time by fingering their buttholes. Most of it got on my beard, so the Hot Black Guy licked it all off, and we kissed some more. By this time there was a crowd of older men circling us, an audience cheering us on, rooting for us two nameless, dick-sucking heroes. Every time we made a man cum, we high-fived each other.

It took a lot of hard work to make the Latino Bear cum. My jaw began to get a little tired. The Hot Black Guy was working on the Indian Man next to me, who was also having trouble cumming. At one point my knees got tired; I'm not as young as I used to be, plus fat, so I popped a squat, but lost my balance and fell backwards. It could have been bad, but I felt a strong hand catch my lower back and gently push me back into place. It was the Hot Black Guy multitasking! He had not even stopped sucking the dick he was sucking as he reached out to save me with his left hand. I felt so supported—was this truly queer community? Later, Hot Black Guy lost his balance as well, and I reached out with my right hand to support *him* as he readjusted, keeping the dick in his mouth. Both men cum, the Latino Daddy and the Indian man. We exchange "YES, BITCH!" and "GURL! YOU ROCK!" High-five each other, then turn to the last man standing: the Silver Muscle Daddy, with the biggest dick in the room. He tries to wave us away, saying he's enjoyed watching, but that his old cock was not what it used to be, that we probably would not be able to make him cum, that he didn't want to disappoint us, that he was "too old."

"I think you're just trying to talk yourself out of a good orgasm," said the Hot Black Guy.

"Yeah, why don't you at least let us try. Even if you don't cum, we'll have enjoyed sucking on that big old dick," I said, gently patting him on his muscley thigh.

"Okay, knock yourselves out." said the Silver Daddy.

The Hot Black Guy turned, and in one swift movement grabbed some of the red pillows lying around the old Eros on Market Street, sticking them quickly under our knees. "Gurl, we're gonna need these!"

"Right! Thank you!" I said. "I'm 36, but 86 in gay years."

On our knees we held hands.

"We can do this, if we work together" he said

"We gonna make this daddy cum?" he asked loudly.

"We are going to make this daddy cum!" I said.

"I CAN'T HEAR YOU!" he screamed.

"WE ARE GOING TO MAKE THIS DADDY CUUUUM!!!" I screamed.

And we became one, two bodies, one mind, in sync. We began to suck the Silver Daddy's long, 11-inch cock, using both our mouths formed into a fleshlight. Up to the tip, down the shaft. His right hand pulled on the Daddy's balls; one of my hands had two fingers up the Daddy's ass. The other hand cupped and slapped the Daddy's right butt cheek.

"Oh my god," the Daddy moaned.

"You're doing it!" the crowd cheered.

We were like glowing, transforming Sailor Moons, all the members of Voltron formed into one, Captain Planet by gay powers combined.

"You're! Really! Doing it!" the Daddy began to pant. You could hear him through the whole club.

We were two crystal gems fused into one.

"I'm going to cum!"

We were made of love.

"Don't stop! I'm CUMMING!!!"

Two of our hands reached up to the Daddy's nipples and pinched harder than we've ever pinched before. Releasing screams of pleasure from the Daddy's mouth, we leaned back, as jizz sprayed out of his enormous cock and over us. We raised our hands for the communion, letting the ropes fall all over our bodies. Never in my life had I had semen *actually* rained on me. When the cumming stopped, the by now large crowd of men that had become our audience erupted in cheer! The Daddy kept thanking us and thanking us. The Asian couple was still there, clapping. the Latino Bear was there, clapping. The White Bald Guy, the Indian Guy, their arms over each other, all happy, all clapping and cheering. The Hot Black Guy and I fell into each other's arms, our cocks pressed into each other and we kissed. From all the edging and now frottage we both finally orgasmed and fell on a bed to hold each other as man after man came by to pat us on the shoulder or butt, saying "Great job!" "Amazing!"

"That's how you do it!" The Hot Black guy has his eyes closed, his head on my shoulder. My arms wrapped around him, my knees on fire, both of us too exhausted to move, we don't say a word as the now full club began to dance with the sexual energy that we had pulled down from the slut cosmos. The man in my arms was so tired, he completely passed out. I held him even closer, feeling our cum-covered bodies glue to each other. Eros played a fast-paced techno remix of *If you are going to San Francisco*. I closed my eyes. The song sang, *You're gonna find some gentle people there!*

Sam Cohen

Like a Star

My flight was delayed, so it was two in the morning when I landed in Vienna. My phone didn't work even though it did in Poland, so I took a regular cab from the airport to an address Johanna had texted me, an address composed of numbers with slashes between them in front of a street name I couldn't pronounce. I showed my phone to the driver and asked him which number among the slashes was the apartment number. "Thirty-eight," he said. I took my bags and went to the door.

Next to the thirty-eight button was Johanna's last name, another word I couldn't pronounce but which I felt relieved to see. When I learned this last name in the middle of our Madrid affair, I couldn't understand how the arrangement letters made the sounds they did, so I started doing Duolingo. It wasn't because I was obsessed with Johanna, I told myself. I just liked language, I wanted to know how letters worked together. I returned to Johanna in Madrid five weeks later able to say "I have a dog" and "I want coffee." Johanna said "It is very heavy that you speak German now." That was four years ago. Now I press the button next to the thirty-eight and Johanna buzzes me in without saying anything. When I'm in the elevator I realize thirty-eight doesn't indicate a floor in any way, so I ride from floor to floor, looking around.

On five, Johanna is standing with the door open. She hugs me and laughs and laughs.

"It is very funny that you're here," she says.

I feel a little self-conscious because I'm not sure why I'm in Europe in the first place. I came because some friends in Poland invited me but mostly because my girlfriend said we should meet here after her conference presentation in Amsterdam. But then we broke up right before the trip, which makes standing here in Johanna's doorway at 2 a.m. feel insane. At the same time, I feel comforted by the laughing, the deep smile that accompanies the laughing, the way Johanna's eyes fix on me. I forgot how it felt to be looked at by her.

"I like your hair color," I say.

Her hair is bleached on the top, almost white, and shaved to near translucence on the sides. She's skinny, boyish but creasing around her mouth and eyes and I'm not kidding, her eyes fix on you and then they sparkle, like she's some kind of Icelandic elf. I'm wearing a strappy pink tent dress I'd changed into earlier in the day when I was dying of heat and walking around the old Jewish quarter of Krakow and which is making me feel like a zaftig gay Carrie Bradshaw, which is to say, *ultraglamorous.*

"Do you want some water? Bier? Wein?" she asks. Because of Duolingo, I understand that she says beer and wine in German. "Also where will you sleep, with me or on the couch?"

"I didn't know my flight would be so delayed," I say. "I thought we would have more time, to hang out, see the vibe."

"Yes, right?" she says, laughing again. "Well anyway, we can figure it out later. What do you want now?"

"I would love a water and a cigarette, then a beer and a shower.'

"Since when do you smoke?" she asked. "This is very un-American."

"Always," I said. "I smoked in Spain, you would always have some of my cigarette."

"I don't remember this," she said.

I shrugged. "I hid it from you for a few days because it's a deal-breaker for a lot of people in the US," I said.

"Yes, in the US smoking is worse than heroin," she said, handing me a glass of water which I drank in a single multi-swallow gulp. "Americans are very stupid."

"Once when you were mad, you told me I was the most American person you had ever met," I say.

"I said that?" she says. "I was obviously trying to be very mean to you. I have met so many Americans. Some of them are very awful." She takes a swig of beer. "Anyway, it turns out no."

"Because of the smoking," I say.

"Yes, because of the smoking."

I love how she talks, without contractions, replacing every w with a v and every v with a w, or else an f. Every consonant is over-pronounced and words have spaces in between. "I no longer believe in non-wiolence," she would say later, and also, "I LOFF the new album of Taylor Swift." "I vould like to come wisit you in LA," she had said once before, but then she'd started ignoring my texts.

"I'm going on the balcony," I say

"No, just smoke in here."

"That's crazy. No."

"Oh my Gott."

"Fine, but I'm sitting on the window ledge." I hop up and prop myself in the frame. Europeans, it turns out, have not heard of screens.

"Are you aware," she says, "that this is the fifth floor?"

I laugh, light my cigarette.

"I am serious, get down from there."

"Tell me how it feels to be back in Vienna," I say instead, blowing smoke and enjoying wearing my pink dress, hanging a bare leg over the room-side of a European apartment.

"It feels very good," says Johanna. "Every year it feels so good to return and I wonder if I made a mistake moving to Madrid. I am in a bit of a crisis, I think. I am wondering if I missed my train stop."

I feel comforted by her immediate honesty. This is part of why we connect, I think, both of us always trying to say the truest thing. Unless it's about each other—we both understand the important of subtle moves in our dance of seduction. "You can always come back to Vienna," I say. "You have this apartment, even. Anyway there are a million train stops."

"I don't know," she said. "Last year I was invited to apply for a job at the university in Vienna, but I wasn't ready to come back, and now what will I do here?"

"Why didn't you apply?"

"I don't know, because all of my friends here have babies. Anyway, I think I am done with the university. Everyone there is so boring."

I hop down off the window and sit in the corner of the sectional.

"You will never do this again," Johanna says, gravely. "I hated every moment of this."

"Fine," I say. "Do you still want a baby?"

"No, I am over that. The moment has passed and now it is too late. You want another beer?" She goes to the mini-fridge to get one. She has a dishwasher but not a full-sized fridge, which strikes me as very European.

"So you didn't go to Berlin?" she asks.

"No," I say. "Jamie and I broke up."

"Yes, I thought this might have been the case when you said that you would no longer go to Berlin."

"Yeah."

"And why did you break up?"

"A lot of fighting," I said. "A lot of problems. And maybe we wanted different kinds of lives, I don't know." I'll tell her more later, when I'm not so tired.

"There were always a lot of problems in this relationship," she said. "I have thought for a long time that it would not work."

"Who are you seeing? Still the clown?"

"No, not the clown," she says, "You were right that a clown is not a good match for me." I wait. Johanna is always seeing someone, always in a way that seems turbulent and temporary. I've gone into the encounter this time reminding myself of this—that I'm there because we have fun together, because we understand each other, but that no matter what happens or how good it might feel, I cannot get caught up. I tell myself I know about Libras now.

"Natalia," she says. Of course, a princess name. "And no I think she is really great, the problem is just that she has this job, director of photography, where she goes to shootings for one full week and it is impossible to reach her. And I wonder, I don't know, what is the point of having a girlfriend who you cannot reach."

"Maybe her absences will feel more okay once it's more established. How long has it been?"

"Six months."

"Exclusive?"

"Ehm," she says, "I donno." I understand this to mean she wants to fuck.

"I'm going to take a shower now," I announce.

"And then where will you sleep?"

I pause. I know I want her, but I don't think it should be now; I think we should actually sleep. At the same time though, being out on the couch alone instead of crawling into bed next to her feels like a psychotic, self-punishing choice. I know I'm smiling idiotically. "Um," I say.

"Look, this is probably very obvious," she says, and fixes her Icelandic elf eyes on me for a long time, "but if you sleep with me, we can just sleep."

"Okay," I say. I take it as a rejection, but one I can handle.

I get in the shower and in a couple minutes there's a knock.

"Sam?" she says. It's harsh and German whenever she says my name. "Did you close the door?" She means lock, I know, because of cerrar. I can reach the doorknob from the shower, so I unlock it, pop it open a crack. "You closed the door, you are such a weird person," Johanna says. "Anyway, tell me how thick you would like your quilt." She extends a blanket at me. "This is option one. Grab." I grab it. "Okay and this is option two." She extends the same blanket, folded over this time.

"One's good," I say. "Thank you." Jamie basically never invited me over, so I am thirsty for this kind of lesbian care.

I get in bed and Johanna takes off her shirt to change. I'd forgotten what her tits looked like, small and triangular, with long nipples pointing downward. She has tattoos near her clavicle, big hawks and hearts, a lot of circular moles and a spray of freckles on her ribcage. Somehow butches always look the most butch to me shirtless, the way they move with their shoulders and tits. Johanna's body has a lot of hard parts—jutting shoulders, visible ribs—and then the tits. I'd forgotten the details of this body that I loved to touch and the visible flash of it makes me feel something. I remember then that we spent significant portions of the pandemic video-fucking, giving each other orders and making live bespoke porn from apartments across the planet. The memory makes me react to Johanna's body, the real live body I jerked off to so much onscreen, its *hereness*. Plus I now remember the intense perviness of Johanna, her willingness to do crotch shots and demand them in return, to give a graphic play-by-play of how she wanted me to touch my body, to whimper and moan when I'd do it.

Then she has a t-shirt on again. She gets in bed and I flip off my lamp.

"Good night," I say, and within moments we're face-to-face, rubbing each other's backs.

"Maybe we should just sleep," she says. "You want?"

"I want to touch first," I say.

"Do you care," she says, "if I am in an exclusive relationship?"

"I don't care for myself," I say. "I feel like it's up to you whether you want to respect your relationship."

"What a horrible thing to say, if I want to *respect my relationship.*"

I smile as she rolls on top of me, slides off her rings and puts them on the headboard. She wears four silver rings, and it feels like the whole point is so you can watch her take them off when she's ready to fuck.

"Are you okay?" she asks, while she's fucking me. It feels unlike her, how I remember her, to ask. But I know I'm different, too.

"Of course," I say. "I'm good."

"It's just that first sex after a breakup can feel weird."

She's right, it feels weird. I've gotten used to the same hand, the same movements, the same kind of ramping up. I loved the predictability of partnered sex, the certainty of the next phase helping me fully inhabit every part. There is an off-ness, now, the unfamiliar shape and rhythm of the hand inside me. I know I'm not going to come so I flip Johanna and start fucking her. I'd forgotten how she cried out in this way that sounded starving and anxious, how her body trembled and thrashed. Once she comes I slow down, let her ride it out. I still my hand then and hold her, letting her thrash a bit against my fingers until she stops.

I maybe pull out and pass out at the same time. It was the shortest sex we ever had. Last time in Madrid, we'd been hungry in the same way and there was something both alluring and terrifying about it. The first night we met, we fucked for hours, back and forth and at the same time. Then we were inside the fuck, pretty much, for five days.

At noon, I put on a hot pink sheer lace dress I got at a Polish thrift store the day before and read Sally Rooney on the couch. I bought this dress imagining this scene, morning at Johanna's. It fits in a loose way, the way it's supposed to, and I like how you can see the hints of nipples, the dark of a pubic triangle, but how these are also obscured by the lace pattern. My friend in Poland gave me the novel to read, said she'd liked Sally Rooney more than she anticipated.

"Hey," Johanna says when she wakes up and comes in, sleepy and smiley a half hour later.

"Good morning," I say, looking up from my book.

"You want coffee?"

I smile. "Yeah."

I continue reading while she does some things at the kitchen counter, and then she comes over and sits next to me. "This is a very old book, no?"

"Like five years," I say. "But I didn't read it then."

"You like it?"

"Yes," I say. "It's about heterosexuals, but it's very smart about relationships and status and class and the ways single lines of dialogue can shift everything."

"Okay," she says, "This is a good pitch. Maybe I will read."

I go back to reading and she sticks her hand under my dress and rubs between my thighs. This is my dream, I think: to be interrupted by someone's desire. I keep reading but moan and smile, occasionally throw my head back. These sounds and movements are a natural result of letting my body do what it wants, but also, I consciously want Johanna to feel my appreciation.

The kettle whistles and she leaps up. "Milch?" she asks, grinning at me.

I groan. "Oh come on," I say. Then I smile. "Yes, milk."

"What is this dress?" she asks, coming back from the kettle with two coffees.

"I got it at the Polish thrift store," I say, and this makes her laugh.

"Yes, now that I see it that way, it looks very much like what some Polish housewife would wear. But on you it is somehow very queer and very hot."

"Thank you," I say.

She pushes me down then and pulls the dress up around my waist, rubs twice and then starts fucking. Within five minutes, I am gurgling from my throat, which I know is pretty much a sign I'm about to release cupfuls of cum but I don't say anything. She moans while she fucks, as though the fucking is about to make her come, too. Then right after the gurgling she's going *oh fuck*. This is what Jamie always said when it started to happen, too—she could feel it before I could, coming from somewhere high up where her fingertips were. The squirting is new—it didn't happen yet when I was in Madrid, but it does now.

"Keep your legs here, I will get a towel," she says.

"Sorry," I say.

"No, it's good," she says, already going and coming back, shoving an orange towel with Troll dolls on it under me. "Lift more," she says, and I do. She adjusts the towel and says, "okay there." Then she jams her fingers back in. I squirt again, soaking the towel. I start to fuck her from below. She comes quickly, collapses on me, kissing my face everywhere, and we stay like that, collapsed together. I tilt my head back and examine her bookshelf while she lies on my chest. "What are you thinking about?" she asks.

"I'm thinking," I say, "about how I'm pretty sure Chimamanda Ngozi Adichie's *Americanah* is a regular size in English, but the German version is the biggest book I've ever seen."

She laughs. It's relieving, maybe, that I haven't entered a state of melancholy, or of an excessive, fixated type of desire. It is something I am working on.

"You want breakfast?"

"Sure," I say. "Thank you."

She starts opening packages of Austrian cheese, soft and hard. Dense brown bread. Eggs, tomatoes, avocados. She pours vanilla yogurt into a bowl from a glass jar and covers it in blueberries. She puts water to boil and takes tiny ceramic egg cups out of the cabinet. I haven't had a lover make me breakfast in years, since my exclusivity with Jamie, and so each opening of a package, each pour, feels like she's creating a magic potion for me.

"You want strong cheese or delicate cheese?"

"Both," I say.

"You are vegetarian, yes?"

"Yes."

"For this, I did not get ham."

"Thank you."

She takes out butter, a jar of jam, a cherry cake her mom made.

"Have some cake," she says, so I cut myself a piece, this yellow cake with perfectly spaced cherries like it came out of a package.

When everything is ready, she makes a spread. The ease of this makes me emotional. I spread European butter on the dark bread. I bite. I spread seedy, dark jam over the butter and bite again. I peel the top off my egg and scoop the thick liquid of the orange yolk into my mouth.

"All the food is so much better here," I say.

"I know," she says, "I have been to your country."

When everything is gone, I wash the dishes.

"You want to go to the river?" she asks and I nod. She's been telling me about the Danube for years, her favorite place, one she has sent me photos of.

We change into our bathing suits.

"Bring underwear and something warm for later," she says.

Outside, she hands me a helmet and I climb onto her motorcycle.

"Be careful your dress," she says. "Lift the bottom."

Every time she can see my potential future and wants to make it better—I might get cold, my dress might get ripped—I want to kiss her face and so I do.

I feel electrified, riding through the streets of this European city on the back of this motorcycle, a femme dyke on bike, an inhabitant of a world from old, working-class dyke literature, some femme of Leslie Feinberg's or Pat Califia's. This is something Johanna and I share, I think, wanting to be in a dyke novel, wanting life to feel like a fantasy version of life, wanting to feel like dykes. It feels rare now, these old genders we want to inhabit, the ways we want to follow the contours of an existing narrative about women loving women and living outside the patriarchy and maybe organizing workers or something if we can ever get our shit straight. We zip by buildings with tiny lions under every window, with faces making different specific expressions all along the facade. She points out the first district, which we are driving past, with its emerald city domed roofs and crazy spires twisting into the sky. I wonder what it would feel like to grow up somewhere that looks like this. I decide I am a fundamentally different kind of person because I didn't, someone who feels untethered from history. Maybe this is what Americans do in Europe, though, try to re-tether ourselves a bit. But we're distracted by the cheeses and the fucking and then we go home.

The wind blows and the sun heats my skin and my hands push firmly on Johanna's thighs. This feels like life, like the meaning of life. I think about a part in *Stone Butch Blues* where the narrator says you can tell what a femme will be like in bed by how she is on a bike. *Millie was very, very good on a bike*, Leslie Feinberg writes. How do I be good? I wonder. I hook my fingers in Johanna's belt loops and scooch so my crotch is directly against her back. I stay still, make sure to lean with her on the turns. Later, I switch it up: wrap my arms around her waist, press my thighs hard against her hips.

At the river she tells me that because Austria is a social democracy, there is cheap river access, tennis courts, and parks for the working class. In addition, old people can be on a waitlist for summer cabins by the river. This is a fact that, as an American, I find incredible. We find a patch of remaining sun—it is almost five—and she takes off her shirt. What *is* this country where you can be a hot topless butch in the sun by the river, where recreation for the working class is considered a social need?

"I think I find you hot in this pornographic way now," I say, "because we've had so much video sex."

"What do you mean?" she says, not sure whether to be offended.

"I mean I've just seen you on screen so much, that in a way you've become like a fantasy person."

"Like a star," she says and smiles.

"Yes, a star," I say. Johanna loves stars, and almost no female star is deemed unworthy of her love. She loves Ellen, Taylor Swift, the Real Housewives of Beverly Hills, and Selena Gomez.

"Let's swim," I say and take off for the river. The water is warm and I submerge myself easily. The Danube shows up a lot in novels and history books, but I can't remember any of the details. Now I am in it and it feels like summer camp—semi-opaque water, pebbles, mulch.

Johanna follows me in and we swim out far, under the buoys, which she says are just for kids anyways. The water is shallow and waveless and moves almost imperceptibly slow.

"You liked the motorcycle?" She asked.

"I loved it," I said. "I felt like a femme from classic lesbian lit."

"Yes, I am a bit of a stereotypical dyke."

"I like that," I say. "I once had an ex who called me a lesbian fetishist, kind of derisively."

"Meaning?"

"Meaning I get off on like *the idea* of two women together."

"Ahh but this is a nice thing, no?" She says. "A very nice thing. I like this about you."

"Well that person turned out to be trans."

"Ah yes," Johanna says. "Then I can see how there would be a problem."

I backstroke out more.

"What do you think about nonbinary?" asks Johanna.

"You're nonbinary," I say.

"Sure," Johanna says. "But sometimes you think you're nonbinary, too." She raises her eyebrows and smiles. She is mocking me.

"Because I think all dykes are nonbinary!" I splash her. "But I am aware you're *more nonbinary* than me. I'm not an idiot."

"Okay so you are right. Monique Wittig already told us in the 1980s that lesbians are not women. So it is done. We do not need this word nonbinary. We have lesbian."

"I think people feel different ways about different words," I say. "But I like being lesbians with you."

We lie out more. There are maples, willows, a lot of single women on camping chairs, reading books. I am often a single woman reading a book outdoors, surrounded by families, and I love this place where it's normal to be a woman alone reading.

"I am starving," she says. "I guess you want to try Austrian food?"

"At some point," I say. "Could be tomorrow."

"Let's get it over with," she says. "I hate Austrian food. Let's have it now and then we don't have to have it again."

At the restaurant, Johanna gets a one-euro Gruner Veltliner and I get a giant mug of beer and she points out things that are good on the menu. They are mostly salads.

"But after the salad, we will have a thing which is the best thing ever. A dumpling of apricots."

The salad is a giant bowl of potatoes covered in avocado and pumpkin seed oil, and we eat it while Johanna complains about bisexuals.

"I also like to be lesbians with you," she says. "With the bisexual girls, usually it is different."

"I mean a lot of femmes are kinda bisexual," I say. "I've noticed a lot of femmes in their 40s start fucking men. Maybe I'll do it when I get back."

"Well, you'll still be a dyke though," she says, surprising me. "Not really bisexual. But this makes me very angry still. I consider this traitorous."

"Johanna." I set my mug of beer down. "Femmes in our 40s have spent *over twenty years* having our hearts *fucking shredded* by butches."

"Fine," she says. "I don't know. Anyway, these bisexual girls do not fuck."

"What do you mean they don't fuck?"

"They are accustomed to having to do nothing in sex, and so they don't."

"They do *nothing?*" I ask, incredulous.

"Not nothing," she concedes. "They go down."

"That's something," I say.

"Yes, something," she agrees.

I eat potatoes from the salad.

"Sometimes they fuck, but they do it without passion, not like a butch. This is why sometimes I fuck butches," she says.

"What about me?" I ask.

"You fuck like a butch," she says. I grin. I have no idea if it's true, but it feels like a compliment to aspire to. I take it as an invitation for later, to fuck like a butch.

When the apricot dumpling arrives, Johanna divides it in half and I'm not that into it, it's obvious, as my half still mostly remains after hers is gone. I say I'm just very full which is also true. I did not expect the salad to be a bowl of potatoes.

"Help me finish?" I say.

"Fine, but then you have to stop eating the apricot out of the middle," she says.

I laugh. It's true that I was doing that.

Back at the apartment, she asks again about Jamie. I tell her we fought a lot.

"But fighting is okay, no?" she says. "I think you are a fighting person. You fought a lot with me, even. I'm a fighting person, too."

She decides she wants to scan her texts, look for our fights. "Oh my *GOTT*," she says. "This is so mean, *look*. I ask you, 'Will you ever respond to my text?' And you say, 'Probably not.'"

I don't feel like telling her I was bristling with hurt, *dying* with hurt, so I just say, "Yes, that is very mean."

"I am very happy to have you finally admit this," she says.

"Wait look," I say. "The next text is you sending a screenshot of my ass with a butt plug in it," I say. I am also trying to set an alert for later. "I think I must have called you and apologized and then we had video sex."

"Wow, all the way in June of 2021," she says. "I did not realize our relationship lasted so long."

"Weird. I was already with Jamie."

She takes a cigarette out of the pack, lights it on the couch. She drags on the cigarette, ashes in a candle. "Anyway, maybe you are a bit high maintenance, but I find that hot."

I think for some reason of this time in Madrid when she asked who my best friend was, and I explained that I'd recently had a falling out with my closest friend, that I felt very alone. We were walking along the river and I started crying, describing the situation. She held my hand and walked me to the river edge, where we sat on the stone pavement. Moonlight made the whole surface of the water shine and Johanna shoveled cake into my mouth while I cried. It was really good cake, cake she had bought earlier while we were walking around the city and had been carrying around. I remember this feeling strange to me, this idea of buying slices of cake and putting them in your backpack. I remember feeling loved then, crying and telling the story of my friend breakup while this light spongy cake with buttercream kept entering my mouth without my having to ask for anything.

I put my cigarette out in the candle, grab her by the back of the head and kiss her hard. She pulls me close, fills my mouth with her tongue. I lead her to the bed and push her down, decide I'll fuck her first. As I fuck her, she moans: "my Gott Sam" and "oh *FAHK*." She bucks her hips and I use the momentum to lift her off the bed from the waist down so I'm supporting her hips and legs in the air with one arm while I'm fucking her with the other hand, some kind of weird reverse wheelbarrow that I hope makes her feel like just a hole, like I'm fucking her like a butch. Suddenly she lifts her head and bites me hard. I yelp. I add a third finger and then look down. Blood pools where my fingers meet my hand.

"You're bleeding," I say.

"Is it okay?" she says.

"Yeah of course," I say and go harder. When there's blood all over my wrist and on both sides of her thighs I say, "I think we should get a towel though."

I leap up and she says, "the cum towel is on the couch, the orange one."

I return with it and see her splayed open, blood darkening her pussy and all over her inner thighs. I've never seen this on anyone but myself—most of my lovers have been too butch to feel secure bleeding all over their thighs and my hand, I think, then wonder why I associate butchness with lack of mess, with clean edges, contained fluids, quiet orgasms. I shove the orange towel under Johanna's butt and lift it again to fuck her.

I go in instantly, three fingers, hard. She wails, cries out, bites the pillow, bites me.

After she comes, she grunts hard, removes my hand, flips me over and holds my forearm down. Being fucked has activated something animal in her and now she is fucking me, hard. My spray hits her body this time, then drips downward. She shoves the bloody towel under me, and then uses its edge to wipe my hand which looks like I've recently delivered a baby or killed someone. *Birth, death, fucking,* I think. She uses a full palm to spread my cum around my thighs and ass crack, and then once my ass crack is full of cum, she uses it to push a finger in my ass. "Okay?" she says.

It feels like she got my alert. "Yeah," I say. "Okay."

In the morning we eat toast with butter, dark seedy jam, avocado, tomato, and cheeses. No eggs, we decide. I change into shorts and a mesh shirt, all black which I think will look cute on the bike.

"We will go to the first district," she says. "You would like to see the tourism places of Vienna, no?"

"Yes," I say. "I would like that."

We park the bike by this domed cathedral that looks like a mosque, with this turquoise-y green roof that a lot of the Viennese buildings have, and Johanna starts talking about Hapsburgs.

"Who's that?" I ask.

"You don't know Hapsburgs? Maybe they are called something else," she says. "Hapes-burgs?" I like that she doesn't make a big deal out of my American ignorance. She grabs my ass. I had recently announced to my friend Shuli that all I wanted in life was someone who would grab my ass in public. "I could have sex right now," she says.

"I forgot how pervy you are," I say. "It's my favorite thing about you."

I realize my phone is gone, that my phone is not only my phone but my only way of paying for things.

"Just don't worry about it," Johanna says. "You can use my phone for photos and pay me back at the end of the day for whatever we do."

We look at Stephen's Cathedral. I like how there are gargoyles and then the parts that were destroyed in the Nazi era have been replaced by more modern roof tiles and stained glass. Or at least that's how I make sense of what I'm seeing. We walk through a Viennese coffeehouse that Johanna calls "alternative" and then look inside the traditional, palatial one where Lenin and Trotsky met, which now has a wraparound line of tourists.

"There is a feminist bookstore here," Johanna says. "There is also very good ice cream."

"It is my goal to see every feminist bookstore worldwide," I say.

"We can get ice cream after," she says.

When we walk in, she grabs bell hooks *All About Love* off the shelf and says, "this is the worst book."

My jaw drops and I mock clutching my pearls. In the US, no one criticizes bell hooks.

"I like that book," I say.

"It has nice parts, okay, like that love is a verb," she says. "But in this book, she defends Bill Clinton for his relationship with Monica Lewinsky!"

"I don't remember that," I say.

She makes some European *pfff* sound.

"Do you like any bell hooks?" I ask.

"Her book on pedagogy is very good," says Johanna.

We walk into fiction. "I am very into this revenge fiction now," she says. "I used to believe in non-violence but not any longer. I like to read about killing men."

"Did you read the book I left you?" I ask.

"Which one?" she says.

"Baise-Moi."

"Yes of course."

"Did you like it?"

"Yes it was very good."

"I would like to read this book that you are reading," she says. "But it seems they don't have it here."

"Ask," I say, gesturing to the dyke at the counter. They talk in German for awhile and then the dyke goes in the back and returns with the book.

Johanna smiles. "Now I can read your book."

The ice cream parlor is old-fashioned, with tables where you can sit and be waited on, a long menu of sundae options in German and English.

"You pick," she says.

"Hot raspberry," I say.

It comes in a glass cup: vanilla ice cream covered in hot raspberries you can tell have been cooked in the back and not, like, scooped from a jar. Whipped cream with a chocolate drizzle on top.

"This ice cream dish is also called Hot Love, here in Austria."

Exactly what I came here for, I think about saying, but don't, even though I feel pretty sure Johanna would like it. It's hard to say the word love. Instead, I scoop up vanilla ice cream and raspberries and stick the spoon near her face. Her mouth opens.

It's so easy with her it's like it's choreographed. I wonder if something permanent could feel like this, or if the commitment is what would ruin it for both of us, if the second we decided to belong to each other we would start to work on destroying each other.

We look at the National Biblioteka, the museum of some famous queen, the iconic opera. Everything is so elaborately carved, covered in faces and statues. I don't understand a time when there was time and resources for this, how it even happened. It's hard to imagine being someone who lived in a place constructed by unimaginable people with unimaginable power structures and economic structures and lives. Or maybe if you lived here, you simply could imagine those things.

The art museum has a retrospective of one of Johanna's favorite artists, Valie Export, an Austrian feminist artist working from the '60s until now. When I see the size of the show, I announce that I have to pee before I can go in. "You should go into the show though, start looking."

I go up the escalator and wander through the ornate, curvy, pastel and gold halls of the museum to find the bathroom. I don't think I have ever seen a space dedicated to contemporary art museum housed in such rococo conditions. When I come back, Johanna is standing in the exact same place, looking at her phone and my heart radiates warm waves, outward. Something about seeing her there waiting, standing in the same spot looking at her phone—this patience, this commitment to looking together.

We go into a room where hundreds of TVs show the same repeating image, a needle of a sewing machine going in and out, in and out. I think *repetition, feminine labor, penetration, monotony, blah blah blah,* but then the repetitive needles start to feel intense and scary, and I guess something about this is working. We're the only ones in the room so we make out a little.

When we walk outside, it's drizzling but the sun's out. A giant rainbow arcs into the green dome of the roof in front of us.

"Johanna!" I screech, and point.

"This is very beautiful, this rainbow," she agrees.

We are both hungry and need to eat before we go to the *Barbie* movie. It's the night of the premiere and we're both excited.

We sit outside at this pan-Asian place where we get the international combination of red tofu curry with a veggie bun bowl and end up talking about our mothers.

I was going to avoid the topic of our mom issues, but she asked first.

"Not great," I say, "the same. How are things with your mom?"

"The same," she says.

She talks about the ways her mom enabled abuse in her childhood and I think about all of the men who have fucked us up: me and all the dykes and girls and former dykes and former girls I've tried to love. I imagine Johanna and I traveling the world on a train that never stops, fucking each other and killing them all.

Our weird meal lands on our table. I divide the white rice in half with a chopstick and put some in a little white bowl for her.

"I feel like I cannot have a normal relationship because of this abuse," she says. It's the first time I've heard her say she can't have a normal relationship.

"I feel like I can't have a normal relationship because of my mom," I say.

"Yes, for me in reality it is because of my mom, too."

It is weirdly pleasurable, I am finding, to toggle between the hot curry and the cold noodles. The noodles have fish sauce, but are kind of flavorless overall, and I like the rotation, warm and spicy, cold and bland. I need to focus on this because I am finding myself wanting to promise to love her forever and well.

"Do you know your attachment style?" she asks.

"Anxious," I say. "You?"

"Mine is the worst one," she says. "Disorganized."

I laugh. "You are totally disorganized!" I say.

"I know," she says, "I said so."

"I think I was hurt by that, last time, in Madrid," I say. "It was so intimate, and then so walled."

"Yes, I can get very very close and then, how do you say it, detach?"

"It's harder for me," I admit. I feel my eyes burn a little. "Once I am close, I want to stay close."

"But just because you have a lot of intimacy doesn't mean you have to have a relationship."

I feel my throat fill with something.

The waitress brings a free dessert, bowls of coconut milk with tapioca. I take a bite. Johanna finishes hers with apparent delight, so I slide mine over. She eats it, too.

At the *Barbie* movie, we're on the balcony of an old Viennese theater. Girls come into the theater tossing their hair in hot pink bustiers and ass-tight lamé, Johanna goes "Is this feminist?"

I narrow my eyes. "Do you mean is it *anti*-feminist?"

"Yes, this. Like this kind of femininity is constructed by the patriarchal gaze, no?"

"Oh my god," I say before launching into a tirade about how pink and glitter are not tools of the patriarchy, and how, while they might be forced on us in childhood, at some point we learn that they are uncool, frivolous, dumb, etc., and that there is something beautiful about all these women—these *international* women!—coming together to celebrate frill.

"Thank you for this lecture about pink," Johanna responds.

I roll my eyes.

"I am serious," she says. "I had not thought about it this way because I felt very forced into pink. I see it a different way now."

During the movie, she turns sideways and leans into me in a way so that I am almost spooning her. I hold her and laugh a lot at the movie. She is a good follow-up laugher, laughing when I laugh. I love when people do this, like they just needed a little invitation to fully experience the humor they were sensing.

I am beaming after. "I loved it!" I say.

She smiles. "I think I loved it, too."

She reaches for my hand and we walk into the hallway holding hands. Then in the lobby, she drops my hand and turns to me. "I think I am nonbinary, no?"

"I mean, duh," I say.

"Let's go to the lesbian bar," she says.

It feels so good to be a femme on a bike riding through Vienna on the way to the lesbian bar after seeing the *Barbie* movie. After we park, Johanna complains that there are straight people outside, but when we walk in, it is all pairs of makeup-less women sitting on plush furniture around small, round tables—candles, and colors like *burgundy, carmine*. It's like we're in a lesbian period piece where something both very intellectual and very erotic is happening. There are lesbian oil paintings and, because it is Vienna, I don't know if they are more modern reproductions, or like, unearthed old things. I don't ask. Instead we get a high top in the back and talk about Barbie. Johanna loved male guitar music on the beach as the ultimate symbol of patriarchy, but hated that Kate McKinnon had to be the ugly, weird one.

"No but it's smart because it acknowledges that lesbians *are* considered ugly and weird in a Barbie-type world, that we have to live on the margins!"

"I guess. Also there was too much Ken," Johanna says.

"There was way too much Ken," I agree.

We go outside so I can smoke, and Johanna sees someone she knows. I ask if she wants to say hi, but she doesn't. The person always hits on her.

"Well if she does that I'll definitely step in and claim you," I say.

In response, Johanna grabs me and kisses me and kisses me.

In the apartment, my phone is right on the kitchen counter. We open a bottle of wine she bought before my visit, that we haven't gotten to. It's an Austrian Riesling which is somehow not gross. Johanna decides it is time for me to pay her back.

"You said you have PayPal, right?"

"Yes," she says, and I PayPal her.

She tries to transfer it and can't figure it out.

"You'll figure it out tomorrow," I say. "Come on, it's almost two and I have to leave for the airport at four." But she's no longer in sexy mode, she's in bank mode. I smoke a cigarette on the windowsill again.

"Do not fall out," she says, "Or I will go after you. I cannot live with the guilt of such a thing."

I smile but she's already in bank mode again, waving her hands around, verklempt.

"Do you want to send it back to me and go to the ATM?"

"No," she says.

"Fine," I say after I decide at least forty minutes have passed. "I'm gonna sleep for an hour before my flight."

I exit for her room, then get under the covers without taking anything off or brushing my teeth. A minute later she comes in. "Sam," she says in her serious German way. "You are asleep now?"

"Yes," I say.

"Come on, let's go to the ATM."

I throw off the covers dramatically and sulk the whole way down the block.

"Are you mad?" She asks.

"Yes," I say.

"Very mad?"

"Also yes."

"Okay that is fine."

The ATM works for phones, but an error keeps happening with my particular transaction. I try machine after machine in the bank's vestibule and sigh to the point of wailing.

"Come on we will figure it out later," she says.

On the way back, she spanks me.

I barely react. "Is that my punishment for sulking?" I ask drolly.

"No, it is a love spanking," she says. "Do you feel the love?"

She does it again on the stairs and in the elevator until we're in her room and she's fucking me from behind. She is still fucking me when my alarm goes off. She doesn't stop. I hit snooze.

"I have to go," I say. My thighs and ass cheeks are covered in cum.

I push her out of me and then hold her for a minute before rolling off to get dressed.

In the living room, I'm wearing clothes and we hold each other, standing, for a long time.

When I let go, her face is shiny with tears.

"Do you remember," I say, my face inches from her face, "how I asked you if I could come and spend the quarantine with you?" It's pushing something to say this, I know, a way of wanting her to consider that we could have a totally different life by now.

"No," she said, "I don't remember this at all. I don't think this happened."

"It happened," I said. "I was at that artist residency when the pandemic started."

"You were?"

"Yes, remember they paid for my return flight from Madrid? Anyway, I had just left your apartment a few weeks before and you tried to get me to stay with you, to not go to the residency. But then a few weeks later, I suggested I come back, get stuck in Madrid with you for whatever the quarantine was. I mean, I don't think I understood it would last so long."

Her eyebrows knit together. "But how would this have been possible?" she asked, suddenly angry-sounding. "This would not," she said, "have made any sense at all."

Jenny Fran Davis

Parachute Time

At a mermaid-themed bar in Great Falls, Montana, an adult woman in a Walmart bra, plastic swimming goggles, and a skirt made of iridescent scales twirled and shimmied in a huge tank of water, disappearing every forty seconds to gulp fresh air from the top of the tank (she had no gills).

A fellow bar patron revealed his private fantasy to me and my lesbian boyfriend over the chorus of a rushed-tempo Ariana Grande song: a contest in which thousands of shimmering goldfish were released, and hordes of buxom mermaids holding nets in their mouths pushed off into a mad dash to capture all the fish, tails flapping and nets swishing in the fray.

We didn't really know how to respond to this. Like all fantasies, it seemed specific to his particular perversity.

But to me, the hottest part of the movie *Heathers* is when Heather Chandler vomits, and Veronica tells her to lick it up ("Lick it up, baby. Lick. It. Up!"), and so I intuited the eroticism of this man's goldfish game, which to me signified a desire to watch women's bodies underwater.

Not just underwater, but underwater competitors—to see them as shiny predators, gulping through the water after every last bite.

And I intuited the eroticism of the tank—of the way the woman dressed as a mermaid catapulted herself through the water, suspended, flicking her shiny blue tail as she somersaulted in the water, and the eroticism of the chlorinated billows she displaced, yanking herself up and down, a slow, one-woman performance for the potbellied men in red and white hats sipping rum at the bar and for the women with them, the women tenuously holding the men's attention, the men whose sad eyes flickered between the mermaid and the women.

I intuited the eroticism of the mermaid's confines, her limitations, her separation, her sequestering, her difference, her strong, fleshy tail, her feet, her prowess in the water and her helplessness on land.

What I want to tell you about Montana is that it is the biggest place in the world. It goes on forever. The mountains there are blue and green and yellow and purple. There is not enough space to fill up every part of it. Seeing all of it, you get the feeling of having at once nowhere and everywhere to look.

What I want to tell you about me is that sometime in the 1930s, the acclaimed lesbian starfucker Mercedes de Acosta bought a bracelet in Berlin because she'd read an article in a German magazine about how Greta Garbo favored heavy bracelets.

As one story goes, Greta Garbo once traced her foot for Mercedes. Greta put her foot to paper and gently dragged a pencil around it to capture the shape of the appendage; everyone said she had big feet and she set out to prove them right, she even took care to define the slipper she was wearing in the sketch, an act of tenderness that was not lost on me as I studied it for clues that what I'd heard was true, that the rumors could be believed, that the stories about her were not just fantasies but a portrait, however blurry, of some reality of courtship and obsession and the movement of a pencil across a page.

Mercedes de Acosta slept with Marlene Dietrich too, or so they say, and Mercedes actually had footwear items from both stars in her archive: a stocking of Marlene's (suggesting, one historian says, a striptease in progress) and Greta's sketch, the two mementos lying side-by-side in the archive as a sort of parallel fetish; one wonders if Mercedes had a particular thing for feet or if feet are universally sexy, feet after all are gateways to the leg, and these women—Greta and Marlene—are both known for their phenomenally slender, sexy legs.

Mon grand amour, the letters from Marlene to Mercedes read, and *femme adorée*, the direct addresses are in French "because it is so hard to speak to you of love in English," all the letters from Marlene are written in green ink on silver stationary, and most are sealed with green wax and the official Marlene Dietrich monogram, and that is how one knows they are legitimate.

I think I'm much like Mercedes de Acosta in that way, Mercedes who bought a heavy bracelet because Greta liked such things.

I think I'm much like Mercedes de Acosta because I have a thing for legs.

Great Falls—home of the Sip 'n' Dip Lounge—is located in what's been described as the least gay-friendly city in Montana. Population hovers at about 59,000. There is a river that splits the town in half and a decent Goodwill on one of its banks, squat blue homes that could belong in Minnesota or Maine, anywhere near a body of water.

Kiss me, I instructed Tess when we were seated at our ketchup-smeared table, facing the bar behind which the mermaid twirled in the water.

Before us were two limp veggie burgers and an electric blue drink that we'd established I would drink most of, because Tess was driving (I had no license), but I could hardly stomach the drink and kept sliding it around in the small pool of water collecting at its base.

Tess glanced around the dark bar without kissing me.

Kiss me, I begged.

And then, when she still refused, I said something like, What, you're worried we'll get gay bashed; would that really be so bad?

I explained that I'd always liked inhospitable places.

No, no, no, Tess said, and further insisted that I definitely didn't want to be gay-bashed, I didn't know what I was talking about, that was a stupid thing to say, and that I should definitely lower my voice.

Actually, she thought it was cute that I'd said that, but she was serious—no kissing in the Sip 'n' Dip Lounge, not even in the bathroom, where the music thumped quieter, as though we were underwater.

Actually, kissing was okay, and she pressed me up against the wall inside the bathroom stall and wedged a leg between my legs.

Tess and I had driven to Great Falls from Helena, where we were staying with Tess's relatives, some of her mother's cousins, the husband a professor at a small Catholic college in Helena and the wife, Louise, an avid crafter of clay mice that represented members of the family.

The daughter, who'd recently changed her name from Sophia to her Hebrew name, Ruah, was a horse-wrangler and mortician-in-training. Ruah lived with her fiancé in a trailer with two horses named Spirit and Trooper.

Tess and I slept in a tent outside the trailer. In the tent was an air mattress and a string of fairy lights and a night table on which some books about the Jews of Montana were stacked neatly.

At the Sip 'n' Dip Lounge, I drank the blue drink, which made me shake, and we were back in our borrowed car by nightfall, because Louise had warned us about the wildlife that ran periodically onto the roads, her friends and acquaintances who had been thrown into their windshields in desperate attempts to stop short before hitting them.

On one of Mercedes's teenaged birthdays, at the beginning of the twentieth century, I remembered, she wished that she would meet Greta Garbo in Hollywood, though famously Greta never wanted to meet anyone; she was antisocial, misanthropic, and very, very private. But much later, after Mercedes's wish came true, Greta practiced her role in *As You Desire Me* for Mercedes, who by that point was her lover, before acting in front of the camera. Greta could play any role.

When people talk about her specialness, they usually say something like that.

Mercedes de Acosta loved actresses from childhood. As a girl she lived right by Maude Adams's apartment in New York; Adams played Peter Pan onstage and de Acosta was obsessed with her, delighted in telling people she'd saved Maude Adams from a fire.

She was determined to get a little silver thimble from Maude, who often gave those away to children who waited outside the theater; the thimble represented a kiss, which was what Mercedes wanted more than anything.

Greta and Mercedes exchanged gifts and letters, vacationed together, sunbathed naked, lived together, shopped together. Mercedes was hyper-visible; one historian says she "dressed to be seen, to be identified in the papers"; this troubled Greta, Mercedes's visibility backfired, "the double-butch two-shot," one historian writes of the GARBO IN PANTS image, "gave Garbo a new kind of visibility," Mercedes even pasted photos of Greta into her Bible, but in 1946 Garbo abruptly stopped their relationship, writing in self-mockery of her Swedish accent, *I vant to be alone.*

As part of our mission to find gay things to do in Montana, we had Ruah drive us to Missoula, the liberal college town that housed the University of Montana. A friend who'd gone to college there tipped me off to a bar where lesbians—college athletes, my favorite—might congregate, so we headed there.

In Missoula, I bristled at the enormous *M* spray-painted onto the side of a mountain. *M* was the initial of Tess's recent ex and also what we called her to avoid conjuring all of her.

In our tent at night I looked her up to see if any new pictures had been posted. *M.* had a gaggle of girlfriends that all looked like her, Jewish and exclusive. I tried to look away, but there were *M*'s painted everywhere, on every hillside.

To Missoula I wore a denim dress with a ropy velvet corset and bought a furry black skirt that looked like a bearskin.

The bar we chose was populated by a friend group of lesbians in their forties whose style could be best described as Mexicali Blues off its antidepressants: ropy knapsacks slung around solid bodies, shredded miniskirts in muted tones swinging around muscular quads and dingy wool legwarmers colliding with blocky water shoes or hiking sandals. A mix of taut and pudgy faces, outdoor lesbians of varying fitness levels.

It was the birthday of one of the friends, the ringleader of the group around whom all the friends clustered. Her plain face was surrounded by fringes of gray-brown hair. All of their faces were plain and gaping; none stood over 5'5", and as we danced awkwardly into the center of the room, I felt like a neon pink Air Dancer outside a car dealership.

One of the women—not the ringleader, but an intimate friend of hers—exclaimed that it was Parachute Time. She extracted a rainbow parachute from a basket in the corner of the bar and everyone began screaming and hollering and making their way to the center of the room.

Tess and I screamed with excitement, too, not exactly sure what was about to happen. We all grasped the perimeter of the parachute and yanked it up and down until it billowed rhythmically. We all quickly sat down, and in the few seconds that the parachute still puffed around us, the lesbians proceeded across the circle doing old disco moves or the worm.

Under the parachute, that parachute time that we were so lucky to be present for, our peers danced and shimmied. We traded places with each other. People leaped into the center and did the worm. Everyone chanted.

Before we left, Tess and I debated if we should say goodbye to the leader of the pack, the middle-aged lesbian in the skirt and legwarmers. We approached her like a scam artist approaching his first victim.

We just wanted to say thank you for parachute time, Tess said.

She eyed us, and I thought, She is bored of us, she is so bored by us.

But then she cried out, *Wait!*

We stopped.

She looked deep into our faces, trying to understand what we were, and finding nothing in our faces that betrayed such information, held out one rough hand.

I didn't know if she wanted me to shake it or slap it, so I grasped it in mine, and she clenched back. We stood like that for a moment, until the pulse in our hands spread to the pulse between my legs, and I blushed.

We run a hot spring outside of town, the woman said finally in her brassy field hockey coach voice. Do you want to come with us there?

The way she'd constructed the sentence was curious and weirdly appealing—*do you want to come with us there?* It seemed impossible to say no, so we did. We went with them there.

At the hot spring, the steam lifted off the water in great plumes, and women bobbed up from the surface, shiny like candy apples, topless and plaster-haired and eyes-closed and red-faced, like baby mice.

They were all white and old.

It was nighttime, and a few big lampposts reflected on the water, big blurry pools of light shifting as the women glided through the hot bath, wrinkled breasts floating out from their torsos, sagging upper arms motoring through the ripples, faces tipped up to the moon.

The leader of the Parachute Time pack—Wendy—rested her tattered garments in one easy yank and then sank, at the end of the same motion, into the pool in a pair of gray underwear, gray pubic hair sprouting at the sides.

And then she was among the masses, gliding in easy patterns—not quite circles, but somehow no one rammed into anyone else—in the hot bath.

The water they displaced with their strokes simply lapped back down as they moved through the bath, prompting another woman's bobbing, so that there was no real "wake," and so the whole thing, their gliding, took on a timelessness, a lack of before and after, that seemed at once eternal and very young.

I watched them for a long time, until my eyes grew wet with steam and my face flushed.

Come in, a voice beckoned, and I peered into the pool, unable to discern who had said it.

But then they were all saying it:

Come in

Come in

Come in

until it was something of a wordless melody, a sound without shape, a whisper and a yell, urging me towards the hot spring.

It was one degree off from being painfully hot, and that meant that it was the most delightful temperature, like a bath without the grime, the cold outside air bouncing off the steamy surface and then blowing off on its way.

Greta Garbo's masculinity is much discussed by historians, who allege that she "got in drag" when she performed high-femme, heavy-glamor roles; one writes about her getting into drag, that it happened "whenever she melted in or out of a man's arms, whenever she simply let that heavenly-flexed neck—what a magnificent line it makes: like a goose's rather than a swan's—bear the weight of her thrown-back head."

There is Greta's androgyny.

She used to climb ahead of Mercedes in the Sierra Nevada mountains, she would "leap from rock to rock on her bare Hellenic feet"; Mercedes describes her as a "glorious god and goddess melted into one."

Greta is goddex, a gender-neutral god, lit up by the brilliant scenery, the beautiful view.

There is her athletic prowess.

Often, Mercedes recounts, she'd row them both across a lake to a lumber camp, where they'd buy dairy products and talk to lumbermen who'd mistake them for schoolgirls on holiday.

"And at night," she says, "in a fantastic silence and with dark mountains towering around us we would go out in the boat and just drift."

Other things we did in Montana:

We went to a barn-bar on the side of a highway and danced to country music songs.

We stopped in a craft store in a small town and bought candy-colored knitted baby shoes, or rather I pressured Tess to buy them for me, and she did.

We fucked in our tent, me in the electric blue lingerie I'd bought at a Christian gift shop, until the air mattress puddled beneath us.

We examined a massive pit, a depression as vast as a whole city, in Butte, and went to an Italian gourmet shop.

We managed silence on long drives across the state, minutes-long stretches with no other cars on the road.

We missed the annual Strawberry Festival in Billings, for which I'd packed an elaborate outfit.

We were shown all of the figurines that Tess's great-aunt made every holiday season, a mouse family to represent herself, her husband, and Ruah.

We learned that at Christmastime Tess's great-uncle called himself, in nondenominational spirit, the Great Bear of the North.

Our last night in Montana, back in Helena, we played croquet with a couple of the neighbors, including a twelve-year-old girl who rattled off the plot of her novel in progress.

The girl's parents looked at me expectantly, as though I was supposed to tell this girl she was a good writer. Tess's aunt took picture after picture of us, stumbling around the croquet set to capture us from all different angles.

We wielded our croquet sticks proudly, liking that they were yellow and blue, crisp and stark colors like the ones in the movie *Heathers*, before we retired to our tent, we fed the horses treats from our palms.

It was chilly.

I was wearing Tess's butch horse-girl jacket.

We looked at all the pictures that had been taken of us on our trip.

In the picture I took of Tess during Parachute Time in the bar in Missoula, she looks at me, gleeful and shocked, as she grasps the parachute and yanks it up and down.

Her face lit from some external source and her butch horse-girl jacket coming off one shoulder, she is looking at me and not at them, and she is beckoning me to come over with one arm, she is saying, Come on, Come on, get off your phone and come join Parachute Time.

I don't remember now why I was removed from the scene, why I was checking my phone at that moment.

I must have gone to check my texts and then decided to take a single photo, which was unlike me; Tess was the one who was always remembering to take photos.

Either way, I am glad I have it.

At some point Greta looked at Mercedes's bracelet and said something like, What a beautiful bracelet.

"I took it off my wrist and handed it to her," Mercedes recounts. "'I bought it for you in Berlin,' I said."

There is a picture of me in front of the wooden placard with MER-MAID CROSSING etched into it.

In the picture, I am making fun of the place and myself, saying, This is a spectacle.

The placard is positioned just in front of the tank, which is behind the bar at which a lone, elderly female bartender poured liquor into tall plastic cups with shaking hands.

In the picture, I'm wearing Tess's butch horse-girl jacket over a spotted grey and blue dress. I wore that jacket, which she'd bought in a thrift store in LA, every day that week in June.

It was just after mud season, when the nighttime temperature dipped into the 40s and daytime temperatures soared to the low 80s, burning our skin because of how close we were to the sun.

In the picture, the adult woman in the goggles—which is to say the mermaid—is a vague shape behind the dirty glass, mid-flip, not looking.

I can look away?

I can look away?

I vant to be alone.

Hedi El Kholti

Before I Met You

There's this guy I meet at the Roosterfish. He lives in a motel nearby and I hear he's a meth dealer. He's kind and generous and always offers me lines. We're standing near the pinball machine. Playing pinball is something I'm good at. He's impressed with my moves. I make quick nervous motions but avoid tilting the machine. That's what I did often instead of going to school. There were all these disreputable cafés next to our lycée in Casablanca, full of pimps and prostitutes and pinball machines. I loved the louche atmosphere. Deals were made, people were playing card games. It felt very cosmopolitan, like the Fassbinder movies I'm starting to watch. I go back to his room sometimes at the Jolly Roger Motel on Washington Boulevard and do a line or two. We talk about our lives, but don't have sex. I am here for the drugs. I don't really get the whole motel living thing. The way he justifies it as a choice feels very suspect, like he's running away from something. I have standards, I think. I'm trying to slow my inevitable fall so that I can fully enjoy it, as if in slow motion.

There's this other guy. He's a bit older, in his late thirties, and wears a hairpiece. He lives in Santa Monica in a small apartment, filled with crystals. He believes in something called the Course in Miracles, and wants to design his own set of cards, filled with daily spiritual affirmations tailored towards homosexuals with PTSD and survivor's guilt. He's making very slow progress, and I try to be supportive of his efforts when he reads the cards to me, even though it feels completely foreign and alienating. We date for a short while. We take a weekend trip to Santa Barbara and stay at a fancy resort but it's a bit of a scam and there's a confusing moment where he trades a bottle of wine for our stay. He knows the owner. It's like a favor. I make a mixtape for the road as if we're going to the end of the earth. Red House Painters, Kristen Hersh, the Pixies, Love and Rockets . . . I probably still have it. His dick is fleshy, soft and cumbersome. He takes me to Numbers sometimes, a hustler bar in West Hollywood, I am not sure why. Maybe he sees something in me I'm not yet aware of. The mirror-tiled entrance functions as a camera obscura, giving the customers a furtive glimpse of who's descending the staircase. I pay his rent once. He disappears. He drops a pair of expensive leather boots with a note in my backyard as repayment. They don't fit me and I drop them at the Salvation Army. I never hear from him again.

I'm at loss with language. I listen to Tricky a lot. He's left Massive Attack and released a solo album. I buy his debut album *Maxinquaye*, and all of his imported singles at Vinyl Fetish on Melrose. The crystalline beats of Massive Attack's *Protection*, released six months earlier, to which Tricky contributed two songs, have turned muddier, and feel degraded, as if the master tapes were left outdoors, exposed to the elements. I feel confused in the early nineties, but happy when I arouse someone else's desire. *You want to be with me? I've nothing to give.* The record is titled after his mother, who committed suicide when he was four, and it feels at times like a séance to contact her from beyond the grave, with Martina Topley-Bird, his collaborator and romantic partner, acting as the possessed medium. *Your eyes resemble mine, you see as no others can.* His mother wrote poetry that was lost and never published. Tricky tries to imagine or recover those lines that he probably never heard. The record is violent and sensual in equal measure. I love the way he overdubs his coarse asthmatic voice on the track, often at the wrong places, overpowering the song, like he's whispering loudly in my ear, a garbled fractured incantation. *I can't breathe and I can't see. MTV moves too fast, I refuse to understand. You go your way and I'll see mine. Feels like wasted time.*

There's this other guy I meet at the bar. He invites me to his place nearby. We do a line of speed. He likes me a lot and the sex is amazing. I like meth in the early nineties. It doesn't seem like a plague yet as far as I'm aware. I don't read alarming pieces about it in *Frontiers*, or *the Advocate*. He tells me he puts a small amount in his coffee every morning, like a dietary supplement. He makes it sound very healthy. The apartment is really organized, but the style of the furniture feels old fashioned, as if the place was already furnished when he moved in. He's an out-of-work actor and very good-looking in an Italian sort of way. I'm in love. I leave in the morning. At dawn, the streets are empty. It's magical to see the sun rise in Venice and I can't believe my luck, basking in the afterglow of really good sex on drugs. On my way home I find a giant green velvet chair that looks like a prop for a music video. I imagine it was discarded after a shoot. I pick up a lot of things in the street in the early nineties. I put it in the back of my car and take it home. But the dogs viciously attack it and rip it apart—pieces of foam get strewn everywhere on our courtyard. Sitting in my giant green throne I felt that I lived in a Depeche Mode video set for a brief moment. I was so disappointed when I took it to the curb. I ran into him months later and he was really sad that I never called him back.

There's the other guy that picks me up at the bar. I go to his place in Marina Del Rey. Nice condo. He has an amazing collection of CDs. A whole wall of floor to ceiling of every British indie pop record ever released, imports and Japanese pressings. Eyeless in Gaza, Felt, In Embrace, every 4AD, Sarah, and Factory release . . . His record collection makes me want to spend the rest of my life with him. We'd be old by the time we'd listen to all of them. Sadly, a few days later he reveals that he has a boyfriend, a trust fund baby who's about to come back to town. He had left his job, at the boyfriend's insistence, so they could travel the world. And they did go to Australia. Maybe Key West too. The boyfriend has become resentful of having to pay for everything and he's trying to cut him loose or make him a bit more of a responsible adult. Or maybe he wants to be loved for himself. When I meet them both at the bar a few days later, the boyfriend accuses me of trying to destroy their relationship. I tell him that I didn't know about his existence, but he doesn't believe me. We become friends. I go with him to get tested for HIV for the first time and he comforts me. I'm terrified that if the results are positive, my green card will be denied, and I'll get kicked out of the country. He moves out of the condo after a while and rents a much less glamorous place in a nondescript neighborhood in midtown. I pay his rent a couple of times. He never pays me back and disappears. Is he on Facebook or dead? Or both.

I come out to my dad. He instigated the meeting on the last day of his trip. My stepmother and little sister stayed in Venice or went shopping. We're sitting in a café in Westwood. It's like he knows already, and maybe he's the one who asks. I don't remember even though I brought a tape recorder with me that I hid in my backpack. I have the feeling this is the last time we'll ever speak and I want to remember the moment. I want to be able to replay it. Maybe I could use it later in a video, but I didn't label the tape and most likely lost it in subsequent moves. He's remarkably calm and if he's upset, he hides it well. The only thing he asks me is if I am a top or a bottom. I find the question strange, but he explains that if I'm a top this could be just a phase but if I am a bottom there is no turning back. When I drop them at the airport the next morning, he seems diminished and older, as he disappears in the Tom Bradley terminal. I drive to work directly from there, and "Ode To My Family," a new single from The Cranberries, plays on the radio. I start crying. I'm deeply ashamed that I've caused him pain, that I have disappointed him. Everything was all right as long as it remained a secret. I have a sense that I've done something irreversible.

There's the other guy I met at the bar. He's much older and strange. He has an art studio in Venice with no art inside of it. Art is an identity. He has huge color-coded jars full of glass beads for future potential pieces that he has no intention of making. Also rows of videos. He documents every minute of his life. It's like reality TV before it became a thing. All the tedious moments labeled. He lives in an apartment in a high rise by the beach on Pacific. I drive past his window often when coming back from work. There's a blue light outside. When I get the results of the HIV test for my green card, he films it. He puts his fingers in my mouth and violently squeezes my tongue. I tell him to stop but he tries to convince me that I like it.

I'm not so sure but maybe. He's endowed with what I learn later is called a beer-can dick; short and fat, an oddity I find mesmerizing. I just googled beer-can dick, but the internet doesn't do my memory justice.

I go see Tricky at The Viper Room. His second album has been released as an import only a few months after his debut but under a different moniker, Nearly God, which explains why the club seems so empty. I go alone and the show starts really late. I vaguely remember him saying that he had come directly from the airport to the venue. The bass is loud and overwhelming, too loud for comfort. It makes the space tremble, and I feel physically ill, as if it's triggering a panic attack. The sense of dread is not attached to anything specific, until I can almost hear the 911 call that Joaquin Phoenix made when his brother River was dying right outside the club, a couple of years prior. I had the poster of *My Own Private Idaho* in my room in Paris the last year I lived there. I feel his presence hovering over the space, and I remember how much his fearless, unapologetic interpretation meant to me then, and how the movie gave me the courage to come here.

Brontez Purnell

The Queen and Trade

I, Brontez Purnell, singularly, (I really can't speak for you other bitches, and wouldn't DARE try to, thank you very much) have stamped myself with that particular coven of gay men who consider life in society at best an utter bore; I therefore bide my time with literature, poetry, (responsible) drug use, and late night hook up website shenanigans with other (reasonable) sex addicts. I suppose I should say with all honesty that I do not identify as a hedonist. I am just a forty-year-old man who stands at the precipice of irreversible erectile dysfunction, and I'm trying to kick this party up a notch for what I wager is the third to final act of my sex life—which, I can honestly say, has been fucking up to this point. But as I have spent what feels like a lifetime stuck in the seventh circle of hell of sexual ponderance— What does the sex that I am having *say about me*? What does the sex that I am having *say about the world around me?* I can't seem to come to any real conclusions. It will have to be enough to tell you what I have witnessed in this body, for that is all I can tell you.

At the age I am now, I have nothing invested in "being sexy" anymore; I no longer go to sex to "feel sexy." I approach it like any bodily function that must be done on time and efficiently enough to release a certain pressure valve and get on with my daily business. I have gained somewhere around eighty pounds since Covid and know by the rule books of the gays that some part of me should feel diminished by this, but by all accounts, am having the rawest, roughest sex of my life. I can only theorize that this weight gain puts out certain signals to a direct group of men—it reads as "breedable," or, "his fat ass can take some dick." Either way, it's a far cry from when I was twenty-eight and 160 lbs, spending five days a week in the gym but also in the dismal abyss of San Francisco pre-online discourse around, like, you know, race politics, body positivity, my "black life mattering" etc. All I know is that when I had muscles, mostly everyone wanted me to top (which, like, ew)—and even if you had the muscles, you couldn't *just* have the muscles, those queens wanted you to have the muscles, the nine-inch dick, the apartment, the degree from an Ivy League, etc. I look back at pictures from that time period and, little did I know it at the time, but I was for *sure* the sexiest boy in San Francisco—none of the other bitches could even *compete* with me. "How did it feel, being the sexiest boy in SF in 2006?" One may ask? Answer: It wasn't enough.

I have had to find some solace in the fact that being on Sniffies has put me in this weird silo of mostly having sex with DL men; I haven't had sex with an out gay man in a minute. From what I gather, DL men don't really operate out of agenda, just more sexual urgency: "Damn—you're built like a *woman*—can I come over?" is how they seem to operate, but I'll say more on that later.

When I was clued into Sniffies, sometime around quarantine, it was a breath of FRESH AIR. Quarantine was an interesting time for sex because only the TRUE sex addicts came out, the bitches that were PERECTLY WILLING to risk death for dick (I being one of them). Suddenly, we were back at a weird polarizing sexual point in history. Not to diss the other app, but Grindr wasn't gonna cut it this time. I have NO fucking clue why it's called "Sniffies" (which I sure will change after this is published) but I have always been keen on the tag line "*FOR THE CURIOUS.*"

Let me say, with complete humbleness, that I have thrown my body into the ritual of sex more so than the next bitch, I'm certain of it. One thing I have definitely learned is that there is this self-segregating realm of sex, curiosity vs. agenda. You cannot have an *agenda and* be curious. I remember back in the days before PrEP where I lived in San Francisco and spent most of my online cruising oscillating between Adam 4 Adam and Bareback Real Time. Boys I knew who were on Bareback Real Time quite often did not disclose on more public-facing apps their love of bareback sex. I tend to think more interesting things and bolder choices happen in a sexual chaos realm that has the cloak of anonymity, rather than one that is public-facing. The ultimate problem with Grindr is that it is public-facing; like, you literally HAVE to show your face. You are more likely to see your friends, co-workers, public officials, etc., and you can't get down like a dirty bitch. Even during the Black Lives Matter moment I was SO DISGUTSTED to see how many fucking white dudes had #BLM in their profile, but I literally wasn't getting any more white dick. Not that allyship should include a dick-down, but fuck, like, doesn't it help?

When I switched to Sniffies it suddenly occurred to me that more white men had hit me up to top on that app than any other app I had ever been on ever. This is just *one* facet of this new realm that I notice. I had been on Scruff once, for a year, and literally had NO responses. Essentially, it's like a white boy otter app, and I'm a TOTALLY hairless black man, so I get it, but I am always curious as to how the perimeters of the spaces we play in directly correlate to, say, society, the bodies we inhabit, socio-politics. What does the sex that I am having *say about me*? What does the sex that I am having *say about the world around me*? There was something about Sniffies, where men are literally just allowed to show their dicks, butts and assholes, and where anonymous, pictureless profiles are basically encouraged, that led me to this new world of sex. And after being disappointed with sex apps for a while, I thought it was worth attempting to document how much (and also *how very little*) sex means, and what it says about us.

Warhol superstar Penny Arcade once declared (poignantly) "The sexual revolution cheapened sex" —oh, how I concur! I would first like to admit that at the time of this writing, I am sitting in a very dirty bedroom (my own) in sunny Oakland, California. I have held up in my room for a few days trying to complete work on my eighth book, *Diary of Dead Bachelors,* in which I profile (in poems) the life of forty men who die alone. Perhaps not the healthiest of mental states to put oneself in, but the artist life chose me and I did accept. But I digress. I am currently trying to condense the two years since the start of the pandemic—the time I discovered Sniffies, and certain epiphanies that came with it—until my current now, when I stand at the brink of a new year and am deeply contemplating—for the first time in my life—a long stretch of self-imposed celibacy and deleting all my cruising apps. But let me not get ahead of myself.

I am currently sitting in the Sniffies global chat LOL'ing at the audacity of some of these bitches. What I have noticed in the last year is a very stark shift in the general crowd of Sniffies (at least in my VERY SMALL BUBBLE of Oakland) over the last year. What seemed to be a large crowd of DL guys has now being colonized (and yes, let me use that very political word) by the out gay man crowd—latecomers who have exhausted the possibilities of their old apps and bring with them the expectations of that culture: vitriol for DL men in their profiles, every third profile wanting a muscular, dominant, hung, alpha, top. First of all, any bottom thinking they can be choosey is fucking laughable to me. If a top isn't to your liking you can always close your eyes and get fucked doggystyle and pretend he's someone else. This is the *true* joy of being a bottom, next to the fact that you aren't the one that has to maintain an erection. Secondly, I am constantly amazed that, in the Bay Area of all places, the spiritual nexus of tech-bro and homelessness, that anyFUCKINGone would subscribe to these lofty, laughably delusional goals. Like, I could see if this was, say, Los Angeles, but muscular *and* hung? In this dystopian hellscape? Sweetie, read the room. You have to pick *one*.

This goes back to my first point "the sexual revolution cheapened sex." Let me telescope back a bit and explain . . . but then sometimes, maybe I get too stuck on the past? I often to go to this with these sepia-toned, out-of-date pics of (presumably) homosexual couples from the early part of the previous century. I'm always trying to put myself in the headspace of before we had access, before we had won the visibility war and created hierarchical realities where we could self-segregate and abuse each other. Was there ever a time where we were just fucking happy to *find* each other, period? Say, for instance, if I'm a miner during, I don't fucking know, the Gold Rush, and just happen to find another gay miner in the desolate vastness of the Sierra Nevada—even then would I be like, "Meh, his dick's not big enough, guess I'll die alone . . ." What I'm to understand is how access, *seemingly* endless options, and visibility has warped our orbits.

Sluts

DL Alvarez is an artist/writer who utilizes film, drawing, language, and ephemera to tell stories about betweenness. Their writings have been widely published and their artwork is housed in such collections as SFMOMA, The Berkeley Art Museum and Pacific Film Archives, the Met, Whitney, and MoMA in New York.

Vera Blossom is a proud Filipina American and transfemme monster. Her work explores desire, pleasure, gender, ritual, friendship and death with explicit vulgarity and frank humor.

Chloe Caldwell is the author of *Women* (Harper Perennial, 2024). She lives in Hudson, New York.

Cristy Road Carrera is a Cuban-American artist, writer, and musician. Her work explores survival, sexuality, culture, punk rock, and thriving in a broken body and depleting system. She published *Green'zine* from 1997–2004, and since has released three graphic novels; as well as countless illustrations for music, publishing, and social movements. Her most recent projects are the revolutionary *Next World Tarot*, and her music with *Choked Up*. She's currently writing songs and dystopian romance in New York City.

Sam Cohen is the author of the story collection *Sarahland* (Grand Central Publishing, 2021). Her short fiction is published in *Bomb*, *Electric Literature*, *O Magazine*, *Fence*, *Diagram*, and elsewhere. Before coming to Oberlin, she taught at the University of Southern California, UCLA Extension, CalArts, and many Los Angeles community colleges.

Tom Cole's work has been presented at Participant Inc, Thread Waxing Space, Dixon Place, Clocktower Gallery, ICA Boston, Performa, and Howl Arts. He has collaborated extensively with Anohni, most recently appearing in *She Who Saw Beautiful Things* at The Kitchen. His work has been anthologized in *Pathetic Literature*, edited by Eileen Myles.

Lydia Conklin has received a Stegner Fellowship, four Pushcart Prizes, a Rona Jaffe Foundation Writer's Award, a Creative Writing Fulbright, a grant from the Elizabeth George Foundation, and fellowships from MacDowell, Yaddo, Hedgebrook, and elsewhere. Their fiction has appeared in *The Paris Review*, *One Story*, and *VQR*. They are an Assistant Professor of Fiction at Vanderbilt University. Their story collection, *Rainbow Rainbow*, was longlisted for the PEN/Robert W. Bingham Award and The Story Prize. Their novel, *Songs of No Provenance*, is forthcoming in 2025 from Catapult in the US and Chatto in the UK.

jimmy cooper is a poet, hardcore singer (in the band Texture Freq), editor (at furious beautiful zines), and bookseller (at the Book House in Minneapolis, Minnesota). You can find his work most recently in *Responses to "Forbidden Colours"* (Pilot Press, 2023), *Responses to* Untitled (Eye with Comet) *by Paul Thek* (Pilot Press, 2023), *Make the Golf Course a Public Sex Forest* (Maitland Systems Engineering, 2023), of which he was also an editor, and ongoing in Razorcake magazine and the furious beautiful review of books.

Lyn Corelle is a filmmaker, photographer, and writer based in Minneapolis. They co-edited the 2023 anthology *Make the Golf Course a Public Sex Forest!* In 2021 they released *A Corpse Among Corpses*, an essay film on the legacy of asylum graveyards around the Midwest. They can be found on Instagram @lyncorelle and Twitter @sex_forest.

Jenny Fran Davis is the author of *Everything Must Go* (a novel for teenagers) and *Dykette*. She lives in Brooklyn. Her next book comes out in 2025.

Cyrus Dunham is the author of *A Year Without a Name* (2020). His writing has appeared in *The New Yorker*, *Granta*, and *The Intercept*, among other publications and anthologies. He is a co-founder and editor of Deluge Books.

Hedi El Kholti is a co-editor at Semiotext(e), alongside Chris Kraus, where he created the publication *Animal Shelter*, an occasional journal of art, sex, and literature and the Intervention Series. Hesse Press published *A Place in the Sun*, a book of his writings and collages, in 2017.

Robert Glück is a poet, fiction writer, critic, and editor. In the late 70's, he and Bruce Boone founded New Narrative, a literary movement of self-reflexive storytelling that combines essay, lyric, and autobiography in one work. Glück is the author of the story collections *Elements* and *Denny Smith*, the novels *Jack the Modernist*, *Margery Kempe*, and *About Ed*, and a volume of collected essays, *Communal Nude*. His books of poetry include *La Fontaine* with Bruce Boone, *In Commemoration of the Visit* with Kathleen Fraser, *Reader*, and *I, Boombox*. With Camille Roy, Mary Berger and Gail Scott, he edited the anthology *Biting the Error: Writers Explore Narrative*.

Miguel Gutierrez is a multi-disciplinary artist based in Lenapehoking/Brooklyn and Tovaangar/Los Angeles. His work centers attention as a material form and as a means to unravel normative belief systems. His performance work has been presented internationally for over twenty years. His writing has appeared in Lambda Literary, InDance, Creative Time's *Invitations Toward Re-worlding*, In Terms of Performance: A Keywords Anthology (ed. Shannon Jackson and Paula Marincola), and his book *When You Rise Up* is available from 53rd Street Press. www.miguelgutierrez.org

Gary Indiana is an American writer, actor, artist, and cultural critic. Best known for his classic American true-crime trilogy registering the debased state of American life at the millennium's end (*Resentment*, *Three-Month Fever: The Andrew Cunanan Story*, and *Depraved Indifference*), Indiana has been described by the *Guardian* as "one of the most important chroniclers of the modern psyche."

Hailing from her native Los Angeles, **Taleen Kali** composes romantic punk songs wrapped in layers of shoegaze, psychedelia, and grunge, creating a cosmic sound that's dreamy and defiant alike.

Cheryl Klein is the author of *Crybaby: Infertility, Illness, and Other Things That Were Not the End of the World* (Brown Paper Press). She's also a co-editor and contributor for *Mutha Magazine*, a nonprofit worker, and a lifelong Angeleno.

Gabrielle Korn is the former editor-in-chief of Nylon Media and the author of *Yours For The Taking*, *Everybody (Else) Is Perfect*, and *The Shutouts*. She lives in LA with her wife and dog.

Jeremy Atherton Lin is the author of *Gay Bar*, recipient of the National Book Critics Circle Award for Autobiography, and the forthcoming *Deep House*. He is based sometimes in Los Angeles and mostly in the English town of St Leonards-on-Sea.

Nate Lippens is the author of the novels *My Dead Book*, which was a finalist for the Republic of Consciousness Prize, and *Ripcord*.

Meredith Maran is the 72-year-old sexpot, grandmother, and author of 14 books and bazillions of book reviews, features, op-eds, think-pieces, and feel-pieces for *The New York Times*, *Washington Post*, *LA Times*, *O Magazine*, and other outlets. She lives in Los Angeles and Palm Springs.

Carta Monir is a writer and erotic performer living in Ann Arbor, Michigan. She is very beautiful and you are in love with her.

Amanda Montell is the bestselling author of three nonfiction books, *Cultish: The Language of Fanaticism*, *Wordslut: A Feminist Guide to Taking Back the English Language*, and *The Age of Magical Overthinking: Notes on Modern Irrationality*. Her books have been praised by *The Atlantic*, NPR, *The Washington Post*, and more. In addition to creating and hosting the hit podcast Sounds Like A Cult, Amanda's writing has appeared in *The New York Times*, *Marie Claire*, *Harper's Bazaar*, and elsewhere.

Carley Moore is the author of *Panpocalypse*, *The Not Wives*, *16 Pills*, and *The Stalker Chronicles*.

Bradford Nordeen is a writer, curator and the founder of film platform, Dirty Looks Inc. His publications include *Because Horror* (with Johnny Ray Huston), *Check Your Vernacular*, *Dirty Looks at MoMA*, and *Fever Pitch*. He is presently completing his debut novel, *Blessed Western*, and a companion screenplay, to be produced by Lior Shamriz, about his experience living in a hotel in Santa Cruz while pursuing a PhD in Film and Digital Media at the University of California.

Baruch Porras-Hernandez is a writer, performer, organizer, professional MC/Host, curator, stand-up comedian, and the author of the chapbooks "I Miss You, Delicate" and "Lovers of the Deep Fried Circle" both with Sibling Rivalry Press. He had the honor of touring with the legendary Sister Spit Queer poetry tour in 2019, is a is a two-time winner of Literary Death Match, a regular host of literary shows for KQED, and was named a Writer to Watch in 2016 by *7×7 Magazine*. His poetry can be found with Write Bloody Publishing, The Tusk, Foglifter, Assaracus and many more.

Kamala Puligandla is a writer and editor in LA, who writes autobiographical fiction and essays on queer love. She has published two books, *Zigzags* (Not A Cult, 2020) and *You Can Vibe Me On My FemmePhone* (Co-Conspirator Press, 2021), and works at the Feminist Center for Creative Work.

Brontez Purnell is the author of several books, most recently *100 Boyfriends*, which won the 2022 Lambda Literary Award in Gay Fiction, was longlisted for the 2022 Mark Twain American Voice in Literature Award and the 2021 Brooklyn Public Library Literary Prize, and was named an Editors' Choice by the *New York Times Book Review*. The recipient of a 2018 Whiting Writers' Award for Fiction and the 2022 Foundation for Contemporary Arts Robert Rauschenberg Award, he was named one of the thirty-two Black Male Writers of Our Time by *T: The New York Times Style Magazine* in 2018.

Liara Roux is a sex worker, writer, and organizer currently living in Paris with her beautiful and famous dog. Her memoir about her experiences as a sex worker, *Whore of New York*, was published in 2021.

Andrea Sands is a musician and writer living in South Gate, California. Andrea has a cat named Cecil. Andrea currently sings and plays instruments in 4 different bands.

Daviel Shy wrote and directed *The Ladies Almanack*, starring Guinevere Turner, Hélène Cixous, and Eileen Myles, and *The Lovers*, a seven episode series currently in post-production. Shy's writing has been published by Taylor & Francis, University of Chicago Press, in chapbooks and online. She runs L.M.N.O.P: Lesbian Movie Night Ongoing Project, now celebrating its twelfth year.

Jen Silverman is a novelist, playwright, and screenwriter. Their books include the debut novel *We Play Ourselves*, story collection *The Island Dwellers*, and *There's Going to be Trouble*, upcoming from Random House in April 2024. Honors include fellowships from the National Endowment for the Arts and the Guggenheim.

Anna Joy Springer (she, they) is a lifelong Californian whose artistic work uses fantastical, speculative, and other figurative modes to explore the nature of interbeing and to register lesser cultural currents through writing and pictures.

Laurie Stone is author of six books, most recently *Streaming Now, Postcards from the Thing that is Happening* (2022), long listed for the PEN/Diamonstein-Spielvogel Award for the Art of the Essay. She was a long time writer for the *Village Voice*. She is currently a contributor to *Paris Review*, and she writes the Substack *Everything is Personal* (lauriestone@substack.com).

Michelle Tea is the publisher of DOPAMINE Books, creator of Drag Queen Story Hour, founder of Sister Spit, and instigator of other queer literary interventions. She is the author of *Valencia*, *Black Wave*, *Modern Tarot*, and many other books.

McKenzie Wark is the author, among other things of *Raving* (Duke), *Reverse Cowgirl* (Semiotext(e)) and *Love and Money, Sex and Death* (Verso). Her correspondence with Kathy Acker was published as *I'm Very Into You* (Semiotext(e)).

Zoe Whittall is the author of the bestselling novels *The Fake, The Spectacular, The Best Kind of People*, the LAMDA-winning *Holding Still for as Long as Possible*, and *Bottle Rocket Hearts*. Her latest books are *Wild Failure (Stories)* and her fourth poetry book, *No Credit River*, is forthcoming in fall 2024. She works as a TV writer.